Mood Swing

The Bipolar Murders

This book is a work of fiction. Any resemblance to actual events or persons, living or dead, is entirely coincidental.

"Mood Swing: The Bipolar Murders," by Julie Lomoe. ISBN 1-58939-885-8.

Published 2006 by Virtualbookworm.com Publishing Inc., P.O. Box 9949, College Station, TX 77842, US. ©2006, Julie Lomoe. All rights reserved.

Manufactured in the United States of America.

Sept. 10, 2006

To Don —

Mood Swing

The Bipolar Murders

by

Julie Lomoe

Thanks for being the first to make this a book club selection!

Julie Lomoe

To my husband Robb,
whose faith and love have sustained me
through thirty-three years of mood swings,
and to my daughter Stacey,
whose adventures in homesteading
on the Lower East Side
helped enrich this novel.

Chapter 1

*R*ishi was halfway out the window and onto the fire escape when I tackled him. Arms around my dog's massive shoulders, I groped for his choke chain and yanked hard. Half a dozen pigeons flapped skyward, squawking.

"Bad boy!" I paused to catch my breath, stroked his neck. "Don't chase pigeons! I don't want you catching bird flu or God knows what else."

The window shouldn't have been open, I realized with a jolt. I'd had it cracked last night, but only a couple of inches, and I was positive I'd closed it. My heart hammering, I led Rishi on a tour of my office.

He kept straining to get back to that window. The iron security grate was swinging open on its hinges. The padlock lay on the floor and the key was gone from its nail beside the window frame. I'd already given any burglar in the vicinity more than enough time to get away, which was fine with me. Despite my weekly self-defense class, I see no point in courting danger.

I was thankful Rishi was there to protect me and lend me courage. He's leaner and rangier than a German shepherd, stockier than a Doberman, bigger than a Rottweiler. Despite his forbidding looks, he's a basically friendly beast, but sometimes it's in my best interests not to let people know that. Now he was panting, drooling saliva from his enormous jaws, tugging at his heavy-duty choke chain.

"Okay, Rishi, let's see what you're so excited about," I said as he dragged me back to the window. Whimpering urgently, he put his paws on the window ledge, thrust his enormous head out, and peered down into the back yard.

I followed his gaze. A motionless figure lay sprawled face down on the black asphalt in the courtyard below. The blackness threw the silhouette into high relief. The curly brown hair, the plaid flannel shirt were familiar.

Stephen Wright! My stomach lurched. I was virtually positive it was Stephen. He wore that shirt constantly, like a talisman, believing it had special protective powers. I'd tried to talk him out of it on more than one occasion, and he'd explained the symbolism. Ragged, stinky, too hot for summer – he knew, and he could care less. I had backed off. As a member of WellSpring Club, he had the right to dress as he pleased, within reason. And as Director of the psychosocial club for mentally ill adults on Manhattan's Lower East Side, I had the obligation to let him make his own choices, also within reason.

Passing out in the back yard was not within reason. Stephen had been going to AA religiously, and he hadn't passed out in months. Now he'd obviously fallen off the wagon. I felt a wave of fury mingled with guilt and regret – obviously our program hadn't been enough for him.

I leaned further out the window. "Stephen, wake up! It's Erika!"

No response. Evidently my voice didn't carry down to the courtyard from my second-floor office, but I didn't dare call any louder. It was early, just seven thirty, and people in the nearby tenements were probably still trying to sleep. Some of them were already dubious about having a psychiatric social club as a neighbor, and screaming would only make matters worse.

I pulled Rishi away from the window and out of my office. We careened down the two flights of stairs to the ground floor, through the dining room to the door that opened onto the back yard. I unlocked both dead bolts, climbed halfway up the concrete steps to the yard, then stopped aghast.

It was definitely Stephen. His face was hidden, but I recognized his build, with the masculine shoulders that tapered to a body so thin, I was always halfway tempted to take him out and treat him to a meal. But there was something awkward about the angle of his limbs, and a halo of thick, ropy blood surrounded his head and splattered across the asphalt.

I shut Rishi in the kitchen, crossed the asphalt and knelt, feeling Stephen's neck for a pulse. Nothing.

My guts told me he was dead, but my mind wouldn't buy it. Frantic, I dredged my memory for the CPR I'd studied at the hospital but never had to use. First step: "Stephen, can you hear me?" No response. Next step: call for help. Damn! My cell phone was upstairs, in my purse. I raced inside to call 911, then back to Stephen's side. I rolled him onto his back, tilted his head back to open the airway and listened for breath. Again, nothing. I wiped his mouth with a tissue, placed my mouth on his. Two breaths. Was there a pulse? I placed two fingers at the side of his neck, felt only stillness.

Damn! How many chest compressions? Fifteen when I'd trained, but now it was thirty. I placed both hands on his sternum, pressed down, started counting. Thirty compressions, two breaths, thirty compressions, two breaths . . .

My body took over the rhythm. Still no response from Stephen, but I refused to think about that. Minutes stretched into what felt like hours. Where the hell were the EMTs? My heart was thudding heavily, and I was gasping for breath. I couldn't keep it up much longer.

Was this an accident? A suicide attempt? Stephen was diagnosed bipolar, and his illness put him at high risk for suicide. I understood the danger all too well. No one at WellSpring knew it, but I shared Stephen's diagnosis. I too was bipolar.

All at once, from inside the kitchen, I heard a wild salvo of warning barks. About time! I ran inside, grabbed Rishi's leash and headed upstairs to the lobby. I opened the door and confronted two cops, a man and a woman. "Where are the EMTs?" I asked. "I told the operator a man may be dying."

"They're on their way, ma'am," the man said. Even as he spoke, an ambulance was pulling up at the curb. "I just need to check out the scene first. Where is he?"

I led them into the back yard. The woman rushed immediately to Stephen's side and squatted down, feeling for a pulse. Then she stood murmuring to the other cop. I couldn't make out the words, but the way she shook her head confirmed my worst fears.

Two Emergency Medical Technicians burst into the yard, lugging their paraphernalia. "You'll have to step aside, ma'am," said one. "We need room to work."

"I've been doing CPR ever since I called 911." My breath was still coming in gasps. "I don't know how long. It felt like ages."

The woman officer approached me. "You did the best you could," she said softly. "Why don't I take you inside now. There's nothing you can do." As she caught hold of my arm, I took a long last look at Stephen. A shaft of sunlight pierced the gloom of the yard, and goldenrod and Queen Anne's lace framed his head in a funereal display. Stephen would have liked the picture, I thought. He had a lot of artistic ability.

When I got back to the lobby, the front door was open. Outside on the stoop, two young white cops were talking with Stan Washington, an enormous man with mahogany skin and a grizzled beard, who virtually ran the club when I wasn't around. Apparently they had all arrived at the same time. The cops were trying to figure out where to go and Stan wouldn't get out of the way. I heard him saying something about a warrant and quickly stepped in to defuse the situation before it turned into a physical confrontation.

"I'll take it from here, Stan," I said, sidling between him and the cops.

"Down here," said the woman officer, who had been right behind me. The new cops followed her while I explained the situation to Stan. "I want you to keep the club members outside while I work with the police, okay?"

"The police should not be in this club without a warrant," he growled. Stan pretty much managed the daily operations of the club, but he was also a club member. Like the others, he was saddled with a heavy-duty diagnosis. Paranoid schizophrenia, in his case. I knew he'd had some bad experiences with the police in the days before he got his illness under control.

Standing so close to him, I felt as though I was bellying up to a sequoia. "Please, Stan, just keep the club members out and let the police in, okay? We owe it to Stephen."

He stared at me intently. "I understand the necessity. Now that the soul has fled, the body belongs to the government. How did he die?"

"It looks as though he fell." I almost mentioned suicide, but I stopped short. Could it have been an accident? Maybe murder? Too soon to tell. I was giving Stan a quick summary of the situation, trying hard to be objective, when one of the police officers returned with some yellow crime scene tape and strung it across the door. Great. Now Stan and I couldn't get back in.

A few seconds later the cop was back, glaring at Rishi. "I want you to remove this dog from the premises," he said.

"No way. I'm Director of this club. This is my dog and he stays with me."

The policeman was standing stiffly with his hand on his service revolver, looking far too jittery. I realized I'd better modify my stance. "If you want, I can lock him in my office."

Just then a lanky man with a shock of red hair and a nubby gray sports coat materialized beside us. "Is the dog friendly?" he asked.

"Yes." I figured this was no time to suggest Rishi was anything other than a loveable cream puff. "You can pet him if you want."

"I'm Detective Dennis Malone." He knelt down and gave Rishi a good rub around the ears. My dog groaned with pleasure. "Good dog. I'll be in charge of this investigation, okay fella?" He stood up and looked at me gravely. "I understand you found the body. Let's go someplace quiet where you can tell me about it."

"Okay. I'm Erika Norgren, by the way. The club's Director."

He lifted the yellow tape and we ducked under. Then Rishi and I led him up the steps and into the lobby. "We might as well use the group room," I said. "It's right through here." I opened a tall, golden oak door at the back of the lobby and ushered him through, then watched as he scanned the space.

"This room is our pride and joy," I said. "It was the main parlor back when this building was a townhouse. We use it for our community meetings, and the members like to hang out here, drink coffee, read the paper."

"I can see why. It's a beautiful room. Nice high ceilings."

"Yes, and it has the original moldings. The fireplace is bricked up, but it has a great view of the backyard." *And of Stephen Wright's body. Stop playing tour guide, Erika. This isn't the time.*

We found seats at a table. Rishi crawled beneath it and settled down.

Dennis settled back in his chair. "So, Erika. I'm familiar with some of the people here, but we haven't met. How long have you worked here?"

"About five months."

"This must be a heck of a thing to be faced with when you're new on the job."

I wasn't about to play damsel in distress. "I've had better days," I said crisply. "So what's the procedure going to be? When can I start letting members back in the club?"

"First, tell me what happened. Then you can show me around the building, and we'll see. Why don't you start with how you found the body?"

"Actually Rishi found him first. As soon as we got to my office, he took off across the room and tried to climb onto the fire escape. I thought he was after the pigeons."

"Do you always let him run loose around the club?"

"Not when anyone else is here. But it was early, and no one was around, so I didn't see any problem. I had no idea the window was open."

"What were you doing at the club so early?"

"The air conditioner in my apartment conked out, and the heat was unbearable. I checked the forecast on TV, and that weather guy who gives the irritability ratings said today was going to be a nine out of ten. That's why I didn't want to leave Rishi at home. It would have been cruel and inhumane to leave him stewing in that oven. The club has great air conditioning. Besides, I wanted to come in early to get a jump-start on the day. I often find I can get a lot more done –"

"Okay, Erika, I get the idea. Now let's get back to what happened in your office."

I told him what I remembered, then he took me over it again in more detail. Polite but thorough. Detective Malone was the archetypal Irishman – red hair, pale skin, startlingly green eyes. Not normally my type, but he got along with my dog, and I liked the way he was handling this. As a trained counselor with a master's degree in social work, I appreciate good interview skills. He was pulling information from me I didn't know I had.

"Our club secretary Gloria Valdez and I locked up the club last night after we'd seen the last members out, and as far as I knew, it was empty. Gloria checked the top two floors while I did the three lower ones."

Malone kept going over the bit about the window. Why was it open? "I don't like canned air all day." Did I usually leave it open? "No." Had I ever left it open before? "No" Why was it unlocked? "I don't know." Do you know where the key is? "No. The last time I noticed, it was hanging on a nail near the window, but it's gone now." Then he wanted to know about Stephen. Can you identify the victim? "Yes. Stephen Wright." Who would want to hurt him? "I can't think of anyone." Was he suicidal? "Not to my knowledge." Who would know? "His psychiatrist."

He stared at me stonily. "You're not helping me, Erika."

We were interrupted by a uniformed officer, who wanted access to the roof. It took me a couple of minutes to find the ring of keys that Gloria kept stashed at the back of a file drawer, then locate the one labeled "roof." I extricated it from the ring, handed it to the cop, then put the other keys in an envelope and stuffed them in my pocket.

"Okay," said Malone. "You can walk me through the club now."

"All right. Let's start with the roof."

Club members maintained a small roof garden where they grew flowers in buckets, broken pots and a couple of big wooden wine barrels. Watering the plants was a hassle, but the roof got full sun, so they preferred it to the backyard, which was usually in deep shade. In the early September heat, the roof was ablaze with showy annuals grown from seeds the members had ordered from catalogs and started indoors back in the spring. Pink and purple cosmos and cleomes were favorites, along with petunias, geraniums and dusty miller.

I started for the parapet, intending to look down into the back yard, but Malone grabbed hold of my arm. "Don't go over there. We don't want to mess up the roof till the crime scene people check it out. Don't touch anything, and don't say anything to the club members until we've had a chance to interview them."

His presence was reassuring, but his manner annoyed me. Or maybe it was the heat up on the roof, where the sun had already begun to feel like a plumber's torch on the back of my neck.

"You're not going to interview them all, are you? That's really going to upset some of them."

He glared at me. "I patrolled the streets around here before I got my detective's shield, and I can tell you some of the people you've got here are real hard cases."

"They are *club members*, Detective, not *hard cases*. Many of them are also extremely vulnerable. They are dealing with serious disabilities, and generally doing it rather well. I do not want you messing with them. Understand?"

His eyes narrowed almost imperceptibly. "We will be interviewing people. That's our job, Erika. But you can make it easier on everyone concerned by helping us out. We'd like an interview room, and once forensics is finished with the crime scene, I'll need you to identify the body. Now, we're going to walk off this roof exactly the way we came on."

I showed him the layout of the building floor by floor, top to bottom. We agreed the conference room at the front of the second floor would be a good place for interviews. "That's about it," I said at last. We were on the ground floor in the dining room, right near the phone where I had first called 911.

"What's over there?"

I followed his gaze to a barn-red door near the stairwell. "Oh, that's the door to the basement. The boiler's down there, all the mechanical stuff. There's a pool table and a couple of weight machines, but we keep it locked unless someone wants to use it. It's not really renovated, and we can't seem to get rid of the musty smell. Stan's in charge of the key."

"Okay, we'll check it out later."

Uniformed cops seemed to be everywhere. A woman officer was stationed at the front door with a clipboard, making a note every time someone entered or left the building. "She's the recorder," Malone explained. "Everyone coming in or out gets logged in."

"How long will the crime scene tape be up? How long do we have to keep the members out of the building?"

"Until I say so, Erika." His lips curved in absolute confidence.

"You're going to have a street full of very hot, upset people. Do you think I could give them a time?" With a wave of my hand, I indicated the growing crowd outside. "Two hours, say?"

He shrugged. "Whenever there's a body, there's always a crowd. Just so you know, this is my crime scene until I say otherwise. Once I decide you can let your folks in, I'll expect you to keep them away from the backyard, the roof, and anyplace else we have a ribbon up. That means you keep out, too. The doors stay locked and off limits. Understand?"

"Okay. But they like hanging out at the tables in the group room, and the windows look out on the back yard. What if somebody looks out and sees the body?"

"No problem. We'll be interviewing your patients anyway, and anything they see may help jog their memories. Or do you call them *clients*?"

"At WellSpring, we never use the term *client*, let alone *patient*. The people who come here suffer from serious mental illness, but they're able to function independently in the community, and they come here of their own free will. We provide a therapeutic environment, a safe space where club members can decompress, get their lives together, socialize, eat a good meal, maybe do some painting or writing. We also provide job training and career counseling. And we prefer the term *member*, or *consumer*."

Detective Malone presented his palms in a placating gesture. "OK, but we've got a job to do here and member or consumer both sound awkward. How about if I just call them *people*, or maybe *folks*?"

Finally, a breath of cool understanding. "People or folks will do just fine," I said with a smile.

Chapter 2

*W*hen Malone went off to start the interview process, I retreated to Gloria's office just off the lobby, where I put in a call to my boss, Ocala St. Claire, to let her know our building was now a crime scene belonging to an NYPD detective. Ocala is the head of Compassion House, an umbrella organization that runs WellSpring and half a dozen other community-based operations around the City. When I reached her voice mail, her deep contralto informed me she was unavailable. I left a message, then dialed her secretary, who reminded me that Ocala was away at a conference until tomorrow but promised to contact her.

I went out to the street where club members were milling around, sitting on the curb, the stoop. Many were smoking, muttering nervously as the police led away first one, then another to interview. I walked among them, trying my best to act reassuring while saying as little as I possibly could.

At about ten o'clock, Malone escorted Gloria Valdez down the steps and brought her over to me. Our club secretary was whimpering softly, gazing imploringly at me like a puppy who'd just been beaten to within an inch of her life.

I glared at the Detective. "Have you been mistreating my secretary?"

He glared back. "Just a standard interview. I had no idea she'd get so stressed out."

I had questions of my own for Gloria, but it would be useless trying to get anything out of her during one of her crying jags. "This situation is hard on all of us," I told her. "Why don't you take the rest of the day off? Go home and rest up for tomorrow."

She flashed a tremulous smile. "*Muchas gracias*, Erika. *Hasta manana.*"

Somehow the rest of the morning crept by. The police began letting the members in around eleven. Stan brewed coffee, decaf and regular, then brought the carafes up to the group room. People began to congregate, chatting quietly and reading the newspapers. There were hushed whispers and glances toward the windows in back, along with glances toward Stan, who had positioned himself like a high-school study hall monitor at the door to the group room.

I crossed the room to him. "How are things going? I assume you put Rishi back in his closet."

"Yeah, but he wasn't happy about it. I hope he doesn't piss all over those file cartons you got stacked up in there. But I don't want those cops messing with him. As far as the members are concerned, I've been doing what Malone suggested, telling them that Stephen had a fatal accident and that we can't talk about it until the police have finished."

"Thanks, Stan."

Stan opened his mouth, then shut it again, at an uncharacteristic loss for words.

"What's wrong, Stan? Is there something you're not telling me?"

He frowned. "People liked Stephen. He was a good man, and we should have a memorial service for him."

"You're right, I like that idea. But maybe it's a little premature. There hasn't even been a positive identification yet."

Stan grunted, sighed deeply, then folded his massive arms. In the silence that followed, I studied the black and blue tattoos that twined menacingly around his wrists and up his forearms. I'd never deciphered them, never had the nerve to ask for an interpretation, and this was hardly the time to start.

It was just before lunch when Detective Malone beckoned to me from the doorway. I crossed the group room self-consciously, acutely aware of all the curious eyes watching me with the handsome detective. He inclined his head down toward mine. "The crime scene technicians are finished, and they're bringing the body out now. I need you to take a look before they take the remains away to the morgue."

I felt suddenly shaky. All morning I'd managed to maintain a calm, professional veneer, but the charade had finally run its course. Meekly I followed Malone into the hallway, where a black body bag lay atop a metal gurney. He gave me an inquiring glance, I nodded, and he nodded in turn to a young woman dressed in a tee and khakis who stood near Stephen's head. Wordlessly, with latex-gloved hands that looked incongruously delicate, she tugged on the industrial-size zipper. As the face came into view, I caught a whiff of blood and excrement that was only partially masked by the new-plastic fumes of the body bag.

The face was serene, angelic, unmarred by so much as a scratch, but the curly brown hair was matted with dried blood, tangled like a crown of thorns. "That's definitely Stephen Wright." I felt suddenly dizzy. "I'd better sit down."

I turned around and there was Germaine Lavendre, all five foot six, 280 pounds of her, standing saucer-eyed and trembling. "That's Stephen," she said. "Is he OK?"

I put my arm over her shoulder, which helped steady me, and led her into the other room. "Stephen has had an accident," I said.

Julie Lomoe

"He looked dead," she said, in a high, flat voice. "I like Stephen. I'm sorry he's dead."

"We're all sorry," I said.

Malone caught up with us and shot me a warning glance. "We've asked Ms. Norgren not to discuss the investigation for the time being. When we learn more, we'll let her know and she can pass the information on."

He turned his gaze to me. "We're about finished here. Erika, in the course of your work, you have a lot of conversations with these folks, right?"

I nodded. "Of course."

"But it's not privileged communication, is it?"

"Maybe not in a legal sense, but we respect people's confidentiality," I said stiffly. "Trust is essential to the way we work here. And their files are off limits to anyone outside the agency."

He paused, studying me a long moment, probably wondering how far he could push. "I understand," he said finally. "But if you find anyone who knows anything or saw anything, you call me, understand? If you can think of why he might have committed suicide, that would help."

"All right. I'll do what I can, Detective." Or not. I felt an overwhelming need to be alone. "Can I go back into my office now?"

"I'll take you up there in a minute. But remember to keep people out of the back yard and off the roof until I give the okay. The crime scene tape will stay up for the rest of the day, at least."

"What about the plants?" squealed Germaine. "Without water, they'll die just like Stephen. He wouldn't have liked that. He liked flowers. He was an artist, you know."

"No one goes on the roof. Not this one here," he said, pointing to Germaine, "not you," pointing to me, "no one, understood? I expect you to keep it locked."

"But the plants," wailed Germaine in her high, grating voice.

14

"The plants can survive without water for a day," I said. "But we'll water them first thing tomorrow morning, I promise."

Malone shot me a glare. "No one else goes up there until we get this sorted out."

Sensing the street cop inside the dapper detective was yearning for release, I decided to cooperate. I let him escort me up to my office without voicing any of the complaints that were on the tip of my tongue.

As Malone closed the office door behind us, Rishi whined from the supply closet. "I'll leave him in there for now," I said. "He's used to it. There's plenty of room, and he has a blanket and some water."

"Whatever. Anyway, so far this looks like a straightforward suicide, but you never know. The cause of death could be anything from a heart attack to a hard shove in the back that pushed him over the edge."

He paused, watching me. I didn't give him any reaction, so he went on. "There are marks on the window ledge that could be footprints, although we'll have to wait for the lab guys to verify that, and there are marks where we think he went off the roof. He would have had easy access to the fire escape, because you keep the key to the window grate hanging beside the window." He skewered me with a look that spoke volumes about the foolishness of people who leave keys in obvious places. I felt myself flushing and his little twitch of a smile told me he noticed.

"Do you know of any reason this – " He paused to look down at his notebook. "This Stephen Wright might have wanted to take his own life?"

I hesitated. "I don't feel comfortable sharing confidential material with you."

"I could get a warrant, but it'll be a lot easier if you tell me what you know."

I chose my words carefully. "Stephen Wright had a long history of mental illness with several acute episodes. His diagnosis was bipolar disorder."

"That's the same as manic depression, right?"

"Bipolar disorder is the currently accepted term, yes. People with a bipolar diagnosis are at high risk for suicide. One out of ten actually succeeds. You might say that suicide is part of the landscape of their mental illness. On the other hand, many bipolar people are amazingly high achievers. When they manage to harness their creative energy, they can be incredibly imaginative and productive, so there's an up side as well."

He was gazing at me quizzically. The gleam in his green eyes unnerved me. "I'm something of an expert on the subject," I said. "I'm diagnosed bipolar too."

No sooner were the words out of my mouth than I regretted them. What on earth had possessed me to go blurting out information I shared with practically no one?

His eyes narrowed almost imperceptibly. "No kidding," he said. "You seem so together, I never would have guessed."

I felt myself getting bristly, combative. "Is that supposed to be a compliment?"

He actually had the grace to look embarrassed. "I didn't mean it the way it sounded."

"Detective, what I just told you is strictly confidential. No one here at the club knows I'm bipolar, not even my boss. I'd like to keep it that way."

"Understood. This interview is part of an official investigation. Anything you say here is off limits to anyone not working the case."

"Anyway, back to Stephen," I said. "If I recall his file correctly, he made a couple of serious suicide attempts a few years back, and both times he was admitted to the Bellevue psychiatric ward. He also had problems with drugs and alcohol. But he's been well stabilized since I've known him."

"Any recent problems?"

"As far as I know, his life was going well. He was earning money. He had the respect of his peers, attended AA meetings, and took his medications. That's a prescription for success, not suicide."

Malone frowned. "Whatever it was—heart attack, a slip and fall while attempting a burglary, too much alcohol, suicide, homicide—there are a lot of possibilities."

When he asked me to get him a list of the names and addresses of club members, I told him I'd have to check with Ocala St. Claire at Compassion House. He made a note and then looked at me with an intense but inscrutable stare calculated to make even Mother Theresa feel guilty. I let him look.

"Thanks, Erika," he said, finally. "That's enough for now. I'll let you get back to your members." He grinned, and his pale face reddened. "No offense, but the word *member* sounds like a reference to a body part. When I was a street cop, we used that in reports. Like, the complainant said the suspect waved his member in an exaggerated manner at her while urinating on the curb in front of 417 East 3rd Street."

I had to stifle a laugh, because I knew the people he was talking about. In my job, I probably know almost as much about the neighborhood as the local cops, and this particular pair had a notorious feud going. "I agree that *member* is an awkward term," I said, suppressing a grin. "But it's politically correct, so I guess we're stuck with it till the powers that be come up with something better."

He had me look over my office again to see if anything was missing, but he wouldn't let me touch anything. The place looked okay to me.

Malone and I left the room together. I stood silently watching as he put the crime scene tape back across the door and headed for the stairs. Not a bad looking guy, I thought. Jacket a little tight across the back, nice butt, probably works out.

Once he was out of sight, I walked down the hall to a small library that we like to show visiting dignitaries. The next big hurdle would be the morning community meeting. I could feel the stress building in my head, and an intense little whirlwind of grandiose thoughts starting to build. Maybe I could find a way to stop all bipolar suicides everywhere. Sure I could.

I needed some time alone to decompress and center myself. Years ago, I learned the hard way that time spent alone is a crucial coping mechanism for people with bipolar disorder. Back then I didn't allow myself that time. I suffered what my ex-husband called a "nervous breakdown" and did some things I later regretted. I know better now, but days like this can send me spinning if I'm not careful.

I locked the library door, put on a Keith Urban CD, and let the country music wash over me as my racing thoughts drained away. Twenty minutes later, I felt grounded and ready to face the world again. As I unlocked the door, I reminded myself to practice that attitude of detached concern that had been drummed into me in my social work internships—empathic and caring, yet with an invisible screen that keeps me from overstepping the boundary that separates professional from patient.

By the time I got down to the group room, the community meeting was already in progress. Typically, these meetings dealt with housekeeping details—who's on what work crew, when is the next van trip to the shopping mall in Paramus, are we short of art supplies, and so on. Gloria usually kept the minutes, but today Germaine was acting as secretary.

The club president, who was elected once a year, ran the meetings. This year it was Jeff Archer. A gifted artist, bipolar like Stephen, Jeff could be a little scattered at times, but generally he did all right. When he asked for unscheduled business, I stood up and gave a brief summary of the morning's events. I told them the police thought Stephen may have had an accident, and that I'd be available this afternoon if anyone wanted to talk with me about it.

The club members seemed surprisingly calm about Stephen's death. The isolationist tendencies so common to mental illness, combined with the medications that mask symptoms and mute emotions, probably had something to do with it. But maybe these folks were also more accustomed to sudden death than I was. Many of them had spent time living homeless on the streets.

The meeting ended just before lunch. We had a full time dietician who prepared one hot meal a day for the members, and I usually ate with them. Today, with only limited access to the kitchen, lunch was cold cuts and sandwich bread, served buffet style in the downstairs dining room.

After lunch, I walked Rishi while Stan supervised the clean-up crew. Heat rose in shimmering waves from the concrete sidewalks, the air was steamy and the few people who were outside shambled along at half speed. On the shady side of the street, shirtless men and women in tank tops and shorts lounged on fire escapes and front stoops, swigging beer from cans hidden in paper bags or chugging from plastic liters of soda. The street was like a giant comforter, an unpredictable but familiar mother enfolding me in its arms. Or an incubator of delusions.

I tried to picture Stephen just before he died. Had he really broken into my office after hours, climbed out my window and up the fire escape to the roof, then thrown himself off the parapet? It wasn't impossible. Could someone else jump off? Definitely. Maybe I should make it off-limits or try to talk Compassion House into installing a fence up there. Maybe I could launch a campaign to get the city to put up fences on every rooftop. *Simmer down, Erika. Grandiosity is a red flag for mania.*

Rishi brought me back to reality by crouching unexpectedly beside a spindly oak tree and producing a gigantic turd. Walking a dog in New York City means carrying a plastic baggy. When your dog does Number Two, you put your hand inside the bag, grab the turd, and roll the baggy off your hand with the turd inside. I prefer zip-lock bags, but lots of people use plastic supermarket bags, and I know a couple of devout ecologists who use the brown paper variety. I scooped the poop and we headed back to the club.

By the time we got back at one-thirty, most of the cops had gone, leaving yellow tape blocking the entrance to the back yard, the door to the roof and my office. Two officers remained to make sure no one messed with Malone's crime scene. I stopped by the file room and pulled Stephen's folder. Chart in hand, I locked myself in the library with Rishi, who went to sleep under a table.

I brooded over Stephen's record. The more I thought about him, the more I studied his case, the more puzzling his death became. There had been so many facets to his character, he was like a shape-shifting creature born of Hollywood special effects. Just when you thought you knew him, he would morph seamlessly into somebody else. Some days, he was a regular one-man theater repertory company. The only thing that never changed was that shirt of his. But even when he was hamming it up, there was an appealing, childlike quality to Stephen, a playfulness that people gravitated to. He was always involved in some project or other, and I made a mental note to find out what he'd been working on.

At this point, I didn't thank there was anything suspicious about his death. I just wanted to understand it. People are all too quick to dismiss the actions of mentally ill people as "crazy," but that's just another way of saying they don't understand. There's always a reason.

By now the police had canvassed the neighborhood, but they couldn't find any witnesses. Malone got Stan to identify the club members who knew Stephen best, and detectives interviewed them in our second-floor conference room. By mid-afternoon, Malone was gone, and there was only one cop left on the scene, making sure no one got into the back yard. By four o'clock, she was gone too.

I asked Stan to help me close up for the night. We let Rishi off his leash, and the three of us went through every room in the building, carefully, starting at the top, looking for anything unusual or out of place. I made extra sure the grate on my office window was padlocked, and I locked my office door, too. We left together and stood talking after I set the alarm on the front door.

"What do you think, Stan? Did Stephen kill himself?"

Stan peered down at me over his small, steel-rimmed glasses. "He was a happy man in recent days. The Lord works in mysterious ways, but this is a hard one to understand."

"What was he into lately? Was there anything in particular he was happy about?"

"Well, he was excited about some mosaics he was designing for the stairway in that squat where he lives, and he was making some benches for the community garden down the block, the one that lady runs. Ariana Birdsong. Some people call her the Garden Nazi, but I like her well enough."

"What squat was he living in?"

"Nine Squat."

"Where's that? I don't know the squats all that well."

"On Ninth Street, off Loisaida." That's now the official name for what used to be Avenue C until someone in City Hall decided the popular Spanglish term for the Lower East Side would be a good way to gain some political brownie points. Stan paused, and his eyes narrowed. "You're not going over there, are you? Bunch of alkies and crusty punks in that building."

"Rishi and I will be OK."

Stan squinted appraisingly at Rishi, who rubbed his muzzle against the man's imposing thigh, angling for an ear rub. "This dog looks bad. Maybe they won't realize he's just an old sweetie. Anyway, most of the people in Nine Squat are harmless enough. Besides, they probably won't even let you in."

Chapter 3

*T*wenty minutes later, Rishi and I stood on the sidewalk staring at a heavy steel door and graffiti-decorated plywood where windows should have been. Nine Squat was a boarded up building next to a vacant lot. Stan had briefed me about the place. It had been abandoned by the owner and taken over by New York City years ago for back taxes. For awhile, it was used by drug addicts as a crack house and shooting gallery. After it was damaged by fire, the City boarded it up. Then about ten years ago, squatters moved in and began renovating the building without getting permission from the City, much less paying rent to anyone. In a way, I admired the city's squatters - they were the only folks I knew of who managed to create a viable life style while evading Manhattan's exorbitant rents.

By now most of the squats had been legalized as coops, and the squatters were landed gentry after their own eccentric fashion. But this squat looked more eccentric than most, like a six-story brick fortress with the drawbridge up. Gentrification had not reached this far east. The façade was painted a dusty, matte black, and black vinyl shrouded the windows. A few posters and some random graffiti provided tentative bits of color, but failed to make inroads on the overall impression of a post-apocalyptic bunker under siege, like something out of a Mad Max movie.

I marched up to the front door and rapped with my knuckles. That hurt and made hardly any noise. If anyone heard me, they didn't respond. With no bell or buzzer, I was at an impasse. Should I yell up at the windows? The block was practically deserted, except for a tall man dressed in black who was walking a dog toward us down the block. I switched to a tight, two-handed grip on Rishi's leash and braced for a possible confrontation.

The man and his dog approached slowly, sizing us up. The dog was a pit bull, and they give me the creeps. I'm an inveterate dog lover, but I make an exception for this particular breed. There's something unnerving about the way they skulk around with a sullen expression, as if they're suffering from a lousy self-image and are just waiting to bolster their egos by attacking you. Rishi didn't much like the pit bull either; both dogs stood tensely, staring silently at each other.

Up close, the man appeared younger than at a distance. His skin was pale and his thin, tattooed arms protruded from an open leather vest. As he got closer, the swaying vest revealed a skeletal white chest and pierced nipples. He wore artfully torn black dungarees, and a nose ring, an eyebrow ring and multiple lip rings embellished his sweat-drenched face.

We recognized one another at about the same time. He gave me a hint of a smile and I gave him the same. "Don't I know you?" I asked. "Aren't you Joshua?"

"Joshua Gordon, yes. And you're Erika. You run WellSpring Club, right? I didn't expect to see you over here." He glanced down at his dog. "Don't worry about Mugsy. He only attacks when I give the command; otherwise he's a sweetheart. Can I help you? Are you looking for Stephen?"

The polite inflections of the young man's speech were pure Ivy League, distinctly at odds with his threatening image.

I hated to tell him. "Do you know Stephen well?" I asked.

"He lives here. One of the originals, you know? If he hadn't sponsored me, I wouldn't have a place to live right now."

"How do you mean, *sponsored?*"

"In this squat, you have to be voted in, and you can't do that without a sponsor. So are you looking for Stephen?"

"I'm afraid I have some bad news." I paused, searching for the right words. They didn't come, so I just blurted it out. "We found Stephen's body this morning in the back yard behind the club."

He seemed to recoil and curl in on himself. His aura of black-leather badness evaporated, replaced by a wide-eyed little boy with trembling lips. "No!" He fell silent, then shook his head vehemently. "No, it's impossible. I mean not impossible, but unbelievable. Not now, after everything he's been through. He was doing so well. Are you sure? How did it happen?"

"We don't know. It could have been an accident, or suicide. We'll have to wait and see what the Medical Examiner has to say." I gave him a brief summary. Stephen's chart had revealed no traceable next-of-kin, and someone should share the burden of grief.

"Stephen spoke very highly of you," said Joshua at last. His eyes glistened with unshed tears. "It's not that I don't trust you, but I don't see Stephen jumping off a roof. He didn't do drugs anymore, but he still liked beer. It could have been an accident or a stroke or something. I can't see suicide, but hey, what do I know. I'm not a shrink."

"Neither am I, and I'm not sure how he died. That's why I came over here. Maybe if I can understand more about him, where he lived and what he was into, it'll shed some light on what happened."

"That would be great. Stephen was a good person. He doesn't deserve to be brushed aside and forgotten."

"Do you think you could let me in to take a look at his place?"

"Sure, I guess so. But be careful and watch your step. It's dark inside, and the hallways and stairwell are kind of rustic."

Rustic was putting it mildly. Once he unlocked the deadbolt and ushered us in, I stood uncertainly while my eyes adjusted to the darkness. He pulled out a gigantic flashlight and shone it at my feet so I could get my bearings. "Don't worry, there's electricity in the apartments," he said. "The circuit must have tripped again for the main hall, and our electrician is out of town right now."

"This building has its own electrician?"

"Oh, definitely. It takes a lot of skill to hook up and maintain the electric without the hassles of dealing with Con Ed. Me, I'm more into carpentry and sheet rocking. Everyone has to contribute something. Now Stephen, he was really artistic. See here, at the base of the stairwell, all the mosaics? He was planning to tile all the risers, at least up to his apartment on the third floor."

His flashlight illuminated a rainbow of ceramic colors, big chunks of crockery fitted into a freeform, undulating mosaic. "I've never seen anything like it," I said, "except once in Barcelona when I saw the works of that architect—"

"Gaudi!" he broke in. "Stephen loved Gaudi's work, claimed he was his biggest inspiration. You're the first person who ever made that connection."

We gazed in silence at the intricate patterns. He let the light travel slowly around and over the mosaics, then up the stairs. Rishi and I followed Josh and Mugsy up a couple of flights, until the mosaics stopped. A little further up, so did the stairs. "What happened here?" I asked.

"We haven't finished yet. We were replacing the treads, keeping a couple of days ahead of Stephen. I don't know what will happen now. Every time we work on the stairs, it'll remind us of Stephen. I hope people don't lose heart. "

"I hope so too. But in the meantime, how do you get to the upper floors?"

He pointed to some steep wooden steps, little more than a ladder, that rose up and disappeared in darkness. "You want to see his room?"

I gazed into the inky blackness above, and my heart contracted into a clenched fist. Heights aren't my thing. Besides, I rationalized, my long denim skirt and sandals were ill suited for climbing, and I couldn't very well leave Rishi tied here in the hallway of a building where no one knew him. "Thanks, I'll take a rain check. But tell me something. You say Stephen was actively involved in this project right up till the end? He hadn't gotten discouraged and given up?"

"Not at all. In fact he put in a few tiles last night, right before he went out." He waved the flashlight around, illuminating random bits of Stephen's mosaic work. "It doesn't make sense, does it," he mused. "Why would someone so gung ho about something suddenly turn around and off himself?"

I couldn't come up with a reasonable answer. "You're right," I said. "It doesn't make sense."

As I headed home with Rishi, thoughts ricocheted around my brain like popcorn in a microwave. Normally I enjoy walking through the Lower East Side. The streets are full of murals, many of them memorials to dead recording artists – Jimi Hendrix and Bob Marley are perennial favorites – or to popular locals who had died. Some of the paintings are small, taking up only a five by six-foot section of wall, while others take up the whole side of a building. I love those murals. The vibrant colors, the beautiful faces and bodies, the high-energy compositions celebrate the glory of life. In their way, they are as profoundly moral and beautiful as the art I saw in medieval cathedrals when I went to Europe years ago.

I like the smells, too, wafting from the Chinese and Hispanic restaurants, and from the occasional yuppie pub or vest-pocket restaurant. Tonight, though, I was indifferent to the pleasures. Despite the heat, I strode purposefully along, eyes scanning the sidewalks and doorways, ears alert for footsteps and unusual noises. Ten years in the city along with a few martial arts classes had honed my self-preservation skills, and it was second nature to project an aura of confidence that proclaimed I was no one to mess with. But tonight the façade was fragile, and I was relieved when I reached the comfort of my apartment on Tenth Street near Avenue A.

My trip to Stephen's squat preyed on my mind as Rishi and I trudged up the four flights of stairs to my apartment, which was like an oven. Once in the solitude of my own space with the long police-lock bar holding the door against all intruders, the images in my mind began to intensify, feeding on themselves and growing like a malignant tumor. The sight of Stephen's body with his chestnut hair in a puddle of blood on the asphalt, blood splatters glinting in the early morning sunlight, replayed in my head like a mantra to some ugly primeval god that demanded human sacrifice.

Unwilling to give in to the nightmare, I wandered over to my Yamaha keyboard, untouched for over a month. Lately I'd been pouring so much creative energy into my job that I had little left over for my music. I turned on the machine, punched in the "Galaxy" sound and began noodling, letting my fingers meander through fragments of jazz and rock songs, experimenting with the dozens of voices and rhythms that were electronically embedded in the machine. But my improvisations kept segueing into minor-key dirges, which led inevitably to thoughts of Stephen.

Since the music wasn't working its usual magic, I decided to give in to my addiction to FreeCell. I flicked the switch and let the computer boot up while I opened a window, poured a glass of wine, and loaded my CD player with Alan Jackson, Keith Urban and Tim McGraw. My musical tastes are eclectic, but there's nothing like country and western to divert me from my demons. I also tried pounding on the air-conditioner a few times with no results and swore to buy myself a fan in the morning.

Determined to ignore both unwelcome thoughts and the sweat running down my ribs, I hunkered down with my computer for an evening of mindless distraction with Double Free Cell, a game that involves manipulating two full decks of cards into four orderly piles. As I play, I often find myself running a fantasy drama in my mind.

Tonight's script was about a foiled robbery, fire escapes and rooftop battles. After several losses, I got on a roll and was on the verge of winning my third game in a row when I realized what puzzled me most about Stephen's death. Not the probability of suicide – bipolarity and suicide often go together. It was the logistics. How did Stephen get into the club after hours? Could he have stowed away someplace while Gloria and I did our closing walk-through? And if he wanted to go up on the roof, he didn't need to break into my office and go through the window. He could have taken the key from Gloria's ring of room keys, which the regulars knew about, and gone up the stairs.

And if he had wanted to commit suicide, why throw himself off a relatively low building into an empty courtyard? A four-story building isn't all that high. Instead of dying, he stood a good chance of breaking a bunch of bones and lying in agony for hours before anyone found him. Would he have risked that? And what was he doing in the club after hours anyway?

I thought about Gloria's tearful act that morning. I had let her take the day off because it's WellSpring policy to make accommodations for persons with disabilities, but I wasn't convinced she was losing it mentally. As Administrative Secretary, she had access to every nook and cranny in the club. She could be hiding something from the cops, or from me. It was getting dark outside, but still not too late to get some answers. I decided to pay Gloria a visit.

Chapter 4

As I slipped into my sandals and grabbed my purse, Rishi jumped to his feet and bounded to the door expecting another walk. I was tempted to bring him, but I didn't want him distracting Gloria while I interviewed her. "Be a good boy," I told him. "Guard the place."

Outside, the evening air was a good ten degrees cooler than in my apartment, and a gentle breeze helped dissipate the oppressive heat. It seemed everyone in the neighborhood was out on the stoops and sidewalks enjoying nature's air conditioning. In the street, kids played ball and showed off their in-line skating and skate boarding skills while parents watched from the sidelines, no doubt as reluctant as me to hole up in their stifling apartments.

Gloria lived just two blocks east, in an old tenement building about the same vintage as mine. But my building had been painstakingly rehabilitated, while hers was decidedly down at the heels, its facade and hallways encrusted with what looked like a century's worth of grime. I'd been there before, because several club members had one-room apartments in the building.

The place was owned and operated by Vito Pisanello, a local slumlord who liked to allude to his mob connections. According to the neighborhood grapevine, he was holding onto this and several other buildings as tax write-offs and investment properties, waiting for an opportune time to make a killing when the real estate market was close to peak. I'd met Vito a couple of times, and found him instantly infuriating.

"Hi, Erika! What are you doing here? Did you come to visit me?"

My musings had brought me to Gloria's doorstep, and the lilting voice was hers.

Standing next to a skinny young man, she was looking slightly wobbly and holding an open can of Budweiser. From the looks of things, she'd been drowning her sorrows, and quite successfully at that.

"Yes, as a mater of fact, I did, Gloria. Do you have a few minutes to talk?"

"Sure. Come on, there's plenty of room right here." She plopped herself down on the top step of the stoop and patted the cement beside her.

"It would be better if we go inside where we can have more privacy."

Her liquid brown eyes grew suddenly wary, and she glanced away. "You want to talk about Stephen? I cannot, is too upsetting. All day I was crying, I couldn't stop until finally Ricky here bought me a couple of beers and helped me calm down."

Sinking down beside her, I put my hand on her shoulder. "I've been upset too. Maybe it would help us feel better if we talk together. We both knew him pretty well, and we might have a lot to share."

She looked directly into my eyes, then sprang to her feet. "You're right. Come on, I'll show you my place." She smiled at Ricky and thrust out her chest importantly. "Thanks for the beers, Ricky. Sorry I got to go, but my boss and I need to talk."

I had the distinct feeling she was glad for an excuse to get away from Ricky, and that he wasn't happy about it. Whatever dynamics were going down, it was fine as long as she opened up to me.

Gloria had a studio apartment on the third floor at the rear. It was a single room with a sofa bed, the kitchen a mere closet-sized alcove with louvered doors, but I sensed her pride as she showed me around. Her housekeeping was much better than mine, and the room vibrated with color – posters for salsa musicians and singers, green plants, baskets of silk flowers. A parakeet with brilliant turquoise plumage chirped from its cage as I basked in the cool breeze of the air conditioner.

After a brief but futile attempt to talk with the parakeet, I plunged ahead. "I'm uncomfortable about Stephen's death. The police haven't determined whether it was suicide or something else, and since you knew him so well, I hoped you might have some ideas about it."

"What kind of ideas? I don't know what you mean." Her voice held a nervous quaver.

"I'm not sure. I don't know what I'm looking for. Just anything out of the ordinary, I guess."

She sank onto the sofa, buried her face in her hands. Her shoulders were shaking.

I hated to pressure her, but despite the air conditioner, I hated the thought of staying here for hours even more. I made my voice stern. "What is it, Gloria? You have something you need to tell me, don't you."

Silence, then muffled sobs. She still wouldn't look up. At last I sank to my knees in front of her, clasped both her hands in mine and pulled them away from her face. "Please," I said. "For Stephen's sake."

She gazed at me with big spaniel eyes. "Okay. I am a good person, an honest person. Ask anybody, they'll tell you. I cannot live with secrets and deceptions, and I cannot live with Stephen's death on my conscience. In a way, I'm afraid I may have played a part."

This was more than I'd bargained for. I moved to the sofa beside her and waited silently for her to continue. Silence is often the most powerful way to elicit information, for counselors as well as cops.

"I gave Stephen the keys to the club so he could go up to the roof. And I told him the combination to the alarm because he needed to go in and out after hours. If not for me, he wouldn't have been up there at all. He might still be alive."

I took a deep breath, then another. I wanted to ask why, but the word *why* makes people defensive. Better to be empathic. "You must have had a pretty good reason for doing that," I said softly.

"Well, it seemed like it at the time. He was making mosaic planters up there, you know, and he wanted to work late in the afternoon or early in the morning, before it got too hot. He said the sun dries out the mortar too quick, so the tiles don't stick right."

"I thought he finished those planters a month ago."

"Maybe also he sleeps up there on really hot nights. He told me he liked the plants and seeing the sky at night. The windows in his place are painted black so he can't see out, and he doesn't have an air conditioner. He says it's like hell when the temperature gets above ninety."

"I can imagine," I said in the most soothing voice I could muster. In fact, I was seething. No one had even hinted at something like this.

"So I loaned him the extra key to the roof door. He wouldn't steal anything, you know."

I was not at all sure of that. I had a brief fantasy of pierced and unwashed squatters partying on the roof of the club when it was supposed to be closed.

"Are you okay?" She looked worried.

"I understand." I said. "So who else knew about it?"

"Only the people he told where he was. He had a lot of friends, you know."

"Do you think he was depressed?"

"Oh no, not at all."

"Then do you know if he had any enemies? Anyone he was fighting with, or who might have wanted him dead?"

Gloria was silent, and I could almost see the wheels turning behind her luminous eyes. "No," she said at last. "You know Stephen. He was usually excited about something, and he got along with everybody. When he was depressed, he just kept to himself. And he never mentioned any problems with anybody."

"That's my impression too." Suddenly exhausted, I stood and stretched. "It's after ten. I'd better get home."

She looked relieved. "So you're not mad? You're not going to fire me?"

"No, but I need to know if there are any more keys floating around, either to the roof, the front door or anywhere else."

"Just the two keys I gave Stephen. And only me and Stanley know the alarm code."

I made her promise not to give away any more keys or codes, and I promised myself to have the doors re-keyed and the alarm code reset first thing in the morning. Gloria would no longer have access to the alarm or doors leading to the outside. We talked for a couple of minutes about the mosaic planters Stephen had made and agreed it was a shame to lose a fine artist like him. Then I left Gloria sitting on the stoop with Ricky and his beer.

Back in my apartment, the message light was flashing on my answering machine. It was Detective Malone, asking me to meet him. From his tone, I couldn't tell if this was a business call or a man looking to spice up an empty evening. I dialed the cell phone number he left, and he picked up on the second ring. He asked me to meet him at Tag, a new bar just down the block that had purple and red neon scrolled over the facade like graffiti. I hadn't been there yet, and I was curious to see the inside of the place, but I waffled demurely until he told me the place had great air conditioning. "See you in half an hour," I said then.

Was this a date? No matter – my workday clothes were clinging sweatily to my body, and I badly needed a change. I sniffed one armpit experimentally, decided I smelled too funky even for the East Village. I slipped into the shower, then into a black Victoria's Secret thong, a skimpy green sundress and some spiky mules.

I studied myself in the full-length mirror on my bedroom door. *Not bad for thirty-three.* Maybe some blusher, some shadow to bring out the blue of my eyes? No, forget it. I didn't want Malone thinking I'd gone out of the way to look good for him, and besides, I was running late. I ran a brush through my unruly blond hair, spritzed myself liberally with Obsession, and headed out the door.

When I arrived at Tag, Malone had already commandeered a table near the window and was brooding over a half-empty mug of beer. When he glanced up and saw me, his eyes tracked the length of my body and his face flushed slightly, belying his cool, offhand demeanor.

My face grew warm in response. Aha, I thought: the plot thickens. His fair Irish looks were starting to grow on me, and with the sensitive, brooding expression he wore this evening, he could have sprung full-blown from a TV cop show. I ordered a gin and tonic. We indulged in some chitchat. Then he pulled out a pen and steno pad and placed them deliberately on the black lacquered table between us. *The knight throws down his gauntlet,* I thought.

"You've been holding out on me," he said flatly, confronting me with his green eyes. "I need everything you know about Stephen Wright."

"That's a change," I said. "This afternoon I got the impression you were ready to write Stephen off as a suicide. What's going on?"

"First you answer my questions, Erika. Then I might answer some of yours. But keep in mind this is a potential homicide investigation, and I'm responsible for making this case."

"Okay, Dennis, shoot," I said, flashing him a quick smile.

"Let's start by you telling me what he was doing on the roof and how he got into the building."

I sighed and gave him a rundown on everything I'd learned from Josh and Gloria. Then I asked him if he knew yet how Stephen died.

"According to the ME, it wasn't the fall that killed him."

"No?"

"No. It was the sudden stop."

Detective humor, I thought. *Ugh.*

"In other words, he wasn't stabbed, or bludgeoned, or poisoned," Malone went on. "He didn't die of a stroke or a heart attack or an overdose. He fell. I was at the autopsy this afternoon, and the ME couldn't find any signs of a struggle, no marks where he had been shoved, nothing but garden dirt under his fingernails, no sign of sexual activity. But get this. His belt was riding very high on his stomach."

He paused to see if I got the importance of his statement, but if this was a pop quiz, I flunked. I gave him a puzzled look.

"When I was a rookie," he explained, "we had a DOA that got bounced from a club and hit his head, which killed him. Now the thing is, bouncers learn to eighty-six a guy by grabbing the back of his shirt and his belt and literally lifting the guy up in the air as they walk him to the door. If your roof was a club, I'd say he could have gotten bounced. Some of your people are strong enough to do that, aren't they? Maybe that guy Stanley Washington?"

My first reaction was to jump to Stan's defense, but I couldn't quite get the words out, because it was just possible, if he came back to the club for something and found Stephen on the roof, that it might have led to a fight. "I don't think so," I said, choosing my words carefully. "Stan's history indicates he's violent only when he's in a delusional state. And it's always accompanied by substance abuse. To the best of my knowledge, he's been on the straight and narrow for several years. I'd know if he was becoming delusional again."

"Maybe. What about the others?" Malone reached down and pulled a file folder from a bag at his feet. "You wouldn't believe how much we know about people. Once you get into the NYPD's computers with your own identification system number, you're ours for life. We talked to a lot of your people today, and I've found rap sheets on half a dozen."

"Where are you going with this, Detective?"

"I think one of your members is probably our killer. What do you think, Erika?"

I was about to tell him exactly what I thought, in not very nice terms, when I was saved by a slight, wiry man who appeared suddenly at Dennis's shoulder.

"Hey, Erika, what are you doing with this jerk?" My eyes were approximately level with the man's black-denim crotch. When I raised them, I found myself staring into the icy gray eyes of Arthur Drummond, an occasional member of the club.

"Hello, Arthur," I said, putting some ice in my voice. "Sorry I didn't get a chance to talk with you earlier today, but now's not a good time. Are you coming to the club tomorrow?"

"I split right after lunch. Nothing worth sticking around for. But you haven't answered my question. What are you doing here?"

Dennis broke in. "You want something, Zapata? Spit it out or take off."

"I didn't know you hung out with cops," Arthur said, trying to ignore Dennis. "I'm disappointed in you, Erika." His voice had a harder edge now, and I knew the effect was deliberate. Arthur used his voice, his words, and his good looks to charm or intimidate, in keeping with the occasion. I hated to admit it, but his ferocity scared me a little.

I tried to sound casual. "We're just relaxing, trying to revive after a long, hard day."

"I don't recall inviting you to join us, Zapata," Dennis said, fixing him with one of his blinkless stares. "Why don't you take a hike?"

Arthur stood rigidly, his eyes fixed on the distance somewhere above our heads. "I don't take orders from no cop," he hissed.

"Don't make me mad, Zapata. You got about five seconds before I arrest your ass for menacing." His tone was curt and decidedly unfriendly until he turned back to me. "Now where were we before we were interrupted?"

Arthur glowered briefly, then turned tail and left.

I held my tongue till he was safely out the front door. "I gather you two know each other," I said. "Why do you call him Zapata?"

"I busted him a couple of years ago. At that time he was walking around with a droopy mustache, a sombrero, and a sword. Called himself Zapata after a character in an old movie."

"The movie was *Viva Zapata*, and the actor was Brando," I said. "And his real name is Arthur Drummond."

"Whatever. I'm sorry to say this about one of your members, but he's both a nut case and a dirt bag. He's spent some time on Riker's. Drunk and disorderly, robbery. And he has a history of harassing women, getting obsessive about them."

"How do you mean?" It was all too easy to picture Arthur as a stalker, a rapist or worse. Evidently my uneasiness about him had been right on target. These unsavory details had not been in his file at the club.

"When he's attracted to a woman, he's been known to follow her, phone her, write letters. Nothing worse than that, so far as we know. But with sociopaths like him, the antisocial behavior often escalates over time, isn't that right?"

"Not always. When people with mental disabilities take their meds and keep up their therapy, they can often keep their symptoms under control and live normal lives."

"Like you, for example."

"You're going to keep throwing that in my face, aren't you? I shouldn't have told you I was bipolar."

"Sorry, I couldn't resist needling you. Can I buy you another drink by way of apology?"

The man was infuriating, but I was tempted. "Better not," I said at last. "God only knows what else I'll tell you if you loosen my tongue with more alcohol."

"Well, don't say I didn't offer. Anyway, Erika, I asked around about you and the wire is you know how these people tick. They tell me you even helped us out a few times when you were a social worker at Beth Israel. What happened that you ended up at WellSpring?"

None of your business. My years helping distraught people who came into hospital emergency wards were far behind me. "That was a long time ago," I said. "A different job. "

"Has he come on to you yet?"

"Arthur? He's complimented me a couple of times on my clothes, things like that. Once he asked if I was involved with anyone. I told him yes."

"Are you?"

Was the question personal or professional? I tried for an inscrutable Mona Lisa smile. "Does it make any difference?"

He leaned back in the booth, his arms folded. "It might."

I smiled. "Finish your beer, Detective. Have you seen any good movies lately?"

He hadn't. Neither had I. So much for small talk. I insisted we split the check, which he didn't like, but then I let him walk me back to my apartment, which made him feel better. We shook hands at the door, and I went upstairs alone.

———

I postponed the lonely night ahead by treating Rishi to an hour-long walk. That bled off some of my nervous energy, but there was plenty to spare when we got back.

Images kept swimming in my mind's eye, slipping in and out of focus: Stephen's lifeless body sprawled in the courtyard. Arthur's malevolent glare when he saw me with Dennis, and the concern on Dennis' face as he questioned me about the club members.

Stephen's death nagged at me more than ever, but I wasn't sure what if anything I could do about it. Dennis Malone's information only ruled out death by natural causes, leaving suicide, murder and accident as possibilities, although Dennis was clearly leaning toward murder as the explanation that fitted the facts. I really wanted to talk with someone about it, but it was after midnight, and I no longer had friends I could call on late at night.

A sudden hunger pang reminded me that I'd completely forgotten about dinner. I slathered some chunky peanut butter on a slice of seven-grain bread, made Rishi a similar entree, poured a glass of Merlot to keep me heart-healthy and flipped on the TV to catch the local news.

I paid less attention to the news than to Rishi, who was opening and closing his jaws, licking his lips, still in the throes of his peanut butter experience. "Was it as good for you as it was for me?" I asked, unsure whether he was enjoying himself to the last taste or trying to cleanse his mouth of the sticky stuff.

I was waiting for the weather and debating whether to stay up for Jay Leno's monologue when I heard the word *WellSpring*. I glanced up to see a shot of the club's facade just over the announcer's shoulder. Then all at once there was footage of some members out on the sidewalk in front of the club. The streetlights were on but there was still some daylight, so the TV news team must have been there while I was talking with Gloria. A young blond woman was interviewing them. "Stephen Wright's suicide was a terrible tragedy," she said as she thrust a microphone in Germaine's face. "Do you have any comments for our viewers?"

"He was a really good guy," said Germaine in her squeaky rasp. "It's hard to believe he'd do something like this."

"But I understand he was bipolar, or what people used to call manic depressive. Doesn't that put him at high risk for suicide?"

"I guess. I don't know," she mumbled.

Stan suddenly appeared and draped a protective arm around Germaine's shoulders. "Don't answer her, Germaine." He turned to the camera. "A man's medical history is personal and confidential, and it should stay that way," he said, with a righteous ring in his voice. "We focus on people's strengths, not their weaknesses."

Good for you, Stan, I thought.

"But you must have medical staff who can monitor how everyone's doing?" The reporter's upbeat, chirpy style struck a false note that set all my alarm bells ringing.

"No," said Stan. "This is a place people come for help with social problems and work training. They – "

"You mean they are totally unsupervised?" said the reporter, cutting him off. "Completely without medical care?"

"They get their medical care elsewhere," said Stan.

"I'm afraid we're out of time, but that's an area we'll explore in more depth as this story unfolds. This is Nancy Welcome for News Channel Eight. Now back to the studio."

I zapped the TV with my clicker and thought about what I'd just seen. The reporter was not simply asking random questions, she was going after something. I couldn't tell if she was just misinformed, or deliberately trying to provoke a reaction.

When I worked at the hospital, a detective told me he was required to wear a suit because the news stations monitor police radio calls and could show up on the scene at any time. I remembered a sign the public relations director at the hospital where I first worked used to keep taped to the inside of her desk: "The Media is the Enemy."

Chapter 5

"*H*ey, Erika, what's up?"

Ocala's deep voice jerked me away from Stephen's chart. It was ten the next morning. I'd already written up the incident report on his death and was poring over his records when I looked up to see her looming in the doorway.

"I didn't expect you back so soon," I said.

"My secretary paged me at the conference yesterday and filled me in a little. All those panel discussions about Medicaid were boring me to tears, so I decided to come back a day early. Flew into Kennedy at three in the morning, and I'm exhausted. But I got here as soon as I could."

"I'm so glad you're back." I had a sudden urge to jump up from my desk and hug her, to draw strength from the pillowy warmth of her embrace, but I managed to restrain myself. She was my boss, after all.

Ocala St. Claire exuded power and strength. A black woman with deep chestnut skin, she carried her 250-plus pounds with the confidence of a pro wrestler on her nearly six-foot frame. Like a wrestler, she cultivated a flamboyant personal image and talked with intimidating vehemence when she was getting a point across. She grew up in a housing project in the Bronx, and her street smarts showed. But I'd seen occasional glimpses of a softer side, and I suspected that much of her public persona was a carefully cultivated act, one she used with tremendous effect to crusade for her multiple causes.

I'd met Ocala a few times when I was a psychiatric social worker at Beth Israel Hospital. I saw some of her Compassion House clients in the emergency room, and she must have liked what she knew of my work, because she saw fit to hire me as Director of WellSpring five months ago. I was long gone from Beth Israel by then, having suffered a conspicuously manic meltdown. But if Ocala knew that unsavory part of my history, if she even suspected I was bipolar, she never mentioned it during the interview process, and I wasn't about to broach the subject.

As for the major gap in my professional resume between Beth Israel and WellSpring, I'd taken refuge in a series of low-stress clerical temp jobs. Burnout, I told Ocala. A radical understatement, but she appeared to buy into my explanation, along with my assurances that after taking stock, I'd recommitted fully to my social work career.

In the five months I'd been at WellSpring, I'd come to love the place and the people. Ocala didn't give me much feedback, but all in all I was confident I was doing a decent job. With any luck, I would pass probation and become a permanent employee in the near future. There had been some rocky moments, a few crises, but nothing like Stephen's suicide topped off by Nancy Welcome's muck raking newscast. I hoped my luck wasn't about to run out.

I invited Ocala to sit, got us some coffee, and filled her in on what I knew of Stephen's death. She agreed we had to re-key the system immediately and restrict after-hours access to the building. For the time being, only I and the administrative staff at Compassion House would have access. She was also bothered by the garden on the roof, but decided closing it should have to be my call. There was no money to put up a fence.

Closing the garden would mean killing the plants, but the risk was real. I told her I'd inform the members of the bad news at our meeting that morning.

Then she got to the hard part. "I saw Nancy Welcome's interview last night. Did you know anything about that?"

"Not until it aired on the eleven o'clock news. Judging by the way the light looked, it must have been around sunset. I was interviewing Gloria about that time."

"What's with that reporter bitch?" Ocala shook her head, reminding me of an angry mama grizzly. "I don't want you saying anything about how this cop thinks one of our members might have gotten murdered right here in the club. Know what I mean?"

I nodded in agreement.

"And if that Nancy Welcome and her Eye on the Apple news team show up again, call me right away. You are the only one who talks with her from now on. You tell Stanley and all the other club members, they should just walk away when she comes calling."

"I understand."

It was almost time for our morning meeting, so I invited Ocala to stay.

She grinned. "You don't get me that easy. I have to be uptown before noon. A couple of suits from the Zebulon Foundation are treating me to lunch at Tavern on the Green. If I play my cards right, Compassion House might just get some significant crumbs from the table. Maybe get you a fence up there, keep people safe. Anyway, your meeting might go better without me. Put on your therapist hat and do some group processing around that boy's death."

The agenda for the morning community meeting was fairly informal, with reports on current happenings and upcoming events, then open discussion of whatever issues might be on people's minds. Usually the majority of those present were fairly passive, preoccupied with their inner imaginings or subdued by the powerful medications that controlled their psychoses. Keeping them involved yet on topic was a constant challenge.

Jeff Archer's vague leadership style was not enough to keep things together. Today he was wearing a pink button-down shirt with the collar buttons missing, shopworn chino pants and untied basketball shoes. His lank brown hair was in need of washing, and his gangly body was constantly in motion. Neither his appearance nor his soft-spoken manner commanded attention. Members wandered off for coffee or conversed quietly, generally ignoring the meeting in progress.

When I accepted the job as director of WellSpring, I'd been looking for something low key, not too stressful, but challenging enough to rekindle my professional skills. "I like your style," Ocala had told me. "You're upfront but never condescending. That's why you'd be perfect for the job. The club is run almost entirely by the consumers. The members make most of the decisions and run the day-to-day programming. I don't want someone on a power trip who would pull rank all the time."

Up to now my understated style had worked out well, but with so much going on, I decided it was time to adopt a more assertive leadership role. Empowerment for club members did not mean abandoning common sense. For awhile I sat silently, studying the carved wooden moldings and window frames of the high-ceilinged group room, imagining the elegant Victorian parlor it must once have been, while I waited for an opportune time to introduce the subject of Stephen's death. I didn't want to undermine Jeff by jumping in and taking over his meeting unnecessarily.

Ultimately Jeff chose the moment for me. "Erika, do you have anything to report about yesterday's incident? A lot of people are wondering."

I inched forward in my cracked red vinyl chair, took a deep breath and began. "There's no easy way to say this. You probably know what happened here yesterday. The medical technicians were here, and then the police—"

Arthur Drummond cut me off. "Spit it out, Erika. How did Stephen end up in a body bag?"

"He fell off the roof," I said, and paused to watch the reactions – mostly stunned sadness or foggy confusion. For a long moment, no one made a sound. Then Germaine clapped her hands to her cheeks and let out an unearthly shriek. She'd seen Stephen's body yesterday, even been interviewed on TV, but something about the mention of the roof seemed to get to her. The floodgates opened, and people began talking all at once. I raised my hand, and slowly they all fell silent.

"At this point the police are still investigating," I said. "They haven't decided yet if it was a suicide, an accident, or something else. A lot of you talked to the police yesterday, but they'll need to talk with some of you again, and I think it's important that everyone cooperate."

"Don't do it, guys," said Arthur. "Open your mouth, and you're liable to be framed for murder."

Jeff started to say something but Stan cut him off. "You're out of order, Mr. Drummond. Don't go planting crazy ideas in people's minds."

Arthur laughed. "What harm would that do, Stanley? Everyone here is crazy already. Except me, of course. I just stop by for the free lunch."

Stan and Jeff rolled knowing eyes at each other, but no one dared contradict Arthur. I stood up to get their attention. "Helping the police with this investigation is important. In the meantime, if anyone has any information that might help us understand Stephen's death, please let me know."

Germaine got to her feet and waved her arms in the air. "Listen up, people!" Her kaleidoscope eyes glittered madly. "Arthur is right to say *murder*. Stephen was one of my best friends, and no way would he have killed himself. Someone murdered him. I'm sure of it." She choked back a sob and with a deep sigh leaned against a wall, withdrawing into herself.

"I know many of you are finding this hard," I said. "Stephen's loss hurts us all, and it might help to talk about it. This afternoon we'll have a group meeting in the conference room to share our feelings, and my door will be open all day to anyone who wants to talk with me."

Now, what about the roof garden? I felt too wrung out to broach the subject, so I chickened out and delegated to Jeff. While the club members talked, I pulled him aside and said we would have to close the roof until we could get a fence put up. I suggested he might want to ask the members how we should dispose of the plants. Some folks might want to take some flowers home with them.

Then I went over to Germaine. Once Jeff got the meeting going again, I took her hand and gently led her upstairs to my office. I let her sit on the couch while I took one of the side chairs. "So what do you think about all this?" I asked.

Instead of answering, she burst into sobs. I gave her some tissues to wipe her eyes and waited. Finally she said, "It's like when my father died. It's so sad. I want to make something to remember him by."

"Remember your father or Stephen?"

"Both, I got to do both. Like a plate, maybe. Could I go do ceramics now?"

———

I walked Germaine upstairs to the ceramics room, where she and two older women friends pretty much ruled the roost. Then I began my morning walk-through, checking each room in turn to make sure everything was OK. This was the part of my job that I liked best. In some organizations, they call it "managing by walking around." It gave me a chance to chat with the members and make sure everything was under control.

The craft rooms on the third floor were alive with activity. In addition to the ladies addicted to ceramics – which was a lot better than what they had been addicted to – we had a couple of dedicated painters, a guy who spent all day every day carefully constructing sailing ships inside old wine bottles, three women who quilted together for an hour each day, and some men and women who used the rooms for everything from appliance repair to jewelry making.

From the crafts rooms, I descended the stairs back down to the group room on the first floor. The meeting had broken up by now, but the atmosphere was electric. A dozen people were clustered around the television, staring at the black and white snowstorm on the screen. Stan was crouching at the console, fussing with the controls of the VCR, and the crackling static aggravated the pounding in my overtired head. I badly needed coffee.

Gloria was wearing a Cheshire cat grin as she came over to greet me. Her enormous brown eyes gleamed with excitement. "Did you see Stan on the eleven o'clock news on Channel 8 last night? He came off looking pretty cool, huh?"

"He sure did," said Anne O'Dowd, a young woman who suffered from chronic schizophrenia and was usually lost in her own world. Not today. "Stanley Washington, you look mighty fine on that tape," she cooed. "I'm gonna call you Denzel. Play it again, Stan." She gestured toward the TV where Stan had restarted what was evidently a videotape of the interview. "Germaine should have washed her hair, you know? But – "

"Excuse me, Anne," I said. "In answer to Gloria's question, I did see the interview, but purely by chance. Why didn't anyone tell me about it?" My irritation probably showed, because everyone fell silent.

Germaine appeared in the doorway. Her green-gold eyes, which always reminded me of shattered crystal, darted from side to side. "I saw it by accident. I always watch Apple news in case there's something important, you know, like a terrorist attack. No one told me anything."

"Okay," I said. "No one told me anything either."

So that was what all the excitement was about – Stan luxuriating in his fifteen minutes of fame. He crossed the room to join us, thrusting out his chest and taking long, fast steps as he walked, like some gigantic toy soldier out of *The Nutcracker*. His body radiated tension, and his shoulders gave an occasional involuntary jerk, probably a side effect of his medication.

"I hope you don't mind, Erika," he said. "I thought Ms. Welcome might run the story at eleven, and I had my VCR ready to roll. Just in case you missed it."

"I caught it, but thanks, anyway."

"How did you like my little sound bite?" he asked, with a jerk of his left shoulder

"Not bad, Stan, and I liked how you got Germaine off the hook, too. What's your take on that Nancy Welcome?" Stan had already survived more incidents on the city streets that any three average people are likely to see in their lifetimes, and I'd learned I could trust his ability to read people.

He frowned. "Ms. Welcome is crafty. She wants something from us."

"Any idea what?"

"Some people are just prejudiced, Erika. Sometimes it's about the color of their skin or the way they talk and sometimes it's about the different way a man's mind works."

"How do you mean?"

He thought for a few seconds, head bowed, lips pursed. Finally, he looked off into the distance over my shoulder and announced in a stentorian voice, "I do believe that woman is afraid of people with mental illness. Best to avoid her. There's no telling what a person like that will do when she's afraid."

"Stanley, you're just weird about women," said Gloria. She put her hand on his arm. "Not to worry. I'll talk with that reporter if she shows up again."

"No, you won't," I snapped. "This is not the time for ego tripping. In fact, this incident raises some important issues. Before anyone talked to the media, Ocala or I should have been consulted. This kind of publicity could damage the reputation of the club and everyone associated with it."

A spasm rippled across Stan's upper body. "We didn't tell the TV people, Erika. The news crew just showed up in their van and started taking pictures, right in front of our building. I was walking past the end of the block when I saw the floodlights, and I thought I should see what's up."

"A good thing you did, too," I said, "but next time, just walk away and page me. That goes for all the club members."

Stan's face took on a look of wounded indignation. "That Welcome woman told me they left a message on your answering machine, but that you never got back to them and they didn't have time to wait around. Tell the truth, she was real pushy."

"There was nothing on my machine. Did she say who told them about the story?"

"No, and I didn't think to ask. I'm sorry, Erika. I didn't mean to cause problems." Stan's jaw was clenched, and a discernible tic had surfaced in the vicinity of his left eye.

"No need to apologize, Stan. You did a good job with that reporter."

His face relaxed once more, and the tic vanished as suddenly as it had appeared.

I sighed in relief. Stanley Washington was important to WellSpring. He did more than supervise the members who did the cleaning and other work around the club. WellSpring was his life, and his strong, imposing presence was an integral part of the club's atmosphere.

"I'm glad you're okay with the tape," he said. "Is it all right if I play it once more? Not everyone's seen it yet."

I suppressed the urge to rip the tape from the VCR and stomp it under foot. Destroying the tape wouldn't make the story disappear. And I was curious to see the clip again; maybe it wouldn't seem so unnerving in the light of day. "What the heck," I said. "Go for it, Stan."

Gloria was right, Stan did look good on camera, and I could see why he liked replaying the tape. He had taken off his glasses for the videotaping, and Anne had a point. Take away fifty pounds, and he did bear a passing resemblance to Denzel.

Chapter 6

*T*ill now, I'd loved my office at WellSpring. It was a sanctuary, an oasis where I could retreat and renew myself when other people's demands threatened to overwhelm me. Stephen's death changed that. The question of who had been here, and why, nagged at me. I carefully went through my desk drawers, checked the little room where Rishi lay fast asleep on the floor, and took a quick inventory of the bookshelves and my diplomas on the wall. Nothing seemed out of place.

I switched on my computer, logged onto the Compassion House network and opened up Microsoft Outlook to access my e-mail. My personal mailbox had a couple of e-mails about purchasing and a memo from Ocala with a hyperlink to a new directive from the State Office of Mental Health, which I saved to read later. Then I opened the WellSpring mailbox.

Usually, the new mail was minimal, maybe a dozen items at most. This time, the window was completely full, and as I scanned the "from" column, I didn't recognize any of the senders. The subject lines were downright nasty – things like "re: dead crazy" and "UP YOURS SCUM" and "Get Out." We'd been flamed big-time.

I opened the first message and read in disbelief: "You people ought to be ashamed of yourselves, wasting tax payer money on the dregs of society. That guy who killed himself did the right thing. The rest of you should do likewise."

And another: "Your club for crazies is a blight on the neighborhood. We're trying to make the Lower East Side a better place to live, and your presence here is bringing down the property values. Why don't you all go back to the nuthouse where you belong?"

And yet another: "Bitches. The good work is began. Stevie was first. Therr'l be more. count on it."

Sick at heart, I clicked on one after another. The more I read, the angrier I felt. The notes varied in literacy and language, but a common theme ran throughout: a mean-spirited prejudice against the mentally ill and a deep-seated anger at the notion that public funding was helping them stay afloat. There were over 50 e-mails, and most mentioned last night's news story.

Evidently I hadn't been the only one with insomnia last night. People had been up till all hours, composing these tirades while the city slept. I scanned the names again, looking for patterns. Some of the screen names were repeats, but the majority were from different senders, or at least different e-mail accounts.

How had so many people gotten WellSpring's e-mail address in the middle of the night? It wasn't confidential. In fact, it was printed on our brochures and fliers, but our clients came through professional referrals for the most part, so our promotional materials weren't widely available. The computer literate could find us with a search engine, but some of those e-mails were far from literate.

I'd only gotten a couple of hours sleep, and I was beginning to feel the effects—groggy, headachy, unfocused. Impulsively, I decided to skip lunch and clear my head by taking Rishi for a romp in the dog run at Tompkins Square Park.

Had my head been clearer, I probably would have avoided the dog run. Rishi and I have tried it before with unfortunate results. He's well trained, and he generally gets along with other dogs when I'm there to discipline him, but he does not back down when challenged. Once he got into a serious fight with a Weimaraner who was running loose with no owner in sight. That time, I broke up the fight with the pepper spray that I generally carry in my purse.

This morning as we approached the chain-link enclosure, Rishi began straining at his choke chain, turning every so often to bounce at me and nuzzle my hand, grinning in amazement at his good fortune. I led him into the foyer: the designer had thoughtfully built in a little gated space to prevent dogs from pushing their way in or out. After carefully latching the outer gate, I unlatched the inner one, then unhooked the lead from his choke chain and let him loose.

Delighted to be free, he barely glanced at the other dogs before taking off at a run, streaking in an enormous oval around the perimeter of the enclosure like a superbly conditioned athlete on the track. After three laps, he bounded over to me, panting happily, still full of energy. Then he turned his attention to the other dogs. Setting his sights on a nearby trio—a white poodle, a golden retriever, and a shaggy brown mutt of indeterminate origins—he bounced over and began sniffing their behinds. They reciprocated with appropriate doggy etiquette, circling and sniffing, tails stiffly aloft in full alert.

Suddenly a small but sturdy, dark-haired mutt with a curly tail darted in and bit Rishi's leg. Big mistake. Rishi whirled, his enormous jaws clamped down on the mutt's neck and he began shaking it in the air.

Disaster! I reached into my purse for the pepper spray, couldn't find it.

A woman came running up and swung her purse at Rishi's head. "Out, out, get out, stop," she screamed. "Get that dog out of here!"

I pulled with all my strength on his choke chain with one hand, tried to unlock his jaws with the other. While the mutt's owner battered Rishi with her purse, I tried everything I could to separate them, but it wasn't working. If I couldn't get this settled in the next couple of minutes, that leg-biting little brute might not survive.

A deep male voice said "Great scene. Wish I had a camera." I looked up to see a chunky man in a beige linen suit hovering beside me with an amused smile.

"I have two rottweilers," he said as he stripped off his jacket and slung it on the fence. "Let me help." He leaned down, grabbed both of Rishi's rear feet, and pulled. Then he began walking backward in a circle, forcing Rishi to balance on two legs. Suddenly Rishi let go. The smaller dog's owner scooped it up in her arms and ran out of the pen.

The rottweiler handler was still swinging Rishi around to avoid getting bitten. "Get his head," he ordered. I grabbed Rishi's collar with one hand, and with my other arm I put Rishi's head in a bear hug. The man dropped my dog's rear feet, and it was all over.

As I hooked the lead onto Rishi's choke chain, the small dog's owner, now safely on the other side of the fence, screamed that she would sue me and have my dog destroyed. I was infuriated. After all, it was her dog that had started the fight, but I figured answering would only make things worse. I swallowed my anger and led Rishi away from the scene of his indignity.

"That's a magnificent dog you have there," said the rottweiler man, catching up with us. "But it looks as if he's a bit much for you to handle."

The comment got my hackles up again, but under the circumstances, I was hardly in a position to quibble. "He's great with people," I said. "It's just a dog dominance thing."

"Then why bring him to the dog run? Is it a vicarious way of getting your aggressions out?"

I sidestepped the question. "Maybe you didn't see what happened. The smaller dog started it. Rishi doesn't attack other dogs. He's gotten more mellow with time."

"Like fine wine, you mean? Dogs don't age like that. They age more like strong cheese. Their individual characteristics get more pronounced, including their bad habits when they're not properly trained."

I was silent a moment, studying him. He was good-looking in a craggy kind of way, a couple of inches under six feet with a muscular build suggestive of endless hours at the gym. His pale blue shirt was obviously custom fitted, his expensive jacket slung casually over one arm. Blond hair that called California beaches to mind. Not bad, in other words, although I didn't normally go for the body building type.

"He's trained," I snapped, "but thanks for the help." I gave Rishi a heel command and we started back toward WellSpring, but I couldn't shake my new friend.

"Going back to work? I'm headed that way myself. Why don't I keep you company?"

I was puzzled. "How do you know where I work? Have we met somewhere?"

"I make it my business to know what's going on in the neighborhood." He smiled and extended his hand. "Sorry, I should have introduced myself. I'm Kevin Winthrop. I have a couple of real estate investments in the neighborhood, and I've seen you around. You're Erika Norgren, right? You direct that club?"

I felt absurdly pleased with the recognition. "I wasn't aware I was that well known."

"It's a surprisingly small world down here. I've seen you walking your dog, once when I was driving my car and a couple of times when I was visiting my buildings. You probably didn't notice me."

That didn't explain how he knew me, but I let it drop when he asked about Stephen. "A real shame, that young man dying. It must be hard on you." I felt myself frowning. "As the director, I mean, coping with that kind of thing. Your members must be upset."

"Look, Mr. Winthrop," I said, "I appreciate your concern, but I'm on my lunch break, and I'd like a few minutes of solitude, just me and Rishi, while we walk back to the club."

"Fair enough, but call me Kevin." He bent to stroke Rishi's head and scratch his ears. Despite his earlier manhandling, Rishi arched his neck and luxuriated in the sensation.

"Nice meeting both of you," Kevin said. "I'll be in touch." He turned and walked briskly out of the park. As he swung his arms, his sweat-soaked shirt clung to the muscles rippling on his back. No wonder he was able to pick up Rishi so easily.

Walking back to WellSpring with Rishi, I thought about Kevin Winthrop. The unexpected attention was flattering, and it reminded me of the loneliness I'd been feeling lately. I began brooding about the directions my life had taken since my acute bipolar episode three years ago. I'd quit my hospital job, lost my husband, and after a few mania-driven shopping sprees, lost my credit rating as well. With medication and therapy, I'd been able to begin resume functioning fairly normally, but it had been rough. Those two years of dumbed-down temp jobs had taken a toll on my self-esteem.

I was so preoccupied with the past, so oblivious to my surroundings, that my heart lurched alarmingly when a deep voice called my name. "Hey, Erika, aren't you going to say hello?"

It was Arthur Drummond, loitering beneath the awning of the bodega near the club. A Pakistani family ran the little corner store. The men wore turbans and around meal times you could smell curries cooking in the back where the family lived, but the store still carried Malta brand malt soda and other Caribbean favorites for their customers, along with some canned Chinese foods and things I couldn't identify. Mostly, they made their money selling Lottery tickets and cigarettes.

I don't normally think of people as "loitering," because the word is judgmental and I like to give people the benefit of the doubt. But Arthur had the ability to loiter conspicuously, like a small locomotive ready to go charging off at any time. He let his right hand rest casually on the corner of the stand full of cut flowers, which the bodega had begun selling in response to the increasing gentrification of the neighborhood. One of the proprietors stood in the doorway glaring while Arthur ignored him.

When I first came to WellSpring, one of the men who ran the store complained to me about our members hanging out in front and scaring away his customers after the club closed. Ocala had made it clear that we needed good community relations, and the crew who lounged around outside the bodega was my first real challenge. I asked Jeff to bring it up in one of our morning meetings, and the members had agreed they would just buy stuff and leave. So far, it was working out, and I was annoyed to see Zapata, as Dennis called him, breaking the agreement.

Arthur projected a subtle aura of menace, and I sympathized with the storeowners.

"Oh, hi, Arthur. I didn't see you. How are you doing?"

He stepped cautiously into the sunlight, his eyes fixed on Rishi. "Not bad, but that dog makes me nervous. Does he bite?"

I smiled. "Only when I tell him to." Then I realized Arthur might take me seriously. "Just kidding. Let him check you out for a minute, and he'll be fine."

As if understanding every word, Rishi began a thorough inspection, while Arthur stood tense and frightened. I yanked Rishi back when he began sniffing thoughtfully at Arthur's black-denim-clad crotch. The dog knows better, but he likes to push his limits.

"I thought you were ignoring me on purpose," Arthur said. "You've been keeping pretty fancy company, hanging out with that rich dude at the dog run. Not to mention that stinking cop."

I'd left the dog run less than ten minutes ago. Had Arthur been watching, maybe even stalking me? Remembering Dennis's warning, I felt a sudden chill. "I'm not hanging out with anybody," I said indignantly. "Not that it concerns you anyway."

"On the contrary, it concerns me a great deal. I don't want anyone treating you with disrespect. You're a special lady, and I've been thinking about you a lot lately. I was kind of hoping you and I could go out sometime."

For some time now, I'd seen this moment coming. In a way, it was a relief getting it over with, and it could have been worse. Arthur was playing the perfect gentleman, and we were standing on a sunny sidewalk, with plenty of passers-by, in front of a busy deli. Yet as I paused to frame a diplomatic answer, I found it hard to meet the gaze of his cold gray eyes.

"That's not possible, Arthur," I said. "Our relationship is professional, not personal, and it has to stay that way. Nothing against you personally, but it's a matter of professional ethics."

"Hey, that's cool, I understand. But no one has to know. We could keep a low profile. Like you could invite me over for dinner; I'll bring the food and cook."

I looked into those icy eyes of his and gave him my one-half-watt smile. "Thanks for the invitation, but no thanks. I don't cut corners with ethics."

Anger flashed in his eyes and he took a step toward me. Rishi, who had been sitting comfortably at my feet, jumped up with a low growl, and Arthur quickly retreated.

Turning away, I found myself gazing at the masses of fresh flowers arranged in tiers outside the store. While we talked, a teenaged girl had come out of the store and begun tending them carefully, adding fresh blossoms and removing wilted ones while the turbaned store owner supervised.

"Look at those Stargazer lilies," I exclaimed. "And all those roses and baby orchids. It's amazing the variety of flowers these places sell. But they all have pretty much the same assortment at any given time of year, so they must all get them from the same source."

I was trying to change the subject, but Arthur was having none of it. "Hey, Erika, look at me, and stop being so nervous. I have patience. I can wait. But you know I'm going to have to keep an eye on you, make sure you don't get into any trouble."

I squirmed away from his touch. "I appreciate your concern, but that's not necessary."

He smiled thinly. "Oh, but it is. I've seen that guy from the park around the neighborhood before, and the wire says he's a heavy hitter— a major player, if you get my drift. And that cop, Malone, he's on the take, as crooked as they come. Both those guys pretend to be smooth as silk, but they've got a nasty side you wouldn't believe."

Arthur's tone had taken on an angry new urgency, and I wasn't about to argue the virtues, or lack thereof, of two men I barely knew. He might have paranoid delusions about them, in which case debate would be pointless. Or perhaps he was just trying to intimidate me into letting him play my protector. But for that, I had Rishi.

"You know a lot about what goes on in the neighborhood, don't you?" I asked. He nodded gravely and a little smile twitched at the corners of his lips. "So what can you tell me about Stephen that I don't already know?"

His smile widened. "He slept on the roof. Got drunk up there, too. That's probably how he fell off."

"I thought you said he was murdered."

"That's possible too. Somebody could have pushed him off. I don't like to say this, and you have to promise to keep it quiet." He waited until I gave him a nod of agreement. "It could have been

Stanley. He's got the history, you know. I saw him once—this was maybe five years ago —he was in Tompkins Square Park just sitting on a bench talking to himself when a cop came along and hit him in the shins with his club. For nothing. Stanley picked that cop up in the air, held him over his head, and went running through the park, screaming at everyone to get out of the way because he'd caught hold of Satan and was going to crush him under foot." Arthur gave a cackling laugh, looking pretty satanic himself.

I suppressed a smile. "So what happened?"

"The cop kept trying to reach his gun, but Stanley was swinging him around too much. Then a bunch of other cops ran up, jumped on Stanley and beat the crap out of him. And by the way, one of those cops was your friend Malone."

"That was a long time ago. Do you have anything more recent?"

Arthur scowled. "What do you mean more recent? You don't trust me?"

He was getting edgier, and the time had come to wrap up this discussion. "Thanks for telling me about that," I said. "Why don't you walk us back to the club?"

"Okay, but first, just a token of my appreciation." He turned to the banks of flowers, selected three Stargazer lilies, and extracted some bills from his jeans. Before I could protest, he flagged down the girl, the deal was done, and Arthur was thrusting a paper cone of flowers into my hands.

"For you," he said.

"The lilies are gorgeous, Arthur, but I can't possibly accept them."

"Too late now, you have to," he said, fixing me with his intense stare.

As I looked down at the three extravagant blossoms nestled in the paper cone, I felt my resolve weakening. The creamy white petals striped with shades of pink and crimson were outrageously beautiful in their sensuality. "Let's put them in the lobby at WellSpring, so everyone can enjoy them," I suggested.

"Whatever. Keep them anonymous if you want. But every time you look at them, I want you to think about me, and how we're going to get together one of these days."

"Not in this lifetime, Arthur," I said, refusing to give him the last word. "Let's walk."

Chapter 7

*W*hen Arthur, Rishi and I entered the club, Gloria greeted me enthusiastically through the open door of the administrative office, where her desk was placed so she could monitor traffic in the front hallway. Arthur thrust the flowers into my hands, and Gloria's expression darkened. "They're very pretty," she said. "Are they for Stephen's service?"

"What service?"

She lowered her eyes. "Oops. I guess we should have checked with you first, but you weren't around. We were talking at lunch, and we agreed we should hold a small memorial service."

"You're right, you should have checked. When were you thinking of having it?"

"Today at five thirty."

My stomach lurched. "That's impossible!"

She shot me a sheepish grin. "Not to worry – Stan's already on top of it. You'll see, it'll all come together."

Over my dead body, I almost said. But hey, this was their club. "You've known Stephen a lot longer than I did," I said. "I suppose it's your call. So Arthur, what do you think about using the flowers for Stephen's service?"

He fixed me in his icy glare. "They're yours now. Use them however you want." He turned tail and strode out the front door into the street.

I started to hand Gloria the flowers to put in a vase, but she shrank away and shook her head so vehemently her wavy brown hair flew in all directions. "No! I'm sorry. I have this thing about flowers. I love to see them living and growing, you know, in the park or in flowerpots is fine. But I can't stand to see them cut off so young and beheaded."

Gloria was acutely sensitive to the plight of every living creature. I knew she refused to eat or wear anything that came from animals, but I hadn't realized her sympathies extended to plants. "Someone else cut them before Arthur even thought about getting them," I said. "So I refuse to feel guilty."

"That's like saying it's okay to wear leather shoes because you're not the one who slaughtered the cow."

I took a deep, cleansing breath to chase away the irritation, then exhaled slowly. "I hear you, Gloria. But let's talk about this some other time, okay?"

Gloria rolled her eyes and shrugged, tossing me a bit of attitude. "Hey, Erika, I didn't mean to dump on you. Anyway, you had a bunch of messages while you were out. They're on your voice mail. And people called from some TV news shows, following up on last night's story. I told them about the memorial service. I hope that's okay."

I took another cleansing breath, but the extra oxygen just fueled my growing anxiety and anger. "Are you playing games with me, Gloria? I told you all media calls should go to me."

"But you weren't here," she retorted. "I did the best I could, it's not fair to blame me. I was just doing my job."

Ocala would have a cow, but the damage was done. "In future, Gloria, when I say all calls from TV people and newspaper reporters, I mean every single one of them. No exceptions. Is that agreed?"

She nodded. "Yes. *Lo siento mucho.* I'm sorry." Her eyes filled with tears. Soon they were spilling down her cheeks, and her hands were starting to shake.

I realized I was laying too much on Gloria. Despite her flamboyant dramatics, she was fragile at heart, and I had to cut her some slack. "We'll just make the best of it," I said in the most reassuring tone I could muster. "No need to worry. And Gloria, thanks for doing such a good job with the phones. You really do excellent work."

She beamed, her eyes cleared, and the storm clouds scudded past. Now it was time to track down Stanley Washington and find out what the hell was going on.

———

"You said you liked the idea of a memorial service," said Stan a few minutes later.

"Yes, but I would have waited a few days. That would have given us a chance to notify Stephen's friends and let the media story cool off."

He frowned, folded his massive arms and leaned back against the copy machine. It groaned in protest. "I was going to bring it up at the morning meeting," he said, "but you went bombing out of there with Germaine. When I went out for a smoke afterwards, I ran into Ariana Birdsong. You know, the woman who runs the community garden down the block?"

"The one who dresses like vintage Stevie Nicks? I've seen her around. How she can wear lace-up boots and capes in the middle of summer is beyond me. Her garden is beautiful, though. I often stop and look at it, because Rishi likes to pee on the cast iron fence."

"Well, Ariana and me, we go way back. She suggested we use her garden for the service. We went into the back of the garden where it's all shady, and she did some kind of psychic thing. She told me tonight is the most favorable evening for a memorial service, so I thought why not? We talked it over at lunch and decided to go with it."

"It's awfully short notice. You think you can pull it off?"

"I'm positive. We've already got people lined up to sing and read some poetry, and Susan is typing up the program even as we speak."

"That's great, Stan." I always marveled at his ability to work with Susan Harvey, the reclusive middle-aged member who'd done clerical work for the club at minimum wage for more years than anyone cared to count.

"I've drafted people to bring over some chairs and to act as ushers," Stan continued. "And I told everyone to go home to shower and put on clean clothes before the service. We don't want anyone neglecting their activities of daily living and showing up all stinky."

"It sounds as if you've got everything covered," I said. "Stan, you never cease to amaze me. Your management and leadership skills are so good, you could do very well for yourself in the corporate world. I really depend on you at the club, but sometimes I wonder why you're content to hang out here instead of setting your sights on something higher."

Stan's lips curved in a slow smile. "Now and then I've considered making a change. I've even gotten a couple of offers. Just last spring a cat from an African-American record company offered me a job as a kind of all-around guy Friday."

"I never knew that." I could easily picture Stan duded up in custom-tailored clothes that showed off his intimidating physique, squiring hiphop artists around Manhattan. "Why didn't you take it?"

"Believe me, Erika, I was sorely tempted, and for many a long night I prayed for guidance. The Lord told me to research the company and study the music, and I realized the Devil lurked in the lyrics. Nothing but sex and violence."

He spread the fingers on one massive hand, ticked off a point with his index finger. "Besides, the members depend on me, and I know some of them would be really upset if I left. Then too, I'm comfortable with the job, and I'm afraid something more high pressured might be too stressful and cause me to decompensate." Another tap, the middle finger this time. "The pay is lousy, but it's low enough so that I can keep my SSI disability benefits." Tap. "And I've established a certain reputation. People respect me in spite of my disability – maybe even because of it. In a way I'm a role model for a lot of these folks. If I went to work for some company, I'd have to conceal my mental illness." He tapped his little finger and laughed. "I could go on, but I'm out of fingers." He nodded, gave a thumbs up sign. "Above all, God wants me to do this work."

————————

At five, sunshine slanted across the cast iron fence at the front of the garden and bounced off the brick wall of the building to the east. But after I passed through the filigreed gates, I was swamped by shadow. Hemmed in by tenements on either side, the long narrow plot of land saw sun for only a few hours at midday. Near the front, rectangular raised beds held tomatoes, zucchini, Swiss chard and other edibles, all carefully aligned in rows and mulched with wood chips. Halfway back, the garden underwent a personality change, as geometric order gave way to flowing romanticism. Straight paths grew suddenly curvy as they snaked around clumps of hostas and astilbes. Plants I couldn't identify hugged the ground along the walkways, and the creamy white patterns on their variegated leaves gave off an eerie glow in the deep shade. Enormous rhododendrons and azaleas, long past their season of bloom, soaked up the light with their glossy green leaves.

The paths were punctuated with handcrafted benches of concrete inlaid with glass and pottery mosaic. Sections of the walkways with similar mosaics converged at a raised pond in the center. Clearly the pond was a work in progress. Mosaic tiles climbed one side, but the rest was incomplete, with the black plastic liner still exposed. The water was green with algae. I remembered the mosaic work in Stephen's squat and wondered if he'd had a hand in this creation as well.

"How do you like my garden?" The low, melodious voice made me jump. Ariana Birdsong had materialized unexpectedly beside me, dressed in frothy layers of black satin and lace, with knee-high lace-up boots of black leather. Pale hair cascaded in a platinum wave down her back.

"I love it," I said. "I've never been inside before."

"It's not generally open to the public. Especially the public with large, galoomphy dogs who pee on the plants."

I felt myself blushing. "Oh, I don't let Rishi pee on the plants. But I'll admit he likes the fence."

"You didn't bring him tonight, I take it?"

"No, I took him home before the service. I thought he might be too distracting."

"Just as well." She smiled and extended a hand swathed in black lace. "I'm Ariana, by the way. Are you into gardening?"

"I'm Erika Norgren." The lace scratched my palm. "I wouldn't say I'm exactly into it, although I love looking. I used to have a few plants on my fire escape, but it's too labor intensive for me. This garden is wonderful, though. Is it all yours, or do other people help you with it?"

"Various folks have helped out over the years, but basically, it's my baby."

"I'm truly impressed."

Just then Stan came over. "Ladies, the service is about to start. Kindly follow me."

While I'd been absorbed in studying the garden, Stan and the others had set up folding chairs along the paths near the pond, and Gloria had begun handing out candles. "Four colors," she said. "White, yellow, red and blue. Take the one that most reflects your mood right now, and light it from the candle here on the table."

Stephen's death had cast a definite chill over my psyche, so I chose Nordic white. It wasn't that my feelings were frozen. Far from it. But I was doing my best to stay calm and objective, and white fit the cool, collected image I was determined to project.

Ariana lit a bundle of dried sage, and its pungent aroma wafted over us as we followed her single file, then found seats along the winding paths. A young man played aching laments on an acoustic guitar. People sang, read poetry, spoke of their memories of Stephen. As the late summer light faded, I fell deeper under the spell of the ceremony and felt the tensions seeping from my body. As we had hoped, honoring Stephen in ritual brought a sense of peace and completion. Perhaps now I could begin to put this tragedy behind me and move ahead.

Impulsively, I decided to trade my cold white candle for a red one. Turning away from the shadows and toward the table by the gate, I was momentarily blinded by the glare of the photofloods that heralded the arrival of the media. Three cameramen and at least as many reporters presented a united phalanx across the front of the garden.

Arthur stood in front of them, playing security guard. "Kindly have the decency to wait here till the end of the ceremony," he was saying, in a tone of clipped menace. Evidently the aura of danger he projected so well was having its effect, because the news crews were acting uncharacteristically submissive, hanging back along the fence.

Then one of the reporters caught sight of me and broke ranks. It was Nancy Welcome, the woman I'd seen on the eleven o'clock news. "Miss, could I ask you a few questions?"

"This is Erika Norgren, the Director of WellSpring," said Arthur helpfully. So much for changing candle colors, I thought – I'd probably need my Nordic cool for awhile longer.

Her video man had turned on his camera and was advancing steadily. The others followed like circling sharks. She shoved a mike in my face and began without preamble. "We're down on the Lower East Side at a memorial service for Stephen Wright, the young man who died after falling from the roof of WellSpring, a social club for mentally ill adults. I'm talking with Erika Norgren, the director of WellSpring. Erika, this is an unusual service. What's the significance of the colored candles? Is this some sort of occult ceremony? Perhaps voodoo?"

The image of Ocala's glowering face when she'd warned me about Nancy Welcome flashed across my mind's eye. My boss had made it crystal clear that I should call her immediately if the newscaster showed up again. But it was too late now.

"Ms. Norgren, what's the meaning of the candles?" Nancy's voice took on an imperious edge. "What exactly is going on here?"

Ocala hadn't expressly forbid me to talk with Nancy – she just didn't want the club members doing it. "This is a memorial service for Stephen Wright," I said. "Now, I'd appreciate it if you hold your questions for afterwards. I'd be glad to talk with you then."

"What about that scent in the air? Are you using a certain illegal herb as part of the ritual?"

I almost grinned, and Arthur cracked a rare smile. "No, that's sage," I said. "Native Americans use it in purification ceremonies, for the same reasons priests use incense at St. Patrick's Cathedral, or you use deodorant. It improves the atmosphere." I drew myself erect, the better to project my voice. "Now I have to insist that you turn that camera off so we can continue the service. That goes for all you media people. This is a private memorial service, not a public spectacle."

Like a tenacious terrier, Nancy Welcome continued to advance. "What about this garden? Is there a permit for its operation, or is it like the ones the City has been closing down?"

Candle or no, I began to see red. So did Arthur and Stan, who closed ranks on either side of me and began to advance on the reporter. "You heard the lady," Stan said in a rumbling bass. "Why are you messing with the memorial service?"

Suddenly not so intrepid, Nancy stepped quickly back, her stiletto heel impaling her cameraman's instep in the process. "Shit!" he exploded. "Damn it, Nancy, give it a rest!" Then he flipped the switch on his camera and the little red light blinked off.

With the reporters momentarily at bay, I turned and reentered the garden. While the guitarist played Pachabel's Canon, Ariana was doing a slow, lyrical dance involving several yards of gossamer black chiffon. I took a seat in the shadows next to some giant hostas as I pondered my next move.

Chapter 8

A s I watched Ariana working wonders with her black chiffon, I puzzled over the TV crews hovering outside the gates, and how to cope with Ocala. Should I call her on my cell phone? It was well after five, and the answering service would probably pick up. I could try her cell, but even if she answered, the memorial would most likely be over and the reporters gone before she could get here. I'd caught sight of crews from at least four different channels. If I carried it off right, this was an ideal opportunity to put a positive spin on a tragic situation, to garner some positive PR for WellSpring. Ocala would probably be furious if I let the opportunity pass.

I knew I should have invited Ocala to the service, or at least told her about it. But Stan and the others had been so speedy in putting it together, literally while I was out to lunch, that I'd had no idea it would turn into such an ambitious happening.

Ariana's dance segued into a final chant. As she extinguished the candles to signify the close of the service, I rose and moved quietly through the garden and out the wrought iron gates to confront the camera crews.

Nancy Welcome was waiting front and center, wearing a suit of tangerine wool that showed an extravagant length of leg and looked far too warm for the season. Beads of sweat shone through her makeup, and she was dabbing at her forehead with a tissue. "Ready when you are, Erika," she said. "But let's get Stan Washington, the guy I interviewed before. He was great on camera. Maybe some of the other club members too."

"Unfortunately, that's not such a good idea. People's attendance at the club is strictly confidential. Because of the stigma attached to mental illness – "

"Hold it right there, Erika. That's a good angle, but I'd like to get it on tape before we talk any more. It'll sound fresher that way."

She signaled the cameraman, who aimed his lens at me and began filming. Nancy walked casually into the frame. "I'm speaking with Erika Norgren, Director of the WellSpring Club. The memorial service for Stephen Wright has just ended. Behind us, people are leaving, including many members of WellSpring, the social club for mentally ill adults. Ms. Norgren has requested that we not show these folks on camera. Why is that, Erika?"

"People's attendance at the club is strictly confidential, Nancy. Some members hold jobs, and they may not have told their employers about their illness, for fear of repercussions. Even if they're upfront about their own illness, their family and friends may be embarrassed and not want it discussed."

"So there's a lot of secrecy involved with WellSpring Club, how it's run and who comes here," Nancy stated.

"Unfortunately, some secrecy is necessary," I replied. "But that's because in our society there's still a strong stigma associated with mental illness. For that to change, we need more honesty and open communication about the subject." I took a deep breath, then a totally unpremeditated leap off the high dive. "For example, I've been the Director of WellSpring Club for almost six months, yet no one at the club knows that I'm officially diagnosed with bipolar disorder. It's well controlled with medication, and not even my boss knows about it. I guess she'll find out on the news tonight."

Her eyes took on a predatory gleam. "That's very interesting, Erika. I appreciate your sharing it with News Channel 8. Any reason you decided to go public about your illness at this particular time?"

"I'm an honest, upfront person in general, and I've been feeling more and more hypocritical about keeping this important part of myself under wraps, especially since I became Director of WellSpring Club and began working alongside a lot of wonderful people who face their illness bravely and openly every day. So I'm hereby making it official – I'm one of the crazies, and proud of it."

Closing ranks on either side of me, Stan and Gloria began to cheer and clap. Still filming, the cameraman pulled back for a long shot as other members arrived to check out the commotion.

"I never knew coming out of the closet would be so exciting," I said. Then everything turned soft and swimmy, and my knees went suddenly weak. But the sensation passed in short order. I didn't fall swooning to the ground in the wake of my revelation. No fireworks exploded, no comets streaked across the sky. The handful of club members who had gathered around gave me a round of applause and a couple of thumbs up, but that was it. At last I had made the public confession I'd dreaded for so long, and nothing had changed at all. Not yet, anyway.

The next few hours passed in a hyperkinetic blur. Although the memorial service brought some measure of peace and closure to my feelings about Stephen's death, I kept obsessing about my on-camera revelation and what its impact might be. I paced the blocks of the East Village with Rishi, went home, tried to eat but couldn't. My usual diversions failed me and I kept checking my watch impatiently. But at long last, watching myself on the Channel 8 news, the reality of my revelation finally hit home. I looked good, I thought smugly, and I was pretty damn eloquent. This interview was a defining moment, one that would shape my life from this point forward, for better or for worse. I just hoped Stan was taping it for posterity.

Too elated to sleep, I managed to doze off near dawn. Walking to WellSpring with Rishi that morning, I was still surfing the wave of the night's euphoria. In my mind's eye, I pictured the club members arrayed on both sides of the stoop, cheering and showering me with flowers as I made my grand entrance. Now that my bipolar diagnosis was out in the open, no longer a shameful secret, I could finally be fully authentic in my dealings with the members, and there was no limit to the heights we could scale together.

Sad to say, the reality when we reached the club fell considerably short of my fantasy. No one was waiting on the steps to herald my arrival, but then that wasn't surprising, since it was still early, only a few minutes after eight. The only surprise was an unnerving one: Ocala's silver Chrysler parked outside the club.

When I walked in, Gloria was already at the reception desk, with Stan standing beside her. "I don't think there's anything to worry about," he was saying, but he stopped short when he saw me, and an expression of guilt flitted across his face.

Ocala stood at the desk, her fingertips drumming impatiently on the fake walnut veneer. She acknowledged my entrance with a cursory nod, then turned back to Stan and Gloria. "Good talking to you both. Keep up the good work," she said. Then her tone dropped to a lower register. "Erika, let's talk in your office. Can you leave the dog out here?"

She'd never complained about Rishi before. This was not an auspicious omen, but I reluctantly complied.

Once in my office with the door closed, she got right to the point. "Erika, if there's one thing I can't stand, it's having my employees spring surprises on me. It's even worse when I find out in a way that makes me look like an idiot."

"I assume you're referring to the news on Channel 8 last night."

"Damn right I am. I wouldn't even have known about it, except a friend called me up to say there was a story about the club. I tuned in just in time to hear your big confession about being manic depressive."

"I believe I said bipolar."

"Whatever. Erika, it's bad enough that you staged a media event without giving me a heads-up first. But what bothers me most is that you failed to let me know about your illness before going public with it. We should have talked it over, and discussed when and if it would be appropriate to reveal it."

My heart began pounding harder. "Are you saying it's so shameful, I should have kept it under wraps?"

"Not at all. But the way you chose to reveal it on TV smacks of self-aggrandizement."

"Ocala, that's not fair! I didn't choose to reveal it; it was completely spontaneous. For that matter, so was the memorial service. The members planned it themselves; I was hardly involved at all. And I had no idea it would turn into a media circus, with all those news crews there."

"What do you mean, all those news crews? You mean it wasn't just Channel 8?"

"No, there were some others. But I don't know how much footage they got, or whether any of them ran anything. By the time I finished the interview with Nancy Welcome, they'd already drifted away. Maybe they decided the story wasn't that big a deal." I forced a smile. "And they were right – it wasn't."

She didn't smile back. "Girl, you got that right. Who wants to see some woman standing up there blowing her own horn? I didn't catch the whole thing, but I'll bet you didn't even mention Compassion House."

"I don't remember." I paused. "But Ocala, I need to ask you something. I seriously considered telling you about my bipolar diagnosis when you wanted to hire me for this job, but I wasn't sure how it would influence your decision, so I chickened out. If you had known, would you have hired me anyway?"

She was silent, gazing at the floor. "Of course I would have," she said after a moment. "I was convinced you were the best person for the job. And it would have been shameful to discriminate against you because of a diagnosis of mental illness. Just as shameful as discriminating on the basis of age or race. It would go against everything I believe, and everything WellSpring stands for."

"That's what I thought," I said. "Thank you." I let it go at that. She talked a good game; after all, her eloquence was one of the strengths that had brought her such success. But that momentary hesitation had told a different story.

"I guess that's about it," she said. "But I'll be in touch. The way things are going, Erika, you can expect to see a little more of me from now on. In all fairness, I have to tell you I have concerns about your performance as Director. The way you let the members go off half-cocked with this memorial service, for example, without even running it by me first. I'd been planning to sign off on your probationary review, make you a permanent employee, but after these recent events, I'm having second thoughts."

"Is that a threat? Ocala, I don't – "

The buzz of the intercom cut me short. I grabbed the receiver, grateful for the distraction. "Gloria? What's up? I'm in a meeting with Ocala."

"I know, but there's this man here who wants to see you. His name is Mark Levitan. He says he's a lawyer."

"I don't know any Mark Levitan, and I'm not expecting any lawyers." Across the desk from me, Ocala sat a little straighter, and her eyes widened.

"He said you wouldn't know him. He just dropped in on the off chance you might be available." Gloria's voice dropped to a melodramatic whisper. "I think you should see him, Erika. He's really hot."

Had I heard right? This day was shaping up to be a lulu, and I hadn't even had my second coffee yet. "Okay," I said after a moment. "Tell him to have a seat. I'll be out soon."

Ocala rose as I replaced the receiver. "Mark Levitan, huh? Girl, you'd better be on your best behavior. That man is a heavy hitter."

Was it my imagination, or had her mood just taken a radical turn for the better? "Why?" I asked. "Do you know him?"

"You better believe it. He's one of the strongest advocates around when it comes to mental health. Always up in Albany, lobbying and schmoozing with the politicians. He runs his own not-for-profit, the Empire State Coalition for the Mentally Ill. We've been on various committees and panel discussions together over the years."

"You must know him pretty well then."

She chuckled. "As a professional colleague, maybe. I wouldn't exactly call him a friend. We've gone toe to toe on a few issues over the years, but he's a good man. Someone you'd definitely want on your side." She paused. "Tell you what. Let's put our previous discussion on the back burner for now. Buzz Gloria and tell her to send him in. I'll introduce you."

Moments later, when Mark Levitan entered the room, I felt all the breath leave my body in a long slow exhalation, and I couldn't seem to catch a breath to replace it. The man was stunningly attractive, with lean, chiseled features, dark brown hair and beard streaked with gray. His smile as Ocala introduced us had a mischievous quality, and his hazel eyes were aglow with intelligence. Gloria was right: he was definitely hot.

"I'll leave you two alone to get acquainted," Ocala was saying. I had a moment of panic as she headed for the door. What could I possibly say to him? Minutes had passed, and I had no idea what we'd been talking about.

My boss left, closing the door behind her. "I was really impressed with the way you handled that interview last night," Mark said once she was out of earshot. "And especially the way you disclosed your bipolar diagnosis. That took a lot of courage."

"Courage or idiocy – I'm still not sure which."

He grinned. "I see Ocala was here bright and early. Was she busting your chops about it?"

I felt my skin flush. "Well, she had some concerns – "

"I'll bet she did. Don't let her get to you. She's a good woman, her heart's in the right place, but she flies off the handle at times. She'll get over it."

"How do you know – " I choked on my words.

"How do I know how she reacted? Erika, I've been an advocate for the mentally ill for many years, but more important, I've been in the place you are now. I've been diagnosed bipolar since I was twenty-three years old, but I managed to conceal my illness for many years. As time passed, I got more and more disgusted with all the lies and subterfuge. Finally, in my late thirties, I had the guts to go public about being bipolar. I've never regretted it, but it wasn't easy, especially at first. I can relate to what you must be going through. In fact, you were on my mind when I woke up this morning, so I decided on impulse to drop by and see if you were in."

"I'm glad you did." *Understatement of the century.* If only I weren't feeling so tongue-tied. "Sorry if I seem a little distracted, but I've got a lot on my plate right now. Ocala just informed me my job is in jeopardy. And Stephen Wright's death really bothers me."

"He was bipolar too, wasn't he?"

"Yes, and I know that put him at risk for suicide, but he was doing so well, I can't believe he killed himself. The police think someone may have killed him. Maybe someone at the club."

His eyes narrowed. "Do you believe that?"

"I don't know what to believe. How can I do my job if I think we've got a murderer wandering around WellSpring? My relationship with the members is built on openness and trust. I can't operate out of fear."

"True. And the cops are much too eager to blame violent crimes on the allegedly crazy, although that's all wrong statistically. Even so, Erika, I think you should watch your back."

Suddenly I was no longer tongue-tied. All my suspicions, all my insecurities and sorrows came pouring out in a torrent. When I paused to glance at my watch, nearly an hour had passed. "I'm sorry, I didn't mean to go on like that," I said, "but you're such a good listener, I lost track of the time."

"I've been in and out of therapists' offices all my adult life," he said with a smile. "I suppose I've picked up a few tricks of the trade. Seriously, though, it's obvious we've got a lot more to talk about. Let's get together for lunch or dinner one of these days."

Gazing into those hazel eyes, I couldn't imagine anything I'd like more. Although come to think of it, maybe after dinner we could come up with something even better. No, Erika, I thought. Chill out, take it slow. "That would be great," I said, trying hard to sound nonchalant.

He handed me a business card. "I'm pretty swamped right now, but I'll call you soon."

Damn! Was he blowing me off already? With this man, as far as I was concerned, "soon" was much too late.

Chapter 9

When Mark Levitan left my office, he left a gigantic vacuum in his wake. I felt utterly limp, as drained of energy as if I'd just run a marathon. The man radiated such vitality that I was keenly aware of his absence. But how could that be? How could I already be missing a man I barely knew? No, that wasn't right – I did know him, more intimately than many people I'd known for years. We'd spoken for scarcely an hour, but we were soul mates. I was sure of it.

No, wait a minute – this was ridiculous. Here I was, swooning away, constructing fantasy castles around a relationship that hadn't even begun. But he must have felt it too – why else would he have come over so quickly? He claimed to have stopped by unannounced because of the courageous way I'd disclosed my illness in the TV interview. But maybe there was more to it – maybe he'd been smitten at first sight, vowed to come flying to my side as soon as humanly possible.

Cut it out, Cinderella, I cautioned myself. It's a cruel world out there, and bona fide princes are in short supply. I took a deep breath, turned on my computer, and vowed to get on with my day. First, what about some coffee? No, if I left my office, Gloria would undoubtedly flag me down and quiz me about my dashing visitor, and I wasn't up for that yet. I wanted to savor my thoughts of Mark Levitan in solitude.

I floated through the rest of the day, concentrating on creating an atmosphere of calm and normality. Maybe Stephen's memorial service and the hour of venting to Mark had restored my professional objectivity. Let the police deal with Stephen's death, I decided. There was no obvious proof of foul play. He'd probably committed suicide after all. Tragic, but I had to attend to the other people at the club, help them move on.

Back home that night, some of my objectivity deserted me. But when negative thoughts assailed me, I banished them by conjuring up images of Mark. All in all, I slept better than I had in ages. Next morning I walked to the club with Rishi. He sniffed around, picking up news of the dog world, while I took in deep breaths of air that had been scrubbed partly clean by the night. I admired the community gardens, savored the varied smells of multiethnic frying and baking, while Rishi lifted his leg to leave scented souvenirs of his passage. *I love Loisaida*, I reflected as I said good morning to some of the regulars who staked out pieces of sidewalk along our route.

As we rounded the corner onto East Fourth Street, I stopped a moment to study the club from afar. Its brick façade was painted a fading cobalt blue, but other than that it blended unobtrusively with the other late 19th century tenement buildings on the block. The low-profile look was deliberate. In terms of neighborhood harmony, advertising our presence would have been counterproductive.

Heading down the block, I felt buoyant and energized, ready for a fresh start. Then I reached the club, and saw the graffiti on the stoop:

BURN IN HELL STEPHEN WRIGHT!

DEATH TO THE CRAZIES!!!

The spray paint gleamed wetly, and the chemical smell of toxic pigments and propellants still hung in the air. My heart pounding wildly, I froze in my tracks and stood staring at the ominous message. Rishi sniffed cautiously, sneezed, then angled himself against the balloon letters, lifted his leg, and began giving the stoop a purposeful watering. Normally he knew better than to pee on people's porches, but he seemed to sense that some stranger had marked his territory and to feel the need for a retaliatory response.

Unlike the neighboring stoops with their elegant wrought iron railings, the front steps at WellSpring were flanked by low masonry walls. The expanses of battleship gray cement made an irresistible canvas for graffiti artists, and this was by no means the first time the stoop had been defaced. But to the best of my knowledge, the area had never before been decorated with a death threat.

The glossy black letters were emblazoned on both sides of the stoop. The calligraphy was in the balloon style favored by so many graffiti artists, the bulbous black letters haloed in lurid red and purple. There was no signature. Who had committed this abomination? Was it simply a prank, albeit in appallingly bad taste, or a genuine warning? My sensible left-brain self told me it was probably one of the members acting out their ambivalent emotions about Stephen's demise, but the sick feeling in the pit of my stomach told me to take it very seriously indeed.

What to do next? Brewing a pot of coffee seemed like a reasonable start. I yanked Rishi away from the graffiti and started up the steps. Before I could make it to the top, an ear-splitting whistle stopped me in my tracks. Not a whistle of appreciation, but the two-fingered, taxi-flagging variety.

Wheeling abruptly, I saw Vito Pisanello, the mini-magnate of neighborhood real estate, standing on the sidewalk and glaring balefully at the graffiti. His black Armani suit and black silk shirt were a tad too tight, and his ample belly spilled over his belt buckle. "What did I tell you?" he sputtered. "This place is bringing down the neighborhood."

I stood my ground on the third step, the better to look down onto the bald spot the little man tried to hide with a bad comb job. "I have no idea who did this," I said, "but I'll make sure it's cleaned up today."

"You better. I've sunk a small fortune into my buildings on this street, but this dung heap is dragging the whole block down. These wackos have no pride in ownership."

"This building is owned by Compassion House, not the members, and I resent your using words like that."

"I'll use whatever words I want, lady. I'm just calling the shots like I see them. You should keep your crazies on a shorter leash, like you do with this dog here."

"They're not crazies, Mr. Pisanello, let alone wackos."

I paused for a gulp of air as the adrenaline coursed through my system. I was itching for a full-blown confrontation, but there was nothing to be gained by open warfare, so with a supreme effort I summoned my social work skills, took a deep breath and let him vent, acknowledging his ranting with an occasional nod or "uh hum". Addressing him as Mr. Pisanello seemed to take the edge off too. The phony deference cut deep against the grain, but I had absolutely no desire to know him on a first-name basis, so I could live with the hypocrisy.

When he started alluding to his influential acquaintances in Little Italy, however, I knew it was time to leave. I excused myself by saying I needed to call the police about the graffiti, then climbed the stairs, punched in the new code for the front door and headed with Rishi to my office.

Dennis Malone picked up on the first ring, listened carefully to my report, then told me he'd be over soon to check out the graffiti and take some photos. In preparation for his visit, I locked Rishi in my office. No point in his desecrating the crime scene any further.

Half an hour later, Dennis was on the doorstep, digital camera in hand. "I'm all done," he said. "I snapped a few pictures, but I don't know what good it'll do. You got any coffee?"

I escorted him downstairs to the dining room and poured him a Styrofoam cupful. "Cream? Sugar?"

"Black is fine." He took a gulp and grimaced. "I hate to say it, but this stuff is vile."

"What do you expect? We get it from a wholesale supplier." We headed back upstairs and outside, where I fixed him with what I hoped was a steely-eyed stare. "So anyway, Dennis, what's up with Stephen's investigation?"

"The case is still officially open, but we haven't come up with anything to suggest it wasn't a suicide. I don't think this graffiti proves anything different. Offhand, I see nothing to tie it directly to Stephen's death."

I felt a surge of anger. "You mean aside from the fact that it mentions him by name and warns of more killings to come? How much more direct can you get?"

His mouth twitched in annoyance. "The graffiti is pretty vague. It doesn't say anything about killing, precisely. I'll confess, Erika, I came over mainly to humor you and because the morning was starting out to be pretty boring. I thought seeing you would be a pleasant way to jump start the day."

"You arrogant bastard! You think Stephen's death is just some kind of sick joke? Or maybe you think suicide is just an occasional side effect of mental illness – unfortunate but inevitable."

He laid a hand on my forearm and smiled into my eyes. "Calm down, Erika. You have to trust me."

I pulled away. "I hate it when people tell me to trust them. In my experience, it usually means they're lying through their teeth."

He laughed. "You certainly are feisty, especially for so early in the morning." Then the smile evaporated, and I thought I saw something like sympathy in his green eyes. "Seriously, Erika, we're not giving up on this case. I'll keep you posted if there are any new developments."

"In the meantime, I gather we'll just have to wait around until someone else is hurt or killed."

"Erika, we have no reason to think that will happen."

"At least we can paint over the graffiti. The members shouldn't have to confront this message whenever they come in or out of the club."

"You're right, it doesn't exactly project a welcoming message. Might drive some people away, and I don't imagine you want your attendance to go down."

Dennis had a point. WellSpring was dependent on the health of its bottom line, with feelings and finances inextricably linked. Mental health professionals referred the members, who were free to choose whether or not to attend on any given day. Once a month I tallied the attendance figures in a report that went to Ocala. To me, the monthly statistics were merely a minor hassle, and I always had to remind myself they were vital to the club's survival.

"Yoo-hoo, Erika?" Dennis was studying me quizzically.

"Sorry. I was just thinking about the attendance. I wouldn't want –" I stopped short as I saw Stan and Gloria walking up the street, followed by several others.

Dennis edged closer and spoke softly into my ear, generating a tickling sensation that turned into a quiver. I hoped he didn't notice. "We may as well let your folks get a good look at it," he said. "With any luck, maybe someone will know something about who might have done it, or be able to identify the artist's style."

"I'd hardly call this person an artist," I said.

Stan approached, stopped in his tracks and stared at the message on the concrete piers. Others followed, and soon there were eight of us in a ragged semicircle, studying the graffiti.

What could I say? The desecration spoke for itself all too clearly. I stood in silence, trying to come up with something midway between reassurance and paranoia. Fortunately, Dennis stepped into the breach. "Does anyone have any ideas about who might have done this?" he asked.

Eyes shifted uneasily from the graffiti to the sidewalk and back again. No one said a word.

"Okay. If something occurs to anyone later, give me a call." Reaching into a pocket, he extracted a handful of business cards and dealt them out to everyone present.

Just then Jeff Archer ambled over. "Hey, what's happening?" His voice was casually cheerful. Then he saw the graffiti. "Oh, shit. That's disgusting. Anyone know who did it?"

I frowned. "Not yet, unfortunately."

Jeff leaned over to scrutinize the stoop at close range. "It doesn't look like the style of the graffiti artists I've seen. Too sloppy and amateurish."

Stan stepped forward. "You should know, Jeff. You're probably the best artist around these parts, especially now that Stephen – " He stopped abruptly, switched gears mid-sentence. "Erika, what are we going to do about this mess? Can we paint over it?"

"Detective Malone and I were just discussing that. I'd say the sooner the better."

"I nominate Jeff Archer as foreman," said Stan, with a sweeping gesture in Jeff's direction. "Provided he accepts my nomination, of course."

"I accept with pleasure," said Jeff, "but only if I can have total artistic autonomy."

"That depends," I said. "Aren't we just talking about a simple cover-up in some basic color that would blend with the building? Jeff, why don't you and Stan go over to the hardware store on Second Avenue, come back with some color chips, and we'll discuss it at the morning meeting. When it comes to anything that affects the building's overall appearance, we need to give all the members a chance for input."

Jeff's smile evaporated. "Whatever," he mumbled. "I should have known no one here appreciates my talent." With his long auburn hair and huge brown eyes, he looked like a choirboy who'd just lost his brand new puppy.

Jeff was a master at the art of manipulation, skilled at using his boyish good looks and dramatic flair to make his way in the world. Even so, my heart went out to him. Beneath Jeff's mercurial charm cowered a fragile, frightened child, and the last thing I wanted to do was inflict still more pain on a being who had already had more than his share. I persuaded him to stick around and present his plans at the morning meeting. After Dennis left, Jeff spent a few minutes scrutinizing the stoop with such intensity, I could almost see the wheels turning in his head. The other members watched awhile, then wandered off one by one.

Finishing his inspection, Jeff turned back to me. "I'd like to do an organic design, kind of art nouveau in feeling, in keeping with the era when the building was built. Mostly abstract, but with some plant motifs."

"Sounds good to me," I said. "If you present your ideas at the morning meeting, you probably won't have any trouble. I'll be there for moral support, just in case."

He fixed his enormous brown eyes on me. "Erika, thank you for backing me up. You really think people will give me permission to do it my way?"

"I hope so, because I'd like to see this abomination painted over as quickly as possible. Preferably by tonight."

He grinned. "You got it. At least I can slap a base coat over it, and then see where it goes from there."

Just then Gloria appeared at the top of the steps, waving a pink message slip in my direction. "Erika, there's a man on hold for you. I told him you were busy and tried to take a message, but he wanted to wait. Says it's important."

Hallelujah! It had to be Mark Levitan. I flew up the steps, and she thrust the slip at me. She had printed the name in block letters: Kevin Winthrop.

I drew a momentary blank. Then it came back to me – the guy from the dog run. Oh well, better luck next time.

She gave me a conspiratorial grin. "New boyfriend? He has a sexy voice."

I shrugged inscrutably and dashed inside. Minutes later, I was committed to a dinner date. Kevin told me to be ready at seven, and to wear something "dressy but not formal." As for where he was taking me, he wanted it to be a surprise.

———————

At the meeting, Jeff articulated his ideas with impassioned eagerness, illustrating his points with several whirlwind sketches in oil pastels.

"Jeff, you're fabulous!" Germaine exclaimed. "Just like that guy who paints mountains on TV!"

"Even better," said Stan. "That guy's a bore; all his paintings look the same."

Arthur Drummond voted against the project, and Susan Harvey abstained, but nearly everyone else voted in favor, and Jeff had the club's approval well before lunchtime.

I was just finishing dessert when Stan and Jeff approached my table. "Could you give us a voucher for the hardware store?" asked Stan. "And a hand truck would be good too. We should be back in an hour, and then we can recruit people to help work on the primer and base coats."

I felt a twinge of apprehension. Was I leaving too much to Jeff's discretion? After all, his artwork could be pretty strange. But then I thought of that morning's conversation with Vito Pisanello, and his condescending comments about the building and its inhabitants. The stranger the better, I decided – we might as well give him something really worth getting upset about.

"Okay," I said. "Go for it."

Amazing, I thought. A few hours ago, I'd been staring in foreboding at a threatening eyesore of a graffiti, and now here we were, about to give the club's façade a major facelift. Working in a small, loosely run organization definitely had its advantages. But come to think of it, I'd better give Ocala a call, and bring her up to speed. I couldn't afford to alienate her any more than I already had.

Chapter 10

I was famished by the time Kevin buzzed me on the intercom. Grabbing my bag and a sheer, hand-woven stole, I said goodbye to Rishi and clattered down four flights of stairs to the street.

Kevin was lounging against the side of a black SUV. Its flawless finish suggested it was the recipient of regular tender loving care. Its equally flawless owner wore a linen jacket of pale beige, with shirt and pants in understated, sandy tones that harmonized well with the blazer and complemented his blond hair and deep tan. He looked like the supporting actor in an epic movie about privileged white colonists in Africa, primed for an evening of socializing at the country club before tomorrow's safari.

The image made me smile, and Kevin caught my mood. "You're smiling like someone with a delicious secret," he said. "Care to share it with me?"

"Oh, nothing special. Just looking forward to this evening. I've been working so hard lately, I haven't had time for much in the way of diversion."

"Tell me about it. I've been working eighty-hour weeks since God knows when. But I'm my own boss, so I've got no one to blame but myself. Anyway, let's not think about work tonight." He eyed me appraisingly. "You look fabulous."

I'd chosen a dress of sheer silk in sage green, with overlapping bias cut layers that floated with my slightest movement, accented with a strand of jade and malachite beads. "Thanks," I said. "You look pretty elegant yourself."

"I made reservations at The Founders Club. I hope that's all right with you."

"Great! I haven't been there in ages."

"Oh, you've been there?" He seemed momentarily crestfallen, disappointed at the ease with which I seemed prepared to slip into his elegant world. When we'd met before, I'd been dressed down in my typical WellSpring mufti, so perhaps he'd hoped to win me over with unaccustomed luxury. And in fact he was succeeding, although not in the way he'd planned.

There's a secret side of my psyche that takes inordinate pleasure in expensive fashion, wining and dining, a side that my husband cultivated in me and that I've pretty much vanquished from my present world. Ostentatious spending seems politically incorrect, and in any case I don't have the financial wherewithal to indulge. Perhaps most important, I associate lavish spending with those manic phases when I've run up my credit card charges with reckless abandon. In the end I paid dearly, so I take pains to avoid that trap. On the other hand, I have no qualms about indulging my taste for luxury every now and again if someone else picks up the tab.

Scrambling into Kevin's Range Rover in my silk dress and high heeled sandals was a challenge, but by the time he realized I could use some help, I was already perched on the black leather seat. More black leather padded the walls and the dashboard, and a screen of heavy metal mesh partitioned off the cargo space behind the back seat. The total effect suggested the set for a bondage flick.

He watched as I glanced around. "Pardon the inelegant transportation. I use this vehicle to haul my dogs around. The black leather stands up well to abuse, and their hair doesn't show so much when they shed."

"You said you had rottweilers?"

"Yes, two females – Greta and Gudrun. You'll have to meet them one of these days."

"I love dogs, but I have to admit that's one breed that intimidates me a little."

"Their nastiness is much exaggerated. Mine are really sweet, affectionate dogs. As long as I tell them someone is okay, they're fine."

"What if someone's not okay?"

He grinned. "Then all bets are off."

——— ——— ———

The Founders Club was every bit as elegant as I'd remembered. The maitre d' seated us on an intimate banquette in a far corner, and as I sank into the soft mauve plush and studied the menu with its astronomical prices, I remembered the times I'd been there with my ex-husband Richard. Like Kevin, he had been smug, self-satisfied about being able to afford a place like this. The price of one bottle of wine on the list Kevin was perusing could probably feed a small family for a week.

But this wasn't a night for self-induced guilt trips about social injustice, so I decided to relax and enjoy myself. Kevin insisted we indulge to the utmost, with a different wine to complement each course, and we spent most of the meal making like restaurant reviewers, tasting, commenting and exclaiming over the subtle medley of flavors.

Sometime within the few minutes after we ordered dessert, my appestat finally kicked in and warned me not to eat another bite. A moment later the waiter arrived with plates holding elaborate constructions of chocolate mousse, pastry, and meringue drizzled in rivulets of raspberry sauce that flowed in carefully calibrated curves onto the plates. "This is far too impressive to eat," I said. "It looks like a maquette for a sculpture. Enlarge the scale by maybe a hundred, cast it in bronze, and I could picture it in front of one of the corporate headquarters over on Sixth Avenue."

Kevin laughed. "Erika, you've got a really quirky imagination. It's one of the things I find most fascinating about you." All at once he reached across the table and covered my hand with his. "You remind me a lot of my sister. It hit me when I met you at the dog run. There's something about your expressions, your vitality, that's very much like Barbara. And your coloring is a lot like hers, with dark blond hair and blue eyes."

He was gazing at me intently, and I felt myself blushing. "Does Barbara live in New York City too?" I asked.

"She did, yes. But she died three years ago. She was only twenty-seven." His eyes grew moist. "It still gets to me. I guess there are things about her death that I still haven't processed completely."

"That's natural. Grieving for someone you love can go on for a very long time. There's no one standard period of mourning that's right for everyone." I paused, aware how pompous I sounded. "Kevin, I'm truly sorry. And forgive me for sounding like a social worker there for a minute."

"That's all right. You *are* a social worker." His grip tightened on my hand. "I was already drawn to you, but I was really blown away by that interview the other night, when you admitted you were bipolar. That was Barbara's diagnosis too, although I'm not sure it was correct." Releasing my hand and leaning back against the banquette, he sighed deeply. "I'm positive her so-called treatment by the mental health system played a major role in bringing about her death. She killed herself three years ago this fall."

My breath caught in my throat. "I'm so sorry."

"It never should have happened. If she'd stayed clear of the psychiatric establishment, I firmly believe she'd be alive today."

His revelation left me stunned. The information was doubly unnerving because Kevin's sister had killed herself at twenty-seven, the age I'd been when I was first diagnosed bipolar. I knew only too well what it was like to feel suicidal.

Untouched before me, my elaborate dessert was beginning to soften and slump, the chocolate and raspberry sauces merging into a murky mess. Absently, I picked up my spoon and began etching jagged new contours through the brown and red, exposing the white china beneath.

"Maybe I shouldn't have brought it up," said Kevin. "But I feel this strange bond with you, and I would have felt dishonest keeping it to myself."

"I'm glad you told me." I laid my spoon down on the plate with a clink. "It's just a shock, that's all. You were saying her psychiatric treatment was partially responsible for her death?"

"Yes, but let's drop the subject for now. I wanted this to be a relaxed, pleasant evening, not a time for soul-searing revelations."

"Fine," I said. "I'm ready to try some of this scrumptious dessert now, before I turn it into a Jackson Pollock."

"Good idea, I'm ready for mine too. Let's have an after-dinner liqueur with it, maybe some Courvoisier, then call it a night. I know we've both got a busy day tomorrow."

———————

Back home before eleven, I walked Rishi, then poured myself a giant glass of Tropicana to counterbalance the expensive wines I'd been imbibing all evening. Then I stretched out on the sofa and tried to process my feelings about Kevin.

With his blond hair and rough-hewn features, Kevin Winthrop was an attractive man. Even so, I was relieved that he'd wanted to make an early night of it, and I wasn't sure why. Maybe it was the unsettling comparison with his sister. Or maybe he was simply too straight, too successful. I've always been drawn to men who lived on the alternative edges of society, usually men involved in the arts. More often than not, they've been tormented in one way or another and chronically short of cash. I've had more conventional suitors, and I've tried to open my mind and heart to them, but when they got serious, I ran the other way.

There was one noteworthy exception: my ex-husband, Richard, was conventional to the core. I didn't realize it for a long time, because I was fooled by his hip façade. The marriage began to unravel almost before we finished the wedding cake, but we stuck it out for a few years. Our split was polite and perfunctory, but the whole experience left me even more leery of men in suits than I'd been before.

But what about Mark? He wore a suit, looked damn good in it, in fact. He was even a lawyer, like Richard. But his advocacy for the mentally ill, his upfront attitude about his own illness, gave him that alternative edge I liked. All in all, a potentially devastating combination. He hadn't called, though. Maybe I should call him. But no – best not to appear too needy. In the meantime, I resolved to give Kevin the benefit of the doubt.

———

In the days that followed, Jeff Archer virtually took up residence on the front stoop at WellSpring. It was fascinating to watch his creation evolve. He began by obliterating the harsh black and red of the graffiti with a variety of greens. Hints of vegetation began to take shape, gigantic leaves and curving vines. On the second day he added fragments of tree trunks, and on the third day, flowers appeared.

At the end of the first week, I was in my office cleaning up odds and ends of paperwork when Gloria buzzed me. "Ocala's outside talking to Jeff," she said. "Maybe you'd better go check out what's happening."

My heart sank. I wasn't up for an unannounced site visit, and Jeff was so fragile. What if Ocala was out there tromping all over his ego?

I needn't have worried. When I arrived on the scene, they were both beaming. "This mural is a bit more than I bargained for," Ocala told me. "It's kind of flamboyant, but Jeff explained it's still in the early stages, and the colors are going to blend together more. It's a big improvement on that grubby old blue paint."

I gazed at the wall. Long before my time, the facade had been painted cobalt blue, but now it was grimy and starting to chip. "Before painting, ideally, the building should have been sandblasted down to the original red of its Victorian brickwork," I told Ocala. "And the terra cotta detailing at the roofline and around the windows should really be restored before it deteriorates any further."

She laughed. "Dream on, girl. Compassion House doesn't have Vito Pisanello's deep pockets. Given our shoestring budget, you're lucky we were able to squeeze out a couple hundred dollars for the paint."

"I know. Thanks for approving this project, Ocala. I think Jeff's creation will do us all proud."

As the late afternoon sun glinted off the fresh paint, I felt a wave of warmth and affection sweep over me. For Jeff, for Ocala, for everyone at the club. The oppressive heat had finally broken, and there was a fresh hint of autumn in the air. The threatening graffiti was still there, but invisible beneath the shimmering surfaces of blue and green, like a shark in the ocean's depths. On a gorgeous day like today, it was easy to forget it had ever existed.

———

Back home that night, I walked Rishi, then poured a glass of Merlot and nuked myself a frozen pizza, supreme with all the fixings. To cut down on the outrageous calorie count, I gave Rishi half. Then I sat down at my Yamaha keyboard and began to play. My mind kept drifting to Jeff and his mural, to the playful, unfettered creativity that flowed from his brushes.

With a jolt, I realized I was jealous. How delicious it would be to spend my days creating in solitude, stopping only to imbibe the praises of occasional passers-by. Although I loved my work as a therapist, I wasn't fully confident I was cut out for my new role as administrator, and the nonstop interpersonal intensity of WellSpring was getting on my nerves. I craved the counterbalance of solitude.

These two sides of my psyche were like yang and yin, I reflected: yang the bright, assertive, expansive light of day, and yin the dark, inward-turning, receptive silence of night. Ideally, they formed a balanced, harmonious whole, like the intertwined symbols of the circle. But as I improvised, it occurred to me that since I'd been working at WellSpring, my yin and yang energies had been slipping out of kilter. The yang kept screaming for more space in my brain, demanding attention and sucking energy from the yin, the darkly mysterious female side that I drew on for my creativity.

True, I needed to nourish my creativity. But no more for tonight. I was exhausted, and sleep was calling. I switched off the Yamaha, shrouded it in the colorful throw that served as its dust cover, then headed for bed.

———————

In the second week of the mural's creation, the hours of light were growing ever so slightly shorter. But Jeff's workday was steadily growing longer. On Wednesday morning, he asked for a key to the club in order to get his materials first thing in the morning and lock them up at night.

I flashed back to Stephen, his long, lonely nights creating mosaics on the roof, his ultimate fall from the edge. "Sorry, Jeff, but no. I trust you, but we're taking tighter security measures these days. Besides, I don't want you getting too hyper and losing sleep over this project. That way lies madness. Believe me, I know – I've been there myself."

He rolled his eyes, like a teen-ager enduring a lecture from Mom. "That's you, not me. Cut me some slack, Erika." Then he regained his customary manners. "I'm sorry. I mean, I understand where you're coming from, I've experienced that kind of mania myself, but seriously, there's no problem. I'd recognize the symptoms. I just want to get on with my work."

"Okay, let me think about it."

"Let's ask Stan. I'll bet he wouldn't mind letting me in and out. He's here at all hours anyway."

———

Jeff got his way. With Stan's endorsement, he even talked me into springing for a halogen work lamp on its own tripod for working after dark. Now he was well under way when I showed up each morning, still going strong when I left at night. To keep away from wet paint and avoid disturbing the artist at work, we began using the door at the ground floor level instead of the main entrance. I paused often to greet Jeff and check on his progress. Usually he took the opportunity to step back and stand alongside me, studying his work from a different perspective. "I'm letting the work tell me how it wants to evolve," he told me one morning. "And it's telling me it needs room to grow up over the door frame and further across the walls. Does that sound okay to you?"

"I like what you've done so far," I said, "and the East Village has an long, venerable tradition of mural painting. What the heck, go for it."

And go for it he did. As if by wizardry, the tropical vines and tendrils snaked higher over the doorframe, out across the masonry to the window frames and beyond. He began adding bits of background color interspersed with the foliage, using sunset colors of pink and orange. Exotic birds perched in the branches, and a pair of monkeys swung limb to limb.

By the first day of autumn, the project had expanded to cover the entire ground and first floors of the façade. To my eyes, it looked virtually finished, but Jeff insisted there was more to do. "It's my gift to WellSpring, so it has to be as good as I can possibly make it," he explained one day. "This place has given me so much that I feel the need to give something back. Something for people to remember me by when I'm no longer here."

He had just dropped a bombshell, and my heart sank. I decided to be direct. "Talking about being remembered – does that mean you aren't planning to stick around?"

"You mean do I intend to kill myself like Stephen did?" He smiled quizzically, letting the question linger in the air as he waited for my reaction.

I forced myself to outwait him, knowing my silence would be more likely to elicit an honest response than would a barrage of anxious questions.

Sure enough, the silence didn't sit well with him. "Erika, you can rest assured I'm not going to do anything drastic like offing myself," he said at last. "I believe suicide is a viable option in certain circumstances, like when your life has absolutely no redeeming qualities whatsoever. But that's not me. At least not this week."

Chapter 11

*M*y heart did a weird double-time beat, and I was still speechless. It wasn't deliberate therapeutic strategy this time, just sheer panic.

Jeff laughed. "Jeez, Erika, you should see your face! I knew that would get a rise out of you. I'm not planning to kill myself. Not this week, not next week, not in the foreseeable future."

I could have strangled him. "Then stop jerking me around, Jeffrey! Suicide's nothing to joke about. Make those kinds of comments to the wrong people, and you could find yourself in Bellevue under suicidal precautions."

"There's no need. Seriously, Erika, I've been feeling great, and this mural is making me feel even better. I know it's good, and what's really exciting is that other people know it too. There's a nice old lady who stops by to cheer me on and bring me coffee and bagels. A couple of people asked about me doing murals on their buildings. And a woman who owns a gallery in Chelsea saw it and said she might give me a show. Maybe she thinks I'll be the next Jean Michel Basquiat."

"That graffiti artist who turned into an overnight sensation in the art world? I certainly hope not. He was a good painter, but he flamed out and died far too young. Of a heroin overdose, if I recall?"

"Yes, but you don't have to worry about that with me. I've been clean for three years now."

"That's fabulous, Jeff." I hoped he was being straight with me. At the hospital, I'd worked with more than enough addicts. A few managed to kick, to turn their lives around; the majority didn't. Even with the best of intentions, far too many ended up dead. I opted to change the subject. "You know, as this mural evolves, it reminds me more and more of Gauguin, especially the Tahitian paintings, with all those sinuous curves and tropical colors."

"Thanks. I confess that when I was just starting this mural, I went to the library and studied some books on Gauguin. But I'm not a slavish imitator – I couldn't be, because they wouldn't let anyone take those books out of the library, and I'm too broke to buy any."

The thought of buying Jeff a Gauguin book crossed my mind, but I shoved it away. His charming manipulations didn't cut it with me today, not after the emotional roller coaster he'd just subjected me to. I headed inside to my office, grabbing a mug of coffee en route. Hunkered down at my desk, I felt the acid well up and start to churn deep in my chest, and I knew the club's cheap, bitter coffee wasn't the only culprit.

All week, every week, I played the roles of calm, judicious administrator and sensitive, empathic therapist, and my creative side was suffering serious neglect. What had happened to Erika Norgren the edgy, avant-garde musician? I knew the answer: a few years back, she had succumbed to her distaste for chronic poverty and shelved her fantasies of stardom, yielding to Erika the sensible, bread-winning social worker. On the surface, the sensible Erika was doing a decent job of things, but the outspoken, artistic Erika was smothering inside the respectable shell. Artistic Erika wanted to burst out and be heard.

Watching Jeff's creativity flower day by day was only fueling her jealousy. She was sending those acid waves of pain in protest, screaming "Let me out or else!"

I popped a couple of Tums and started to pace, but my office was too small. Half a dozen steps, and I had to turn back and start over, like a caged lion. Nonetheless, I kept going. Something was tickling at my mind, the hint of an inspiration. The feeling was familiar, but I'd lost touch with it of late. Something new and creative was taking root and growing in my brain. My muse was back, tickling and teasing my mind with a flamboyantly beautiful peacock feather, inviting me out to play.

No sooner did I recognize my muse than I heard her message: She wanted me to stage a celebration at the club, a multimedia extravaganza that would showcase the talents of everyone here. It could mark the official unveiling of Jeff's finished mural, but beyond that, the event would energize everyone at WellSpring, help us move on from the negativity surrounding Stephen's death. As a bonus, it might well garner us some positive attention in the community and with the media. A cabaret, we'd call it. A cabaret to celebrate our face-lifted façade.

I threw open the door and charged down the hall, eager to share my revelation with the world, or failing that, with whoever happened to be around. I headed downstairs to Gloria's office, where I found her reading a romance novel. She'd make a perfect test subject.

"Gloria, I've had a scathingly brilliant idea," I said. "What would you think of our putting on a multimedia show in honor of our new façade? A kind of cabaret where the members could show off their talents – singing, dancing, acting, whatever they like?"

She leaned back and pursed her lips in thought. "Sounds good. But do we have that many talented people here?"

"Of course! Everyone has some kind of talent, even if they haven't discovered it yet. And if they haven't, I'll help them figure it out.

Anyway, this show won't be about judgment or competition. It'll be a light-hearted, playful kind of thing."

"It sounds exciting, Erika. Could I sing something?"

"Absolutely, and I can accompany you. What do you want to sing?"

"Something by Christina Aguilera? Or no, Madonna. I could dress up like her, too."

I laughed. "Which Madonna? She's been through so many image changes, you've got a lot to choose from. Maybe you could even do a medley."

"Great! Count me in."

"Okay, but do me a favor and keep this under your hat for a bit. I want to clear it with Ocala before I discuss it with the rest of the members."

———————

Ocala was more receptive than I had expected, especially when I told her of my plans to invite the media and garner some positive publicity for WellSpring. "We should pick a date at tomorrow's community meeting," I said. "I want to do it sometime in October, while the weather's still good and before people start getting preoccupied with the holidays. Maybe right before Halloween. I'd really like you to be there, so tell me if there are any dates that are bad for you."

"Why, Erika, how thoughtful of you," she said, sounding like a teacher praising a slightly backward child. She'd never patronized me like this before she learned I was bipolar, I reflected. And I'd never before felt the need to indulge in such shameless brown nosing with my boss.

My negotiating strategy paid off. Ocala not only approved the cabaret; she authorized me to spend up to five hundred dollars for expenses. "It'll be worth it if you can get us some positive P R," she said.

"What with Stephen's death and that negative publicity, it feels as if the club has been in a downward spiral. I'm counting on you to turn things around."

———————

Stan was chairing the community meeting the next morning. Jeff had abdicated the responsibility for the time being, claiming it interrupted the flow of his painting. When I floated the notion of the cabaret, some members were skeptical.

"Sounds like a lot of work," said Stan. "Do you think we have time to put something respectable together?"

"Today is September 22nd, and I'm thinking late October, so that makes about five weeks," I said. "That should be plenty of time."

"Hey, Stanley," said Gloria. "Think of Stephen's memorial service. We pulled that together in less than a day."

Stan frowned. "It turned into a media fiasco. Ocala would have a fit if that happened again."

"She's already approved it," I said. "She agrees with me: the positive media coverage could do wonders for the club."

"Yeah, Stan, stop being such a wet blanket," said Arthur.

The muscles in Stan's jaw twitched. He folded his massive arms and glared silently at Arthur. I broke in. "Let's brainstorm about this for a few minutes. All suggestions are welcome, no matter how far-out or ridiculous they might seem. I don't want anybody putting down anyone else's ideas. Gloria can act as recording secretary. What we want now is unfettered inspiration. Then later we can discuss all our ideas and decide how realistic they are and whether we want to go ahead."

Germaine piped up. "Could I sing something? I like 'Raindrops Keep Falling on My Head.'"

"You certainly could," I said. "I could accompany you – I like Burt Bacharach, and I know I've got the sheet music around somewhere."

"I want to be the ringmaster," said Arthur. "Or rather the emcee. Ringmasters are for circuses."

"Maybe it will be a circus, who knows? You could be an emcee dressed like a ringmaster. You could talk like one too – 'and now for our scintillating songstress, Gloria, with her spectacularly sultry soprano,' that kind of thing."

Gloria clapped her hands and squealed in delight. "Erika, that's brilliant. Can you wait till I get a steno book? I want to write it down so we don't forget."

I grinned. "Not to worry. There's plenty more where that came from. Once you tap into your inner sources of inspiration, it's like a well that never runs dry."

———————

As the mural neared completion, more and more people stopped to marvel at Jeff's creation. His already long hours were growing even longer, and he took a break only when Stan or I brought him food and insisted he stop to eat. His speech was speeding up, with an edge of elation I understood all too well. Jeff was giving off the signals of someone escalating into a full-blown manic episode.

"You're getting a lot of positive feedback," I said one morning. "I hope you're not letting all the compliments go to your head."

He grinned. "I always consider the source. I value your opinions, for example. But most people don't know what they're looking at, so I don't pay any attention to them. Actually, I'm my own harshest critic. But I know this mural is good. That's what keeps me going."

"Good. It sounds as if you have a solid, levelheaded approach. I'd been worried you might be getting a little too hyper."

"You mean too manicky, don't you? Don't worry, I'm still taking my Depakote. That's what you were leading up to, isn't it?"

I laughed. "You're always a step or two ahead of me."

"I've been in the system long enough. I know the drill. For example, it's okay to say my work is good, but if I say it's going to revolutionize the art world, that's grandiosity."

Just then I saw Arthur loping down the sidewalk. He started down the steps to the ground-floor entrance, then stopped abruptly. "When is this thing going to be finished? It's a pain in the ass to have to keep using the basement stairs."

"Probably in another day or two," said Jeff. "It's in the final stages."

"That's good, because otherwise you're going to be in the final stages yourself."

Jeff flushed. "What's that supposed to mean?"

"Hey, guys, cut it out," I said.

"I will if you can spare some time away from this genius here," said Arthur. "Erika, can we go to your office? I need to talk to you."

Minutes later, I was ensconced in my swivel chair behind my oversize metal desk, which put a solid three feet between Arthur and me. He was staring at me intently. "You spend way too much time with Jeff, talking about that damn mural," he said. "It's beginning to bug people. They feel like maybe you have some kind of special relationship with him."

"I'm sorry if it seems that way. It's true I've been spending a lot of time with Jeff, but the mural will have a major impact on the impressions people form of the club, so I want to be sure it's coming along well. I don't have a special relationship with Jeff, whatever you mean by that. I'm well aware of my professional ethics and responsibilities."

Arthur presented his palms. "Whoa, Erika, cool it. You told me all about your ethics when you refused to go out with me. But I gotta tell you, you're beautiful when you're mad. I'm starting to get really turned on."

My eyes strayed to the door, which I'd intentionally left open. "I feel uncomfortable when you talk like that," I said. "If you don't stop, I'll have to ask you to leave."

He smiled slyly, the wolf salivating over Little Red Riding Hood. "Don't worry, Erika. I would never do anything to hurt you."

Through the doorway, a flash of pale blue caught my eye. It was Susan, unlocking the door to her office across the hall. "Susan," I called. "Can you come in here a minute?"

She turned with a jerk, hesitated, then stepped to the doorway, nervously smoothing the skirt of her polyester print dress. "What is it?" she asked.

I hadn't thought of a pretext, but Arthur disposed of the awkward silence. "I was just telling Erika that she's spending too much time with Jeff Archer and his weird mural, and that it gives people the wrong idea."

Susan's eyes darted skittishly from Arthur to me. "I don't know anything about that. I'm in here all day, just doing my job."

I grabbed a couple of random file folders, then rose and headed for Susan and the door. "I know. I just wanted your opinion on where to file some stuff. You know how I always procrastinate about filing. Come on, Arthur. I need to lock up now."

He shot me that wolfish grin again, and I knew my reprieve was only temporary.

I spent the evening practicing at my keyboard. It was lucky I felt jazzed about the cabaret, because my social life lately was nothing to brag about. Still no word from Mark, and Kevin had told me he'd be out of town for awhile. With Germaine in mind, I opened my old Bacharach and David songbook and went over "Raindrops Keep Falling". Like most of their songs, it had fascinating but devilishly tricky chord changes - that's why I'd bought the book. As for Madonna and the more recent music other members wanted to sing, I was a little out of touch, but that didn't worry me. With my ear, they just had to play me the records a couple of times, and I could easily fake it. Harmonically speaking, pop music was pretty simplistic.

I was playing with the rhythm tracks on my Yamaha, experimenting with a hip hop groove, when the phone rang. I glanced at my watch – twelve-thirty a.m. No one I knew would call so late. Probably a wrong number. Let the machine get it.

"Erika, are you there? Pick up, please. Erika – hello?"

The voice was Stan's, but the panic wasn't like him at all. I punched the stop button on the keyboard and waited in the sudden silence.

"Erika, this is Stan. I'm calling from the club. It's an emergency. Please pick up."

My heart pounding, I crossed the room and lifted the receiver to my ear. "Stan, this is Erika. What's wrong? What's happening?"

"It's Jeff. I found him on the steps of the club. It looks like he's ODed."

"God, no! But you found him in time? He's going to be all right?"

There was silence at the other end, then the keening of an ambulance siren growing steadily louder. "I called 911," said Stan. "They just got here. I'd better go."

"I'll pull on some clothes and get over there as fast as I can."

"Thanks." There was a click and the line went dead.

I realized Stan hadn't answered my question, at least not in so many words. But his silence had told me more than I wanted to know.

Chapter 12

E'ven before my cab pulled up at the club, I knew it was bad, because the scene was much too calm. The cops and paramedics stood talking quietly next to an ambulance parked with the rear doors agape. Behind them I caught a glimpse of Jeff's brown hair, his body lying limp on a gurney.

I turned away and rummaged in my handbag, then handed the driver a ten. I told him to keep the change, in the irrational hope that my generosity might somehow make the nightmare disappear.

Stan emerged from the shadows to help me out of the cab, with Ariana close behind. Standing shakily at the curb, I forced myself to look in Jeff's direction. One glance told me my symbolic gesture had been futile. He lay full-length on a collapsed gurney, wearing his usual paint-spattered jeans, his well-worn Nike sneakers and the same tie-dyed tee shirt he'd been wearing during the day, a riot of rainbow colors emblazoned with a Grateful Dead logo. His lank brown hair flopped over his forehead, and his expression was serenely angelic, but his skin was deathly pale. On the stoop, half a dozen cans of paint stood open, the brushes stashed in a can of solvent. The halogen lamp lay smashed on the sidewalk below.

A slight young cop stepped forward, and I introduced myself. "What's going on?" I asked.

"My partner and I were first on the scene. When I couldn't get a pulse, we called the paramedics and started CPR. They were here within five minutes, and they injected him with Narcon. That's a powerful antidote to heroin, and it would have brought him back if anything could. If we'd been even a few minutes earlier, we might have saved him. But the heroin that's on the street these days can be really lethal, especially the way they cut it with all kinds of garbage."

"Why do you think it was heroin?"

"We won't know for sure till after the autopsy, but all the works were right next to him, including the needle. See, they're still up there, at the top of the stoop."

I looked, and my stomach lurched sickeningly. "But I'm virtually positive he wasn't doing drugs," I protested. "He had a lot of good things happening in his life. This mural, for example. He planned to finish it in the next couple of days. He'd told me how heroin damped down his creativity and he never touched it anymore."

"Sorry, ma'am, but with all due respect, if he was an addict in the past, anything he told you about staying off the stuff was essentially bullshit." The young officer studied the sidewalk. "Unfortunately I've seen a lot of cases like this. It's not unusual for people to kick, then get sucked back into it despite their best intentions. Especially when they're under stress or depressed. Of course we can't make a definite determination yet. We've left the scene intact. We're waiting for the detectives and – "

"I know. You can spare me the details." The homicide detectives would be here any minute, followed by the crew that dealt with the technical detritus of death – the crime scene examiners, the photographer, the medical examiner. A few weeks ago, I wouldn't have known what to expect, but Stephen's death had taught me more than I wanted to know about this type of scenario. It was the kind of on-the-job training I could gladly have done without.

An unmarked car pulled up and Dennis Malone climbed out, looking bleary-eyed and rumpled. "I'm glad you're here," I said.

"I'm not. What is it with this place, anyway?" He scratched his head. "Have a seat in my car while I check out what's happening. I'll be with you soon."

It was an order, not a suggestion, so I let him help me into the back seat of his blue sedan while his partner exited the front.

"Don't worry, Erika, I won't lock you in," Dennis said with a sleepy half-smile. "I'll just close the doors so you can have some peace and quiet."

It hadn't entered my mind that he might imprison me. As soon as he left, I tried the door, and it opened easily. Relieved, I shut it again, then rested my head against the cracked vinyl seat and closed my eyes in a fruitless attempt to blot out the horror lying just a few feet away.

Much later – it could have been hours or minutes, I had no idea – the muffled rumble of an engine jolted me alert, and I opened my eyes to the sight of the medics raising the gurney on its spindly metal legs. Atop the day-glo orange mattress lay a black plastic body bag. As I watched them wheel it to the idling ambulance and load it inside, all at once I was floating up and away from my body, viewing myself and the whole scene from a great distance, through a light fog. Like a near-death experience, except that I wasn't near death. Perhaps Jeff had had one; I'd have to ask him. But no, I couldn't – he wasn't coming back.

Once the ambulance had pulled away, Dennis Malone came over to the car, trailed by Stan and Ariana. The detective opened the door and extended his hand to assist me out. "I need to ask you all a few questions," he said.

"I should think so," snapped Ariana. "Because I'm absolutely positive Jeff didn't kill himself. I know, because I was close to him the whole time until the cops arrived."

Dennis cast her a hard look. "Was he still alive? Did he say something?"

"No, I couldn't get a pulse. But I could sense his aura, and it was still pure and strong. Not the aura of someone who would OD on heroin."

The detective's lips twitched almost imperceptibly. "We don't know for sure if that's what it was. We'll have to wait for the autopsy."

"The works were right there beside him," said Stan. "It looked pretty incriminating. And he did have a history of drug abuse, although he's been clean for several years."

"I can't comment on his personal history, since it's confidential," I said. Good – my professional veneer was kicking in, precarious as it might be. "But tell me – how did you happen to find him?"

Dennis shot me a green-eyed glare, and I realized I might be trespassing on his turf. Saying nothing, he shifted his gaze to Stan, who crossed his arms and cleared his throat, then fixed his eyes on the sidewalk. "I stopped by about ten o'clock to help Jeff lock up his paints and stuff, like I've been doing the past week or so. He told me he needed a couple more hours. You know Jeff. Once he gets going, he keeps right on, like the Energizer bunny – " He stopped abruptly, aware of his mistake in tenses.

Ariana took up the story. "So Stanley called me, asked if I wanted to get something to eat. We went to Rosie's, that vegetarian place on St. Marks. Then we walked back to the club to help him lock up. When we saw him lying there, we thought he was dozing, but when Stan called him, he didn't answer." Her eyes began to mist over.

"It was twelve twenty-two," said Stan. "I remember, because I looked at my watch. I went up the steps, called his name and shook him, but he didn't respond. So I let myself into the club and called 911. I called Erika, and then we carried him down the steps and tried doing CPR. We kept it up till the cops got here, and then the medics. They tried everything they could, but nothing worked – they couldn't save him." He let out a gargantuan sigh, his eyes glistening behind his round glasses.

"That's enough for tonight," said Malone. "I'm going back to the station to check out some things, but I'll want to talk to all of you tomorrow. Some of the other club members, too. " He folded his lanky frame into the front seat of the sedan and started the engine.

A profound exhaustion swept over me as I watched him pull away. "I'm too tired to think clearly," I said, "but Ariana, I agree with you. Something isn't right about this."

"If there's any justice in the world, the police will do a thorough investigation," said Stan. "But justice is a rare commodity sometimes. I'm not going to hold my breath."

We stood huddled together, reluctant to go our separate ways. Down the block, looking toward Second Avenue, the streetlights were few and far between, and the street was swallowed by shadows. By day, the neighborhood around the club felt familiar and benign, but now, at two in the morning, every stretch of darkness held the potential for unknown horrors.

"We'll walk with you till you get a cab," said Stan. "You shouldn't be alone this time of night." His tone left no room for objections.

"Thanks, I appreciate it."

Just before we set out, I turned to look at Jeff's mural. In the darkness, the curvilinear shapes twined across the façade of WellSpring like ominous creatures from the ocean depths. The biomorphic plant forms, so decorative by day, were monstrous tentacles, ready to seize and strangle anyone foolish enough to wander near. Jeff had already perished in their grasp. With my heartfelt support and encouragement, he had created a devouring monster that ultimately destroyed him.

——— —— ———

Back home, I filled my biggest coffee mug with Merlot, then rushed to the phone and speed-dialed Ocala's number. As I sank into the overstuffed armchair next to my desk, Rishi jounced me and red wine splashed all over my chest like a bloody, incriminating stain. Serves me right, I thought. I'm the guilty one – if not for me, Jeff would still be alive.

Ocala answered just as Rishi planted his huge paws on my thighs and began licking the wine off my shirt. Pushing him back, juggling the phone and the mug of wine, I began telling her about Jeff.

She cut me off. "Slow down, girl! Are you all right? You sound hysterical."

"No, I'm not all right. The whole thing is my fault, and now I've got the blood stains to prove it."

"What's your fault? Take a deep breath and start over – I haven't understood a word you said. Is somebody hurt? Should I call 911?"

"No, Stan already did that, but it was too late. Jeff Archer is dead." I began to cry, gasping out narrative fragments between sobs.

When I finished, there was a long silence at both ends of the line. At last Ocala spoke. "What a nightmare! You poor child – no wonder you were upset."

"I can't help thinking I was to blame. For not picking up the warning signs, or for letting him take on such a big project with so much responsibility. The whole thing might have driven him back to drugs."

"Whoa, Erika, wait a minute! That kind of thinking is not only unproductive; it's downright dangerous. The last thing you want to do is start rumors that reflect badly on you or on WellSpring. If you parade around in a hair shirt, flogging yourself and proclaiming your guilt, people will not only believe you, they'll expand and elaborate on everything you say. Save the soul searching for your therapist. As an administrator, you need to show a thicker skin."

"What you say makes a lot of sense," I said. "I'll try to remember it."

"You do that. I don't think we can do anything else tonight, so let's both try to get some sleep." She paused. "One more thing. What was that you said at the beginning, about the blood stains?"

"Oh, that was nothing. Right before you picked up, Rishi bumped into me and made me splash red wine all over my shirt. It was just a metaphor."

"I see." From Ocala's tone, I could tell she didn't. Thankfully, she said goodnight and let me off the hook.

I still craved human contact, but I couldn't think of a living soul to call. Mark Levitan, maybe, but not at this ungodly hour of the morning. Ocala had suggested I speak with my therapist, which would have been a grand idea, except that right now I had no therapist, just a psychiatrist to write my prescriptions and keep tabs on my lithium level every three months. Far too wired to sleep, I managed to avoid my bed in the few hours left before dawn. Instead, I moved restlessly from my keyboard to FreeCell on the computer, then to old movies on cable TV and back again.

I knew insomnia this extreme could portend a flight into full-blown mania. On the other hand, who could blame me? The reality of Jeff's death could well send anyone round the bend. I brewed myself some coffee and waited impatiently for sunrise. I needed to be at the club early for damage control.

———————

In the early-morning sunshine, the club looked deceptively ordinary. The sky was a brilliant autumnal blue, the air crisp and motionless, and the street as deserted and frozen in time as an Edward Hopper painting. Gravitating to the spot where I had stood talking with the others last night, I gazed at the stretch of sidewalk where Jeff's gurney had lain, then willed myself to look up at the corner of the stoop where he had been found, but there was absolutely nothing to suggest what had happened here. No yellow crime scene tape, not even so much as a chalky outline of his fallen form.

But Rishi found the site intensely fascinating. His nose to the ground, he snuffled excitedly as far as his leash would let him reach, coming repeatedly back to the stoop. The hair on his shoulders was erect and bristling, and every so often he whimpered softly.

I lowered myself gingerly onto the steps. "What is it, baby? I wish you could tell me what you smell." Obviously his nose was picking up all sorts of information. After all, he was half German shepherd, and shepherds were the breed of choice for tracking criminals, ferreting out bombs, drugs, and cadavers.

Rishi shoved his wet nose against my cheek, licked my face. I gave him a big hug and buried my face in his fur.

"Erika! Hello. Are you all right?"

I looked up to see Stan staring down at me. "As well as can be expected," I said glumly. Then I remembered Ocala's advice: today was a day for the proverbial stiff upper lip. "We need to present a united front. We'll have to tell people about Jeff's death, but we don't know what really happened, so I don't think we should say anything about the overdose theory."

Stan's jaw dropped. "Theory? It's more than a theory. I saw the syringe, and . . ."

"I know you did, Stan. But we should wait for the autopsy results, just to be sure."

He began wringing his massive hands. "I wonder, Erika. Do you suppose this was some kind of set-up? Maybe someone wanted Jeff dead, and staged the whole thing with the drug paraphernalia to make it look like an overdose."

Stan had just given voice to a notion that had been lurking half-formed at the back of my mind, but I wasn't ready to confront it quite yet. "No!" I snapped. "We've got to avoid speculating. Let's wait for the facts. Otherwise we'll just be feeding the gossip machine."

The news about Jeff blazed through the club like run-away fire. People were accustomed to seeing him hard at work on the mural when they arrived each morning, and his absence fueled speculation. Perhaps Stan let something slip. In any case, the rumor mill was going full blast, so I decided to move up the community meeting to ten o'clock.

When I announced Jeff's death, Germaine let out a shrill scream that segued into deep, wrenching sobs. Her crying was contagious. Soon several women were weeping openly, and the men's eyes were moist. For what seemed an eternity, the crying was the only sound in the room. Then, hesitantly at first, people began to talk. The voices mingled in a cacophony of sound.

I stood silent, letting the waves of noise wash over me, telling myself it was good to let them vent, uncertain how to channel the energy filling the room. Certain words kept recurring, floating free, hanging suspended in the stale air of the group room. *Jeff, dead, heroin.* And more ominously, *murder, jinx, curse.*

The venting had gone far enough, I decided. Time to turn down the heat and put a lid on the pot. I motioned Stan over to sit beside me, and together we told the members the facts as we knew them. "The police are investigating," I said, "and they may want to question some of you. The autopsy report should be ready in a couple of days. Until then, we shouldn't speculate about the cause of death."

"I heard it was a heroin overdose," said Susan Harvey.

"That's one possibility, but we don't know yet," I said.

"I bet Jeff was murdered," said Gloria. "There's no way he would have ODed."

"I agree," said Phil Lafferty, an owlish man in his thirties who usually kept to himself. "And I bet the same person murdered Jeff and Stephen. There's no way they could have both offed themselves, when they both were doing so well."

"Or maybe there's some kind of jinx or curse over the club," said Gloria. "Maybe we should have an exorcism."

"Whoa, hold it everybody," I said. "This kind of speculation isn't productive. We don't want to frighten people unnecessarily."

"Right. Then they might stay away from the club, and heaven forbid that should happen." The new voice belonged to Arthur, who had just arrived and was slouching against the doorframe, wearing a supercilious smirk. "You wouldn't want to put a damper on your monthly statistics, or it might affect your funding streams."

Stan drew himself erect. The muscles in his massive neck were twitching. "I'm sure that's not what Erika meant," he said.

"How do you know what Erika meant?" said Arthur. "I'm sure the lady is quite capable of speaking for herself."

The exchange threatened to degenerate into an alpha male pissing contest. "Thank you, gentlemen, but that's enough," I said. "It's time to bring this meeting to a close. Stan and I have told you everything we know, and I'll keep you posted on any new developments. In the meantime, I'll be in my office if anyone wants to come see me. Even though we don't have facts, we can still talk about our feelings."

"Thanks," said Gloria. "But please, Erika – don't forget what I said about murder, or about the club being cursed."

"Don't worry, I won't." How could I? Deep down inside, I was beginning to suspect she was right.

Chapter 13

*I*t wasn't easy escaping the group room after the meeting. People were keyed up and anxious to talk, but I badly needed some solitary down time before donning my therapist's hat. I made it to the sanctuary of my office, where Rishi greeted me with his usual ecstatic enthusiasm. I locked the door, then hunkered down in my armchair and gave him a good solid massage, working from the ears down to the neck and shoulders. Stroking his sleek fur, I felt the tension easing from my own body as well as the dog's.

This would be a good time to study Jeff's chart, I realized. With any luck, it might shed some light on his death. I recalled seeing a decent psychiatric summary in his record when I first arrived at WellSpring, but I wasn't overly optimistic. The charts at the club were amazingly casual, many missing essential data.

With hospital standards still fresh in my mind, I'd complained to Ocala. But she had explained that legally, the paperwork requirements were minimal. "Our whole mission goes against thinking of our members as patients," she reminded me. "We empower them to focus on wellness, not illness, and keeping extensive records is part of the medical model we're opposed to." Her rationale made my job simpler, unless I actually needed some information.

I retrieved Jeff's record from the locked file room down the hall. Fortunately, his was one of the better ones. There was a lengthy psychiatric summary from a hospital stay ten years ago, just prior to his admission to WellSpring, and three others from later hospitalizations. Flipping to the front of the chart, I scanned the data summary sheet for possible relatives and found a sister in Paramus and a stepbrother in Boston. The page was dog-eared and yellow, and the numbers probably obsolete, but I tried anyway. Sure enough, both numbers were out of service.

I was studying the psychiatric summaries when Gloria buzzed me on the intercom. "Sorry to disturb you, but Kevin Winthrop's on the line. He says it's personal."

"Thanks, Gloria, I'll take it."

"Erika, I'm sorry I've been out of touch," he said. "I can't believe it's been two weeks already, but I've been frenetically busy, in and out of town, you know how it is."

"Of course," I said, although actually I didn't have a clue, never having experienced an "in and out of town" kind of lifestyle. Five minutes later, I found myself with a dinner date for the following night. In keeping with my Norwegian heritage, we settled on Trondheim, an upscale place on West 54th Street.

I glanced at my watch: twelve fifteen, and I was late for lunch. Maybe it was my empty stomach speaking when I'd accepted Kevin's invitation so speedily. I'd never been to Trondheim, but I'd always wanted to go. Or maybe it was the thought of alcohol that lured me. Too bad no liquor was allowed at WellSpring, because I could have used a double martini before facing the members at lunch.

I hurried downstairs to see Stan waving from across the dining room. "Erika! Over here! We've saved you a place."

"I got your food for you," said Gloria. "It's meat loaf, and that always goes fast, so I thought I'd better save you some. I knew you were probably still on the phone with that guy I put through." She grinned knowingly.

I wasn't about to discuss my social life, minimal as it was. "I've been studying Jeff's chart ever since the meeting," I said as I pulled my chair up to the big round table.

Gloria shuddered delicately. "Erika, *por favor*. I can't stand to think about him now. Not while we're eating."

She was right – my diversionary tactic wasn't exactly appropriate. "Sorry, Gloria. Let's talk about something cheerier – the cabaret, for example."

Stan scowled. "Do you think we should go on with that, given the circumstances?"

I buried my face in my hands. "God, I don't know. I don't know what to think any more." Then I remembered: stiff upper lip. I put down my hands, picked up my fork and speared a mouthful of meatloaf. Usually I liked the stuff, but today it almost made me gag.

Gloria's huge brown eyes widened as if she'd seen a ghost. "The cabaret might bring bad luck to the club. Bad things come in threes, you know. I still think Jeff could have been murdered. So could Stephen. Having the cabaret now might bring on another murder."

Stan forced a laugh. "Gloria, you're letting your imagination run away with you."

"Don't laugh," she said. "It's not funny. In fact, it's a matter of life and death. I'm just trying to warn you."

"And you have," I said. "But that's enough for now. Everybody's upset about Jeff, and we don't want to make it worse."

"It'll be worse regardless of what we do," Gloria said. "My angel just told me so. He talks to me every night, but this is the first time he's showed up at the club. He knows it's an emergency."

Stan shot me a sidelong glance, accompanied by a slight lift of the eyebrows. His message wasn't exactly subtle, and Gloria and I deciphered it simultaneously. "Don't make fun of me behind my back!" she hissed at Stan. "You're just jealous because you don't have an angel like mine. I'm not crazy!"

"I know, Gloria," he said soothingly. "Chill out. It's all right."

Her anger evaporated, and soon she was smiling back. As always, I marveled at Stan's ability to soothe Gloria's tempestuous moods. I toyed with my food a few minutes longer, then excused myself, returned to my office, and immersed myself once more in Jeff's chart. For over an hour I scrutinized the fuzzy gray copies of old single-spaced psychiatric summaries. They yielded no new insights into his death, but I did manage to acquire acute eyestrain and the beginnings of a nasty headache.

I folded my arms on the desk, cradled my aching head, and thought about what I'd learned. The only family contacts in the record were unreachable, and both parents were deceased. It struck me how isolated Jeff had been, and I wondered if there was anyone at all who would feel his loss and mourn for him, other than his friends at the club. He had never mentioned any significant relationships, but perhaps there was at least a girl friend; I would have to ask the members. And we would need to plan a memorial service, like the one for Stephen just three weeks before.

At the thought of Stephen, I sat up straight. Like Jeff, he'd had no immediate family, and there were other similarities too. Standing abruptly, I rushed to the file room and retrieved the chart for Stephen Wright. There were obvious parallels. Both men were young, in their twenties, with no known family ties. Both were attractive, artistic and intelligent. But their bipolar diagnosis was the most crucial similarity: the euphoric high periods of peak creativity alternating with the devastating lows of a depression so deep, it could easily tip the precarious balance toward suicide.

Neither Jeff nor Stephen had been overtly depressed when they died. But bipolars sometimes kill themselves while in the manic phase. And if Jeff died from a drug overdose, that didn't mean he had deliberately killed himself, but using heroin is almost as suicidal as Russian roulette – the odds of ending up dead are unacceptably high.

Where was I going with this? My musings were leading me in circles. I spun my chair around and stretched my arms overhead, a signal Rishi interpreted as meaning it was time to move. He rose slowly, then stretched luxuriously, raising his head and shoulders in the posture the yogis call the upward dog, then raising his rump and bowing in the downward dog, the pose that says "Play with me."

"Okay, baby, you're right. It's break time." I snapped on his leash and we headed down the stairs and out of the building.

No sooner had we descended the stoop than I saw Vito Pisanello heading our way, waving his arm in a vehement, sweeping gesture as if flagging down a cab. Muttering inaudible insults, I stood my ground and smiled sweetly as he approached.

He didn't smile back. "So you had a lot of commotion here last night," he said, scowling. "Ambulances, police cars, the works. I heard somebody died right in front of the building."

"Who told you that?"

"Come on, lady, I'm the one asking questions here. I have my sources."

Probably one of his tenants had watched the whole scenario from a window. For all I knew, he had a little old lady stationed across the street with binoculars trained on WellSpring. Or maybe a whole cadre of them. But paranoia would get me nowhere; I might as well accommodate him. "Unfortunately, you're right," I said.

"So what happened? Drug overdose? Murder?"

Those binoculars must have been pretty high powered. "They don't know yet," I said. "We'll have to wait for the autopsy results."

"Let me know when you find out. This looks terrible for the neighborhood, and it scares my tenants. I'll have to bring it up at the next Community Board Meeting."

"You mean the one they hold at that school auditorium over on Essex Street?"

"That's the one. It's always the second Tuesday of the month."

Stan had told me about those meetings, offered to escort me to one sometime. I hadn't gotten around to accepting the invitation yet. "Before you go public with your complaints, why don't we discuss them privately?"

"Okay, when? Right now would be good."

"Today's not good. Maybe sometime next week?"

His mouth twisted as if he'd just bitten down on a sourball. "Next week. Yeah, sure. I'll get back to you on that."

"Look, Mr. Pisanello, this situation isn't exactly a picnic for us either. It's not as though we planned it."

"Yeah, but the kind of people you attract to your social club for psychos, you got to expect that things like this are going to happen sooner or later."

He was starting to push my buttons. "Excuse me," I said, "but I just came out to walk my dog, and he's getting anxious." Actually, Rishi was standing calmly at my side, gazing at the little man with moderate interest. I was the one getting anxious, and I'd better exit before I blew my cool. Without another word, I yanked Rishi's leash, turned tail and began leading him down the block.

He shouted after me. "Hey, come back here! I got a few more things to say to you."

I threw him a brief backward glance. "Sorry, but I don't think so."

"You'll be even sorrier if you don't come back here and finish this conversation. Next week, my ass! Nobody treats Vito Pisanello with such disrespect. Nobody!"

So now we were on a first-name basis. I supposed that was progress of a sort. Resisting the urge to say, "Ciao, Vito," I kept walking so he couldn't see me smile.

——— —— ——

By ten after four, I was home, sprawled on my sofa, clicking the remote from Oprah Winfrey to Judge Judy and back again. I'd never left work this early, but I'd come dangerously close to blowing up at Vito Pisanello, and there was no telling who my next victim might be if I hung around the club. My self-control was marginal, and it wouldn't take much for me to become completely unhinged. No one at WellSpring had ever seen me that way, and I wasn't about to let them.

Oprah was doing one of her socially uplifting shows, about the travails of single working mothers, and Judge Judy was berating the plaintiff for being stupid enough to let her boyfriend rip her off. Too heavy for me. I clicked the remote and fell rapidly into a deep, dreamless sleep.

When I awoke, night had fallen and I was ravenous. On the way home, I'd had the foresight to buy a container of bacon horseradish dip and a big bag of chips, a combo that's one of my all-time favorites when I'm craving a junk-food orgy. I spent the evening munching, drinking, channel surfing, and trying not to think while I waited for the eleven o'clock news. I wondered if Nancy Welcome would have anything about Jeff Archer's death.

Ever since Nancy had covered Stephen Wright's death and my bipolar disclosure after his memorial service, I'd taken to watching the late news on Channel 8. She was on almost every night. Always elegantly dressed in pale suits, her ash-blond hair carefully curved behind her ears, she was attractive in a post-debutante, ice princess way, but somehow she seemed one step removed from the real-life dramas unfolding on her beat. The more I heard her, the less I liked her, and yet I felt a macabre connection based on her coverage of the club and the fact that she'd interviewed me.

"Good evening, this is Nancy Welcome." Speak of the devil, here she was now, wearing a honey-blond suit that set off her hair to perfection.

"We have a sad and shocking story this evening," she said. "Once again, the WellSpring Club has been the scene of a suspicious death. Just three weeks ago, a young man committed suicide by plunging off the roof of the four-story building. Early this morning Jeffrey Archer, another member of the club, was found dead on the front steps of the building. Sources suggest a drug overdose, but police have declined to confirm the cause of death until autopsy results are released."

A long shot of the building's façade came on. Then the camera zoomed in on Jeff's painting, panning slowly among the details while Nancy waxed eloquent about his talent and the tragedy of his loss. Next, a shot of Nancy standing in front of the stoop, and beside her was Arthur Drummond. Seeing the two of them together, I felt my pulse escalate as I waited for the next bombshell.

I didn't have long to wait. "The death of this gifted young man coming so soon after the earlier tragedy raises some serious questions about this club for mentally ill adults. Are people being admitted into this program who pose a danger to themselves or others, people who more properly belong in an inpatient setting? Is there adequate supervision at WellSpring? What are the credentials of the professionals in charge? And are they actually competent to do their jobs?"

A wave of nausea swept over me. Where was she going with this? Evidently Arthur had some of the same concerns, because he leaned forward and thrust his face toward the camera. "Are you talking about Erika Norgren by any chance? Because I'd like to report that as Director of WellSpring Club, she's doing a terrific job. Whatever problems the club may be having, she's certainly not to blame. Not only that, but she's a really foxy lady." He flashed a smile suggestive of sharpened knives.

Mention Ocala St. Claire, Arthur. Please mention Ocala. If you don't, she'll have my head on a platter in the morning.

"Thank you, Arthur. I'm talking to Arthur Drummond, one of the members of WellSpring. That's it for now, but these questions about management competency are just some of the many questions we'll be exploring in the days ahead."

Damn! Arthur hadn't picked up on my silent prayer. And Ocala was going to be furious. How did this Welcome woman manage to ferret out stories about WellSpring practically before the bodies were cold? Who was feeding her information, and what did she have against the club? Adrenaline was coursing through my body, sending me into a state of hypervigilant rage. Revenge scenarios flooded my brain, threatening to wipe out the last vestiges of reasonable thought. This way lay madness.

I jumped up, clicked off the television, then padded to the bathroom and rummaged in the medicine chest for the Klonepin I'd been prescribed to bring me down from my last manic episode. Normally I avoided the powerful tranquilizer, because it zonked me out too dramatically. But drastic moods called for drastic action. Right now I craved oblivion, and Klonepin was the best way to bring it on fast. For good measure, I took two.

Chapter 14

*T*rapped in a diving bell deep down in the ocean, I was frantic to come back to the surface, but no one heard my screams. Warm tropical water lapped my face. Some alien force had penetrated my solitary cocoon, and I wouldn't survive the pressure once the walls caved in. Weighted down, unable to move, I knew death was near. A strange tranquility crept over me, and I began to let go.

But the walls held firm and the lapping continued. Slowly my capsule floated up toward the surface, and as the water lightened from black to blue-green, I saw the curvilinear shapes of ocean plants and creatures drifting just outside the windows. As they wrapped their limbs and tentacles around my chamber, I realized they were Jeff Archer's creations. Just then Jeff swam into view, did a graceful breaststroke right up to my window, and flashed a radiant smile. "It's wonderful down here!" he exclaimed. "I can create on an enormous scale with living materials. It's far more exciting than paint. Come join me, Erika."

Just as I was reaching tentatively toward Jeff, an enormous weight landed on my chest. I woke to the sound of my own screams and struggled to sit up, but something was holding me down.

I forced myself to look, found myself confronting gaping jaws, fangs, an enormous lolling tongue. Rishi was standing with his forelegs planted across my chest. Awareness came slowly: his tongue on my cheek had been the ocean's warm lapping, and I was safe at home in my own bed. But I was still terrified. The heavy passivity that assailed me in the dream, the way I welcomed death and reached out to Jeff – what that said about my state of mind was more frightening than any nightmare.

I stretched experimentally, pushed Rishi off. He whined, telling me I'd overslept and he urgently needed his walk. A glance at the clock radio told me it was after eleven. Damn those pills! I had known they would knock me out, yet taken them anyway. Maybe the dream didn't express a death wish. Maybe it was simply a warning about the dangers of drugging myself into oblivion.

The ring of the phone interrupted my ruminations. Forcing myself to sit, dangling my feet over the side of the bed, I let the answering machine pick up. "Hello, Erika, this is Gloria." The melodious voice had an edge of tension. "Are you all right? We're worried about you, since you didn't come in. Please give me a call."

I picked up the cordless phone at the bedside. "Hi, Gloria. I'm okay, I just overslept. I'll be in around twelve thirty."

Walking Rishi a few minutes later, I felt as though I were slogging through three feet of muck, lost in the swamp of a Grade B horror movie. But was I the heroine, or was I the monster? The aftereffects of last night's drugs had left me feeling only marginally human. Back upstairs, as I stood under the shower letting the spray blast me back into civilized life, I decided to leave Rishi at home and indulge in a cab.

As soon as the cab turned the corner toward WellSpring, I saw the Channel 8 van idling outside the club. Members clogged the sidewalk, some puffing on cigarettes, others milling in a ragged ring around the center of attention, which consisted of Stan, Arthur, Gloria, and Nancy Welcome, in another of her sugar plum suits – cotton candy pink, this time. She was holding a microphone, and a cameraman was capturing it all on tape.

My adrenaline shot up. I told the driver to stop, thrust a fistful of singles at him, climbed out and hit the ground yelling. "Turn that camera off! What do you think you're doing?"

The cameraman pivoted to catch me in the eye of his lens as the reporter advanced, brandishing her mike. She smiled triumphantly, no doubt delighted to capture my mini-tantrum. "We're in luck. Here's Erika Norgren, the Director of WellSpring."

With a supreme effort, I reined in my anger and shifted into administrative mode. If I made nice, maybe she'd edit out my little outburst. It would be bad enough to be seen flying off the handle on the evening news, even worse to be seen scrambling gracelessly out of a taxi. "How can I help you, Nancy?" I asked.

"I've already interviewed several of your club members, and they've been very helpful," the announcer said. "If you saw last night's story, you probably know I've got some questions to follow up on. I tried calling you this morning, but you were out."

Still mildly stoned from the aftereffects of the Klonepin, I had no response. She drew herself up to her full height. Even in heels, she was a good two inches shorter than me. "How can you judge the effectiveness of your program?" she asked. "Maybe WellSpring is actually doing more harm than good. For example, some of your members might be better off in inpatient settings under closer supervision, where there's less risk of their harming themselves or someone else. And aren't you afraid these recent deaths might inspire other club members to do something equally self-destructive?"

"That's just speculation," I snapped. "I'm calling a halt to this interview. But first I have a question. Where do you get the money for all those expensive suits? Does your expense account cover them, or do the stores lend them to you? If you buy them yourself, your salary must be astronomical."

She nearly choked. "Never mind. I think we've got enough for tonight's segment. But I'll be in touch."

Within minutes, she and her cameraman were back in the van and pulling away. Moments later Ocala St. Claire was parking her silver Chrysler in the space they had vacated. By the way she cut the wheel and angled aggressively into the spot, like a teenage garage attendant on speed, I knew she was on the warpath.

Climbing out, she glared down the street as the news van rounded the corner and disappeared. "Were those the same people who had the story about Jeffrey Archer last night? Who the hell told that bitch about it?"

"I certainly didn't," I said.

"Neither did I," said Stan. "How about you, Arthur? I saw you making nice with that Nancy Welcome. You could hardly keep from climbing all over her."

Arthur grinned. "That was just to make her feel at home."

I glared at Gloria. "Did anyone from the media call today to say they were coming over?"

"No, they just showed up." Her eyes began to tear. "And we haven't called anyone in the media since Stephen's memorial service, have we, Stan? Not since Erika told us not to."

"That's right," said Stan. "We definitely took your lesson to heart."

"Even so, you let her interview you today," I said.

"Enough," said Ocala. "If you all will excuse us, I need to talk to Erika alone."

I hadn't spoken with Ocala since my hysterical call after we'd found Jeff. We adjourned to my office, and I brought her up to speed on what little we knew. "I plan to do some crisis counseling," I added. "Both in groups and individually. I'll touch base with everyone who comes here, talk with them about Jeff and Stephen, and see whether anyone has any unfinished emotional business they need help with."

"That sounds like a plan," she said. Her deep brown eyes drilled into mine. "But isn't it too much for you to handle?"

"I'll give it my best shot and see how it goes."

"Erika, I'm concerned about you, with what you told me about your diagnosis and all. When you called me the other night, you sounded downright hysterical."

"I'd just been dealing with Jeff's death. I think I had the right to be a little hysterical." To my dismay, I felt tears filling my eyes. Determined not to cry in front of my boss, I gulped back a sob and held my breath.

Wheeling her chair closer so that we were knee to knee, Ocala gripped both my hands in hers. "Erika, I want you to go home now. Take the rest of the day off."

"I'm all right. I can stay."

"Girl, I don't want you decompensating on my watch. It's obvious you need some down time. At the club, you have to be always on top of things, available at a moment's notice. I don't think you're capable of that right now. I'll buzz Gloria and tell her you're leaving. Stan can be in charge, with Gloria as backup. I don't want to hear any more arguments out of you, Erika. Take care of yourself. Go home now."

It was obvious: Ocala didn't trust me to run the club. Deep in my gut, something sank like a stone. I felt as though I had just flunked an exam, the kind of exam that comes in dreams, where you cut all the classes and totally forgot to study. Where the questions are impossible and the answers nonexistent.

Once out on the stoop, I realized I didn't want to go home. I dreaded being alone with my thoughts, and it was still hours till my date with Kevin. Maybe a long walk would lift my sagging spirits.

Impulsively, I headed west and zigzagged aimlessly through the East Village until I found myself at the corner of Third Avenue and St. Mark's Place. A horde of early rush hour commuters was hurtling toward me, disgorged by the subway exit at Astor Place.

Crowds make me claustrophobic, and I was hesitating, on the brink of retreat when someone bumped me from behind. Turning to glare at the perpetrator, I found myself face to face with a young man in dark glasses, dressed head to toe in black. Probably an up and coming executive in advertising or TV – people in those fields were especially fond of funereal get-ups like this. He murmured a polite apology, and I nodded noncommittally. No point in provoking a confrontation.

I wasn't about to wimp out and surrender my right to sidewalk space. As I turned east on St. Mark's, an amplified voice boomed out. A red double-decker tour bus was cruising north along Third, and I could see the tour guide declaiming into his mike. "St. Marks Place, famous for its hippies and flower children in the sixties, still a Mecca for folks on the cutting edge. And just to our south, the Bowery, home to generations of drunks . . ." Mercifully, the bus rolled out of earshot.

The man in black flashed a knowing smile, sending a wordless message: aren't we lucky to be true New Yorkers, and aren't those tourists pathetic. I smiled back in silent agreement, then turned away and continued east.

As I walked past the bars, tattoo parlors, record stores and souvenir shops, the stream of commuters was diluted by an infusion of tattooed and pierced young people. Blacks, Latinos, Poles, Ukrainians and Orientals. Young singles, families and old folks. Openly gay couples of both sexes. Drunks, panhandlers and homeless people. Men whispering conspiratorially about drugs for sale. And every so often the unmistakable sweet scent of marijuana. The Loisaida melting pot at a lively simmer, a few degrees shy of a rolling boil.

East of Second Avenue, the crowds and the storefront businesses thinned out, and past First, the street was primarily residential.

Commuters climbed old stone steps to unlock the doors of lovingly restored townhouses, while longtime natives sat visiting on the crumbling stoops of similar tenements which hadn't yet enjoyed the same infusion of cash. People walked dogs and whizzed past on inline skates.

I loved this neighborhood in all its variety and vitality, but the traffic was too much. Today it was backed up all the way to Tompkins Square Park. Up ahead, a cop was directing traffic. Fluorescent orange cones blocked the intersection, and yellow tape was strung across the sidewalk. Had there been a crime? Then I saw the lights on tall poles and the big silvery panels, the trucks lining the curb near the park, and I realized a film or TV crew was shooting on location.

Talk about media hype – I was just about to wade smack dab into a bunch of it! I'd happened on film crews a few times before. Like most New Yorkers, I acted blasé, but I was secretly thrilled at my sudden proximity to whatever superstars were shooting in our fair city. Once I'd watched Pierce Brosnan filming a chase scene in Washington Square Park, and another time I'd watched Hugh Grant strolling up Madison Avenue. As I wondered who might be on the set, I realized that I'd managed to forget about Jeff and the sorrows of WellSpring for at least a little while.

Standing there with stars on my mind, maybe I wasn't exercising my usual street smarts. At any rate, when someone grabbed my arm from behind, it came as a total shock. I whirled in outrage to find myself staring at the impenetrable dark glasses of the man in black who'd bumped me back at Third Avenue. His fingers dug deep into the flesh of my upper arm. I tried pulling away, but he tightened his grip. Something hard nudged the small of my back.

"Don't make a sound," he hissed in my ear. "I won't hurt you if you do as I say. My boss wants to have a little talk with you." So saying, he propelled me toward a black Lincoln idling at the curb. From within, a burly hand shoved open the door and reached out to pull me inside. The dark tinted windows obscured the car's interior, so I had no idea who was attached to the hand.

Time imploded upon itself, and I had the sensation of plummeting helplessly in darkness, like one of those night terrors that yank me from sleep in a panic more profound than any nightmare. Yet there was a sense of clarity and calm, as if I had all the time in the world to ponder my next move. But before I could make a conscious decision, my instincts took over. I stomped down hard on my captor's instep with one heel, then the other, and in the split second he relaxed his grip, I twisted away and ran screaming toward the park. Once my adrenaline kicked in, the momentum kept me going.

Subliminally, I must have remembered the film crew. I had no conscious intention of disrupting the shoot, but I ran past gawking pedestrians, past the crew members who stood watch at the edge of the set, and straight into the center of the scene. I put on the brakes just in time to avoid careening into an actor with dark hair and craggy good looks.

As I stood panting, drenched in sweat, gazing around at the lights, the cameras, the people with clipboards and intercoms, he put out an arm to steady me. "Are you okay?" he asked. "I've had a fair number of fans try to crash the set, but never so dramatically."

I smiled sheepishly. Should I know him? "I'm not a fan," I said, and he looked taken aback.

Whoever he was, he was certainly attractive. "I'm sorry, I didn't mean that the way it sounded," I added. "I was running away from a guy who grabbed me and tried to pull me into a black Lincoln on St. Marks Place. I figured I'd be safest here, with all the lights and people around."

"That's a new one," said a security guard who had just approached, along with a couple of crew members. "Miss, would you mind coming with me now?"

"Yes, I certainly would mind," I retorted. "One abduction attempt is more than enough for one day."

"Let her be," said the actor. "I believe her story, strange as it seems."

"I don't know, chief. She could be a fruit cake."

Suddenly I had second thoughts about rejecting the guard's invitation. After all, the man in black could still be lurking nearby, waiting to try again. A security escort might be just the thing. "Actually," I said, "I'd appreciate it if you walk with me till I find a cab. Those guys are probably long gone by now, but you never know."

"I'll tag along," said the actor. "We've already done five takes of that scene, and I need a break."

He offered his arm, and I took it gladly. Flanked by the tall, dashing actor and the pudgy, middle-aged security guard, I strolled out of the park. trying to project an attitude of fey nonchalance. The two men played along gallantly, as if we were all part of an elegantly over-the-top British detective show. Maybe they thought they were just jollying along a crazy lady, but as I scanned the streets for my would-be abductors, I couldn't have cared less about their motivation. For the moment, they were keeping me out of harm's way.

The actor flagged down a taxi, then opened the door with a flourish. As I climbed in, I saw no trace of the black car or the black-clothed man, but I kept my head down just in case. Just before the security guard closed the door, I asked, "By the way, what are you filming back there?"

The guard gave me an incredulous stare. "*The Blue Line*. This guy here, the one who saved you, just happens to be the star, Paul Mancuso. He plays a homicide detective. I'm surprised you haven't seen it."

The actor bowed and doffed an imaginary top hat, then reached for my hand and kissed it. "Pleased to be of service, Madame." He flashed a wicked grin.

I grinned back, reveling in my fleeting connection with fame. "Thank you so much for helping me out. I'll be sure to watch your show."

He closed the door, and I hunkered down as I gave the driver directions. Paul Mancuso was certainly attractive, I thought, but all things considered, when it came to homicide detectives, I'd take Dennis Malone any day.

It occurred to me that I'd rather be having dinner with Dennis than Kevin Winthrop, but then Dennis would never have sprung for Trondheim. Would Mark? I didn't know - he still hadn't called. Oh well. My little promenade might have taken a bizarre twist, but at least it would give me something to talk about with Kevin.

Chapter 15

My adrenaline was at astronomical heights after my adventure in Tompkins Square Park, and the long hot bath I took once I got home did little to damp down the fires. But what to wear? I attacked my closet and pulled out possibilities till my bed was piled high with clothes. Every outfit had some fatal flaw: a stained dress that I'd forgotten to take to the cleaners, another that had fallen and turned into a heap of wrinkles on the closet floor, a third that needed mending at the hem. I felt as though I'd stumbled into that recurrent dream where I'm trying frantically to get dressed for some important appointment, but the clothes are all wrong. Finally I'm forced to face the world half-naked.

It wasn't the date with Kevin that had me so befuddled, but the accumulated stress of recent events. Jeff's death, Ocala's put-down, Nancy Welcome's intrusive TV coverage, the man in black – the images careened around in a chaotic state of consciousness I recognized as the red flag for a full-blown manic episode. In hopes of slowing down my racing thoughts, I flopped face up atop the pile of clothes and assumed the yoga position called Savasana, the corpse pose. Arms at my sides, palms up, I closed my eyes, focused on my breathing, and soon the tumultuous thoughts began to drift away.

Next thing I knew, the ringing bell and my barking dog jolted me awake. Jumping up, I grabbed a towel and ran to the intercom. Amazingly, I'd slept for an hour, and now my nightmare was a reality: I was late for an appointment, virtually naked with nothing to wear. I couldn't very well make Kevin wait in the street, so I threw on the dress I'd been wearing all day, then buzzed him in.

Well before he reached the fourth-floor landing, I could hear his footsteps pounding on the old wooden stairs. So could Rishi. His big ears swiveled forward and he cocked his head in curiosity, then bounded to the door and began barking in his deepest, most authoritative voice. I shouted over the barking and through the door. "Don't worry, Kevin. Rishi's just doing his standard watchdog bit. Wait a minute while I grab his collar."

"No problem," Kevin called.

Grabbing Rishi's leather collar firmly in my right hand, I unbolted the Fox lock with my left, then pushed open the door. Kevin edged slowly through, giving Rishi ample opportunity to smell him. "Hi, boy," he said. "Remember me? We met at the dog run."

Once again Kevin was stylishly immaculate, wearing a casually cut suit of black linen. "I'll keep hold of Rishi's collar for awhile," I said. "I'd hate for him to mess up those gorgeous clothes."

Kevin smiled. "I understand. This is his turf, and he has to make it clear he's the alpha male around here."

Rishi was intensely interested in smelling the man. He sniffed Kevin's hands, his crotch, both legs, then zeroed in on his elegant black leather moccasins.

I laughed. "You must have been in some pretty interesting places lately." Now Rishi's hackles were bristling slightly.

"He probably smells my dogs, and no doubt I've picked up all sorts of scents on the streets of New York. But most likely he's just feeling protective toward you. As an unfamiliar male coming into his territory, I'm bound to provoke a defensive reaction."

"Yes, that's probably it." Maybe there was something about Kevin that rubbed Rishi the wrong way – perhaps the tangy scent of his Versace cologne. Or maybe it was just that I hadn't had a man up here in ages.

"You about ready to go?" Kevin looked me up and down appraisingly. Judging by the tense set of his jaw, I was about to flunk inspection.

I glanced down at my dress – a gauzy Indian floral print I'd bought years ago at some forgotten hippie boutique. Obviously not the thing for an elegant dinner uptown. "Sorry I'm not ready yet," I said. "It's been a harrowing day. I'll just be a few minutes, but since Rishi's acting a little strange, maybe it would be better if you wait downstairs."

Kevin flashed a taut smile and glanced pointedly at his watch. "Okay. While I'm waiting, I'll phone the restaurant and ask them to hold our reservation. We'll probably be about a half hour late."

I acknowledged the implicit critique with a nod. "I'll be as speedy as I can."

At Trondheim an hour later, Kevin was looking considerably more cheerful. Sipping fine wine and sampling an appetizer platter with six types of artfully arranged herring, we were both starting to unwind. "I've never seen so many kinds of herring before," I said. "It's like Scandinavian sushi."

By the way his eyes kept gravitating to the deep V of my periwinkle cashmere sweater, I could tell I had finally passed inspection. Miraculously, I had found the sweater, along with a silk skirt of the same blue strewn with flamboyant crimson roses, sandwiched between a couple of old coats at the back of my closet. I'd bought the outfit at Bloomingdale's at a late spring closeout sale, then stashed it away to save for fall. I'd forgotten all about it.

"So," Kevin said, settling back in his chair. "Tell me about your harrowing day."

"Well, the highlight had to be that I barely escaped being abducted. Someone tried to pull me into a car on St. Marks Place."

His jaw dropped. "You're kidding."

"Unfortunately not." I proceeded to give him a detailed account, beginning with the bump from the mysterious man in black and climaxing with my escape into the arms of a TV detective.

My tone was light, but the gravity of the situation hooked his attention. "Have you called the police?"

"Not yet, but I'll call first thing tomorrow morning. I need to talk with Detective Malone anyway, to find out the result of . . ." I stopped, uncertain how much I wanted to share.

He leaned closer and lowered his voice. "You can talk freely. I know about the second death at the club. Are the police handling it as a run-of-the-mill overdose, or are they going to investigate further? I can understand how you might be upset. Having two members of your club die within weeks of each other has to be pretty distressing, especially for you as the administrator. Is it impacting on the attendance figures yet?"

I winced. His tone would have been perfect for analyzing sales graphs at a marketing meeting, but it didn't sit well with me. "The attendance figures are the last thing on my mind right now," I said. "I'm more concerned about the loss of two gifted, sensitive men who didn't deserve to die so young. By the way, where did you hear about the second death? I don't know if it's made the papers yet."

"I heard Nancy Welcome talking about it last night on Channel 8. I usually catch her show when I'm in town." He flashed me a sly smile. "I have to confess I have a special interest. Nancy and I dated awhile back, and we're still friends. We get together every so often to have a drink and catch up on each others' lives."

I could picture them together: two blond people with classic good looks, expensive clothes, and carefully cultivated facades. A regular Barbie and Ken. I couldn't resist probing a little. "You must have made an attractive couple. Why did you break up?"

He gazed somewhere over my shoulder. "Basically we were both so caught up in our own careers that we couldn't spare enough time for a serious relationship. Neither of us wanted to play second fiddle. Fortunately, we both had the good sense to realize it wasn't working, so the split was amicable. Since then, I've been playing the field."

"Probably a wise decision. There's something weird about that woman. She seems so driven, at least when it comes to the club. Ever since Stephen's death, she's been on our case. She's always showing up unannounced with her video crew, looking for new angles, making demeaning comments about the way WellSpring is run. She seems to have it in for us, but I can't figure out why."

Kevin began dissecting his vegetables in silence. We were on the main course by now. "Unfortunately I can guess," he said at last. "When Nancy and I were involved, it was shortly after Barbara's death. I was still in shock, obsessing about her suicide, and Nancy endured hours listening to me sound off about everything I detested about the mental health establishment. Maybe some of my bitterness rubbed off on her."

"That could explain it." I ate a few forkfuls of salmon as a new thought took shape in my mind. "Maybe you could do me a favor and talk to her, Kevin. Persuade her to cool it. She's doing the club a lot of damage with her investigative crusade, and my boss is about to have my hide. I've been there just under six months. I haven't even passed my probationary period yet, and I don't want to lose my job."

His lips quirked. "I wouldn't want that either. But trust me, nothing I said would make any difference. When Nancy gets on a roll, there's no stopping her."

"It wouldn't hurt to try."

"Actually it might. We didn't part on the best of terms, and if I ask her to do something, she's likely to do the exact opposite, just to aggravate me."

"But you said you were still friends."

His eyes blazed in sudden anger. "Erika, give it a rest! I said no. God, you're as stubborn as Nancy."

"Never mind. Forget it." Suddenly I'd had enough. Enough wine, enough fish, enough Kevin. "I need to go home," I said. "The past few days have been hellish. I haven't been sleeping well, and I'm really exhausted. What do you say we enjoy the rest of this delicious dinner, then call it a night?"

The anger vanished as quickly as it had appeared, and a flicker of disappointment swept his face. "Of course, Erika. I know you've been through a lot lately, and I certainly don't want to add to your stress. But before we go, let's have some Swedish pancakes with lingonberries. As I recall, they flame them in liqueur right at the table, like crepes Suzettes. Very dramatic."

My appetite trumped my better judgment. "That sounds fabulous, Kevin. Thanks for being so understanding."

―――――――

I played hide and seek with sleep that night. All that rich Scandinavian food was staging a minor insurrection in my stomach, and I wondered how my Viking ancestors had tolerated a diet of fish, fish, and more fish, even if smoked and sauced a zillion different ways. Small wonder they sailed off to discover the New World - they probably wanted something new and different to eat.

On the whole, though, the meal at Trondheim had been delicious, although I intended to steer clear of smoked eel for the foreseeable future. But whenever I managed to snatch a few minutes of sleep, I was assailed by chaotic dreams. In the last one before dawn, endless ribbons of smoky rose salmon and pinkish gray eel swirled around me like gigantic tapeworms. Kevin was there, in a tuxedo, trying to convince me they were actually party streamers and that we were going to some fabulous charity gala. "I've rented a livery service for the evening," he said. "You deserve the best." Then he offered his arm and escorted me to the curb, where a black Lincoln Town Car was waiting. The rear door swung open, and someone's arms reached out to me. But at the ends of the arms, instead of hands, was a pair of cloven hoofs. Kevin was behind me, clutching both my arms and forcing me into the car, when I woke screaming.

I knew getting back to sleep was hopeless, so I got up, made a pot of coffee, and killed a couple of hours until it was time to go to the club. To allow ample time for Stan to arrive ahead of me, I left my place at eight, with Rishi in tow. The way things were going, I no longer wanted to be at WellSpring alone.

As soon as I got to my office, I called Dennis Malone. He was in a meeting, so I left a message, then sipped coffee and browsed through the day planner program on my computer while I waited for his call. Opening the journal function, I began documenting recent events. But I was feeling far too fragile to write about Jeff's death. So when Dennis finally called, I was playing with the program's color scheme, changing the high-priority items from red to magenta and the imitation post-it notes from yellow to lavender.

His tone was brisk. "So, Erika, what's up?"

I took the hint and got right to the point, giving him an abbreviated account of my adventure on St. Marks Place. He listened without comment, and when I reached the end of the narrative, there was a long pause.

"Hello? Dennis, are you still there? Did I put you to sleep?"

"Not at all. You have quite a flair for the dramatic. But it could have been a lot worse. I'm glad to say this isn't a case for me to get involved in."

I was momentarily crushed, until I remembered. "Of course. You're with the Homicide Unit. You seemed like the best person to talk to, and I totally forgot that I would have to be dead in order to qualify for your services."

"That's not funny, Erika." His tone was sharp, but when he spoke again, he had managed to soften it. "This sounds like something that should be handled at the precinct level. I'll call and give them a heads up."

"Thanks, that would be great."

"I'll get right on it. Sit tight. You should be hearing from someone within the hour."

"One more thing," I said. "What about Jeff Archer's autopsy? Have they found out anything yet?"

"Some of the results aren't back from toxicology, but the preliminary findings confirm that he died from a heroin overdose. There's no indication of any foul play, no signs of a struggle at the scene."

"I still can't believe he was using heroin. The investigation isn't over yet, is it?"

"We'll keep it open in case any more findings turn up. But I'll be upfront with you, Erika. Our division is chronically understaffed, and we've got a lot of cases, so don't expect any overnight revelations."

"In other words, you're just going to forget about him, the way you forgot about Stephen Wright? Because they were mentally ill, powerless, with no one to stand up for them and make a stink?"

"Stephen Wright's case is still open as well. Believe me, we're doing everything we can, and the NYPD doesn't prioritize its cases according to mental status." He paused. "Erika, are you all right? You sound pretty stressed out."

"I have every reason to be."

"Well, let me get going so we can get someone over to talk to you. By the way, did you have your dog with you during that incident yesterday?"

"Rishi? No, but he's here with me today." At the sound of his name, Rishi crawled out from under my desk and looked at me expectantly.

"That's good. Take my advice and keep him close at all times. You should have protection, and as a crime deterrent, dogs are hard to beat."

Chapter 16

$\mathcal{A}$n hour later, Sergeant Lillian Golson sat writing in a steno book as I told my story yet again. A fashionably slim black woman, she faced me across the cluttered expanse of my desk, which I had chosen to remain behind, less because it gave me authority than because I felt the need of fortification. Dennis Malone's advice about Rishi had hammered home the reality that I might be in danger, and the speed with which he'd deployed someone here to question me underlined that fact. I was feeling shaky, vulnerable, and for the first time, genuinely scared.

Once I'd finished my narrative, Sergeant Golson took me back to the beginning and coached me through it again, probing for details I might have overlooked. But there was little I could add. "I'm sorry I'm so unobservant," I said. "Maybe I should have been suspicious right when that guy first bumped me."

"Look, Ms. Norgren, don't beat yourself up over this. You're not the guilty party here, you're the one who's been victimized." Her brown eyes gleamed, her voice took on an added intensity, and it occurred to me that she might have a personal stake as well as a professional interest in crimes like this. "Do you think you could identify this guy in black?" she asked.

"I don't know. I only got a couple of quick glances, and he was wearing dark glasses. But I could try."

"All right! Let's take a ride over to the station house, and you can look over a few pictures."

"Can I bring my dog? Detective Malone advised me to keep him with me at all times."

She gave an exasperated sigh. "I guess, if you must. But you'll have to sit in the back seat with him."

"No problem. We can pretend we're the K-9 patrol."

Gloria was all eyes as we paused at her office. "I'll be out for a couple of hours," I told her. "It's personal business, nothing to do with the club." Then I realized that far from damping down her curiosity, I had probably just fanned the fires.

———————

The mug shots were all on computer. I had pictured myself sitting at an old oaken table, leafing through stacks of dog-eared photos, then suddenly shouting "Eureka!" when I recognized the culprit. Instead, I was staring at a monitor, pointing and clicking with a mouse. My eyes were beginning to smart, and the more faces I studied, the more confused I became. To my chagrin, I realized I'd paid more attention to what the man was wearing than to what he looked like. Well-cut black suit, black shirt and tie, dark hair, medium build, in his twenties or thirties – I could have been describing half a million men.

I shoved the chair away from the computer and rose. Rishi crawled out from beneath the desk and we started to pace.

Sergeant Golson was there in no time. "Ms. Norgren? What's happening?"

"This is driving me crazy." I glanced at my watch. "I've been here almost two hours, and the more I look, the more they all look the same."

"Why don't you take a break? Take your dog outside for a few minutes."

"Good idea. But I need more than a few minutes. Overnight would be better."

"How many have you gotten through?" Giving Rishi a wide berth, she walked over to the computer, peered at the screen and answered her own question. "You've still got a lot to go."

"Well, I can't take any more today. I've had it."

"Then you're right to stop. Honey, you look all stressed out. Why don't I drive you home, and you take the rest of the day off. You can come back tomorrow and look with fresh eyes."

"Thanks, I appreciate it."

"No problem. I know how you feel. Even though you got away, you've still been violated. An attack like this robs you of your sense of personal safety, and everyone needs that feeling of safety to be okay living in New York City. The alternative is to be permanently paranoid, and who wants to live like that?"

She actually understood. The realization nearly brought tears to my eyes. Or maybe it was the way she called me "Honey." Politically correct or not, the casual endearment touched me in a way that reminded me how little affection there was in my life.

The dozens of faces I'd been scrutinizing were still swirling through my mind as we left the police station, and I knew they would continue to haunt me in the solitude of my apartment. I couldn't bear the thought of going home alone, so I persuaded Sergeant Golson to drive me back to the club. At WellSpring, I was sure to find plenty of distractions to keep me from brooding about the man who got away. The thought that an unknown stranger might be lurking somewhere in the city, plotting to harm me, was profoundly unnerving, especially because there wasn't a damn thing I could do about it.

I could, however, do something about Stephen and Jeff. Deep down, I was convinced that their deaths weren't as straightforward as they seemed, and Dennis Malone had given me the definite impression that the police couldn't care less. Technically the cases were still open, but both men had been relegated to a limbo where they would languish until their memories faded into oblivion. They deserved better, and evidently it was up to me to insure they got it.

As the squad car pulled up alongside the curb, Rishi scrambled across my lap, digging his nails into my thighs. "Damn!" I exclaimed. I reached for the door handle but it wouldn't budge. In the split second before claustrophobia set in, Sergeant Golson swung around and grinned through the black mesh grating. "Just a precaution. Ms. Norgren, before I unlock the door and let you out, promise me you won't stay at the club too long, and that you'll go home and get a good night's rest."

"I will, I promise."

"Okay. Come back tomorrow and look at the rest of the pictures. You have my card. Call anytime if you have anything to discuss. Take care now."

She fiddled with something on the dashboard, the locks sprang open with a loud click, and Rishi and I made our escape from the black-padded cell that was the squad car's passenger compartment. As we stood on the sidewalk getting our bearings, some club members who had been outside on a cigarette break approached and encircled us, staring curiously.

Arthur crouched and peered into the car as the Sergeant pulled away. "It's a chick! A lady cop. What happened, Erika? Did you get busted?"

"No, nothing like that."

"What were you doing with her, anyway?" asked Gloria. "You left so fast before, I never found out."

"It wasn't anything that concerns you," I said. Then I reconsidered. I hadn't identified my assailant, and essentially I was at a dead end. "On second thought, maybe it does. Let's go inside."

They stubbed out their cigarettes in the butt can at the side of the stoop, and we headed for the group room, picking up a few additional members en route. Once everyone was seated, I began. "Okay, let me tell you about my little jaunt to the police station, and how it came about."

Telling them the story of my adventure on St. Marks Place, I tried for a flip, light-hearted tone, but they saw through my act. Stan and Arthur were especially outraged, and both offered to escort me to and from work. "We could work out a schedule and alternate shifts," said Stan with his typical organizational flair.

"Okay, but I hope the creep shows up on my shift," said Arthur. "I'd ram his head so far up his ass, he'd never see daylight again."

The thought of being escorted everywhere by Arthur was almost as frightening as the thought of my anonymous assailant. "Gentlemen, I really appreciate your concern, but I'll pass," I said. "The police have suggested I keep Rishi with me at all times for protection, and I think that'll be enough for now. But I thought you should all know about this so that you can be alert to any strangers you may see around the club. Let me know immediately about anything unusual, and don't hesitate to call 911 if necessary."

"You think the incident with the guy in black is related to the club in some way?" asked Stan.

"I doubt it," I said. "But at this point, I can't be sure of anything. I also wanted to tell you that the investigations into Stephen's and Jeffrey's deaths are still officially open, so don't be surprised or alarmed if you do see an occasional police officer around the club. Just be polite and cooperative – they're on our side, they're not out to get us."

Arthur stretched his lean body extravagantly and emitted a hearty guffaw.

"Oh, yeah? How much you wanna bet?"

———— — ——

Back in my office, I checked my e-mail and voice mail, but there was nothing of interest. For good measure, I used the remote to access my answering machine at home. Nothing there either. Damn! Day by day, as the pressure mounted, I felt more and more alone. True, I was surrounded by people all day at the club, but my much-vaunted professionalism gave rise to a great divide between me and the members. I cherished the solitude of my nights and weekends, up to a point. But I longed for a good old-fashioned girl friend, someone to gossip and commiserate with, to pour out my heart to.

Maybe Sergeant Golson had planted this insidious longing in my mind. It hadn't even occurred to me to call her Lillian, because I sensed that rank and title were important to her, and that she'd paid more than her share of dues to get them. Somewhat formal and standoffish at first, she had loosened up just enough to reveal a hint of sensitivity and heart behind the uniform. I wondered if she had family waiting for her at the end of her shift, or if she was as lonely as I was.

The plot thickened when it came to men. Ironically, the men most on my mind these days were the men of the club, and especially the two who were dead. I still had vivid memories of both Stephen and Jeff. Their images in death were indelibly imprinted in my brain, and they materialized out of nowhere to haunt me at all hours of the day and night. The way they had looked in life was more elusive. Both had been so vivid, so full of energy, yet I could capture their images only in fragmentary, fleeting glimpses.

Then there were Arthur and Stan. The intensity of their reactions when I had told them about the attack, their readiness to volunteer as my protectors, was more than touching; it was exciting. Having two men care so passionately about me that they were eager to go out and do battle like knights of old – I had to admit it was a definite turn-on. Especially Arthur, with those steely blue eyes and that hard, lanky build – *No, Erika, don't even think about it!*

As for eligible men who weren't ethically and psychiatrically out of bounds, the pickings were slim. Since my divorce, I'd had a number of dates, a couple of fleeting involvements, but I had yet to meet anyone who could truly light my fire. Take Kevin Winthrop. He was attractive, intelligent, successful as well as attentive and lavish with his compliments. For some reason I couldn't respond the way I sensed he wanted me to. But he was a dog lover, a decent conversationalist, and he squired me to fabulous restaurants. So far so good – I'd play along for awhile, see what developed.

Then there was Dennis Malone, the archetypal Irish detective. With Dennis, there was definite chemistry. No out and out fire yet, but the combustible ingredients were all in place for an eventual conflagration. We were both playing it cool, keeping things strictly professional, almost adversarial at times. But the spark in his green eyes, the flush of his fair skin when we got a little too close, told me things could change on a moment's notice. Later for that, I told myself. Maybe after events at the club were resolved.

And what about Mark Levitan? Here I'd thought we were instantaneous soul mates, and I hadn't heard a word. I rifled through my day planner – nearly three weeks since we met. Enough is enough, I decided. With sudden determination, I reached for my Rolodex, found the business card I'd neatly taped at the front of the "L's," and punched in his number.

Naturally I got his voice mail. "Mark, this is Erika Norgren," I said with all the professional cool I could muster. "There are a couple of things I'd like to discuss with you. Give me a call when you get a chance. Thanks." I left him my office and home numbers, but not my cell – three would have been an overload. Putting the handset back in its cradle, I exhaled explosively. There, I'd done it. I was no longer a wimpy lady in waiting.

Feeling suddenly giddy, I snapped on Rishi's leash and fairly waltzed out of my office and downstairs in search of company. I checked in with Gloria first.

"Stan's outside with Germaine," she told me. "He wants your advice on something."

"Okay, thanks, Gloria."

I floated out onto the stoop and down the steps with Rishi, feeling like Maria in *West Side Story* – pretty, witty and bright. Stan was standing on the sidewalk with Germaine Lavendre, studying Jeff's mural.

"What do you think, Erika?" he asked. "We were just trying to decide if this mural needs more work. Jeff said he wasn't quite finished, but I honestly can't figure out why. It looks finished to me."

"Me too," said Germaine. "I told Stan I'd help finish it if I could just fill in the lines or something. I like painting, I do it on my ceramics. But I can't see anything left to fill in."

I scrutinized the mural. "I can't either. I think we should let it be."

"But he didn't sign it," said Germaine. "When I do a painting, I always sign it."

"Good point," I said. "Maybe we can order one of those little commemorative plaques in bronze with his name on it."

"Or Germaine could make something in ceramics," said Stan. "She's good at lettering."

"Miss, excuse me, miss."

I wheeled to find myself face to face with a woman brandishing a fistful of shocking pink fliers. Short and stocky, wearing a tweedy wool suit that had seen better days, she looked to be well over sixty.

Rishi was sniffing her avidly, and I pulled him back "Oh, that's okay," she said. "He probably smells my cats. I have two Siamese."

"Can I help you?"

She stared up at me, ignoring Stan. "I'm an honest woman, I don't like to go sneaking around behind people's backs. So I wanted to give you one of these in person. You're the boss around here, right?"

"Well, I'm the Director, but the club is really a joint venture. Everyone has a say in what goes on here."

"It's for mental patients, right?"

"It's for people who suffer from mental illness. We prefer to call ourselves consumers, or club members, rather than patients."

She squinted at me appraisingly. "Oh, are you one of the crazies too? I've seen you coming and going, and I thought you were normal."

I still wasn't fully comfortable with my out-of-the-closet status. "What's crazy and what's normal? At the club, we try to avoid labeling people, and we definitely don't care for the word 'crazy.'"

"Oh, some of us don't mind being called crazy," said Stan. "It's a venerable old word, after all." He stuck his thumbs in his ears and wiggled his fingers at her. "Ooga Booga!"

She practically levitated in shock, and I was afraid she might go into cardiac arrest then and there. "Stan!" I said chidingly, although I could barely suppress a smile. I turned to the woman, who was panting lightly. She had her hand to her chest as though pledging allegiance. "I'm sorry," I told her. "Sometimes Stan has a warped sense of humor. He didn't mean any harm. Now, you wanted to show me a flier?"

She nodded and thrust a pink sheet into my hand. "My phone number is at the bottom if you have any questions."

"Thanks." Opening the flap to my big leather carryall, I thrust the flier inside. "I'm just on my way home. I'll take this with me and read it there, where I can give it the attention it deserves."

"You do that." She extended her hand. "I'm Miriam Goldfarb, by the way. Nice to meet you, Miss . . ."

"Erika Norgren. Nice to meet you, too." Her hand felt soft and warm.

Rishi nuzzled our clasped hands, but it didn't seem to faze her. "Beautiful dog. May I pet him?"

"Go ahead. He's friendly as long as you don't startle him."

Rishi seemed to like Mrs. Goldfarb, so she couldn't be all bad. She studiously ignored Stan, but I could hardly blame her. "Ooga Booga" indeed!

Chapter 17

Back home, I poured myself a glass of Merlot, kicked off my shoes, and settled down to relax and peruse Miriam Goldfarb's flier. But after a quick glance I exploded off the sofa and began pacing angrily back and forth, muttering to myself. I was glad I'd set the wineglass on the coffee table, because I surely would have thrown it if I'd had it in my hand, and red wine stains are horrendously hard to remove.

The missive was brief and to the point:

SAVE OUR NEIGHBORHOOD!
Recent events have opened our eyes.
The mental patients at the WellSpring Club
are going to destroy everything we've worked so hard for!
Come to the Community Board Meeting Tuesday, October 9, 7pm
Public School #21, East Houston St. at Essex St.
SPEAK OUT ABOUT THIS DANGEROUS PRESENCE
IN OUR MIDST!
East Fourth Street Block Association * 555-6767

The flier was so outrageous that my first impulse was to launch an immediate counterattack. But where to start? Obviously, I needed to talk with Mrs. Goldfarb. She'd said her number was on the flier, and there was only one number there, so I decided to give her a call.

She startled me by picking up after the second ring. Didn't she screen her calls? These days, people who actually answered their phones without subjecting callers to an answering machine seemed positively archaic.

"Hello," she said. "Block Association. May I help you?"

"Mrs. Goldfarb? This is Erika Norgren. We met earlier, outside the WellSpring Club. I'm calling about your flier."

"Oh, yes. How nice of you to call."

"Well, I'm actually not feeling so nice. I was shocked by what the flier said about the club, and about mental illness. It read like rabble rousing of the worst kind."

"Oh dear. That wasn't my intention, but I might have gotten a little carried away. I was having such a good time designing the flier on my computer. It's the first time I've done anything like that, and I was so proud of it."

She was so eager to please, so utterly oblivious to the implications of her words, that I decided to be conciliatory. "Your flier mentions 'recent events'. Were you referring to anything in particular?"

"Two people have died over there since Labor Day. What with all the police cars and ambulances, it's been very upsetting. What kind of place are you running, anyway?"

"We had two tragic occurrences, but they weren't anything we had any control over. It was unfortunate that they happened so close together."

"The first one jumped off the roof, and the second one overdosed on drugs. Isn't that right? I heard about them on the news. Two young men. Such a shame, even if they *were* crazy."

"Yes, it's very sad. They were both genuinely good people, both very talented."

"You poor thing, that must have been horrible for you. Say, I have an idea. Why don't you come over tomorrow? We can have some tea, and you can tell me more about the club."

Why not? "That would be wonderful," I said. "What time is good for you?"

"How about four? That's a nice, proper tea time."

"Fine. Is it all right if I bring my dog?"

"Oh, that would be lovely. But I'm glad you asked me first, because of my cats. I'll take them to visit my neighbor, so your big baby doesn't eat them."

Ideological differences aside, I had a hunch I was going to enjoy getting to know Miriam Goldfarb. I was heading back to the sofa and my glass of Merlot, wondering what to wear to tea tomorrow, when the phone rang. Probably a telemarketer, I thought as I paused to listen. I kept forgetting to get on that "Do Not Call" registry. But miracle of miracles, it was Mark Levitan, asking me to dinner for the following night. We agreed on Romano's, on Mulberry Street in Little Italy.

"The police have advised me to keep my dog with me at all times for protection," I told him. "But that wouldn't go down too well at Romano's, so why don't you pick me up at my place? How's 7:30?"

"Fine. But what's this about protection? Are you in some kind of danger?"

"It's possible. But don't worry, I'll bring you up to speed tomorrow."

———

Too excited to sleep, I stayed up till three and woke early as usual. This insomnia routine was getting on my nerves, but I was powerless to stop the cycle. How big a sleep deficit could I run up before I was terminally and irrevocably overdrawn? This sleeplessness could be part and parcel of an impending mania, but I couldn't afford to dumb myself down with any more Klonepin. Not with men in black lurking around every corner, waiting to get me. Paranoia – another sign of mania. Or in my case, maybe a sign of a healthy survival instinct.

Leaving my apartment with Rishi, I knew I should go to the police station to look at more mug shots, but I simply wasn't up for it yet, so I headed for the club instead. Passing an Italian bakery, I tied my dog to a lamppost and popped in to pick up some pastries for my visit to Miriam Goldfarb's apartment. At the club, I disguised the box in a brown paper bag, scrawled DO NOT TOUCH with a broad black marker, and stashed it at the back of the refrigerator in the kitchen.

The club was relatively tranquil today. No new crises, no one clamoring for attention – the serenity was delightful for a change, although I would have been bored out of my mind if things were this peaceful on a daily basis. I considered talking to some of the members about Stephen and Jeff, but I didn't want to disturb the peace, so I let it slide.

After lunch, when I asked Stan to keep an eye on things while I went to visit Mrs. Goldfarb later that afternoon, he shot me a look of astonishment. "You mean you're actually going to visit that battle ax?"

"Yes. I phoned her last night, and she invited me over. In the interests of good community relations, I accepted."

"Well, good luck, Erika. By the way, I'm sorry about that Ooga Booga thing. I don't know what got into me – I guess the devil made me do it."

I laughed. "Stan, I like your sense of humor, but people who don't know you might get the wrong idea. Some mentally ill people actually do think they're controlled by the devil."

"Believe me, I know. Or by radio waves, or the Internet, or Elvis. But she sounded so damn condescending the way she was talking about crazy people, and I couldn't resist needling her a little."

Miriam Goldfarb lived in a five-story walk-up diagonally across the street from the club. As she'd instructed, I pressed the button anonymously labeled 2B, and soon her scratchy voice came through the intercom, telling me to identify myself before she buzzed me in. It was the same arrangement I used, right down to the lack of a name on the door; we single women in the city have to take precautions.

She was waiting on the second floor landing, standing in the doorway of the apartment at the rear. I got as far as the threshold, then pulled Rishi up short as I stared in amazement. The space behind her was a jungle, with more houseplants crammed together than I'd ever seen outside a professional nursery.

"Hello, Mrs. Goldfarb," I said as I showed her the pastry box in its brown bag. "I brought along something for us to snack on."

"Please, call me Miriam," she said, as she reached out to pat Rishi. He was straining at his leash, doing his best to pull me into the apartment.

"He must smell my angels," she said. "We fooled you, boy – my cats are visiting a neighbor. Why don't you both come in and I'll close the door."

Stepping inside, I glanced around. She was obviously a collector, not only of plants, but of crystal, Hummel figurines, Wedgwood china, demitasse spoons, and countless other objects, all displayed on hand-crocheted doilies atop elaborate Victorian furniture. I shortened my hold on Rishi's leash. "I'll hang onto him for now. One swipe of his tail, and some of these pieces could be history."

"Whatever you think, dear. Now, what did you bring for us to nibble on?"

Taking the box from its bag, I presented it to her with a flourish. "Ta da!"

"Oh, the Milano Bakery. I love their cannoli! But of course everything they make is delicious."

"We must be on the same wave length. I just happened to get cannoli, plus some chocolate cream puffs and Napoleons."

She brought over a little round table and all the fixings for an elegant tea, including sterling silver flatware and Spode china, and we settled back to indulge ourselves.

"How long have you lived in this apartment?" I asked after awhile.

"My husband and I moved here after we got married, in 1953. Both of us were born and raised right in this neighborhood, and we wanted to stay near our families and friends, even though we could have moved someplace fancier. Abe was a wonderful provider, he did right by his family."

"What line of work was he in?"

"He ran a fabric store on Delancey Street. Upholstery and drapery fabric, very high quality, at wonderful discounts. His father started the business, but I had to sell it after Abe passed away. It broke my heart. Next month will make ten years that he's been gone. We were together almost 40 years."

"I really admire that. To me, the idea of being with someone for that long is almost inconceivable."

"Believe me, you'll feel differently when you meet the right person, dear." She peered intently at me over the tea service. "I gather you haven't yet?" As her dark eyes bored into mine, I felt a twinge of apprehension tinged by cynicism, as if I had just entrusted my fate to one of those psychic readers whose storefronts dot the Lower East Side. Any minute now, she would probably bring out the Tarot cards and the crystal ball, then ask for payment up front. *Get a grip, Erika. You didn't come here for a palm reading.*

I decided to ease sidelong into my subject. "Since you've lived in this neighborhood all your life, you must know a great deal about it. Has it changed a lot over the years?"

Her eyes twinkled, and she gave an odd, sneezing sort of laugh. "So! You don't want to talk about men. Very well, we'll talk about East Fourth Street. Of course it's changed. We used to have mostly Poles, Ukrainians, Russians, Jews from all over Europe, but a lot of them started moving out when the Puerto Ricans moved in. And then the hippies, in the sixties. A lot of them looked crazy, with their wild hair and all, and they smoked a lot of marijuana, even right out in the street, sitting on the stoops. But it seemed to make them very relaxed and friendly, so it didn't bother me."

"You sound pretty liberal. Didn't you worry that they were breaking the law?"

She laughed. "They weren't hurting anybody. I'll take a pothead over a drunk any day. They don't get nasty and pick fights the way drunks do. And as for my being liberal, I certainly am. I'm registered in the Liberal Party, although I work for the Democrats sometimes. I'm proud to say I worked on both of Hillary Clinton's Senate campaigns, and I'm glad she decided to become a New Yorker. Her husband's an out and out cad, but . . ."

I could see this turning into a marathon gabfest, so I interrupted. "I'm curious as to why you feel so strongly about the club. That flier was pretty inflammatory. Have any of the members been harassing you?"

"No, they're mostly polite, and they keep to themselves. I'm not crazy about the way they hang around outside and smoke all the time, but it's not that different from when the hippies used to live there, except that tobacco is legal."

"Then what's the problem? Is it just the fact that they suffer from mental illness? Because I can give you some information that might reassure you. For example, studies have shown that mentally ill people are less likely to become violent than the average person."

"No no, spare me the lecture, dear. I'd say anyone who jumps off a rooftop or kills himself with drugs is committing a violent act, wouldn't you? A murder of the self – that's what suicide is, after all. It's a tragedy. But I guess it was really that reporter on Channel 8 who got me thinking. That place can't be very well run if things like this keep happening. I decided she's right – a club like that just doesn't belong in this neighborhood."

I felt the bile rise in my throat. "Don't believe everything you hear, Miriam." How much should I tell her? The police had virtually abandoned both cases, and if I could undo the damage Nancy Welcome had done, I sensed Miriam Goldfarb could be a valuable ally.

I took a deep breath and plunged ahead. "I don't believe those two young men had any intention of killing themselves. At the time of their deaths, they were both feeling hopeful and positive about their lives. And I'd be willing to swear Jeffrey Archer wasn't doing drugs. He was the one who painted the mural on the building, who allegedly died of a heroin overdose. People were impressed by his work, and a dealer even offered him a show. He was much too excited about his prospects in the art world to mess himself up with drugs."

"That was a beautiful mural," Miriam said. "I watched him working on it every day when I walked to the store. He was a hard worker, that boy, and nice looking, too."

"Did you ever talk to him?"

"Of course. And I brought him coffee and bagels sometimes. He never seemed drugged up or anything. You think there was some skullduggery involved with his death?"

"It's possible. The police say he overdosed on heroin, but I think somebody else may have wanted him dead. It's just a gut feeling I have."

The teacup in her hand shivered against its saucer, and she set it down with a clatter. Her hands were trembling. "So maybe Gertrude Reynolds isn't so crazy after all. She's been insisting she saw something, and I thought it was just another example of her senility."

I almost choked on my tea. "What do you mean? Who's Gertrude Reynolds?"

"She lives up in 3A, and her apartment faces the street. She never goes out, and she's more or less turned night into day, staying up till all hours and then sleeping when it gets light out. I visit her every couple of days, and the day after that boy died, she was saying she saw someone take him out of a car and put him there. But she doesn't see too well, and she says all kinds of wild things, so I didn't take her seriously."

My heart began hammering in my chest. "Do you think we could go up and pay her a visit?"

Miriam frowned. "I suppose so. She doesn't get many visitors, only Meals on Wheels and an aide who does her shopping. Her place is pretty disgusting, but we can give it a try."

———————

The stench was the first thing I noticed about Gertrude Reynolds's apartment. Stale urine, rotten fruit and chlorine bleach were the top notes in a blend that pervaded the place. The second thing was the clutter. To reach the front of the apartment, Miriam and I had to squeeze between yellowed stacks of newspapers and magazines, along with enough junk to stock a small thrift store.

Finally, barricaded beyond the walls of paper, I beheld Gertrude herself. Without a doubt, she was one of the fattest women I'd ever seen. She sat near the window on an old love seat, with her swollen, discolored legs splayed out in front of her. A metal TV table stood beside her, holding tissues, a few cups and glasses, and a half-empty bag of Oreo cookies.

"Gertrude, shame on you!" scolded Miriam. "You know you shouldn't be eating cookies, with your diabetes."

"What other pleasure do I have left in life? Nobody cares if I live or die, so I might as well eat what I like." As Gertrude spoke, I studied her round, puffy face and caught a glimpse of the pretty young woman she might once have been.

"You know that's not true," said Miriam in a tone so brisk, I guessed the women had probably had this exchange many times before.

"I'd like you to meet Erika Norgren. She runs the club across the street, and I was telling her about what you saw the other night."

"What I saw? What do you mean? I never see anything. No one ever takes me anywhere."

"I mean from your window!" Miriam snapped. "You told me you saw somebody dump that young man out of a car in the middle of the night, before the police and ambulance came around. Remember?"

Gertrude closed her eyes and sat silently for so long, I thought she had fallen asleep. Then suddenly she revived and stared straight ahead. "Now it's coming back to me. I was looking out the window, like I always do. All of a sudden I saw a black car pull up and stop in front of the club. A man got out, dressed all in black. He went around to the other side of the car and I couldn't see what he was doing for a minute, but then he carried this other man up the steps and set him down at the top of the stoop."

"Did they struggle at all?"

"No, it looked like the one being carried was either unconscious or very very drunk. His body was as limp as a heap of noodles. After that, the other one had his back to me, fiddling around for a minute, and then he got back in the car and drove away."

I could barely contain my excitement. "Thank you very much, Gertrude. That could be extremely important."

She turned her eyes to me. They were a pale, watery blue, and the whites were yellowed. "You're welcome." She did a double take. "Who are you? Do I know you? Oh, you must be the new home aide."

Miriam shot me an exasperated look. I could understand why she hadn't taken Gertrude's story seriously, but my intuition told me there might be something there.

"Gertrude," I said. "When the man in black carried the other man to the stoop, could you tell if the second man was still alive?"

"What man? What are you talking about?"

Stifling the urge to scream, I summoned my most supportive therapeutic manner. "You've been very helpful, but maybe that's enough for today. Just one more thing. May I look out your window? I'd like to see the view of the club you get from here." I crossed to the love seat, perched on one arm, and leaned over with my head next to Gertrude's. The view of the club was perfect, panoramic.

I'd have to call Dennis Malone.

Chapter 18

I glanced at my watch. Six p.m. If I hurried, maybe I could still catch Dennis at work, then head home to get ready for my dinner with Mark. I said my farewells to Miriam and Gertrude, promised to be in touch, then left the apartment with Rishi in tow. I started down the stairs at a rapid clip. Sensing my impatience, Rishi shoved ahead and tugged at his leash. Thrown off balance, I grabbed the banister, slippery with years of accumulated grease and grime.

"Rishi, stop!" I yanked him up short and we continued our descent more sedately. I gave him a couple of minutes to attend to doggy business, then headed across the street to the club. It was deserted by now.

Dennis picked up on the second ring. "Malone here." He sounded exhausted.

"Dennis, it's Erika. I've got some interesting new information." I proceeded to tell him about my visit to Gertrude Reynolds's apartment and her story about the night of Jeff's death.

I heard slurping noises at the other end and wondered what he was drinking. Otherwise he was silent. "Well?" I said finally. "What do you think? Are you going to check it out?"

"Yes, definitely. I'll get right on it. Thanks for the tip."

"Are you going right now? I might have time to go with you, if we make it snappy. But I have to be home by seven. A guy's picking me up at seven thirty."

More silence. I smiled. Maybe the gratuitous zinger had hit home. "No, that's okay," he said at last. "I'll go in the morning."

"I should probably go with you. Gertrude might feel more at ease that way, since she's already met me."

"No thanks. If she's as confused as you say, she probably wouldn't remember meeting you anyway. I'll bring a female detective along. We have someone who's excellent at eliciting information from problematic witnesses."

Next I called Lillian Golson and left a voice mail apologizing for not showing up to look at more mug shots, promising to do it tomorrow. Then I locked up the club, dashed home and jumped in the shower. I'd left precious little time to get ready for Mark, but maybe that was just as well. I was practically jumping out of my skin, feeling much too edgy to execute a competent makeup job. He'd have to accept me *au naturelle*.

At last it was eight o'clock and there I was, face to face with Mark at a corner table at Romano's. Off and on all day, I'd been trying to picture him in my mind's eye with varying degrees of success. He was even more attractive than I'd remembered. His hazel eyes were flecked with gray and green, alight with warmth and energy, and the crow's feet around the corners crinkled appealingly when he smiled, which was often. His lips were full, sensuous, eminently kissable – when he wasn't talking, that is. We both had so much to say, the words poured out in a jumble.

As for Romano's, its Mulberry Street façade was unassuming, and its high kitsch décor featured red flocked wallpaper and mediocre murals of the Italian coastline, but the service was friendly and the food was fabulous. I'd been there with Richard once, and loved it, but he hadn't wanted to return. The place was too tacky for his taste.

Romano's had a weird kind of excitement about it. The place was in the heart of Little Italy, and countless luminaries of the underworld had wheeled and dealed here. The clientele at Romano's included quite a few men in expensive dark suits, some with women in tow, some without. When I'd been here with Richard, I'd filled the conversational gaps by inventing silent scenarios about these mysterious men, casting them as characters in a Mafioso drama. Tonight there was a man across the room who could well have been a don, and the big, burly guy next to him could well have been his hit man. But my imaginary casting game was no longer amusing – not since the men in dark suits were actually after me.

We had barely touched our antipasto appetizers when the waiter approached with our entrees. He moved the antipasto across the table next to the garlic bread and placed the steaming platters before us. Osso buco for Mark, chicken cacciatore for me, and the mandatory side of spaghetti for both of us.

The food was delicious, but I laid down my fork midway through the meal. "I'm going to take a breather. I'm stuffed." I reached for my Pinot Grigio.

"Good idea. I'll do the same." Mark raised his glass to mine and we shared a silent toast.

Our waiter returned. "Thank you for coming to Romano's. For such a beautiful couple, I bring you our special tiramisu for dessert, compliments of the house. Then maybe you come back more often."

"Thank you, that's very nice," I said, "but I doubt if I'll have room for dessert."

"That's okay. If you don't eat it, I wrap it up for you to take home. No problem. Take your time."

Just as my appestat began calling me softly, telling me I could probably handle some tiramisu, a man in black entered the restaurant. Middle aged, portly and short, he looked vaguely familiar. But no, he was probably just prototypically Italian, like one of the characters on The Sopranos. As he came closer and I got a better look, he reminded me of Danny DeVito, or – no, it couldn't be, but it was – my favorite slumlord, Vito Pisanello.

My hand jerked, and wine spilled from my glass. Mark reached over and cupped his hand around mine to steady it. "Erika, what's wrong? You look like you've seen a ghost."

"Shhh, he's coming this way. It's all right, he just startled me." There was no way around it: the little man was heading straight for the hallway that led to a second dining room, and his trajectory would take him right past our table.

Seizing the offensive, I flashed him an ingenuous smile. "Hi, Mr. Pisanello, how are you? I'd like you to meet my friend, Mark Levitan."

The little man scowled, but after a second or two he recovered nicely and gave me a smile every bit as phony as the one I was giving him. "Erika, how nice to see you. But it's a surprise to see you at Romano's."

"Oh, I've been here before. I love it, the food is fabulous."

He beamed, more sincerely this time, and his chest puffed with pride. "It should be. My nephew runs the kitchen, and I own a piece of this place. Now if you'll excuse me, I've got business to attend to. See you around." Wheeling abruptly, he strode into the corridor and out of sight.

"He was more polite than usual," I said to Mark. "Maybe because you were here to protect me."

"He seemed uptight. Or was that my imagination?"

"It wasn't your imagination. He detests the club and since I'm the director, I assume he detests me too. He owns several buildings in the area, and he's afraid WellSpring is dragging down the property values. He claims the recent incidents upset his tenants, and he especially hates Jeff Archer's mural."

"It sounds as if he has some valid concerns. If he sincerely cares about the neighborhood, it might be worth working with him, maybe trying a little conflict resolution."

"Are you kidding? I have a feeling the only conflict resolution he'd go for is the kind that happens at gunpoint."

The unexpected encounter had rattled my nerves, and all at once I felt claustrophobic, hemmed in behind the table with my back up against the red brocade wall. I badly needed to stretch. "I'm going to the ladies' room," I told Mark as I wriggled out of my seat and around the table. "If the waiter comes back, can you have him put the rest of my dinner in a doggie bag? Don't let him forget the spaghetti and garlic bread."

"Of course. I'm sure Rishi will be delighted."

"Rishi? No way! It's for my lunch tomorrow, although I'll probably give him the garlic bread."

The ladies' room was toward the back, along the same corridor Pisanello had taken. With its peeling wallpaper and salmon ceramic tiles on the floor and halfway up the wall, the room was a stylistic throwback to the fifties, but this wasn't a retro recreation, it was vintage original. Dusty plastic flowers in cheap vases graced the counter, and the cloying smell of flowery room freshener failed to mask the odor of urine.

I craved a few minutes of solitary decompression time, but before long another woman entered, violating the tranquillity of my private retreat. As I left the room, I was still jittery, not quite ready to return to Mark, so I decided to go exploring and followed the corridor to the rear of the restaurant. The second dining room was reserved for private parties and special occasions, and I was curious to see what it looked like. I was even more curious to see whether Vito Pisanello was there, and if so, what kind of business he was transacting.

A pair of mammoth doors separated the room from the rest of the restaurant. Made of ornately carved wood in a deep mahogany finish, they had glass panels with etched floral designs. Behind the glass, velvet curtains of blood-red crimson blocked the view beyond. Through the closed doors, I could hear men talking and laughing, but I couldn't make out what they were saying. A faint whiff of cigar smoke escaped through the edges of the doorframe, sending an unequivocally masculine message underscored by the "Private Party" sign on the door. The overall effect was lavish, forbidding, yet juvenile, like a boys' secret clubhouse with a "Girls Keep Out" sign.

I was about to turn back when I noticed a sliver of light gleaming through a narrow slit between the curtains. As the hint of life behind closed doors lured me irresistibly closer, I reminded myself not to act furtive. After all, if anyone asked, I was just exploring the restaurant, admiring the decor, perhaps considering booking a private party or a wedding.

One eye at the opening, I peered into the room. Roughly a dozen men were scattered around three circular tables. After a moment I saw Vito Pisanello seated on the far side of a table, facing the door. He was talking to a younger man beside him. They were both speaking vehemently and gesticulating dramatically, but their words didn't carry through the heavy glass.

Watching Vito, at first I paid little attention to the second man. But as his face swam into sharper focus, it dawned on me. The cut of his jaw, the low hairline, the full, pouty lips all belonged to the man who had stalked me on St. Marks Place. He wasn't wearing shades tonight, but even so, I was virtually positive he was the one. Suppressing the impulse to run, I forced myself to stare a little longer, to engrave the contours of his face indelibly in my mind.

"Can I help you, miss? You look lost."

I hadn't heard anyone coming and the voice at my back startled me badly. I yelped and spun around so wildly that I practically knocked a huge platter of pastries out of our waiter's hand.

"I was just doing a little exploring," I said. My face burned, and I knew I was blushing. "I was admiring these doors. They have an Art Nouveau feel about them, and I was wondering if they're actually antiques from that era, or reproductions. Would you know if the wood is mahogany, or is it stained? And who designed that wonderful floral motif on the glass? It reminds me of Charles Rennie MacIntosh, or maybe William Morris."

"I have no idea, Ma'am. You'd have to ask one of the owners." He was studying me quizzically, and he'd gone from Miss to Ma'am, a sure sign that he'd stopped thinking of me as an attractive young woman and started seeing me as a potential problem.

"Of course," I said, willing myself to slow down and stop babbling. "I'm sorry for taking your time, especially when you're carrying that heavy tray."

"No problem. Now if you'll excuse me, this is a private area, and the gentlemen are waiting."

"Okay. Just one more thing. I saw Vito Pisanello come in. He's a friend of mine, but for the life of me I can't remember the name of the man he's with, although I've met him a couple of times. I just wanted to see what that room looked like, that's why I was peeking in. I realize it might have seemed kind of strange – "

"You're damn right it did." He leaned closer, and his affable mask turned cold. "Take my advice. You don't want to be snooping around, asking about people that don't concern you. That's a private meeting in there, and they don't appreciate people butting in. If I was you, I'd go back to that nice gentleman. He already took care of the check, and he's probably wondering where you are."

Even as he spoke, I saw Mark at the end of the corridor, heading our way. As he approached, I saw worry in his eyes, followed rapidly by a look of relief. He draped his arm possessively around my shoulders. "Erika, you were gone so long, I thought you might be ill or something."

"Your lady friend was doing a little exploring," the waiter said in a condescending tone. He ignored me now, addressing Mark man to man, talking about me as if I were an unruly child, or maybe a mental patient. "I advised her that the back room is off limits. There's a private party in progress, and these gentlemen don't take kindly to interruptions."

"I wasn't interrupting anyone," I snapped. "I was just admiring the workmanship on these beautiful doors."

"Whatever you say. Now if you'll excuse me, I've got to deliver these pastries." Edging around us and reaching for the brass handle on the door, he gave me a long, glowering look before disappearing into the inner sanctum.

I giggled as I took Mark's arm. "He took off like a shot as soon as I mentioned those doors. I guess he didn't want another lecture on Art Nouveau design."

Mark gave me a quizzical look, then shook his head. "I don't even want to hear about it. Let's get out of here."

"But we haven't had our tiramisu. Oh well, let's have him add it to the doggy bags."

———————

Half a block from the restaurant, Mark was ready to talk. "I didn't want to discuss anything too serious at Romano's," he said as we strolled west along Grand Street. It's much too public."

"Mark, what do you suppose actually goes on in that back room? The waiter caught me peeking through a crack in the curtains, and he read me the riot act. Do you suppose the place is teeming with wise guys?"

"Could be. In a place like that, the best policy is to enjoy the food and atmosphere, and just mind your own business."

"When he found me, I started rambling on about the doors, and whether they were actually Art Nouveau or just reproductions. He probably thought I was losing my mind." The thought made me start giggling again.

Mark didn't share my merriment. "Maybe he was right," he said. He gazed at me with concern, then stopped short and stepped in front of me so that we were standing face to face. He rested his hands gently on my shoulders. "Erika, you're trembling."

"That's because I'm laughing."

"I fail to find much humor in this situation. You're awfully hyped up, Erika. I don't know you that well, and perhaps it's none of my business, but with all the stress you've been under, it would be natural for you to decompensate. In the TV interview, you mentioned being on medication. I assume you've been taking it?"

I felt a rush of anger. "Like clockwork, and you don't need to sound so patronizing. With everything that's been going on, this is hardly the time to mess around with my trusty old chemical straitjacket. Heaven forbid I should feel anything too intensely. A couple of people die, I recognize my attacker in the restaurant – so what? It's all part of a day's work. I can handle it, as long as I keep myself thoroughly medicated. I'm not about to – "

His fingers tightened on my shoulders. "What did you say? About the attacker in the restaurant?"

"Shhh!" I scrutinized our surroundings. There was no one within earshot, no one watching us but a couple of big-eyed busts of Jesus in the shop window alongside us. But the savior didn't scare me; I was telling the gospel truth.

"Remember when I told you at dinner about the man who grabbed me and tried to force me into that car on St. Marks Place?"

Mark nodded wordlessly.

"Well, I saw him through the curtains, talking to Vito Pisanello, the one I introduced you to. They were having a heated discussion, with all sorts of dramatic gestures, but I couldn't hear what they were talking about. I asked our waiter who he was, but he wouldn't tell me."

"Of course he wouldn't. You had no business snooping around back there."

"Please don't lecture me. You sound like a sanctimonious old school teacher."

"Sorry. A lot of my livelihood comes from lecturing, so it's hard to turn it off. But Erika, this is serious. What are you going to do about that guy?"

"I haven't decided – no, of course! I'll go back to the police station first thing in the morning and finish looking at those mug shots. And I'll go through the ones I saw already, since I'll have a better idea what I'm looking for this time."

"Excellent idea, Erika. Just promise me that if you identify the guy, you let the police take it from there. I'd hate for anything to happen to you. These guys play rough, and they play for keeps."

Chapter 19

*A*t the station the next morning, I attacked the mug shots with newly aggressive energy. I had a clear mental image of the man I was looking for. The stranger in shades had been a fuzzy, generic stereotype, but this man had a prominent nose, an under-slung jaw, and heavy-lidded eyes beneath thick brows that met in the middle. Strange how the dark glasses and elegant clothes had endowed him with a mysterious glamour, whereas seated in Romano's back room, stripped of the stylish accessories, he was ordinary, bordering on homely.

An hour went by, then another, and I still hadn't found a match. By noon I had seen them all. "Now that I've got a better idea what he looks like, I'd like to check out the ones from the other day," I told Sergeant Golson.

"Good idea. But why don't you take a lunch break first? You'll be in better shape when you look at the photos."

"I'd rather skip lunch and get it over with. I'm not hungry anyway." Just then my stomach let loose an audible rumble, prompting a grin from the Sergeant. "Well, maybe just a little break," I conceded.

I picked up a ham and Swiss on rye from a nearby deli, then headed with Rishi to Tompkins Square Park. Sitting on a bench near some spectacular rose bushes, I soaked up the sunshine and devoured my sandwich as Rishi stood close by, salivating and staring imploringly with those huge brown eyes. "Oh, all right. You've been such a good boy, you deserve a treat." I tore off a large chunk of sandwich and tossed it his way. He caught it on the fly and wolfed it down in seconds.

The mood in the park today was benign and peaceful, worlds away from the day I'd fled terrified into the heart of a TV shoot. In all the years I'd lived in New York, I'd been sensibly streetwise, but deep down, I'd had the irrational conviction that no harm would ever befall me. The mystery man had robbed me of that sense of safety. From now on I would survive in the city, but like the rose bushes caged behind their four-foot fence of cast iron, I could never again flower quite so freely. All the more reason to bring this man to justice. He may not have harmed me physically, but he had definitely messed with my mind.

Back at the station, it was ten after three when I found his picture. His likeness was more than halfway through the photos I'd viewed on the first go-round, so I must have seen it before, but I had more to go on this time. The profile helped, but the eyes were what clinched it.

Elated, I called Sergeant Golson over to the table. "I finally fingered the perp!" I exclaimed. She greeted my news with a smirk and a roll of the eyes, so I decided to amend my statement. "I was dying to say that, but I'll admit it sounds pretty tacky. Seriously, though, I'm positive this is the man. Franco Vanelli."

She scrutinized the picture, then smiled and patted me on the shoulder. "All right! Way to go, girl. We'll get right on it and contact you if we need anything. In the meantime, call if you have any questions. You still have my card, right?"

"Yes."

"Here's another, just in case. You take care now!"

———————

I was delighted to escape the station with its stale, recirculated air and those baleful fluorescent lights that endowed everyone with the bluish pallor of the morgue. I stood on the sidewalk, feasting my eyes on the brilliant blue sky and taking great gulps of fresh air, then headed back to the club. The members had a right to know about Franco Vanelli, in case he showed up at WellSpring.

When Rishi and I reached the club, Stan and Gloria were sitting on the stoop smoking. Arthur was pacing back and forth with the pent-up energy of a caged carnivore, but he froze when Rishi began sniffing his black denim pants. "Hey, Erika, call off your dog," he pleaded.

"He won't hurt you. He's just checking you out to see where you've been." I let Rishi have his way a moment longer, relishing this rare opportunity to see Arthur afraid, but when Rishi thrust his nose into the man's crotch and sniffed deeply, I reluctantly reined him in.

Gloria jumped up from the steps, looking guilty. "Everyone else has gone home, that's why we're out here. I rolled over the phone lines already."

"No problem, Gloria."

"We've been waiting for you, Erika," said Arthur. Now that I'd called off the dog, he had his usual bravado back. "We were just watching the tape from last night's news. We came off pretty well, I thought."

Oh God, the interview with Nancy Welcome, the one that made Ocala more furious than she'd been already. What with everything that had been going on, I'd manage to repress the memory completely.

"They finally ran it last night," said Stan. "Two days after she shot it, but it wasn't particularly time-sensitive, and I guess they had some stories that took priority. Yesterday must have been a slow news day."

I fished in my handbag for a Tum. I'd been consuming a lot of them lately. "Since when have you been so media-savvy, Stanley?"

His mouth tightened. "Since Nancy Welcome started showing up, I guess. Arthur's right, we acquitted ourselves well. Did you see it?"

Eleven o'clock last night, I'd been roaming the streets of Little Italy with Mark, feeling moonstruck. "No, I missed it."

"Want to see the tape?"

"Not right now. There's something else I want to discuss with you. Remember that incident I told you about, when some guys tried to pull me into a car on St. Marks Place? I have some news for you. Come on inside."

In the group room, I told them that I had spent all day looking at mug shots and had identified one of the men. I considered saying I had seen him with Vito Pisanello, but I decided against it. After all, it could have been sheer coincidence that I'd seen them together, and Pisanello might have nothing to do with the incident. He was often in the vicinity of the club, and I didn't want Arthur giving him a hard time.

On the other hand, I was positive that the man I had identified in the photo was the one who had stalked and manhandled me, and the club members ought to know about him. "His name is Franco Vanelli," I said. "I recognized him last night at a restaurant in Little Italy. He wasn't wearing his shades, and I got a more leisurely look at him, so I had a better idea what I was looking for when I went through the pictures today." I described him as accurately as I could.

"That describes a lot of guys," said Stan. "How would we know it was him if he shows up here? And what do you want us to do?"

"If someone you don't know is hanging around, and he fits that description, call the police," I said. "Let them worry about a positive identification, and don't get involved yourself. I still don't know what's motivating these people, but I wouldn't want them bothering anyone else around here. They might be dangerous."

All at once I pictured the fear on Gertrude Reynolds's face as she told me about the man who had carried Jeff's body to the stoop. He had climbed out of a black car. Could it have been the same car they tried pulling me into? Highly unlikely, I thought – in Manhattan, black cars were as commonplace as dark-haired men with heavy-lidded eyes. Even so, our folks deserved to know.

"There's something else I should tell you," I said. "Stan, remember I told you I was going to see Miriam Goldfarb yesterday afternoon?"

"That bigoted old bag? Yes, I remember."

"Actually she was a lot more sympathetic than I expected. And she took me down to her neighbor's apartment. This lady lives on the second floor with a good view of the club, and she claims to have seen someone pull up in a black car and place Jeff's body on the stoop the night he died."

Arthur leaned forward. "The plot thickens. You think it was the same guy?"

"I have no idea. But it certainly raises some interesting questions."

"Yeah," said Stan. "We had such a hard time believing Jeff would OD when he was doing so well."

Gloria's eyes widened. "So he really was murdered just like we thought."

"It's beginning to look that way. The police were going to interview this woman today, so by tomorrow hopefully I'll find out if they learned anything." I paused. "I've been meaning to talk to the three of you, to find out more about Stephen and Jeff. You knew them a lot longer than I did. They had a lot in common, but I wonder if there's anything I'm missing, anything that ties them together?"

Arthur grinned. "Yeah, they both thought they were hot shit. And they were both fruitcakes."

Stan glared at Arthur. "Jesus, man! Have some respect for the dead!"

"Let's all chill out," I said. "I know this is difficult, but we need to think outside the box. Was there anyone who had a grudge against them, for instance?"

Stan was still glaring. "Besides Arthur, you mean?"

"Drop it, Stan," said Arthur. "So anyway, Erika, what are the cops doing about this guy, what's his name? Frank Porcelli?"

"Franco Vanelli. Presumably they'll question him about the incident."

He grimaced. "Right. And he'll deny everything, and they'll let him walk. End of story, until he tries again."

Arthur's scenario sounded all too likely, but I couldn't admit to sharing his cynicism. "I'm sure they won't just let it go at that," I said gamely.

"How much you want to bet? The cops in this burg are lazy, incompetent and crooked, every single one of them." Arthur slammed his fist into his palm for emphasis. "They won't do diddly squat unless there's something in it for them. You mark my words, Erika. Don't hold your breath waiting for the guys in blue to solve your problems. And the courts are even worse. You'll die of old age before you get any satisfaction. If you want justice, you're better off going after it yourself."

Stan frowned. "Are you talking about some kind of vigilante justice, Arthur?"

Arthur grinned. "What ever gave you that idea, Stanley? I was just exercising my citizen's right to free speech and giving my opinion of the NYPD."

My sleep that night was restless, punctuated by dreams that featured Franco Vanelli's face staring out at me from that mug shot. Next morning I was in my office, sleepily sipping coffee and checking my e-mail, when a staccato rapping startled me into instant alertness. It startled Rishi too – he sprang to his feet, barking and ready for action.

"Erika! I have a news update for you." Miriam Goldfarb's voice barely carried over the barking.

"Just a minute, Miriam. Let me get Rishi." I grabbed his collar with one hand and opened the door with the other. He sniffed her eagerly, began wagging as she gave his head a few gingerly pats. "Go lie down, Rishi," I said, releasing his collar and pointing to his lair beneath my desk. He crawled obediently into his cave.

"Thank you, dear," Miriam said. "Your dog is beautiful, but he's so big and rambunctious. God forbid he should knock me over and break my hip. I'd end up like Gertrude, stuck on a sofa forever."

I hoped she wasn't feeling litigious, and wondered if the club's liability insurance covered dog-induced falls. "If you'd called ahead, I could have had him on a leash," I said as I ushered her to the chair beside my desk.

"It was time for my morning walk anyway." As she lowered herself cautiously onto the cheap plastic upholstery, she uttered a sigh of relief, then leaned toward me. "The police were over yesterday to interview Gertrude, and I'm afraid it didn't go terribly well," she said in a melodramatic murmur.

"How do you mean?"

"They wouldn't let me stay in the same room. But I could hear from the kitchen, where I was sitting at the table having coffee. There was a man and a woman, and they both seemed very nice. The woman did most of the questioning, but she had to ask some questions more than once. Gertrude didn't always remember what they were talking about, and a couple of times when they repeated the same question, she gave different answers."

I tried to ignore the sinking feeling in my stomach and to project a mood of optimism. "I'll call Detective Malone and see what he thinks. Maybe it went better than you thought."

"Maybe, but when I was coming out of the kitchen when they were finished with Gertrude, I saw them kind of roll their eyes at each other.

You know how people do when they think someone's crazy." She gasped. "I'm sorry, I forgot. No offense, dear."

I laughed. "None taken."

"I swear, sometimes I think I'm getting Alzheimer's. I heard that interview with Nancy Welcome, where you said you were bipolar, but then I forgot all about it because you seem so normal. But then so do the folks from the club that she interviewed on TV the other night. It's all terribly confusing." She gave an embarrassed giggle. "What did you mean about being bipolar, anyway? Does that mean you have multiple personalities?"

"No, but I do have mood swings. My mood can switch from deeply depressed to elated, and then back again."

"But that's true of everyone! Unless they're dead, comatose, or just plain boring."

"Miriam, you have a delightful way with words. I'd love to talk more, but I have work to do. But I'll be sure to call Detective Malone and follow up on that meeting with Gertrude. I promise I won't let this thing rest."

Miriam was no sooner out the door than I telephoned Dennis Malone, but I had to settle for his voice mail. I had better luck with Lillian Golson; she picked up on the second ring. "Sergeant Golson speaking," she said in a crisp voice.

"Sergeant Golson, this is Erika Norgren. I'm calling to see if you had any luck tracking down Franco Vanelli, the man I identified yesterday."

"Hello, Ms. Norgren." The silence that followed was long enough to arouse my latent paranoia. Didn't she want to talk with me? Most likely she was just distracted.

I tried for a polite, conciliatory tone. "I'm sorry. Did I catch you at a bad time?"

"No, that's all right." Another pause, then an audible sigh. "We sent two units – four officers, that is – out to look for him in Little Italy yesterday evening. He's a known associate of the criminal element in that part of the city. The men on that detail know the area well, and they have informants who keep them apprised of everything that's going on. They know where he lives."

The hint of a shadowy undertone in her voice contradicted the positive message, but I opted to keep things upbeat. "That's great," I enthused. "So what's the next step? Do I have to pick him out of a line-up?"

"I'm afraid the next step is finding him. No one our men spoke with had seen him since the night before. Then they checked his apartment. His wife was frantic, because she hadn't seen him since morning. She'd made his favorite manicotti, and he never came home for dinner."

I flashed on all the men I'd known over the years who were hazy about dinner arrangements. "But that's not so unusual, is it?" I asked. "He probably showed up later on."

"No, they checked again this morning. No one's seen him, and he's apparently a real homebody who shows up for dinner like clockwork unless he tells his wife he has other plans. This isn't typical of him."

I felt a sudden chill. "Maybe he knows I identified him and went into hiding. Or what if he's after me?"

"There's no way he could know you identified him. We don't give out that kind of information."

"But he might suspect, because of the failed abduction attempt. He probably knows who I am and where I work."

"Now, Ms. Norgren, I don't want you to worry unnecessarily. Franco Vanelli has been missing less than 24 hours, and the fact that we couldn't find him probably has nothing to do with you." Another pause. "However, I do believe you should be alert to anything unusual."

"Do you think I should have police protection?"

"We can't justify that on the basis of what's happened to date. But if it makes you feel more secure, you might want to stay with friends, or have someone stay with you, until things are resolved."

A perfect excuse to call Mark, I thought. But alas, I had promised to have dinner with Kevin. Maybe I could invite Mark over later, about eleven.

"Hello, Erika? You still there?"

"Yes. Sorry, I was just thinking about how this situation dovetails with my social life, and which of my many male admirers might make the best body guard."

She didn't laugh, and it occurred to me that my situation might be more perilous than I'd thought. "All you've told me about this Franco Vanelli is that he's a family man who likes to eat dinner on time," I said. "Is there anything else I should know?"

"Well, he has a pretty lengthy record. Burglary, mostly, and a couple of assault charges. He's done time in prison."

"What about murder? Has he ever killed anyone?"

"He's never been convicted. He's been linked to several cases, but there was insufficient evidence, and they never went to trial. But Erika, please don't take this lightly. This man could be dangerous. Call us any time, day or night. And you'd better keep your cell phone on and charged, just in case."

In case of what? I decided not to ask.

Chapter 20

*T*his time when Kevin rang the bell, I was ready and waiting. The day had already contained more than its share of stress, and I had no desire to provoke another face-off between Kevin and Rishi, so by prior arrangement, I met him downstairs.

"Erika, you look lovely as always," he said. "I planned something a little different tonight. How would you like to have dinner at my penthouse in Chelsea? I've lavished a lot of attention on the place, and I'd love for you to see it."

So here it comes at last, I thought. Kevin had been the perfect gentleman so far, but perhaps he had finally decided to put a move on me. I'd have been more intrigued by the idea a few days ago, before my evening with Mark, but my priorities had changed. Even so, I was curious to see his digs. And judging by what Lillian Golson had told me about Franco Vanelli, keeping a low profile might be a good idea.

"That would be great," I said with a smile, whereupon he laid a hand gently on the small of my back and guided me to his car.

We pulled up at his building on Ninth Avenue, and he ushered me into a freight elevator painted glossy black and hung with quilted black mover's blankets. All that forbidding darkness reminded me of Nine Squat, where I'd gone in search of answers to Stephen's death. Why were people of so many social persuasions so enamored of black? It looked good on Rishi, but other than that, it was a non-color I could easily do without.

The elevator came to a stop. "Ready?" Kevin said. "Welcome to my sanctuary. I hope you like it."

Dogs barked somewhere nearby as he pushed back the metal gate and unlocked the padlock on the heavy steel doors, then flung them open to reveal a spectacular expanse of brightness. He took off his shoes and instructed me to do the same. Since the carpet was an off-white Berber weave, I could see why.

I could also understand his wanting to show off his place, because it was absolutely spectacular. The space was enormous, with vast expanses of glass framing panoramic views of the city. On three sides, double doors opened onto a luxuriously landscaped terrace. Inside, the interior design was heavy on off-white, glass and chrome, with a few judicious accents in black, gray and beige. Huge, inscrutably abstract paintings graced the walls, and there was absolutely no clutter anywhere. The overall effect was affluent and austere, as if a crew from *Architectural Digest* was expected for a photo shoot momentarily.

The barking was louder and more excited now. "That's Greta and Gudrun," said Kevin. "Hold on a minute, and I'll get them. I'm sure you'll get along fine." He disappeared into a shadowy corridor as the barks changed to high-pitched yelps of joy. A minute later he emerged with a brace of rottweilers, both straining at their choke chains, their claws digging deep into the luxurious carpeting as they struggled to get at me. I stood motionless, resolved to look relaxed.

"Just let them sniff you," said Kevin. They did, and fortunately they liked what they smelled. My velour top and leather skirt hadn't been cleaned lately, and they were probably picking up on Rishi's masculine aura.

Kevin smiled like a proud parent. "Since the introductions have gone well, how would you like to accompany me and the girls on a walk before dinner?"

"I'd love to. And I doubt if anyone will recognize me or expect me to be in this neighborhood."

"What if they do? Are you on the lam or something?"

"No, I'm just keeping a low profile. I'll tell you later, after our walk."

We walked south, west, then south again, zigzagging past a melange of storefronts, galleries and restaurants. The dogs urged us onward, keeping a steady tension on the leashes Kevin clutched in one hand, too well trained to pull and strain until we neared the meat packing district. "We'd better turn around and start back," Kevin said then. "The scent of all the raw beef and blood gets them a little crazed."

"Then by all means, let's turn around," I agreed. "I've never known any rottweilers before, and Greta and Gudrun are sweet dogs, much friendlier than I would have expected. I'd hate to have to change my opinion."

"The breed has an undeservedly bad reputation," Kevin said. "As long as they're trained right, they're excellent dogs, very intelligent and loyal. I got these two from a breeder upstate. They're sisters, from the same litter. The bloodlines on both the sire and dam's side are full of champions."

As Kevin talked about his dogs, the love in his voice was unmistakable, and he was more relaxed and natural than I'd ever seen him. The mood continued through dinner, which consisted of a delicious array of exotic cheeses, pates and salads from Dean & DeLuca, along with some excellent wines.

As we watched the sun set over the New Jersey skyline, our conversation meandered in many directions. But when at last I told

Kevin about Franco Vanelli, the mood in the room darkened perceptibly. While deep purple clouds swallowed the fiery afterglow of the sun, Kevin gazed at me intently. "I don't want anything to happen to you, Erika," he said. "I think you should stay here tonight."

"Thank you, Kevin, but that's not necessary. I'll be fine if you just drive me home and see me to my door. Rishi will protect me."

"No, I insist. This guy sounds like bad news. As long as he's at large, you could be in real danger. There are a lot of evil people out there, sick, demented souls who are capable of unspeakable atrocities. I don't want you falling victim to one of them." He took both my hands in his. "Tell me you'll stay. I have a spare bedroom you can use, and I solemnly swear I won't sneak in and ravish you in the dead of night."

His eyes burned with the zeal of a possessed preacher, and I felt a twinge of uneasiness. "Kevin, I've never heard you talk like this," I said. "You're getting so intense."

He laughed. "I'm sorry. It's a long time since a woman has been in this apartment, and I suppose your presence has gone to my head. Combined with the two bottles of wine we drank with dinner, it's making me feel a little weird."

In truth, the wine had gone to my head too, but I hadn't realized how much until he mentioned it. I glanced at my watch: ten thirty. The thought of time triggered a gigantic, involuntary yawn.

Kevin laughed. "That clinches it. You're obviously exhausted, Erika. Come, let me show you to your room." Taking my hand, he helped me clamber out of the soft, white leather chair and escorted me down the hall. "This apartment has three bedrooms, and each has its own private bath, so you won't have to worry about being disturbed. My bedroom is here on the right, and the one at the end of the hall has been converted for Greta and Gudrun. You'll be staying in the room across from mine."

He opened a door, flicked a switch, and I found myself looking at a room as warm and inviting as the rest of the apartment was cold. The rug and the comforter on the queen-sized bed were a deep, rosy red. Floral-patterned drapes and pillows echoed the color and added notes of pink, orange and green. A chaise longue upholstered in emerald-green brocade sat near the window, with a telescope on a tripod on one side, a gilded table on the other. On the table lay a leather-bound volume that looked like a journal. The dusty-rose walls were crowded with framed paintings and drawings, and small sculptures and perfume bottles covered every available surface. Somehow it all worked together to create a mood of harmony and joy.

"Kevin, this is fabulous!" I exclaimed as I stepped into the room. "It feels like a rose garden in June."

His eyes misted over. "That's a beautiful description, Erika. Barbara would have loved it."

My breath caught in my throat. "You mean this was Barbara's room?"

"Yes, for the last two years of her life. I hired a decorator to make it exactly the way she wanted it. And it would honor her memory to have you stay here."

"I don't know. I don't feel right about it."

He grasped me gently by the shoulders. "Please stay. It would mean a great deal to me. No one but me has set foot in this room since Barbara died, but it's high time someone did. It might help me get on with my life."

My eyes drifted to the leather-clad journal, and I wondered what she had written there. Curiosity got the better of me. After all, we were sisters in a way. Both of us were bipolar.

"All right, I'll stay."

Kevin smiled. "I'm so glad. I've put new linens on the bed, and there are fresh towels in the bathroom. Feel free to wander around, and help yourself to anything in the kitchen." He walked to the table, picked up the journal, and tucked it under his arm. "I'd better take this."

He let go of my shoulders, then kissed me chastely on the forehead. The way one might kiss a sister.

Lying in Barbara's enormous bed, I couldn't fall asleep. I had no better luck on the chaise. Whenever I began to drift off, amorphous images swirled around me, smoky and wraithlike. In the netherworld between waking and dreaming, I imagined Barbara had sent them, but I couldn't decipher their message. It wasn't until dawn, when the room began to lighten, that I fell asleep.

I woke after ten. When I padded to the door and opened it a crack, Greta and Gudrun came running up the corridor and avidly licked my hands, but Kevin wasn't in evidence. I threw on my clothes and went to the kitchen. There I found freshly brewed coffee, a carafe of orange juice, and a plate of croissants, along with a note saying he had left for work but that I should make myself at home and stay as long as I liked. It was sweet of him, but I vaguely resented the implication that I had nowhere to go and leisure to burn.

Thanks but no thanks, I thought. I chugalugged some coffee and juice, wrapped a couple of croissants in paper towels and stashed them in my purse. Then I checked in with Gloria on my cell, patted the dogs goodbye and split. I rushed home to shower and change, then took off with Rishi for work.

When I arrived, Arthur was standing next to the stoop, waving a tabloid newspaper. "Hey, Erika, look at this! Isn't this the guy you were telling us about? The one who assaulted you?" Coming closer, he thrust the newspaper in front of my face.

"Hey, Arthur, back off," I said. "Talk about feeling assaulted!"

Then I saw the headline: Mobster Slain. There was a murky photo of two cops and a shrouded form on a stretcher, with a Dumpster in the background. At the lower right was a smaller inset photo. I recognized the mug shot. The caption confirmed what the photo told me: the slain mobster was Franco Vanelli.

A wave of nausea hit as the coffee and orange juice collided in my stomach. "Let's go inside," I said weakly. "I can't read this standing on the sidewalk."

Arthur peered intently at me, then snaked his arm around my back. "Are you all right, Erika? All the color just drained out of your face."

"I'm okay." I started to pull away, but stopped when I realized how wobbly I was. "I'm just a little dizzy. Probably low blood sugar; I didn't have enough breakfast this morning."

His mouth twisted in a cynical smile "Sure, Erika. Whatever you say."

I waited for the wave of weakness to subside, then went inside with Arthur. Gloria was at the reception desk, reading the latest *People*, and when she saw me, she jumped up to give me a hug. "Erika, I'm so glad you're here! I've been worried about you!"

"I'm fine." I extricated myself from her grasp.

"Arthur showed me the newspaper, about that guy who tried to kidnap you. I guess he won't be bothering you anymore. That's something to be thankful for!"

"It's hardly appropriate to be thankful for somebody's murder," I said, but on some level I agreed. It might not be politically correct, but deep down, I was definitely grateful.

"Some people are better off dead," said Arthur. "If you ask me, whoever whacked this asshole did society a favor. Erika, how about we go in your office, and I'll show you the rest of the story. There's a whole page about the murder inside."

His gray eyes, usually icy cold, glittered with an unnerving excitement. The story obviously turned him on, and I suspected Franco Vanelli's tangential connection with me was part of the reason why. But discussing the murder with Arthur could only fuel the dark feelings that smoldered beneath his cynical façade.

"Arthur, I appreciate your showing me the paper," I said. "But I'd like to be alone now, so I can read it quietly. Could I borrow your copy? I promise I'll give it back to you."

"Sure, no problem." He handed me the paper. "You can keep it. I want to get another one anyway. The *Post* has the story too, but I'm broke right now, so I only got the *News*. If you like, I can –"

I cut him short. "I'll give you the money. Thanks, Arthur, I appreciate it." I extracted a five-dollar bill from my wallet and handed it to him, then headed with Rishi to my office.

The Daily News devoted a two-page spread to the murder of Franco Vanelli. The basic story was brief and to the point. His body had been found by garbagemen on a morning pickup, lying in a Dumpster behind a factory building on Grand Street, on the fringes of Little Italy. The death appeared to have been caused by multiple stab wounds. No suspects had been identified yet, but the investigation was continuing.

A sidebar gave a sketchy biography. Franco Vanelli was thirty-two years old; he left a wife and two children. Except for stints in several prisons in upstate New York, he had lived all his life in Lower Manhattan, and had been involved in various businesses known to have mob connections.

There was a third article, a bylined feature by a reporter who covered the crime beat. Anonymous informants had suggested this crime might not be mob-related. To begin with, no one knew of anybody who would want Franco Vanelli killed: he wasn't involved in any ongoing feuds or power struggles.

The other oddity was the way Franco Vanelli was killed. Sources described the murder as messy and unprofessional. "This was strictly an amateur job," said one, speaking on condition of anonymity. "The perp didn't know what he was doing, it was like he hacked at the victim with a machete. This was overkill; the level of violence suggests we're dealing with somebody psychotic. And the guy cut off the victim's hands, but he made a mess of that too. Probably didn't have the right tools."

As I finished reading, Gloria's voice came on the P A system, announcing lunch. But the way my stomach was churning, I knew I'd better pass. I stared at the news story until I couldn't stand to look any longer, then folded the paper closed. But the front page with its banner headline and its mug shot of Franco Vanelli was just as bad, so I folded it once more, with the back-page sports story facing out, then placed it on top of my in-basket. Then I bent over the desktop and cradled my head in my folded arms for a catnap, just the way my first-grade teacher taught me. But I felt too edgy, too vulnerable to close my eyes and let down my guard. Too many loose ends, too many horrific images were ricocheting around in my brain.

Still, I must have spaced out for a little while, because when the phone rang right next to my head, it startled me violently. Groggily, I waited for Gloria to pick up, and it took several rings for me to realize it was my inside line.

It was Dennis Malone. "Hello, Erika? I'm glad I caught you in."

"Oh, hi, Dennis. What's up?" Then I remembered. "You must be calling about Gertrude Reynolds. Thanks for getting back to me. How did the interview go?"

"Well, she was pleasant and cooperative, but unfortunately she can't be considered a reliable witness. There were too many gaps and contradictions in her story. She was pretty confused, and both Detective Olstead and I believe she suffers from dementia."

"You're probably right. But people with dementia can have episodes of lucidity."

"That's true, Erika. And she may even have seen something suspicious from her window. But it would be awfully difficult to build a legal case around it. For starters, we'd need to get a psychiatric evaluation to determine whether she's competent to testify."

"That's an excellent idea, Dennis. When are you going to do it?"

"I'm not sure. There's a lot going on right now. The Franco Vanelli case, for one. Sergeant Golson informed me you identified him as your assailant."

"That's right. I'm virtually positive."

"Now that he's been murdered, the case is under my jurisdiction. I'd like to come over to the club and ask a few questions. How's this afternoon, say in half an hour?"

I wasn't up for this. "I'm kind of swamped with work," I said lamely. "Tomorrow would be better."

"We should do it today. It won't take long."

Just then the door opened without warning. Startled, Rishi exploded to his feet, barking, as Arthur cracked the door a few inches, just enough to peer in at me and keep Rishi from getting at him. "Just a minute, Arthur, I'm on the phone," I called. "I'll be out to see you in a minute."

"Okay." He waved a fistful of newspapers through the gap. "I got some extra copies of the *News*, plus the *Post*." He pulled the door shut and was gone.

"I'm glad to hear you've got your guard dog with you," Dennis said in my ear. "I heard you say the name Arthur. Would that be Zapata, by any chance? I mean Arthur Drummond?"

"The very same."

"See if you can keep him around until I get there, along with any other club members who are there. But don't tell them I'm coming, all right?"

"But why . . . "

"See you soon, Erika." He hung up before I could get in another word.

Chapter 21

A s soon as Dennis hung up on me, I locked Rishi in my office and went in search of Arthur. I found him in the group room, the tabloids spread out on the round table before him as he regaled the members with gory details of how the creep who assaulted Erika Norgren had gotten what he deserved.

Arthur would have been furious if he'd realized he was aiding and abetting the police by doing exactly what they wanted: preventing people from leaving the club. I counted eleven members, all sitting spellbound.

No one saw me come in; they were too engrossed in Arthur's narrative. He spoke with dramatic flair, like a preacher describing Satan's descent into hell. "Like John Lennon said, instant karma's gonna get you." He chopped the air with his hand, like the blade of a guillotine crashing down. "For Franco Vanelli, retribution wasn't instant, but it was close enough. This was his karma, to be slashed and stabbed to death in a dark alley, for what he did to defenseless women like Erika Norgren."

Defenseless? No way! This had gone far enough. "Excuse me, Arthur," I said. "Since you mentioned my name, I'd like to join the discussion."

Stan spoke up. "It isn't a discussion, it's a monologue. Arthur's on a tear about this news story. He won't shut up about it."

Arthur glared at Stan, opened his mouth to speak, then evidently thought better of it and subsided into silence. Given Arthur's usually explosive temper, I was surprised at his self-control.

If I could keep a heated debate going for twenty minutes or so, everyone would still be here when the police showed up. I found myself a seat. "Karma's an interesting concept," I said. "But I don't know if it applies in this situation. How do other people feel about it?"

"I think it fits pretty well," said Gloria. "It's like 'an eye for an eye, a tooth for a tooth,' right?"

"Not exactly," said Stan. "Karma is more like 'what goes around, comes around.'"

Germaine piped up in her squeaky voice. "I thought karma was the name of a car, like Honda."

They ignored her. "But in this case, what came around was a little more drastic than what went around," said Phil Lafferty, wiping his Buddy Holly glasses. "I mean, assault is a despicable crime, but it hardly justifies murder."

They were off and running. To my surprise, Arthur opted out of the discussion. He retrieved his newspapers, stacked them neatly on the table, then sat there in glowering silence, one hand drumming restlessly on the scarred wood. He avoided my gaze, and I suspected he was annoyed that I'd redirected the beam of the limelight away from him.

I jumped at the sudden feel of a hand on my shoulder, turned to see Dennis Malone crouching beside my chair. "No need to disturb the discussion," he murmured. "We'll just listen in." Behind him stood a plain-clothes detective I hadn't seen before. A thirtyish woman with red hair cut short and shaggy, she would have looked right at home working in any of the media or arts. Intercepting my glance, she nodded and gave me a tight smile.

Arthur spotted them. Gloria followed his stare and jumped up. "Sorry, I'm usually at the front desk, but I didn't know anyone was coming. May I help you?"

The woman introduced herself as Detective Diane Olstead. The room fell silent, all eyes turned our way.

I wasn't sure how to explain this drop-in visit from the law, but Dennis took over. "I believe I've met most of you, but I'm Detective Dennis Malone, and this is Detective Diane Olstead. You're probably aware of the murder of Franco Vanelli. In fact, I know you are because there's a copy of today's *Daily News* right on the table, and the story made the front page. That's what they call skilled detective work." He smiled disarmingly, but no one smiled back.

He continued more formally. "In a case like this, we need to follow up on every person who has even a remote connection to the deceased. Prior to his murder, Ms. Norgren identified the victim as the man who assaulted her recently on St. Marks Place. We don't know whether it was a random attack or whether he knew who she was. But we need to investigate whether Franco Vanelli was connected in any way to someone at the club. We'll be speaking with each of you individually. Don't worry, it shouldn't take long." He turned to me. "Now, Ms. Norgren, I'd appreciate it if you could show me a couple of offices we can use."

"Mine and Susan Harvey's would be best. They have the most privacy."

"Okay, lead the way." Turning back toward the club members, he gave them a casual wave. "Thanks, folks. Don't go anywhere."

Once we were out in the hallway, he was all business. "Detective Olstead can use Susan's office, and I'll use yours."

"That's fine, but right now Rishi's locked in my office. You might as well interview me first, and then I can take him somewhere else."

He narrowed his eyes, studied me a moment. "We're going to save you for later. And I'm going to have Diane interview you in the other office."

"But Dennis, since I already know you, wouldn't it make more sense for *you* to interview me?"

His lips twitched in annoyance. "I'm calling the shots here, Erika, and I think it would be better for you to meet with Diane. In the meantime, why don't you take Rishi to the group room. There's a phone there with an intercom, right?"

I nodded, feeling increasingly overwhelmed.

"Good. Make me a list of everyone here, with a couple of photocopies. That way Diane and I can call you when we're ready for the next person. I don't want to leave your offices unattended while we're walking back and forth. We'll also need a complete roster of the club's members so we can contact the people who aren't here."

Slowly, as the realization sank in that this was more than a casual social call, the sensation that had started as a mild twinge of nervousness was escalating toward a full-fledged anxiety attack.

———

Over an hour later, I still hadn't met with Diane Olstead, but Dennis's game plan was keeping me moderately distracted. What with answering the phone, reassuring nervous club members, making sure no one left the room, and escorting people to and from the two offices, I had no time to spare for fruitless worrying. Even so, the butterflies in my stomach kept sending up alarm signals, and the Tums I kept sending to calm them down weren't having much of an effect. I didn't even have Rishi as a stress reducer; I had entrusted him to Gloria so he wouldn't interfere with my duties as a receptionist for the two officers.

Two more club members wandered in, making an unlucky total of thirteen. But what about Susan and all the other members who weren't here? This could go on and on, and what was the point? I was virtually positive no one here had any connection with Franco Vanelli.

The intercom buzzed, and Diane asked for Gloria. I went to her office to summon her. "I'd better give you back your puppy," Gloria said as she passed me Rishi's leash. "I can cope with finding Susan's room."

I locked the front door with the deadbolt, then led Rishi back to the group room to rejoin Arthur. He glanced up, then turned his chair away in silence. Strange, I thought. What with this endless waiting, I would have expected him to start ranting about the sorry state of law enforcement. Instead he sat motionless, hunched over the newspapers on the table, his body language sending out an unmistakable "do not disturb" signal.

After an excruciating interval of silence, Gloria returned. "Erika, Detective Olstead asked me to tell you she can see you now. And Arthur, Detective Malone is ready for you as well." She grinned. "Don't worry, guys, it's a piece of cake."

I pushed myself slowly out of my chair, and Arthur followed suit. "Gloria, can you take Rishi back up to your office while I'm in there?" I asked. "I bolted the front door, but if anyone rings, you can let them in."

"Sure, no problem."

Gloria led Rishi away. Then Arthur and I exited the group room and proceeded up the stairs. Just before entering the two offices for our separate but equal interviews, we exchanged a long, loaded glance. I sensed feelings flickering in his eyes – anger, fear, maybe pride – but as for what he was actually thinking, I didn't have a clue.

Diane Olstead greeted me cordially. "I realize you've been through this with Sergeant Golson," she said, "but I'd like you to walk me through everything that happened that night when you were attacked on St. Marks Place. Tell me in detail, as if I'd never heard it before. You never know, some fresh information may emerge."

Her blue eyes were warm and sympathetic as she listened, and I felt increasingly at ease in her presence. As I approached the end of my narrative, I realized how silly I'd been to waste so much energy on needless worry. We were almost finished, and it hadn't been bad at all.

"One more question," she said. "On the day you identified the alleged assailant, what did you do after you left the police station?"

"Let's see. I was feeling upbeat about having identified my attacker, and I walked Rishi back to the club, just to touch base with people. That would have been about three thirty."

"And did you find anyone to touch base with?"

"Yes. Most of the members had left, but Stan, Gloria and Arthur were still around."

"Do you recall what you talked about with them?"

"The Channel 8 newscast the night before, and I told them I had identified the person who – " I stopped short as the realization hit me. "Oh, my God! You don't think that possibly – "

She leaned forward, her face impassive, every inch the professional, but her eyes betrayed her. An imperceptible widening, a sudden gleam – I sensed the excitement of the hunt. "Go on, Erika," she said softly. "It's all right."

From long experience, I know that when people say, "It's all right," they usually mean exactly the opposite. Nonetheless, I plunged onward. "I told them I had identified the man who attacked me, and I told them his name, Franco Vanelli. I thought they should know in case he showed up at the club and threatened somebody else. I told them that if he showed up, they should call the police immediately. But that was stupid, I had no right . . ."

She touched my arm gently. "Don't put yourself down, Erika. You had every right. It sounds as if you shared information in an appropriate way, doing what you thought was necessary to safeguard the club and its members. But you seem upset all of a sudden. What's so distressing to you?"

I took a deep breath, then another. Maybe I should stop, call a lawyer. But why? I hadn't done anything wrong. "What if someone decided to avenge what had happened to me? Maybe not one of those guys, but there's this man I've been dating, Kevin Winthrop. I told him about Vanelli too."

"Do you think any of these men would have the motivation to avenge something done to you?"

I buried my head in my hands, buying myself time to think. Stan? He liked me a lot. He wasn't obsessive about me; there wasn't any chemistry there, at least on my side. But how could I be sure? He kept his feelings under tight wraps most of the time, but he had an intense sense of loyalty and a hair-trigger temper. Arthur, on the other hand, had been all too outspoken about his feelings for me and his anger at my attacker. Then there was Kevin, still an enigma. He was drawn to me, I knew, but was it me he saw, or his sister Barbara?

"Erika? Are you all right?"

I kept my hands to my face and mumbled something noncommittal through my fingers. I couldn't bear the thought that any of the three men had been responsible for Franco Vanelli's murder, and yet I couldn't unequivocally rule any of them out. If I aroused the suspicions of the NYPD about any one of them, I had no idea how he would react, but I was reasonably certain I didn't want to be around to find out.

No, wait a minute. I'd told Kevin about Franco Vanelli just last night, and the murder was splashed across the tabloids this morning. Surely there wouldn't have been time –

The intercom buzzed just as I heard footsteps stomping toward my door. I picked up. "Ocala's here to see you," said Gloria. "I told her you were with the Detective, but I couldn't stop her."

The door flew open and Ocala charged in. "What the fuck is going on here?"

"We're interviewing everyone at the club about the death of Franco Vanelli," said the Detective.

"Who the hell is that?"

"A man with underworld connections who was murdered yesterday. I'm Detective Diane Olstead. And you are?"

"Ocala St. Claire. Executive Director of Compassion House. Ms. Norgren's boss. Would you mind telling me what this murder has to do with WellSpring Club?"

"Probably nothing. We're just exploring some possibilities." To my enormous relief, Detective Olstead took control. By the time she'd finished a concise summary of the situation, Ocala had regained her cool.

All too soon the Detective rose. "Thanks, Erika. I've got what I need for today, but we'll talk again tomorrow."

Don't leave me, I wanted to shout. *I'd rather endure a police interrogation than a confrontation with my boss.* But apparently I had no say in the matter.

"I came by to touch base with you about a couple of things," Ocala said as soon as the Detective had closed the door behind her. "First of all, how are you holding up with everything that's been going on? You told me about that abduction attempt, but we haven't had a chance to talk since."

"I'm hanging in there. Thanks for asking."

"I caught that interview the members did with Nancy Welcome. I didn't want the members talking on camera, but all in all I've got to admit it came off pretty well. Thank God Stan and Arthur are such articulate spokespersons for the club."

They're also prime suspects in a murder investigation. "Yes, they're something else, aren't they? Speaking of spokespersons, Ocala, I've been meaning to ask you about those Community Board Meetings. A woman who lives across the street has been distributing fliers urging people to attend next Tuesday in order to speak out against the club. Do you think I should go with some of the members, maybe check out what's happening?"

"Why not?" She chuckled. "Actually, I can think of a lot of reasons why not. But what the hell, go for it. Just do me a favor and don't get into any shouting matches."

Why was she acting so mellow? Don't ask, I told myself. Just take advantage.

"By the way, Ocala, what about a memorial service for Jeff Archer? We haven't had one yet."

"Memorializing a junky? That's not such a hot idea, Erika. It would just pull in all the media vultures and accentuate the negative all over again." She played with the rings on her fingers a moment. "But maybe you could pay tribute to him by dedicating the mural when you have the cabaret. How's that going, anyway?"

"It was going fine, but it came to a screeching halt when Jeff died. You think we should still go ahead with it?"

"By all means. It was a good idea when you first proposed it, and it's still a good idea. I already have it on my calendar. Friday, October 26th, right?"

"Right."

"As I recall, we talked about how it would generate some positive energy and PR for the club. That's truer than ever now. That is, if you're up for it."

When she put it that way, I could hardly wimp out and refuse. "Okay," I said with all the enthusiasm I could muster. "Full steam ahead."

Chapter 22

When Ocala left, I let out a gargantuan sigh of relief. I was leaning back in my chair, taking a few minutes to center myself, when I heard Rishi's whining outside the door, then Gloria's voice. "Erika? Everyone else is gone, so Stan and I are leaving, but we didn't want to abandon you."

"Thanks, Gloria. Come on in."

As she opened the door, she let go of Rishi's leash. He rushed toward me, sniffed me over, then put his forepaws on my lap and licked my cheeks slowly and thoroughly. At least somebody knew I needed some TLC.

All at once I remembered: Stan Washington was a suspect. "Stan? I thought he already left."

Stan's hulking figure loomed in the doorway. "I was waiting outside on the stoop. I didn't want to leave you ladies alone with just Arthur and the cops."

Susan's office was enveloped in late-afternoon shadow, and I couldn't make out the expression on his dark face. Did he realize he was under suspicion? If he did, he gave no sign. In any case, the thought of staying on at the club alone was unnerving, so I asked Stan and Gloria to wait, and the three of us locked up and left together. Once outside, I assured them I'd be fine walking home with Rishi. We walked to the corner and said our farewells. Then Rishi and I turned north and headed for home.

Fall was in the air, and even the flower display outside the bodega looked autumnal, with masses of chrysanthemums in hues of gold and russet orange, accented here and there by a diminished supply of summery hothouse blooms for those in denial about the coming of winter.

"Hey, Erika, wait up! I see you've still got your taste for flowers."

Arthur took me so completely by surprise, I emitted an embarrassing yelp. "Damn it, Arthur, you startled me. What are you doing here?"

"I wanted to talk with you, and I know you walk home this way."

So he knew where I lived? I shuddered, hoped he didn't notice. "To be honest, I'm kind of talked out," I said.

"Me too. Those cops were something else, weren't they? You must have had a lot more to say than I did, because you were still in there with that detective when I was already done. What did she ask you about?" He was wearing impenetrably black wrap-around shades, so I couldn't read his eyes.

"Mostly about the sequence of events the day I was attacked, things like that."

"Did she ask who you told after you identified the creep?"

My heart began hammering in double-time rhythm. "There may have been something about that. I don't remember exactly."

He ripped off his shades with one hand, grabbed my arm with the other, moving so quickly that Rishi growled. Arthur dropped my arm. "Jeez! Don't worry, pooch, I'm not going to hurt your old lady." His eyes drilled into mine, and he spoke softly with contained venom. "I figure that bitch must have asked who you told, because her crony

Detective Malone was asking along similar lines. And I bet you gave her my name and Stan's."

"But Arthur." I tried for a pitiful, ingenuous tone. "I don't understand. What difference does it make who I told about Franco Vanelli?"

"Don't insult me, Erika. I'm not stupid. Whoever you told, you were giving the guy a motive to murder the creep. Especially if he really cared about you, didn't want to see you in harm's way, and was willing to put his life on the line for you."

I shivered, although the night wasn't that cold. "That sounds kind of far-fetched," I protested. "Maybe that kind of thing happens on TV or in the movies, but I can't see it happening for real."

"Why not? You're worthy of such devotion, Milady." He took my hand and bent as if to kiss it, but Rishi growled again. Arthur straightened and let go. "Your hand is cold, Erika, and you're trembling. You're not afraid, are you? There's no need. I'd never do anything to hurt you."

I forced a smile. "I know that, Arthur. Anyway, there were other people I saw and spoke with later that night, people I told about Franco Vanelli, and I gave the detective all of their names. And there are probably lots of other people who had it in for this guy. Chances are this murder has absolutely nothing to do with me or anyone else at the club. So you don't have to worry about suspicion falling only on you and Stan."

He smiled. "I'm relieved. Just out of curiosity, who else did you tell?"

Kevin's name was on my tongue, but I bit it back. Talking with Arthur, the fear that had begun back in my office was feeding on itself and growing stronger: by sharing Franco Vanelli's name I had quite possibly signed his death warrant. "I don't think it's relevant," I said, "and these people value their privacy. I gave the police their names, and I'm sure they'll follow up. In fact, they're probably tracking them down even as we speak. Now if you'll excuse me, Arthur, I need to hurry." I glanced at my watch. "Oh my God, I'm late. I have a date, and he's probably already waiting for me at my place."

"Why don't I walk you home anyway."

"Thanks, but I'll be fine. I've got Rishi with me, and if we hurry, I'll have just enough time to get in my evening jog. See you tomorrow!" Before Arthur could protest, I took off at a trot. I forced myself not to look back, but as I took great gulps of the cool autumn air, I swore I could feel his steely eyes boring into my back.

———————

Alas, my alleged date was only a spur-of-the-moment invention. Alone in my apartment, I realized how much I would have welcomed company. The blinking red light on my answering machine lured me over to check my messages. The digital display and the sepulchral male voice in the box both told me there was just one. I pressed the Play button, and to my delight, I heard the low, husky voice of Mark Levitan. "Just checking in," he said. "Sorry I haven't been in touch, but I've been swamped with work. Let's get together soon. I'll call you tomorrow. Bye."

I played the message a second time, less for its content than for the way his voice set off good vibrations inside me. My finger was poised over the erase button, ready to strike, but at the last possible nanosecond, I jerked it away, knowing I'd want to hear that voice again. Truth be told, my life had turned so topsy turvy in the last couple of days that I'd scarcely thought about Mark, but the message brought him vividly, viscerally to mind. I realized I hadn't yet told him about identifying Franco Vanelli, much less about his murder.

I jumped up, retrieved my handbag from the sofa and rummaged through it till I found his business card, then dialed his number on the off chance that he was home. Alas, I got his machine. "Thanks for the message," I said. "I'd love to see you, Mark. I've got a lot to report.

Remember that man I saw at Romano's?" I gave him a somewhat rambling account of the events of the past two days, signed off, and poured myself a glass of Merlot. I gulped it down like water, then poured myself another. I kicked off my shoes and paced back and forth as I sipped, murmuring under my breath as Rishi dogged my footsteps.

I was sorely tempted to redial Mark's number and talk some more, maybe invite him to come over tonight, no matter what the hour. But I managed to restrain myself. I'd been long-winded enough already, and I suspected he'd be alarmed. "Pressured speech," the shrinks call it when someone runs off at the mouth too much. Mark might view it as a telltale symptom of mania. For that matter, he might be right.

I was finally starting to unwind when the phone rang. I ran over to grab it, then decided to screen the call first.

It was Kevin. "Erika, are you there? Pick up, I need to talk to you. Now! It's important."

His peremptory tone of voice triggered my rebellious streak, and I waited.

"Erika, pick up! I need to know why you sicced the cops on me!"

So that was it. Just as I'd promised Arthur, the police were already widening their net. I was sorely tempted to lay low and let Kevin rant at my machine, but he'd gone out of his way to be hospitable last night, and I owed him the courtesy of a live response. "Hi, Kevin. The police just interviewed me this afternoon. I gather they talked to you too."

"Grilled me, is more like it. You had no right to get me involved. This Franco Vanelli murder has nothing to do with me." His voice in anger had the metallic overtones of a buzz saw blade.

"I know it doesn't. They're just interviewing everyone I told about his attack on me, looking for someone who might have been motivated by revenge. As if I'm enough of a femme fatale to inspire that kind of devotion." I forced a laugh.

"Maybe you are. Don't sell yourself short, Erika." His chuckle sounded as phony as my laugh. "Anyway, I told them you had spent the night at my place because I didn't want you out there with this guy on the loose, so you've provided me a perfect alibi."

"You don't need an alibi," I said. "I mentioned your name to Detective Olstead, but then I realized you couldn't possibly have been involved. I left your apartment yesterday morning, stopped off at my place, then went to the club. Franco Vanelli's murder was all over the papers by then, and he'd already been dead awhile. So you couldn't possibly have done it."

"Gee, thanks for the vote of confidence." His tone was icy. "You suspect me of murder, then decide I'm not guilty because the timing is wrong, but you sic the cops on me anyway, just to be on the safe side. It's touching you have such faith in me."

"I didn't mean that the way it sounded; I was just thinking out loud. I would have explained it to the detective, but Ocala interrupted us and I got distracted. Detective Olstead left before I could say anything more. I'm truly sorry, Kevin. If you want, I'll call her in the morning and explain."

"I doubt that will be necessary, unless she's an idiot. But I don't like what this says about our relationship. If we even have a relationship."

———————

The talk with Kevin left me feeling unbearably edgy, so much so that I spent most of the evening cleaning my apartment, something I normally go to enormous lengths to avoid. Then I turned to my keyboard for a couple of hours. By one in the morning, still too wired to sleep, I began composing e-mail missives to friends around the country. I kept hoping to hear from Mark, but when he still hadn't called by three, I gave up and went to bed. I lay staring at the darkness for another hour before finally drifting off to sleep.

I was still groggy when I walked Rishi to WellSpring that morning. Three hours of sleep simply wasn't enough, and that's all I'd had for two nights running. I knew I was accumulating an unhealthy sleep deficit, but my internal clock seemed to be ticking speedily along without any rational input from its owner. Fixated on getting up the front steps and grabbing a gigantic mug of coffee, I didn't see the black Lincoln town car at the curb until Vito Pisanello scrambled out of it and came to a screeching halt in front of me.

I jumped. "Excuse me, I'm late for work," I said as I dodged him.

He mirrored my sidestep, moved closer. An image flashed across my inner eye – the two of us locked in an embrace, embarking on a silent fox trot. I giggled. "Sorry, but I'd rather sit this one out. It's too early in the morning for dancing."

The little man's lip curled in a crooked snarl, and I could tell he was not amused. "What are you, nuts? Cool it, Erika. I just need a few words with you."

"Okay, as long as you make it speedy." I reined Rishi in closer, planted my feet and folded my arms so as to look as imposingly grounded as possible.

"Not here," he said. "Come sit in my car with me for a couple of minutes, so we can talk privately."

Feeling suddenly ungrounded, I took a step back. "This looks like the car someone tried to pull me into not too long ago. I wouldn't get in there if my life depended on it." *Which it very well might.* I looked around for someone to scream to.

"Stop being so jumpy. Don't worry, you're not going to get hurt. The car is part of what we need to talk about. The other part is Franco Vanelli's murder. I know you saw me and him talking in the back room at Romano's the other night."

My heart lurched. "How do you know that?"

"I'll tell you, but not here. I can understand your not wanting to get in the car, so how about we go in your office?"

Curiosity triumphed over caution, and I invited him inside. Minutes later, with mugs of fresh brewed but mediocre coffee, we were ensconced in my office. "This place isn't bad," he said, scanning the room. "The original oak trim is still in pretty decent shape."

"Yes, I know." And it's not for sale, I wanted to add. "So, Vito, what did you want to talk about?"

He dropped his pretense of cordiality. "I'll be straight with you. Whoever murdered Franco Vanelli murdered a close friend of mine. I know you saw me and him at Romano's, because the waiter told me about your little spying act. The very next night, the police were all over Little Italy looking for Franco, and the day after that, he turns up dead in a dumpster. You can't tell me it's a coincidence that those things happened one right after another, boom boom boom."

I took a deep breath. "I'll be straight with you too. It was purely by accident that I saw you with Franco Vanelli. I was just checking out the restaurant's architectural details, the way you were checking out the club's just now. But then I recognized him as the man who tried to force me into a car on St. Marks Place. I identified his picture the next day at the police station, but I have absolutely no idea who killed him. I don't think the two things are related."

"Well, they're certainly not related in seriousness. A guy asks a woman to come sit in a car for a little while, but he lets her go when she protests. A couple days later, the same guy gets murdered. Wouldn't you agree that murder's kind of an extreme reaction to a harmless invitation?"

"You call physical assault a harmless invitation?" Then it dawned on me: he'd just offered me a virtual confession. "Vito, are you admitting that was your car, and that Franco Vanelli was working with you to abduct me?"

"That's ridiculous, I'm admitting no such thing." He looked momentarily worried, and I knew the confessional content of his words had dawned on him too.

"But suppose for the sake of argument that a guy does try to get a woman into his car, maybe just to talk to her about something, the way

I tried to do with you just now. He doesn't hurt her or try anything funny, and he lets her go. That's not a crime. Maybe the guy is like me: he loves his car, feels comfortable in it, thinks it's a nice, private place for a talk or whatever."

Virtually positive this hypothetical car-crazy guy was none other than Vito Pisanello himself, I decided to throw him some bait. "Suppose for whatever reason the woman agrees to get in the guy's car. What would he want to talk about?"

Vito smiled, getting into the game. "Probably something about business or the neighborhood. Like maybe she's having a negative effect on the area, encouraging an undesirable element that'll bring down property values."

I tossed him an innocent smile. "But Vito, what if he's told her the same stuff before? Why would he need to repeat it?"

He leaned forward, and his smile hardened. "Maybe she didn't get it the first time. Maybe she needs a little persuading." The smile vanished, and his beady brown eyes went dangerously dead. "Maybe she's too wacked out to realize the kind of people she's dealing with. Not just the guy with the car, but the lunatics she works with at this weird club she runs. Some of these creeps are so far out, they'd do anything for this woman. I'd be willing to bet the wacko who murdered Franco Vanelli goes to this club. He might even be here right now."

Suddenly the room felt colder, and I shivered. "How would the woman know the identity of this so-called wacko?"

"I don't know. That's your area, not mine." He had dropped the third-person pretense. "I'm just a concerned citizen, that's all. Since you've been the boss around here, too many strange things have been happening. Take those two guys who died recently – did the cops ever figure out what happened to them?"

I extended one foot cautiously onto the tightrope this conversation was turning into. "One was a suicide, and the other overdosed. Why? Do you know something I don't?"

"No, but with all the business deals I've been involved in over the years, I've learned not to take anything at face value. Your best friend in the world can turn around and stab you in the back. Maybe somebody wants you to chicken out and quit your job, or even shut the club down."

"Why would anybody want that?"

"Any number of reasons. Maybe they want to buy the building, maybe they don't want the neighborhood full of wackos. Maybe they just hate your guts, or hate your boss, Odessa what's-her-name . . ."

"Ocala St. Claire. But why would someone have it in for me or Ocala?"

"Why not? It doesn't have to make sense. This city's full of psychos, and most of them have never seen a shrink in their lives. Maybe someone's pissed about that TV show, where you told the world you were crazy, and they don't think you're fit to run the club. Look, Erika, I'm just giving you my opinion here, for what it's worth, take it or leave it. But if I was you, I'd think seriously about looking around for a new job, maybe even a new life. Someplace like California." He pushed back his chair, extracted a business card from his jacket pocket and slapped it down on my desk. "Take care now, and let me know if you need anything."

Putting his hands on the chair arms for leverage, he hoisted his body erect, then rummaged in his jacket for another card. "Give this one to your boss. With the run of bad luck you've been having, you might want to think about selling this building. If you do, I'm prepared to make you an excellent offer."

Chapter 23

*O*nce Vito was safely out the door, I sat motionless, taking long, slow breaths in hopes of damping down the adrenaline surging through my body. But the extra hit of oxygen only fanned the flames still higher. In exasperation, I drummed my fists on the desk so forcefully that Rishi jumped out and stared at me in alarm. "It's all right, love," I told him as I rubbed his ears. "I was just expressing myself."

Expressing myself was something I'd studiously avoided during Vito Pisanello's visit. Had I said even half the things on my mind, our meeting would have escalated into open warfare. How dare he tell me to quit my job and move to California? Was this his lust for real estate speaking, or did he truly believe I was in danger? Either way, I refused to be panicked into taking flight.

"Good morning, everyone. Time for the community meeting."

Gloria's lilting voice on the PA system derailed my thoughts onto another track. The cabaret! Despite everything, Ocala still wanted it to happen. So, I realized, did I. Now I needed to make sure the club members were still on board. Leaving Rishi locked in my office, I hurried down to the group room.

Their reactions were mixed. Stan was especially dubious, but I threw all the pent-up emotional energy I'd been expending on Vito into persuading them the cabaret should happen, and before long they came around.

Gloria was especially delighted. "What with Jeff's death and all, I wasn't sure what was happening," she said. "But I've been jotting down ideas in a steno book, and I've got a whole list of possible acts."

Stan cleared his throat conspicuously. "If we're really going ahead with this thing, I'll volunteer as director. Or producer, whatever you want to call it. In other words, I'll take on the organizational piece of it and help keep things on track. With Erika's approval, of course."

"What about everyone else's approval?" asked Arthur, who had just arrived.

Stan made a harumphing noise. "That goes without saying."

"Just checking," said Arthur. "It's cool with me as long as I can still be emcee."

Germaine piped up. "And I still want to sing "Raindrops Keep Falling on My Head."

They were off and running. I settled back to listen as people described what they might do during their five minutes of fame.

"Ocala has approved a few hundred dollars for expenses," I said after a lull. "We need to discuss how we'll use it for food, decorations, invitations, that kind of thing. I'd like to invite the media and see if we can generate some positive publicity for WellSpring."

"Sounds good to me," said Gloria. "How about inviting some people from the music business? There are so many talented people here, maybe a label would want to sign somebody. Kind of like *American Idol*. Let's invite Paula Abdul, or that guy Simon."

"No, not Simon," said Germaine. "He's mean and nasty."

I stifled a laugh. "Let's see how the performance shapes up before we get too ambitious."

"Yeah, Gloria," said Arthur. "In other words, don't go getting delusional and thinking you actually have any talent."

Gloria's jaw dropped and her eyes began to fill, but Stan came to her rescue. "Watch your mouth, Arthur. Gloria has a beautiful singing voice, but even if she didn't, you've got no right to put her down."

"Stan's right," I said. "No one should be criticizing anyone else; this is an equal opportunity performance."

Stan cut in. "Hey, Erika, we've got company. Did you invite this guy?"

Following his gaze to the unannounced visitor poised in the doorway, I felt a jolt of joy. Our guest was none other than Mark. He was looking strikingly attractive, dressed casually but elegantly in deep blues and grays that set off his dark hair and strong features.

"This is Mark Levitan," I said to the room at large. "He's a well-known advocate for consumers' rights and an expert on issues related to society's attitude toward mental illness. This is a wonderful surprise, Mark. Did you stop by to tell us what you're up to lately?"

He smiled. "Not really. I'm just here with some information for Ms. Norgren, but it can wait till your meeting is over."

"Come on in. Sit down and join us," said Gloria, patting the sofa cushion beside her. When he accepted her invitation, I swear she levitated at least two inches in the air. Then again, maybe I was just projecting.

"Now, where were we?" My question was more than rhetorical; Mark's sudden arrival had shattered my concentration.

"*American Idol*," said Arthur.

"Oh, that's right. Thanks, Arthur. I need to touch base with Mark now, but it sounds like you're all on a roll, so don't stop the discussion on my account."

"What's this about a show?" asked Mark. We were walking side by side down the narrow hall to my office, our bodies almost touching, and I was sorely tempted to close the professional distance between us.

Before I could explain about the cabaret, we were at my door. I unlocked and opened it, then stood waiting as Rishi came bounding out from beneath my desk and greeted us ecstatically. Mark rubbed the dog's ears, eliciting blissful groans, then stood erect and gazed into my eyes. "Actually, the show can wait," he said. "I'm here because I'm worried about you. That message you left last night was pretty disturbing. Are you all right?"

"Not really." My memory of last night's message was hazy, so I took it from the top and rehashed the happenings of the past couple of days – Franco Vanelli's murder, the police inquisitions, my frightening encounter with Arthur Drummond, Vito Pisanello's unnerving visit.

"No wonder you sounded so uptight," he said. "I wish I could help. Can you get away for lunch? Maybe we can find someplace more private to talk."

"I'd love to, but I'd better not. The club members are awfully observant, and I think a couple of them have rather strong transference feelings. You know, they project all sorts of emotions and associations onto me, and – "

He laughed. "I know all about transference, Erika. No need to explain. How about tonight? I could come by your place at seven, and we'll take it from there."

"That would be great." Great was an understatement. Gazing into his hazel eyes, I had an urge to throw my arms around him, to kiss him, but I managed to retrain myself.

"Will you be okay till then?" he asked. "You're acting kind of giddy and euphoric. It's charming, but you know it can be a precursor – "

The lust evaporated, replaced by rage. I cut in impatiently. "A precursor of mania. I know, I know. And manic episodes can be brought on by stress, and I'm under a lot of stress. I'm well aware of all that, but I believe I have everything under control. Or rather, I have myself under control, but I can't be responsible for all the craziness around me."

His eyes narrowed. "Meaning what?"

"Don't look at me that way. You think I'm paranoid, don't you?"

"I didn't say that. Look, Erika, I don't think this is the time or place for this discussion. I'd better go. But let me give you my cell phone number. That way you can reach me anytime."

"In case I'm going crazy, you mean?"

He rested both hands on my shoulders, gave me a quick kiss on the forehead. "Crazy's just a word, a relative term. It doesn't scare me."

I wrapped my arms around him, pulled him close for a quick hug, then let go. "Good. See you at seven."

———————

Maybe crazy was just a word to Mark, but it was a scary one to me. I was exhibiting some classic danger signs: sleeping too little, talking and thinking too fast about too many things, inventing grandiose schemes and convincing other people to buy into them through the sheer energy of my enthusiasm. *What we have here*, I thought, *is a storm watch, not a storm warning.* In the parlance of TV weathermen, it's a watch when there's the possibility of a flood or a tornado, a warning when the dreaded event is dead certain. What a brilliant analogy! My cleverness brought on a fit of the giggles – inappropriate affect, another warning sign. *No, not a warning, only a watch. Nothing to worry about.*

Besides, these subtle signs of mania could be considered signs of creativity. Many of the world's most brilliant artists, composers and writers exhibited manic behavior, whether they were formally diagnosed or not. When it came to acting manic, I was in the exalted company of genius.

The very fact that I could step back and scrutinize my own behavior objectively meant there was no cause for alarm. During my handful of full-blown manic episodes, I'd been convinced of the absolute rightness of my every word and deed. Now, I was still capable of entertaining a smidgen of doubt.

———

After work, I was much too wired to head straight home and wait for Mark, and the weather was ideal for an exploratory meander. The air had the bittersweet balminess of Indian summer, with the instant nostalgia that came from knowing that winter's frigid darkness lay ahead.

"Come on, Rishi, let's stroll over to Washington Square and see my old alma mater," I said as we left the building. We headed west toward the park that had been the centerpiece of the old Greenwich Village. The landmark arch still stood proudly, and old men still played chess and checkers at cement tables in the southwest corner. The buildings of New York University loomed to the east and south. Beyond the park, the school's tentacles invaded the Village like a metastasizing tumor, gobbling up old hunks of real estate in its hunger for growth.

I didn't have fond memories of the place. I arrived an outspoken, slightly kooky musician, but my personal style was at odds with the self-contained, professional demeanor expected of social workers. I emerged with my MSW, but my passage through the graduate social work program was like two years in a sausage factory, where a core part of my personality was ground to bits, mixed with foreign ingredients, then stuffed into a smooth new skin that squeezed just a little too tight.

Just looking at the library sent waves of panic rocketing through my system. A gargantuan box sheathed in pink and black granite, the place had triggered some of the worst anxiety attacks of my life. Cramming for exams or researching papers, I spent my breaks pacing around the stacks, trying to avoid the enormous atrium that pierced the heart of the building. But time and again something lured me to the railings of smoked glass and chrome, where I peered into the cavernous space and wondered how many students had hurled themselves over the edge onto the stone floor far below. How could the architects have been so oblivious to the danger of a design that made suicide such an elegant, effortless option?

Rishi nuzzled my hand, and I snapped back to reality. "Thank you, baby," I said as I rubbed his ears. "That was a bad space I was getting into, and I wasn't even inside the building."

We headed through the park and onto LaGuardia Place, the broad street that headed south toward SoHo. Wooden sawhorses blocked off traffic, and on either side, vendors hawked jewelry, candles, and fruit smoothies. Up above, a banner proclaimed the event a "New Age Health Fair."

What a perfect way to exorcise those nasty old images! I guided Rishi around the barriers and down the street between the booths. Halfway down the block, a young Oriental man stepped toward me. "Massage? Special bargain! Only ten dollars. Very relaxing, good for you."

Behind him stood a massage chair, all chrome and padded black vinyl, the kind where you straddle a bench, lean forward and place your head in a horseshoe cushion, staring down at the ground. The device seemed tailor made for an S & M flick, and the thought of being so powerless out on the streets of New York was terrifying. "No, I don't think so," I said.

As I passed half a dozen men with similar chairs lined up one after the other, all shouting out promises of instant bliss, I felt a twinge of regret. I needed desperately to relax, to still the thoughts racing through my mind, and maybe a massage would have helped. I was well into a stretch of craftspeople when I saw another phalanx of masseurs ahead. I set out to walk the gauntlet, resolving to surrender my body to the hands of the first masseur who caught my fancy.

The third man won, less for his sales pitch than for his lithe good looks and the graceful way he moved. I knotted Rishi's leash around the base of the apparatus, ordered him to lie down and stay, then straddled the contraption and dropped my head face down inside its purple padded ring. The white paper toweling around the headpiece and on the seat assuaged my squeamishness about anonymous bodily fluids, but I felt awkward and vulnerable sprawled there so helplessly, staring down at the pavement. But before long, my misgivings melted away under the ministrations of the man's magical fingers. I could easily get addicted to this, I reflected as I surrendered to the pleasures of being stroked, pummeled and kneaded.

When he reached my neck and shoulders, the pleasure yielded to pain, and I gave an involuntary yelp. Rishi jumped up to see if I needed rescuing, and I took a moment to reassure him.

"Your muscles are very tight," said the young man. "Too much stress in your life, weight of world on your shoulders? Take deep breaths; that will help break down tension and expel toxins from your system. Tension very toxic, bad for mental health."

"I know." I let out a gigantic sigh. He was right: deep breathing did help. There was less pain now, less tension, and my body was becoming steadily weaker, succumbing to a profound passivity. All at once I flashed on that dream of drowning in the depths of the ocean, the dream where Jeff was tempting me to join him in death. I moaned, began to weep.

The hands withdrew. "That's enough for one day," said the soft voice at my ear.

Slowly and cautiously, I sat up and looked around. "You weren't hurting me," I said between sobs. "You helped the physical pain go away. This was more like pain of the soul."

"Ah yes, I understand. Many times that kind of soul pain accumulates in the body like poison. It steals your energy and diminishes your life force. Massage can help rid your body of the poison, but you have to do it regularly, like once a week."

I saw where he was headed, but I didn't mind. At ten dollars a session, this was a lot cheaper than psychotherapy, and maybe more effective. Sure enough, he extracted a business card from his pocket; it bore his name, "holistic massage," and an address in Chinatown. "Call me," he said, flashing a beguiling smile.

"I just might do that," I said. "But I can't promise not to cry."

After the massage, my body felt as jointless as Jell-O. I wafted down the street in a state of euphoria, feeling as floaty as a balloon in Macy's Thanksgiving Parade. Heading back toward the East Village, I broke into a spontaneous skip. Beside me, Rishi bounced and pranced with delight.

A trendy young couple, fashionably emaciated and dressed in black, eyed me strangely. He murmured something in her ear and they both laughed, then averted their eyes as if I presented a threat. When my skipping elicited similar reactions from the next few pedestrians, I realized I'd better stifle my girlish glee. If I truly wanted to skip in public, there were two ways to carry it off. I could don serious exercise garb, running shoes, and an intense, no-nonsense expression, and pretend skipping was the latest fashion in fitness. Or I could dress in a gingham jumper and red shoes like Dorothy in *The Wizard of Oz*, and hand out fliers explaining that I was immersed in a performance piece. The images made me laugh. Even so, I had the good sense to stop skipping.

I managed to rein in the physical exuberance freed up by the massage, but in short order all that energy redirected itself back to my brain. I began obsessing about Stephen and Jeff. Their deaths still haunted me, and the official investigation was going nowhere. Was the cabaret just a cop-out, a way of distracting myself from what really mattered?

Suddenly an idea struck me with such force, I came to a dead stop. "Yes!" I shouted. A couple of passers-by eyed me strangely and edged further away on the sidewalk.

The cabaret would be an ideal way of drawing fresh attention to the club. From our referral sources, from the media, and most of all, from the killer, assuming there even was one. People would be coming out of the woodwork to watch the performance, and I, in turn, would have the perfect opportunity to watch the people, maybe pick up some clues as to who had the motivation to murder Stephen and Jeff.

———————

I was still feeling giddy when Mark arrived at my apartment an hour later. He gave me a hug, then backed off to look at me. "How are you doing, Erika?" he asked. "How was the rest of your day at WellSpring?"

"Fine. And I had a dynamite massage on the way home, from this adorable Oriental man on LaGuardia Place. You should try one. It's only ten dollars, and he's probably still there. We could go right now."

"Wait a minute, slow down. I'm not in the mood for a massage right now." He narrowed his eyes and gave me the scrutinizing stare I was learning presaged a lecture. "Are you sure this cabaret project isn't going to be too much for you?"

"No, I can do it. And I realized after the massage that it could be a terrific way to bring the bad guys out of hiding, maybe reel in the person or persons who murdered Stephen and Jeff."

"That's pretty off the wall. Not to mention dangerous."

"The police have done diddly squat. I've got to do something."

"Cut the police some slack, Erika. Give them time. You could be putting yourself at risk, not to mention the club members."

"I won't do anything obvious. I'll just be super-observant, see if anyone unexpected shows up. Maybe pick up some clues."

"I suppose I won't be able to stop you. But Erika, I'm concerned about you. You're still sounding awfully hyper. Have you seen your shrink lately? Had your lithium level checked?"

"Damn it, Mark, stop being so solicitous. My shrink does nothing but write me a prescription every three months. He's only interested in my lithium level, and he only cares about that because he doesn't want me going into renal failure or experiencing some other horrible side effect he might get sued for."

"Maybe you should consider switching shrinks. There's a friend of mine who's a whiz with psychopharmacology, but he's also sensitive to individual needs. He doesn't just write prescriptions; he treats the whole person, body and soul."

"I'm doing okay, I swear it. But it's sweet of you to be so concerned." I moved closer and nestled against his chest, then twined my arms around his neck and pulled him toward me for a kiss.

His lips clung to mine for a fabulous moment. Then he extricated himself from my embrace. "You're a wonderful woman, Erika. I'm really attracted to you."

His eyes were aglow, and his breath was coming in short gasps, so I knew he was telling the truth. But I guessed a disclaimer would follow. Sure enough, it did. "I don't think this is a good idea right now," he said.

My own breath was none too steady. "Why not? I feel the same way about you, and we're both consenting adults. At least we could be."

"I agree. But you're awfully vulnerable right now, with all this stress you're under, and I don't want to take advantage. Let's slow down, get to know each other better."

I felt like crying in frustration, but I laughed instead. "Damn it, Mark, what's going on here? That's supposed to be the woman's line."

Chapter 24

*F*rustration tolerance was never my strong point, but I realized Mark was right. With everything else that was going on, a torrid affair could send me spiraling into a total meltdown. We had exactly three weeks to pull the cabaret together, not to mention the open house for which the performance would be the centerpiece. Maybe we could have shoved the date forward into November, but I really wanted Ocala to be there, and the 26th was the last possible date before her vacation. I convinced myself we had plenty of time.

The dinner with Mark was fabulous, but I came home ready to climb the walls. I spent Saturday and Sunday sublimating all my pent-up sexual energy into creating a master plan for the cabaret. The timetable should be just about right. In the coming week, I'd help people develop their acts. I'd launch a publicity campaign with press releases and public service announcements. We'd send out invitations, and Stan could help nail down the logistics. That would leave two weeks to coach the performers and fine-tune the details.

More than enough time, if everything went right. But that was a gargantuan *if*.

Meanwhile, what about my grand entrapment scheme? How could I use the cabaret to catch whoever had murdered Stephen and Jeff? Be alert, take care with the guest list, track the visitors – what else could I do? And I needed to clear the air with Stan and Arthur. Both had essential roles in the cabaret, and both were still suspects in Franco Vanelli's murder. No way could I work closely with them if I was in a state of perpetual suspicion.

I decided to start with Stan. First thing Monday, I'd ask him to go with me to the Community Board Meeting Tuesday night. Flatter him, butter him up a little, then ease into the subject of the murders.

I knew it wouldn't be easy – not with a paranoid schizophrenic. And sure enough, I was right. Stan was well compensated, stable on medication, but when I brought up the subject of last week's police interrogations, he turned so guarded and hypervigilant, I could almost see the antennae shoot straight up out of his head and start swiveling.

His dark face went even darker. "Are you implying I had anything to do with that mobster's murder?"

"Not at all, Stanley. But we haven't had a chance to really talk since those detectives were here, and I thought we should clear the air."

"Clear the air? That's hopeless if you ask me; it's already too polluted. Malone and that lady detective paid me a house call Friday night and put me through the third degree again. Seems they thought I might have wanted vengeance for that attack on you. Well, let me tell you, Erika – I'm a God-fearing man, and that kind of vengeance is against everything I stand for. Protecting you, looking out for you is one thing, but killing is something else again. Like I told the detectives, it's not part of my world view."

"That was my gut feeling, Stan, but it's good to hear you say it. I've always felt we could trust each other, and I want to keep it that way."

"So do I." He stared down at his fingers. They seemed to have a life of their own, flexing spasmodically atop his massive thighs. He clamped one hand down hard on the other to stop the involuntary movement. "I'll watch your back, and you watch mine."

Too much medication over too many years, I thought. *Tardive dyskinesia.* Best not to mention it, not now. "It's a deal," I said.

"And take my advice, Erika. Don't talk about this stuff with Arthur. You don't want to go getting him all riled up. He doesn't have my self-control."

Good advice, I decided. Let Arthur slide for now.

Next day, when I phoned Ocala for background on the Community Board Meeting, she advised me to get there early to sign up for a two-minute speaking slot. "As I recall, the sign-up sheets fill up really fast, and it's first-come-first-serve," she told me. "People speak in the order they sign up, on any subject they choose. No interruptions or heckling allowed, but people don't always follow the rules. There's no formal agenda, it's pretty much a free-for-all."

"I'm thinking of bringing Stanley," I told her. "I thought about inviting Gloria and maybe Arthur, but they're too unpredictable."

"Wise decision. And whatever you say, keep it short and sweet. Talk about the programming at the club, how people get referrals, the cabaret. Nothing negative or controversial. Same goes for Stanley."

"I'll do my best."

Looking out at the crowded auditorium that night, scanning the room for a friendly face, I tried to remember her advice. I'd jotted a few notes on a couple of index cards, but I hadn't thought through my remarks, figuring I'd wing it. Big mistake. When it came to facing an audience, I was comfortable at a keyboard, performing for friendly folks who were primed for a good time, often prelubricated with liquor. But this crowd looked primed for a fight. Stan had just used his two minutes to cover most of the points I wanted to make. Standing at the battle-scarred wooden lectern, tapping the mike with my fingertips in a fruitless effort to stop its squealing, I tried frantically to marshal my racing thoughts into some reasonable semblance of eloquence.

All at once my eyes fixed on Miriam Goldfarb in the front row. She sent me the hint of a smile – not much, but enough to give me the kick-start I needed. Focusing on her face, I launched into an impassioned description of the club and the upcoming cabaret.

"Don't listen to her! She's a fruitcake like all the rest of them. It's a case of the inmates running the asylum."

The voice was strident enough to carry without a mike. Vito Pisanello – I recognized his whiny, aggravating tone. "Excuse me, but I have the floor, Mr. Pisanello." I gripped the lectern with both hands, reminded myself not to shout.

"Yeah, and you've got an operation that's a blight on the neighborhood. A bunch of crazies always sitting out on the stoop smoking, a couple of very public, unnatural deaths in barely a month – the city ought to crack down and put you out of business before the next disaster happens."

I felt the blood shoot to my head. "That sounds like a threat."

"It's simply a fact. You and your fellow crazies are the threat. Those loonies ought to be under lock and key in a hospital where they belong."

"That's enough, Vito." The gruff male voice was familiar. "Put a lid on it."

I looked up to see Kevin Winthrop striding down the aisle, his tanned face and blond hair aglow in the auditorium's ghastly fluorescent light. At that moment he looked like a knight in shining armor.

When things quieted down, they gave me another two minutes. Looking out at the crowd once more, I saw warmth and sympathy instead of indifference and hostility. *People love a victim,* I thought. Vito Pisanello's off-the-wall tirade had turned them off, tipped the balance in my favor, but Kevin's timely intervention had been the coup de grace. Basking in the round of applause that followed my presentation, I looked around for Kevin to thank him, but he was already gone.

———————

I called Kevin the next morning, but I only got his machine. I left an effusively grateful message, then signed off. Just as well – my mind was already back on the cabaret.

Time flew by in the weeks that followed. I was so preoccupied, I virtually missed Autumn in New York, that glorious season the classic ballad describes so lyrically. I didn't care. Kevin hadn't returned my call and Mark was spending some time on the West Coast, so I had no one to wine and dine with, even if I'd had the inclination.

By mid-October, with the marketing and logistical details under control, I concentrated on coaching the performers and shaping the show. I brought in my Yamaha keyboard and rehearsed with vocalists of wildly assorted styles and talents, covering material from Gershwin through the Beatles to the latest hip-hop hits. Word of the show had spread to alumni of the club who were now holding down day jobs but wanted to come back and perform for old time's sake. We had two comedians, several poets, and people performing tunes of their own composition, from acoustic folk to urban techno.

There was just enough time to revamp acts that were hopelessly misbegotten, but not enough time to get overly perfectionistic. No one was turned away or bounced off the program for lack of talent. Not even Germaine, whose rendition of "Raindrops Keep Falling on My Head" got more excruciating with every run-through. She was essentially tone-deaf, and during one of our rehearsals, I suggested she try something simpler, but she had her heart set on "Raindrops." I let her be, reminding myself that the evening was to be a celebration of the club and its members, not a painstaking attempt at professionalism. I just hoped the audience understood, and that nobody laughed at Germaine.

With his organized mind and steel-trap memory, Stan had a hand in everything that was going right as well as an acute awareness of everything that needed fixing and the smarts to know what to do about it. I would never have dared to undertake the project without him, and on the night of our final rehearsal, I told him so.

"Stan, I want to introduce you and make sure you get a standing ovation tomorrow night," I said. "This cabaret could never have happened without your hard work and organizational abilities."

He glanced away, embarrassed. "Thanks, Erika. But you're the one who put the show together and brought out talents a lot of people didn't even know they had."

I felt my face flushing. "I guess we're a good team. I'm in charge of the frosting and you're in charge of the cake. Without the solid underpinnings, my contribution would be a gooey mess."

Exhausted and more than a little punchy, we both laughed harder than my comment called for. Just then a dark, dashing figure materialized in front of us. "Hey, lovebirds, what's so amusing?" said Arthur.

"Lovebirds?" I repeated. Arthur's comment made me laugh even harder. I reached out to pat Stan's arm. "Sorry, Stan, I don't mean to insult you."

"I'm not insulted," said Stan. "Arthur, don't worry. When it comes to Erika, you've got no competition from me."

I was taken aback. "Stan, what on earth do you mean by that?"

Arthur answered for him. "Stan knows how I feel about you, and he's got the good sense to stay out of my way. Right, Stan?" Arthur shot me an arrogant gaze, looking for all the world like the villain in a nineteenth-century melodrama. For his role as emcee, he had scrounged together an old tuxedo, a top hat and a voluminous black cape.

"Arthur, you look fabulous," I exclaimed. "But you didn't have to go to all that trouble. I trust that costume's just a rental. That way we can reimburse you out of the show's budget."

He threw me a knife-edged grin. "It's not a rental, but you don't have to reimburse me. I'm planning to keep it. It suits me, don't you think?" He swiveled and the cape swirled open, revealing a lining of crimson velvet.

It suited him all too well; he looked every inch the lady-killer. Fortunately, Gloria appeared before I could say anything unprofessional. "Arthur, what a wonderful costume!" she exclaimed. "You look handsome but scary. Like a vampire."

He bowed and kissed her hand. "Thank you, my little chickadee."

Gloria giggled. "I'm saving my costume for the actual show. I want it to be a surprise."

"Have you got everything you need?" I asked. "I don't want you spending a lot of your own money on it."

"I didn't need to. Ariana Birdsong lent me everything I need and helped me put it together."

Visions of black lace flashed before my eyes. "Then you'll be looking more like Stevie Nicks than Madonna."

"Ariana's clothes work well for Madonna too." Gloria flashed a flirtatious grin. "Just wait – you'll see."

Germaine wandered over. "Ariana helped me with my costume too."

I pictured Germaine's boxy, oversized body swathed in lace. Not a pretty vision. I pushed the image away. "Anyway, folks, let's get this rehearsal underway, so we can all get home early and rest up for the big show tomorrow."

I rose, and Stan followed suit. The five of us stood there, a little too close for comfort. I could feel Arthur's black cape brushing my side.

"One more thing," said Gloria. "I have a smudge stick that Ariana gave me. I'd like to light it before the rehearsal, and purify the space for good luck. It's sage. Something the Native Americans do."

I gave her shoulder a squeeze. "I know. We did it at Stephen's memorial service, remember?"

All at once it crossed my mind: I'd never shared my hidden agenda with the others. In fact, with all the frenetic activity involved in preparing for tomorrow night, I'd scarcely thought of it myself. If I was going to warn them to be on the lookout for anyone or anything threatening or out of the ordinary, now was the time to do it. But at the mention of Stephen's service, a shadow flitted across Gloria's face, and I decided to keep my thoughts to myself. They were all nervous enough already.

"Sage helps keep bad spirits away," Gloria said gravely. "And my angel told me to watch out for strange men. They might be evil spirits in disguise."

Stan gave an exasperated sigh. "Gloria, please! Enough with the angels and demons already! We've got a show to do."

"Right. On with the show," said Arthur. "But Gloria, you'd better bring that smudge stick tomorrow too, so you can smoke out the place right before the performance and exorcise any evil spirits that get in over night."

Chapter 25

*T*he next night, barely an hour before the start of the open house, Stan and I were hard at work hanging a brand-new banner. A group effort painted in acrylics on a white sheet, it was casual and crude compared to Jeff's beautiful mural, of which it was going to obscure a considerable portion. But this was a night to celebrate the living as well as to commemorate Jeff's achievement, so the banner deserved a place of honor.

We were still struggling with yellow nylon cord and duct tape when Ocala St. Claire's white Lincoln pulled up outside the club. She was in the passenger's seat for a change, and I caught a glimpse of an imposing black man at the wheel.

I greeted Ocala as she opened the car door. "I'm so glad you could make it. But do you realize you're an hour early?"

"Of course. We came early in case we could be of any help."

Her gentleman friend climbed out from the driver's side, locked the door and strolled around to give her a hand. An enormous man well over six feet tall, he had the build of a professional football player, and it flashed through my mind that he'd be great for crowd control and security. I wondered if we'd need any.

Swiveling around on the honey-beige leather seat of her car, Ocala stretched her legs out toward the curb. "Erika Norgren, I'd like you to meet Howard Springhorn," she said. She flashed him a coquettish smile. "Hold on a minute, baby. Wait till I get my turban on." Reaching into the back seat, she extracted an expanse of colorful cloth and proceeded to twine it around her head, endowing herself with an extra eight inches of instant height. "Now I'm ready," she proclaimed. "I didn't want to squash my headdress in the car." Howard helped her out and she stood posing for a moment, like an African queen awaiting the homage of her subjects.

"Ocala, you look magnificent," I exclaimed. "I wish we had a red carpet for you."

"We should take some pictures," said Stan. "Hold on a minute while I get the camera." He draped his end of the banner carefully over the railing, then charged up the steps into the club.

"Speaking of cameras, Erika, do you know who's coming from the media?" Ocala was smiling, but I knew she was sizing me up, taking my emotional temperature. "I assume you used the media list I gave you."

"Yes, we sent out press releases and invitations to everyone on the list."

"Did you do any follow-up phone calls?"

"No, I didn't know we should." Butterflies fluttered in my chest, and I felt like a contestant on *Jeopardy*. "But we sent invitations to all the agencies and referral sources we deal with, and we put up fliers in the neighborhood. Anyway, our main goal was to do something positive for the members, to stir up some excitement and energy, and I think we've succeeded in that."

Stan returned with the camera, enlisted Howard to help hang the banner. We took turns posing in front of it. "Hi, Neighbors! Welcome to Our Open House and Cabaret," it said in large block letters.

———————

An hour later, the club was full of people, many of them total strangers. So much for monitoring the guests. If we'd expected such a mob scene, we could have put Stan or Howard at the front door with a velvet rope and an "Invitation Only" guest list. But that would have contradicted our entire mission. We'd just have to go with the flow.

From the looks of things, a lot of our visitors had come for the free food. With their cheap, shabby clothes and downcast expressions, they looked like consumers: people from the neighborhood shelters, the addiction recovery centers, the methadone clinic. We had pushed the dining tables against the walls, with food on one side, drinks on the other. The members had opted for standard happy hour fare – Swedish meatballs, barbecued chicken wings, carrot and celery sticks, chips and dips, cheese and crackers. Several had devoted the day to shopping, cooking, and arranging the platters.

By the time I finally made it over to the tables, nothing was left but a few forlorn veggies. Hoping they had remembered to keep some trays in reserve, I settled for diet cola on ice. I longed desperately for something to spike it with, but of course alcohol was taboo at the club.

All at once Ocala was at my side, muttering in my ear. "What happened to the food?"

"Obviously people ate it. But we kept some trays in reserve so it wouldn't all go at once." *At least I hope we did.*

"That's good. We need to save some for the media people and our professional colleagues, assuming more of them get here. So far, I've seen only a few."

"Well, but the consumers are the real reason we're here, right, Ocala? Some of these people probably need this food a lot more desperately than a bunch of human services types. Or have you forgotten what – " A firm hand on my shoulder stopped me mid-sentence, and I whirled to face Mark.

"Mark! I'm so glad you could make it! I wasn't sure if you'd be back from the Coast."

His timing was impeccable; he'd just prevented me from embarking on a major rant. Withdrawing his hand, he stationed himself equidistantly between me and my boss. "I just got back last night. Lucky I had a chance to leaf through my mail today. That rainbow design you used for the envelope really stood out."

Ocala beamed like a proud parent, and I wondered if she was picking up on the vibes between us. I certainly was.

"Congratulations, Erika," he said as Ocala caught sight of a colleague across the room and drifted away. "You really pulled it off. I shouldn't have doubted you. You look great, by the way."

"Thanks." I smoothed the long, clingy skirt of the dress I'd splurged on for the occasion, a silk print in autumnal reds and oranges. Where was he going with this? Was he about to ask what I was doing later? No matter – it was time for some heavy-duty hostessing.

For the next hour I mingled non-stop. I introduced consumers to service providers and set up photo opportunities with the handful of media people who were gradually trickling in, including Nancy Welcome and her crew. The members on kitchen duty kept bringing out more platters of food, but they couldn't keep pace with the growing crowd. As the room grew hotter, it got harder and harder to move through the sea of people without engaging in unwanted bodily contact. My breath caught in my throat as claustrophobia closed in.

Through the crowd, I caught sight of Stan plowing his way toward me. His unflappably cool façade was beginning to crack, and the lenses of his glasses were steamed. "Let's start directing people up to the group room for the cabaret," he said. "That will break up the crowd a little. Right now, it's wall-to-wall people. A fireman would slap us with all kinds of violations."

Arthur joined us, his black and crimson cape swirling dramatically around him. "That's for sure," he said. "It reminds me of those news stories about people killed in crowded dance clubs, when they panic because of fire and get trampled to death trying to get out."

"Thanks for making my day, guys," I said. "But seriously, Stan is right. How about if the two of you start leading people upstairs? I'll round up the stragglers and see you there in a few minutes." Then suddenly I remembered. "Where are Gloria and Germaine? I haven't seen them in over an hour."

Stan smiled. "Don't worry, they'll be here. They went over to Ariana's place to get ready. Gloria told me they planned to get back just in time for the cabaret. They didn't want anyone seeing their costumes and makeup ahead of time."

"I can see Gloria doing that, but Germaine? It's not like her to miss the refreshments."

Stan laughed. "You got that right. I told her I'd save her a plate."

I gave him a high-five. "That makes sense. Well, everybody, let's break a leg – it's show time."

———————

The cabaret was a smash. With Stan as stage manager and Arthur as emcee, the show went off almost without a hitch. There was no stage to speak of. Rather, the performers held forth in the far corner of the group room. People crammed into the long narrow space and overflowed into the hall. We had a captive audience in the true sense of the word, with everyone wedged in so tightly that escape was well nigh impossible. I kept remembering Stan's comments about fire codes, but no one else looked worried. If anything, the hot, crowded conditions seemed to fuel their enthusiasm as they cheered and applauded wildly for each and every performer.

Then came Germaine. Ensconced behind my keyboard, I got a side view as she shrugged off a shapeless beige raincoat to reveal her puffy body squeezed into black leotard and tights with a blood-red bustier. With her theatrical makeup, teased hair and fake eyelashes, she looked ludicrous, a woman imitating a drag queen. Divine in *Hairspray* came to mind, or maybe *The Rocky Horror Show*.

The crowd stomped and screamed their approval. As she began to sing, the wolf whistles and clapping almost drowned her out. Were they mocking, jeering her? I wasn't sure, but as her number came to a merciful close and they rose in a standing ovation, Germaine drank it all in, beaming ecstatically, her green-gold eyes aglow.

Now it was Gloria's turn. I relaxed a little – at least she could sing.

She made a spectacular entrance. Clad in a black trench coat, she posed in the doorway, extending a long leg encased in fishnet hose, doing a few Rockette-style kicks, then made her way to the front. As the pulsing beat of "Like a Virgin" filled the room, she slithered out of the coat and tossed it aside, revealing an outrageously skimpy outfit of black lace and leather.

Most of the men and a few of the women shouted their approval, whistled and stomped. With her full lips and sparkling brown eyes, Gloria was a ragamuffin ingenue in a curvaceous, womanly body. Draped in wispy fragments of lace held in place by a wide black leather belt and strategically tied cords, she looked like some enchanted sea creature cast ashore by the tides, then transported to the club on the back of a motorcycle. Her singing was a little thin, but it didn't matter: she held the audience spellbound.

They gave her a standing ovation. She bowed, smiled, then retrieved the trench coat. Slipping it on, she buttoned it up to the neck and pulled the belt tightly around her, the better to safeguard everything she had just so brazenly revealed. She inched through the crowd to the exit. In the aftermath of her departure, a dozen or so people stood and began inching toward the door.

"The cabaret's not over yet, people," called Arthur. "There are still three more acts to go." Some of the deserters glanced at him and a couple waved cheerily, but none of them stayed. I could hardly blame them. It was getting late, almost nine o'clock, and the heat in the room was stifling.

It was nine-thirty when we ushered the last visitors out the door. Ocala was long gone and so was Mark. Too bad – I could have used his company tonight.

"So here we are, the Fab Four," said Gloria. "We really pulled it off." She had shed her trench coat again.

Stan eyed her uneasily. "Maybe you should go change out of your costume."

"No can do. I left my other clothes at Ariana's." She did a flagrantly sexy bump and grind, and the skimpy lace veils fluttered around her body. "Anyway, I kind of like this look."

"So do I, baby," said Arthur. "You definitely got it, so you might as well flaunt it. Unlike Germaine. Jeez, that was pathetic. All that flab spilling all over the place."

"I have to agree," said Stan. "If we ever do another show like this, we should have a dress rehearsal with the actual costumes, to avoid embarrassment."

"But the audience loved her," I said.

"They were just dissing her," said Arthur. "She was too dumb to know the difference."

He could be right, but I wouldn't admit it. "Where is she?" I asked.

"Probably left with Ariana," said Stan. "Anyway, let's clean up now, so we won't have to face such a mess in the morning. We don't want to leave food around to attract rats and roaches."

I sighed. "I think every scrap of food is gone, but I suppose you're right. I'll go let Rishi out of my office. He's been cooped up in there for hours."

Rishi began to bark, and I knew he'd heard his name.

"That's my cue to exit," said Arthur. "Your dog and I don't get along."

"Come on, Arthur," said Stan. "Help us stay and clean up."

"No thanks. That's woman's work."

"Arthur can leave if he wants to," I said. "He did a brilliant job as emcee, so he's entitled to call it a night." Actually, he had done amazingly well, given his hot temper and antisocial personality. Probably a large part of the reason was his devotion to me, but I preferred not to think about that.

The barking from upstairs was growing louder and more emphatic. "Rishi's telling me he's had enough solitary confinement," I said as I turned and headed up to my office.

By the time I let Rishi out, Arthur had vanished, and Stan and Gloria were prowling the club with plastic trash bags, picking up all the detritus. Rishi tore out of my office with his nose to the ground, checking out the scents of all the people who had been milling around the club in the past few hours. He covered the hallway, then the group room. Next he took off downstairs to the ground floor, snuffling all the way. Having nothing more pressing to do, I followed him.

Stan followed us both. "Rishi's sure excited," he said. "He reminds me of those dogs you see on TV, searching for drugs or bombs."

I smiled. "Most likely he's just picking up the scents of all the people who were here that he doesn't know, not to mention all the food he didn't get to eat."

Now Rishi was exploring the dining and kitchen areas on the ground floor. He greeted Gloria hopefully. "Sorry, boy, the food's all gone," she said. "People were piggy tonight, and they ate every last bit."

Getting the message, Rishi went back to exploring. As he reached the door to the basement stairs, his ears pricked up and he sniffed more intensely, then thrust his nose into the crack at the bottom of the door and began to whine. He gave me a quizzical look, then turned back to the door and pawed it impatiently.

"You can't go down there, Rishi," I told him. By mutual consent, we had kept the basement off limits during the open house. The space housed a recreation area consisting of a pool table, a couple of dilapidated exercise machines and an area for free weights, as well as the boiler and storage rooms. Some of the men enjoyed shooting pool down there, but I avoided the basement. It had scrofulous walls with layers of peeling paint and plaster, and a chronically musty smell that overpowered even the strongest cleansers and disinfectants. Renovating the area would take a strong stomach, enormous stamina, and deep pockets, so it remained essentially untouched.

But Rishi wouldn't give up. He kept scratching the door, whining with the high-pitched fervor he reserves for creatures he wants to hunt down, like cats and squirrels.

"Hey, Rishi, cut it out," said Stan. "You're making gouges on that door, and I just painted it last year." Playfully, he feinted as if to push the dog away. Rishi's hackles rose and he growled softly.

"Rishi! Bad dog!" I exclaimed. "I don't know what's wrong, Stan. Just leave him alone and don't touch him. I'll go get his leash."

"Don't worry, I wouldn't dream of touching him." Stan backed away, keeping his eyes on Rishi. "Erika, do me a favor and check the basement door to be sure it's locked before we leave."

I turned the knob, and the door opened easily. "I guess you must have left it unlocked."

"No way! I distinctly remember checking it before the party. Maybe someone forced the lock, looking for a place to make out or smoke a little dope. I'd better go down and check to make sure no one's there."

"Better you than me." I shuddered. "That basement is like a dungeon. What a creepy place to get locked in overnight!"

"Whoever it was left the lights on," said Stan. Before he could start down, Rishi shoved past him and hurtled full-tilt down the stairs. A moment later, the dog's unearthly yelps told me something was seriously wrong.

I heard Stan's footsteps clatter down the stairs, then stop abruptly. For an endless moment only Rishi's whimpers broke the silence. Then Stan screamed. "Oh, my God, no!"

Suddenly weak, I grabbed the doorframe for support. "What is it? What's wrong?"

"It's Germaine. Erika, you'd better stay where you are. You don't want to see this."

"Is she sick, or hurt, or . . ." Afraid to go on, afraid of what he might say, I started down the stairs.

What I saw made me wish I'd taken his advice. Germaine lay spread-eagled atop the pool table, her wrists and ankles bound to the table with nylon cord of incongruously cheerful yellow. Strips of silver duct tape were stretched taut across her mouth, cheeks and chin. Her remarkable green-gold eyes, rimmed in smudged black liner and mascara, still had the brilliance of shattered crystal, even in death. And there was no doubt she was dead. Blood was everywhere – on her pale skin, on the black tights and red bustier, on the emerald-green felt of the pool table. The clash of complementary green and crimson made me think incongruously of Christmas.

Atop her chest lay a sheet of white paper, with a message emblazoned in red marker:

DIE, CRAZY SLUT!

Chapter 26

*T*ime screeched to a standstill as I stood staring at Germaine's lifeless body splayed on the pool table. Somewhere inside me, a switch had flipped into autopilot, and I felt only numbness. The scene before me was so horrific that I couldn't comprehend it. So I fixated on the visual elements, studying the composition, the interplay of colors and textures, the way I might study a painting in the Museum of Modern Art. Braque had painted billiard tables, but these vibrantly clashing colors were more like Matisse. And the violent hatred directed at the woman – that was definitely Picasso, with a touch of Francis Bacon.

The voice came from a great distance. "Erika? Are you all right?"

No, I'm not. I was silent, shivering.

"Erika! I'm going to call 911. The phone extension down here isn't working, so I need to go up to the dining room. You better come with me."

I turned to see Stan looking at me with wild eyes. A vein pulsed in his forehead and I stared at it, transfixed. "I have to stay here with Germaine," I mumbled.

"It's not safe. Whoever did this may still be here, or he might come back."

Slowly, my mind was shaking off the numbness. "The Novocain is wearing off," I said.

Stan frowned. "What? Erika, are you okay?"

"Yes, I just spaced out momentarily. Go make the call. I'll be all right staying here with Germaine. Rishi will protect me, and it's only right she should have someone with her. She was so alone in life, she shouldn't have to be alone in death."

It seemed an eternity before the police arrived. In reality it couldn't have been more than a few minutes, because the first two were on the scene by ten o'clock. Dennis Malone and Diane Olstead arrived soon after, along with the photographer, crime scene technicians, and medical examiner. The room swarmed with people. They checked in vain for vital signs, measured, took photos, then secured plastic bags around Germaine's hands and taped them closed at the wrists.

Standing beside me, Dennis began to explain. "The bags are to protect any evidence that may be on her hands. If she put up a fight, for example, there might be defensive wounds or traces of blood or skin under her nails."

"Of course," I said loftily. "I've watched enough episodes of CSI to know the drill."

He studied me quizzically, glanced at the crime scene, then back to me. "It looks like things are under control. Let's you and me go upstairs. I need to ask you a few questions."

I laughed bitterly. "Under control? Under the circumstances, I find that a peculiar choice of words."

I glanced over at the table, where the technicians were laying out a black plastic body bag alongside the corpse. Strange how Germaine was being treated with such respect and gentleness. In life, most people had treated her with indifference or contempt. They were handling her with deliberate slowness and a kind of hushed intensity that went beyond anything they'd shown with Stephen or Jeff. Perhaps because she was a woman, but more likely because this time, there was no doubt: the victim had been murdered.

Now they were unzipping the bag and preparing to put her inside. Dennis gripped my arm with one hand, slipped the other behind my back, and guided me deftly toward the stairs. "Let's go, Erika. You've seen enough."

I glanced back at the pool table. "Just let me take one last look. I admit Germaine looks grotesque, but the composition is so beautiful, with all that green and crimson. The complementary colors vibrate off each other. I hope they got some good pictures; I don't want to forget it."

He tightened his grip and propelled me away. "I'm sure the pictures will be fine. Let's go."

"Your hands feel good, Dennis. So masterful and strong. I feel as if we're skating together. Like that Joni Mitchell song about skating away on a river. Except she was singing about skating alone, and I've had more than enough aloneness. I'd rather have togetherness. I wonder when they open the skating rink at Rockefeller Center. It would be fun to go there, don't you think?"

I chattered all the way to my office. Dennis was looking at me strangely, and I knew he was worried about me, but I couldn't seem to stop. I kept up a steady stream of free association, terrified of the dark void that would open up if I fell silent, the cavernous emptiness that would soon be filled with the enormity of Germaine's death and all the images, thoughts and questions it brought to mind.

Once inside my office, I sat behind my desk and placed both palms on the battered oak surface. Rishi hunkered down at my side, still shaking and whimpering softly, and as I stroked his sleek fur to calm him, I felt myself coming back to some semblance of normalcy. "So, Detective, you had some questions for me? You probably want to know if I saw someone skulking around with a machete dripping blood, that sort of thing."

Almost imperceptibly, Dennis recoiled, and I knew I had shocked him. "Yes, that sort of thing," he said. "Or something more subtle – someone who acted suspicious or upset, someone who might have been angry with Germaine."

"No one comes to mind. Germaine suffered from chronic schizophrenia, and she had that kind of flat affect that can come from years of illness and medication. Aside from that, she was diagnosed as having borderline retardation. All in all, she wasn't exactly scintillating company, so I don't think anyone was that close to her. I can't imagine why anyone would have wanted to kill her. They just wouldn't have cared enough."

I paused, and Dennis watched me expectantly as the silence lengthened between us. Then I looked into the void and leapt in. "Unless someone killed her for some other reason. Maybe she saw something incriminating, or maybe she was murdered for what she represented as a member of the club. I think someone is trying to discredit or destroy WellSpring, the same person who killed Stephen Wright and Jeffrey Archer. But those deaths weren't dramatic enough. They didn't look enough like murders, and the media attention died down too quickly, so the killer upped the ante and staged something really dramatic, like a piece of performance art."

Dennis leaned forward, his green eyes gleaming. "You might have something there, Erika. We'll definitely pursue it."

"Do you have any more questions for me?"

"Not right now. Is there anyone who can take you home? You shouldn't be alone."

"I've got Rishi with me. We can take a taxi. I'm feeling better now."

"I'm glad. You had me worried for awhile. But with the murderer out there somewhere, you can't afford to take any chances."

"I could call my friend Mark Levitan. He was here tonight, but he left at some point during the performance."

Dennis reached across the desk for the phone, grabbed the receiver and handed it to me. "Give him a call and ask him to come over."

Mark's machine picked up after two rings. "Mark, are you there?" I said after the beep. "Please pick up if you are. I'm still at the club; there's a problem."

I heard a click, then his voice. "Erika, are you all right? What's the matter?"

"I'm okay. I'll explain when you get here. Please hurry!"

———————

Twenty minutes later, Mark was at the club and I was in his arms, fighting back tears. Once both men were assured I wasn't in imminent danger of collapse, Dennis took Mark aside. "Mr. Levitan, we'll be interviewing everyone who was at the club tonight, including you. I'll talk with you later, but I have one question for now. Why did you leave the open house early? And where did you go when you left?"

"That's two questions," Mark snapped.

"Touché," said Dennis.

Hmm, interesting choice of words. The two men seemed to have gotten off on the wrong foot. Could it have anything to do with me?

Mark's diplomacy skills kicked in. "No problem, I'll explain anyway. I've been in California for a couple of weeks. I got back late last night and saw the invitation this morning. Ms. Norgren had told me about the open house when it was in the early planning stages, so I wanted to stop by and pay my respects. But I'm still kind of off kilter from the change in time zones, and the crowd was getting to me, so I left after the first couple of cabaret numbers." He glanced at me. "Sorry, Erika, I should have said goodbye."

"That's okay, I understand. The crowd was getting to me too. And it was so hot!"

Dennis intercepted the looks we were sending each other. "So I gather you two are good friends?"

"What's that got to do with anything?" asked Mark.

What kind of answer was that? He could have said something more gallant. "We're getting there," I said.

Mark grinned, then sobered again. "This was really Erika's night. I knew she was under a lot of pressure, what with hostessing and directing the cabaret, so I didn't want to distract her."

"I don't see how this is germane to Germaine's murder." *Germane, Germaine. Brilliant!* I laughed at my own wordplay. They both looked at me oddly, and I shifted gears. "Mark, you don't have to answer any more questions. Maybe we should get a lawyer."

"I wouldn't say you need a lawyer at this point," said Dennis.

"But we will at some future point? Is that what you're saying?" I could hear my voice growing more strident, but I couldn't seem to moderate it. "It so happens Mark *is* a lawyer, and an excellent one, especially in the area of human and civil rights, and right now, Mr. Detective Dennis Malone, it feels like you're trampling all over my rights, civil and otherwise."

Mark draped an arm around my shoulders. "Cool it, Erika. What Detective Malone has said so far sounds reasonable enough. There's no need to get defensive." He glanced at Dennis, and the two men exchanged a look loaded with complicity.

"Why are you guys looking at each other like that?" I asked. "I know why – you're thinking I'm some poor pathetic hysterical female, probably about to get my period, and you hope to God you can calm me down before I start crying and screaming."

Their mouths twitched in unison, and I knew I was right. "This has been an extremely stressful night," said Dennis. "Stan and Erika were the first to discover the body, and it was a gruesome sight."

I broke in. "Actually, Rishi discovered the body first. If he hadn't been whining and scratching at the basement door, we might never have gone down there."

Dennis ignored me. "Anyway, she has every right to be upset. Anybody would be. But before you got here, I was concerned that she might be, uh . . ."

I finished the phrase. "Freaking out? Losing it? Going bonkers? You might as well come right out and say it, Dennis. You thought I was going crazy."

Still looking at Mark, he acknowledged my statement with a half nod. "I think she needs someone to stay with her, someone she knows and trusts."

"Talk to me directly, damn it!" I screamed. "Don't be so patronizing, talking right over me as if I don't exist!"

"I'm sorry, Erika," said Dennis. "It's been a long night. I'll go see how the forensics team is doing, and hopefully soon we can close up the club."

"Sounds good to me," said Mark. He flashed me a calculating look. "We'll catch a taxi back to your place, maybe stop off for some take-out food to bring with us. What's your pleasure? Chinese? Thai?"

I realized that except for a few carrot and celery sticks, I hadn't eaten since lunch. Suddenly I was ravenous. "I could go for a gigantic pizza with the works. Sausage, pepperoni, garlic, black olives, mushrooms, anchovies . . ."

Rishi cocked his head and pricked up his ears; pizza is one of his words. Mark was worried about me; I could tell by the way he acquiesced to everything, even the anchovies, without arguing. He ordered by phone from a place on Second Avenue, and a few minutes later we were ready to leave.

Dennis Malone was in the first-floor hallway, talking with Stan and Gloria.

"Erika, why don't you and Mark go ahead," said Stan. "Gloria and I can lock up. We'll talk tomorrow about what to do about the club."

"What do you mean?" I asked.

Dennis replied. "I've informed Stan, and I was just about to tell you, that you should close the club until the interviews and the crime scene investigators are finished. We'll want to meet with you again. I'll call you tomorrow."

I was appalled at the idea of closing the club. But I was even more appalled when I stepped out the door, down the front steps, and smack into the black and yellow crime scene tape that cordoned off the building. Mark raised the colorful plastic ribbon, and I stooped, then scuttled beneath it, feeling like a participant in some children's game for which I'd forgotten the rules.

We walked to Second and picked up our pizza. Then I stood curbside, holding Rishi's leash with one hand and the pizza box with the other. As Rishi and I inhaled the tantalizing aromas of garlic and pepperoni, Mark flagged down a cab.

"Where to?" asked the driver once we were settled inside on the black vinyl seat behind the Plexiglas partition.

As Mark gave directions and the cab took off, I gazed out the window. Except for the pizza place and a nearby bar, the storefronts had their aluminum shutters pulled down tight for the night. The street was nearly deserted, but a lone figure caught my eye. Lean, dressed in black, with a voluminous cape. Even before we drew abreast of him, I knew it was Arthur, and I gave an involuntary gasp. As we came eye to eye, he doffed his top hat, gave a melodramatic bow, and held a finger to his lips to signify silence.

Mark turned to face me. "What's wrong, Erika?"

I couldn't face any more questions or speculations. "Oh, nothing."

"Didn't I hear you gasp?"

"I thought I saw a dog in the road, but it turned out to be a black garbage bag blowing around."

He studied my face, looking worried. "How could anything be blowing around? It's perfectly still tonight. There's no wind at all."

———

Back in my apartment, we drank Merlot and devoured the gigantic pizza in record time, with a generous assist from Rishi. Between bites, I told Mark everything I could remember about Germaine and the open house. The food and wine damped down my feelings temporarily, but soon I was revved up again and pacing back and forth.

"Why do you keep looking at me like that?" I asked Mark. "It's getting on my nerves."

"Looking at you like what?"

"You're doing it right now. Studying me, scrutinizing me, trying to decide if I'm freaking out or not."

He patted the sofa beside him. "Sit down and relax."

I continued to pace. "I'm sick and tired of all your questions. I feel like I'm on trial in some kangaroo court."

"Erika, I thought you needed to talk about what happened tonight, but obviously it's getting you upset. Maybe we should forget it for now. Just let the police handle it."

"I can't do that. It's a cop-out."

"But I don't want anything to happen to you as a result of your involvement with the club. Maybe you should back off and give it a rest."

"What do you mean? Quit my job?"

"Maybe, for your own protection. But at the very least, take some time off. What about a leave of absence? I can see this situation is getting to you. I'm sure Ocala would understand."

"I doubt it. Ever since she found out I'm bipolar, she's been on my case. She'd probably love to get rid of me."

"That's just your paranoia talking."

"Damn it, Mark, that's not true. Ocala's attitude has really changed. It feels like she's always watching me, as if she doesn't trust me anymore. Why is it so hard for you to believe I'm telling the truth? Why do you assume all my perceptions are distorted by my craziness, as if I were seeing everything in some kind of funhouse mirror?"

"Because I've been in a space like the one you're in right now. The paranoia, the hostility, the restlessness, the rapid mood changes – I'm intimately acquainted with all of them. In my case, those feelings usually led to a full-blown manic episode, and I ended up in the hospital. I'd hate to see that happen to you."

I was suddenly close to tears. "But I've been under a lot of stress, so I've been extra careful about taking my meds religiously."

"That's good. But stress can trigger a full-blown manic episode, even if you've been consistent with your meds. And the stress you've been under in the past few weeks has been extreme." He stood, grasped both my hands in his. "I'm sorry I haven't been more available. Maybe I could make that up to you by staying with you until they get to the bottom of these deaths at WellSpring Club. Or better still, you could stay with me."

"I couldn't leave Rishi."

"So bring him along. He and I get along fine."

"This is really weird." I took a step closer, rested my head against his chest. "Here you're talking about moving in together, and we haven't even slept together yet. You're the one who said we should take it slow, remember?"

"Well, the close proximity could be a problem. I might have to reexamine my postulates. But Erika, I'm worried about your safety. There's a murderer on the loose."

Standing this close, I could feel his heart beat. "I'm seriously tempted," I said. "But you're right about my being mood swingy under all this stress. I'm afraid I'd be so horribly bitchy, I'd turn you off and drive you away before we even got started."

"I'm willing to take that chance."

Even as he spoke, I saw the doubt dawning in his eyes. Damn! Why did I have to be so persuasive? "I'll be okay here," I said. "The door and windows all lock, and I have the alarm system, Rishi and some pepper spray. Plus neighbors upstairs and downstairs. And all the deaths have been at the club. I don't think the killer would break the pattern." As I spoke, I flashed on the image of Arthur in his black cape, skulking in the shadows on Second Avenue.

"Are you sure?"

I wasn't, not by a long shot. But I still didn't trust my own volatile temper. And if a relationship was in our future, I wanted a relationship between equals, not a half-baked bodyguard or baby-sitting arrangement.

"I'm positive," I said. Then I kissed him goodnight.

Chapter 27

I bolted the door the instant Mark left. Even before the heavy steel
bars of the Fox lock slid into the sockets, I wanted to kick myself
for driving him away. Slumping against the door, hearing his retreating
footsteps on the stairs, I willed him to return. But his footsteps faded
into silence, and I was alone with Rishi.

Feeling exposed and vulnerable, I padded around the apartment
pulling down shades and turning off lights, with the sole exception of a small
mission-style table lamp. Its amber glass shade bathed the living room in a
warm glow. I hoped it would simultaneously serve as a night-light, convey the
message that no one was home, and help keep the demons at bay.

"I'm asking a lot of you, little light," I said as I outlined its
assignment. "Oh, and you also have to function as a visual focus for
meditation, in the unlikely event that I can sit still long enough to
meditate, and as a memorial votive light for Germaine Lavendre."

Talking to my table lamp – was I finally losing it once and for all?
Not really, not as long as I could still step back and study my symptoms
objectively. A bird's eye view flashed across my mind – a woman

standing alone in her apartment, shrouded in darkness, talking to a 25-watt bulb. I saw her with the clarity of someone undergoing a near-death-experience, flying above my own body and hovering over the operating table. Or pool table, as the case might be.

Get a grip, Erika. If I took good care of myself – ate right, got enough sleep, took my meds, distracted myself with lightweight diversions – maybe I could come through all right. Unlike Germaine.

The anchovies on the pizza had made me fearsomely thirsty, so I went to the sink and gulped two glasses of water, then poured a tumbler of Merlot to mute my edginess. I didn't dare drink too much or zonk myself out with pills – I needed all my wits about me to face whatever lay ahead. But sleep was out of the question – the mere thought of lying helpless in the dark, replaying my mental tapes of Germaine's murder, was terrifying. To get me through the interminable night, I booted up my computer, opened up Microsoft Word and proceeded to type out all my thoughts about the three deaths at the club. Random, free-association stuff, uncensored, as fast as I could get it down.

By three a.m., my ramblings totaled eight pages, single-spaced. I'd written up everything I could think of, but without the charts for Stephen, Jeff and Germaine, I was at a dead end. As I titled the document *Trinity Deaths* and saved it to my hard drive, a zillion loose ends tangled my thoughts and tugged my mind in multiple directions.

Things might be clearer if I went to the club. The charts were there, the computer was faster, and one wall of my office had a dry-erase board that would be perfect for charting out my theories. There had to be something linking the three deaths, some connection I'd been missing. Just a few hours till morning – hell, it *was* morning. I might as well go now.

But what if the murderer was lurking somewhere around the club? It was crazy to go at this ungodly hour. On the other hand, for all I knew, he could be waiting for me here, outside my apartment. I flashed on the memory of Arthur in his dark cloak, waving from the curb on

Second Avenue earlier tonight. I was almost positive he knew where I lived. Better to get out of here.

I saved my meanderings to a jump drive, slipped it into my purse and shut down the computer. Standing, stretching out the kinks from my hours at the computer, I realized I was still in the new silk dress I'd worn at the cabaret. The hot autumn colors, the oranges and crimsons of the floral print had seemed so festive only yesterday, and now I could scarcely bear to look at them. I stripped off the dress, dropped it on the floor where it landed in a lurid puddle. I'd donate it to a thrift shop, I decided, or let Ariana cut it up for costumes.

I slipped into a sweater, jeans and sneakers, checked my pocketbook to make sure my cell phone and pepper spray were handy. Rishi was fast asleep on the rug, his hind legs peddling furiously as he chased some phantom creature through his dreams.

"Rishi! You want to go to the club?"

He blinked open his eyes and gave me an incredulous look. After a moment, he clambered to his feet, shook himself and sneezed.

I rubbed his ears as I snapped on his leash. "What a good boy! Want to do some sleuthing with me?"

He wagged his tail, game for anything. Ever the valiant trooper.

———   ———   ———

We covered the few blocks to WellSpring at a rapid clip. I tried to project an air of jaunty confidence, as if speed-walking my dog at three-thirty in the morning was the most ordinary thing in the world. My act must have been convincing, because the few people we passed, mostly street people and stragglers from late-night bars, gave us barely a second glance. I stayed near the curbs, well away from doorways. A chill wind had picked up, stripping dry leaves from the spindly trees that clung to life amidst the concrete and flinging them through the air.

Turning off the avenue onto Fourth Street, I stopped to scan the few hundred feet that lay between me and the club. The handful of anemic streetlights on the block shed ghostly light on the flat surfaces of the sidewalk and the building facades, but there were far too many patches of darkness, perfect for lurking villains. Should I turn back? No, I'd come too far for that. Rishi was pulling at his leash, eager to forge ahead. And just past WellSpring, across the street, a lone window was ablaze with light. Gertrude Reynolds, I was willing to wager. The thought of the demented old woman alone at her window lent me courage, and I soldiered on to the club.

Yellow crime-scene tape was festooned across the front of the building. I ducked under, keys in hand, and soon Rishi and I were barricaded inside. I unsnapped his leash, rubbed his neck. "You'll tell me if there are any bad guys around, won't you, baby?" Then I let go. He streaked toward the stairs to the ground floor, the locked door to the basement. He whined and scratched at the blood-red steel.

"No, boy. Not there! Let's go up!"

Within five minutes, he'd scoped out the club, top to bottom. Convinced we had no unwelcome visitors, I headed for my office, booted up the computer, and inserted the tiny device that contained my midnight ramblings. Then I retrieved the charts from the file room. I spread out the records for Stephen, Jeff and Germaine on my desk, found a yellow legal pad and a razor-point pen. What next? Uncapping the pen, I began doodling absentmindedly. I'd already pinpointed some similarities between Stephen and Jeff, but how did Germaine enter into the equation? I pored over her chart, but nothing stood out. Maybe a time line would help.

I jumped up, crossed to the white dry-erase board on the wall across from my desk, slashed three vertical purple lines the length of the board, creating four columns. I labeled them: Stephen, Jeff, Germaine and Misc. I scanned the notes on the computer screen, then returned to the charts. I was already familiar with the psychiatric assessments, the basic histories. I'd try the progress note sections this time, write down significant dates, incidents, anything else that struck me about the three victims, then transfer them to the board, see if any patterns emerged.

Brilliant, Erika! Way to go! I began jotting names and dates on the board, coding them in color: red for names, blue for dates, orange for connections among the columns. Caught up in the excitement of my creation, I began feeling that effervescent high that I experienced sometimes with my music, when I was improvising, at the top of my form. A high better than drugs, a high dangerously akin to mania.

The sky was lightening to murky gray when I flashed on a new connection. *B.G.* Two initials, nothing more, but they showed up in the progress notes for both Stephen and Jeff. A woman they'd both known, from the looks of things. According to one social worker's note, Stephen had been so devastated when she left the club four years ago that he had fallen into a spiraling depression that led to a hospitalization. Jeff's involvement with B.G. had been less intense; the notes mentioned her simply as a friend and a source of emotional support.

Confidentiality be cursed! I knew why the social worker had used only initials: it was a breach of confidentiality to spell out one client's name in another's chart. But probably Stan or Gloria would know the identity of this mysterious B.G. I'd call them later this morning. Meanwhile, my mind raced on its merry way. B.G . . . Benny Goodman? Bergdorf Goodman? The BeeGees? *Stop it, Erika!* On the white board, in the columns for Stephen and Jeff, I wrote the initials in orange, a two-way arrow between them.

I glanced at my watch. Seven o'clock – time for a break. No doubt Rishi could use one too. "Want to go for a walk?" I asked him. "Get some breakfast?" He bounced up, ready for action, and we headed down the stairs.

Opening the door, I was prepared for the sight of the yellow crime-scene tape blocking my way. I was definitely not prepared to see Kevin

Winthrop and Nancy Welcome standing at the foot of the stoop, staring up at me. Behind her, a cameraman took aim as she began firing questions at me.

"Are there any suspects yet? Is it true the victim was crucified on a pool table?"

Rishi was straining to get down the steps. I pulled him up short. "Good morning to you too, Nancy."

"This is Erika Norgren, the Director of WellSpring," she said for the edification of the camera. "What are you doing here so early, Erika? Aren't you contaminating the crime scene?"

"Not to my knowledge. Aren't you contaminating the sidewalk by standing there?"

Kevin laughed. "Cool it, ladies. It's too early in the morning for a cat fight."

The nerve of the man! At that moment, I hated him almost more than I hated Nancy. "What are you doing here, Kevin? You told me you'd be out of town for the open house."

"I was, but I got back about one this morning. Nancy left a message about the murder on my machine, because she knows I'm interested in you and the club. Right, Nancy?"

She nodded, simultaneously giving the cameraman a dismissive wave. To my relief, he took the camera off his shoulder. "That's right," Nancy said. "We got some good footage at the open house, but our camera crews were busy with other stories when the news about the murder came over the police scanner. So I decided to follow up this morning. I know it's Saturday, but are you expecting any of the members today?"

"We're closed."

"Just as well," said Kevin. "But Erika, is it wise for you to be alone at the club, with a murderer on the loose?"

Standing behind the yellow tape, I had an acute sense of entrapment. "I've got Rishi," I said. "And I'm expecting some people."

He scowled. "I hate to think of you all alone in there, even for a little while. Tell you what. Why don't you wait out here. I'll go get us some coffee and Danish. Then we can all go inside and have some breakfast. And I'll take a look around, check the windows and things like that."

"The police did that last night."

"They should do it again. In fact, they should be providing you with round-the-clock protection while this madman is still at large. Humor me, Erika. I just want to make sure you're okay."

"All right, on one condition. Bring back an extra Danish for Rishi. He likes cream cheese."

———————

Half an hour later I was back in my office, chowing down Danish with Kevin, Nancy and the cameraman, whom she'd introduced as Ian. Kevin had been right: it felt good having people around.

"What's all this writing on the white board?" asked Kevin. "It's very expressionistic looking. Hard to decipher, though."

"Oh, I was just jotting down some notes about the three deaths at the club, trying to see if there are any logical connections between them."

Nancy leaned forward, suddenly on alert. "Have you come up with anything?"

I glanced at Ian, who was eyeing the videocamera he'd stashed in the corner. "No comment," I said pointedly.

Just then the doorbell rang, and Rishi jumped up barking. Dashing downstairs, my guard dog hot on my heels, I peeked through the peephole and saw Dennis Malone on the stoop. Grabbing Rishi's collar, I opened the door a crack.

"What's going on here?" the Detective said. "You know this is still a crime scene."

"I know. I just couldn't stand staying home alone."

"You shouldn't have come here. I would have gotten in touch when we needed you. And what's that Channel 8 News truck doing outside?"

"Nancy Welcome and her cameraman showed up about an hour ago. They're upstairs now, with Kevin Winthrop."

"Damn!" He slammed a fist into his open palm. "Why the hell did you let them in?"

"Why not?"

"Never mind. I might as well come in too."

I opened the door in silence. "I need your latest roster of club members," he said once he was inside. "Can you get it for me? Don't bother giving me your confidentiality spiel. If you do, we'll just get a warrant. Do you have a sign-in sheet to track attendance?"

"Of course."

"I'll need all of those for the past six months. I'll also need a list of everyone who was at the open house last night, along with their phone numbers and how they're connected to the club."

"That might be tricky. It was awfully crowded, and there were a lot of people I didn't know."

"Just do the best you can."

I heard footsteps on the stoop, the grating sound of a key turning in the lock. Rishi cocked his head and pricked his ears as the door opened to reveal Stanley Washington. He was looking as exhausted as I felt, and I wondered if he'd spent an equally sleepless night.

"You're as bad as Erika, disregarding the crime scene tape," said Dennis.

Stan scowled. "Inasmuch as I manage the club, I didn't think it applied to me. How you doing, Erika? Holding up all right?"

"Hanging in there."

Dennis shrugged in resignation. "Since you're here, Stan, you might as well help Erika get together the rosters and attendance sheets. The open house guest list too."

Stan shot me a look. "I don't know about that."

"It's okay, Stan," I said. "We've got to move fast on this, before something else happens."

Dennis glanced at the stairs. "Meanwhile, I'll go up and tell your visitors they're no longer welcome."

Patting Rishi's head, Stan smiled for the first time. "You mean the folks from Channel 8? I saw the truck outside. They film anything yet?"

"They filmed enough," I said. "Forget about them, Stan. We've got more important things to think about. Before I was so rudely interrupted by the media, I was studying the charts for Stephen, Jeff and Germaine, trying to find some common denominators that might tie their deaths together. It might be nothing, but in the progress notes in Stephen's and Jeff's charts, I came across the initials of someone they both knew about four years ago. Evidently a woman. Stephen got seriously depressed when she stopped coming to the club. The initials are B.G. Do you have any idea who that might be?"

Stan was silent a few moments, his dark face an impassive mask. Then all at once he beamed. "Bobbie Gruenig! That woman was something else."

Chapter 28

We actually had a name! My sleuthing was picking up speed. "Tell me more about this Bobbie Gruenig," I said to Stan.

He fell silent again. Impatient, I grabbed his forearm. It had the smooth hardness of a sun-warmed rock. "Well? Who was she?" I asked. "Tell me about her."

"Calm down, Erika. I'm thinking." He extricated his arm from my grasp. "I didn't know her that well. She was pretty, with long, reddish-blond hair - kind of like you, come to think of it. She liked to write, hung out with the artistic types, like Stephen and Jeff."

"How closely was she involved with them?"

"She and Stephen were going together, but I'm not sure for how long. I don't get involved with that gossipy stuff. It interferes with my work. But you know who might be able to tell you more? Ariana Birdsong. She hung out with that crowd a lot, back when she was a member."

"I didn't know she was."

"Oh, yes. But she doesn't usually let on. Now that she's doing so well on her own, she doesn't like the stigma of being associated with a bunch of crazies. But if you want, I could call her, see if she can come by later."

"That would be great. Thanks, Stan."

The sound of footsteps and conversation cut us short. Dennis was at the top of the stairs with Nancy, Kevin and Ian. "Thanks for your help," he was saying. "I'll be in touch if I need anything else."

"No problem," said Kevin as they started down.

Nancy was uncharacteristically silent as she negotiated the wooden stairs in her high heels. I smiled, pleased that for once she wasn't running the show. She didn't smile back.

All at once I remembered some unfinished business. "By the way," I said to Kevin when he'd descended to my level, "I never got a chance to thank you for your input that night at the Community Board Meeting when you shushed Vito Pisanello. He was really giving me a hard time about the club."

He smiled. "The pleasure was all mine, believe me. I've had dealings with him before, and the guy's a real creep."

"I left you a message the next morning, thanking you, but I don't know if you ever got it."

"I may have, I'm not sure. Forgive me if I didn't call you back."

He was sounding unusually formal, and suddenly I realized why. Dennis was standing there eyeing us both with interest. This was hardly the time for a debate about telephone tag.

We said our good-byes and Dennis ushered them out, then turned to Stan and me. "Now back to business. We were talking about the rosters and the guest list."

"Right," I said. "But first, one question. Can we reopen the club on Monday?"

Both men stared at me open-mouthed, their expressions so similar, it struck me funny. "You think I'm nuts for asking, right?"

They cleared their throats in unison, and I laughed aloud.

"Not nuts," said Dennis at last. "But maybe ill-advised. Are you sure you're up for it? I should think you'd want more time to get over the shock and let things settle down."

"How can things settle down when there's a murderer on the loose?"

"I didn't mean it that way, Erika." He studied his fingernails a moment. "As far as the crime scene investigation is concerned, we'll be finishing up today. Once you give me the lists of names, I'll meet with Diane Olstead at the office to map out a plan. We still have a lot of people to interview, but we won't be using the club for that. I suppose you could reopen if you want to."

"Great. Now if you'll excuse me, I'll just give Ocala a call."

Ocala gave me only a moderately hard time. "It's gutsy of you to want to reopen," she said, "but I'm worried about everyone's safety. What if the killer decides on a repeat performance?"

"I don't think he'll come here in the daytime. All the incidents have occurred after dark. If we suspend our evening programs and close at four thirty, we should be safe enough."

"Still, the idea makes me nervous. I don't know . . . wait a minute, I have an idea. You know my friend Howard Springhorn, who came to the open house? He has his own security business, providing guards for small companies. I'm sure he'd be glad to provide protection for a few days."

"That's an awfully big favor. You really think he'd do it?"

"Hell yes, but not as a favor. I'd pay him his going rate. He's just getting his business off the ground, so I'm the one who'd be doing him a favor, not vise versa. It's a win-win situation all around."

Except for Germaine Lavendre. It's a little late for her. "Thanks, Ocala. I really appreciate it. Nobody would dare mess with Howard. He's one of the most formidable men I've ever seen."

Her laugh was deep and throaty. "Girl, you got that right! Keep him happy, because I want him to stick around."

I had the feeling she was talking about more than his security skills.

We spent the rest of the morning getting the lists of names together, then huddling with Dennis to go over them in more detail. I told him who was most paranoid, who responded better to women interviewers, who was too flagrantly delusional to be trusted.

"What about Arthur Drummond?" I asked Dennis just before he left. "Have you interviewed him yet?"

Dennis frowned. "We're already on it. Why, you think he's likely to show up Monday?"

"Yes, if not before."

"You see that as a problem?"

"I wish I knew. I know he was grossed out by Germaine's costume, but that's hardly a motive for murder."

"What about this friend of yours? Mark Levitan?"

"What about him?"

"Have you been in touch? I think you should be around people this weekend."

So did I. After chasing Mark away last night, the next move was probably mine.

When I finally had the chance to forage for Bobbie Gruenig's chart, Rishi was restless and my stomach was growling, but I couldn't stand the suspense of waiting any longer. "Please be there, Bobbie," I murmured as I entered the file room and unlocked the cabinet that held the dead records. Inactive records, I corrected myself silently. Not all the people whose lives were encapsulated in these musty file folders were dead. Most had been discharged or just drifted away.

269

Gruenig was a distinctive name, and the chart was right where it should be, under the "G's:" *Gruenig, Barbara.* Sending Susan Harvey a silent prayer of thanks for her meticulous filing, I pulled the chart, headed back to my office and began flipping through the pages. I decided to start with the photocopied social work assessment from her most recent hospitalization. Social workers, I'd learned over the years, were more apt to give a comprehensive picture of the whole person, compared to the standardized jargon often spouted by shrinks.

Sure enough, a portrait of Bobbie emerged: an artistic woman of privileged background, who suffered her first flagrantly manic episode in the spring of her sophomore year at Sarah Lawrence. Before that, she had been described as rather neurotic and high strung, but doctors had considered her volatile moods to be a normal manifestation of adolescence.

Her only sibling was a brother nine years older. The social worker noted that after college, he had changed his name from Henry Gruenig to Kevin Winthrop because –

My heart skipped a beat. Kevin Winthrop! So Bobbie Gruenig was his beloved sister Barbara? I flipped back to the face sheet at the front of the chart. Sure enough, there he was, listed as next of kin. Incredulous, I leafed through the other assessments. The name kept popping out at me.

I turned back to the social work assessment and resumed reading. He had changed his name from Henry Gruenig to Kevin Winthrop because he thought the new name was better suited to the distinguished career he intended to carve out on Wall Street. There were allegations that he had sexually abused his sister over a period of many years, stopping only when she went away to college, but these had never been substantiated. On the several occasions when Barbara accused Kevin of abuse, she had been hysterical and barely coherent. Her parents and clinicians believed the statements were delusional, especially since Barbara had such a flamboyant imagination.

My eyes went blurry, and I buried my face in my hands. Hard to believe this time bomb had been lurking unsuspected in the inactive files for so long. This passage explained so much about Kevin – his strangely elusive personality, the reverential way he spoke of Barbara and the shrine he'd made of her old bedroom.

I turned to the progress notes section. The information about her sojourn at the club was scanty, ending almost four years ago. No surprise there – I'd already learned my most recent predecessor didn't like writing progress notes. There was no documentation of an official discharge from the club, nor of suicide.

I scanned the last few notes. Routine, for the most part, but then the initials jumped out at me – S.W. *Stephen Wright!* The notes spoke of their involvement, and Bobbie's mixed feelings about it. Evidently her brother didn't approve of the relationship.

What happened in the months after the notes ceased? Did Bobbie keep coming to the club? Was she still seeing Stephen? I flipped through the record, looking for answers, finding none. But suddenly, in the basic data section, an old photograph stared out at me - a striking young woman with wavy reddish-gold hair and a faraway look in her blue eyes. My heart did an alarming flip-flop as I studied the elegant features. Kevin had been right – Barbara and I could have been sisters.

Holding the chart, my finger marking the place, I left my office in search of Stan. He was at the front desk, on the phone. Too excited to wait, I slapped the record down in front of him, opened it to Barbara's picture and pointed.

He nodded in recognition, then looked away and spoke into the phone. "I'm going to put you on hold a minute. Don't go away."

"You know Kevin Winthrop, that man who was here this morning?" Stan nodded.

"He's Bobbie Gruenig's brother. The chart says he may have abused her. Did you know anything about that? Do you remember ever seeing him at the club?"

He shook his head. "No on both counts. But I've got Ariana on the phone right now. I've already invited her over."

"Great! Tell her to hurry."

Ariana Birdsong made her entrance an hour later in a black cape that reminded me of Arthur's. She doffed it with a flourish, revealing a long, swirling gown. Layers of black lace fell asymmetrically over the purple satin beneath, suggesting the colors of a particularly nasty black eye. Inevitably I thought of Gloria and Germaine. Those damn costumes! If Ariana hadn't gotten Germaine so ludicrously tarted up, the woman might still be alive today.

With effort, I decided to be diplomatic. "Interesting outfit, Ariana. By the way, do you remember the dress I was wearing at the open house last night?"

She nodded. "That was a dynamite print. All those enormous flowers. Silk, right?"

"Yes. I'd like you to have it. I don't ever want to wear it again."

Her eyes widened. "I can understand why. Thanks for the offer, but I'm not sure I could wear it either."

"Then maybe you can use it in an exorcism or something. Burn it, I don't care."

"That's an interesting idea, I'll give it some thought. Goddess knows you could definitely use some help around here."

I hadn't expected her to take me seriously. Burning that dress seemed like such a waste. "Anyway, Stan told me you were friends with Bobbie Gruenig," I said. "I have some questions you might be able to help me with."

"About her relationships with Stephen and Jeff, right? I probably can. But it would be bad karma to do it at the club. In fact, I think we should do a purification ritual here before you reopen. I'm free tomorrow morning if you want."

I suppressed a groan. "So soon after Germaine's murder? I'm not sure it's a good idea. I'm afraid anything that calls attention to the club might bring on more catastrophe."

"Don't worry, Erika. I'm not talking about anything ambitious. Just a small private cleansing ceremony. I'll bring my eagle feather and my sage. It'll just take a few minutes."

What did we have to lose? Things couldn't get much worse, and it couldn't hurt to cover all the bases, no matter how esoteric. "Okay, you're on," I said. "But when can we talk about Bobbie Gruenig?"

"Let's do it tomorrow. You can come to my place after the ceremony. I have a room that's especially propitious for psychic work and exploration. My insights come through more strongly there, and maybe yours will too."

"Why not right now?"

"Right now doesn't feel auspicious. Tomorrow is better, astrologically speaking. Besides, I have a date in a couple of hours." She grinned. "So should you. Go out on the town tonight and clear your mind. You'll be in much better shape for tomorrow."

Just then the phone rang. Stan picked up, listened, then handed me the receiver. "Miriam Goldfarb," he said. "For you."

"Thanks, Stan. Can you transfer the call? Tell her I'll take it in my office." As I headed for the stairs, I mouthed the words "Ooga Booga," but maybe he didn't get it. At any rate, he didn't smile.

"I'm just calling to see if you're okay," Miriam said when I picked up in my office. "Gertrude called me last night about three-thirty. She saw you go into the club with your dog."

"I'm all right. Please thank her for being so concerned."

"Dotty as she is, she doesn't miss much, and the visiting nurses fixed her up with speed dialing in case of emergencies. I'm her number-one contact. But Erika, I'm worried too. You shouldn't be going in that place all by yourself. Especially right after a murder."

"You're probably right, but I couldn't sleep, and I wanted to look up some stuff."

"You shouldn't be alone, young lady, not right now. Isn't there some nice man you can call, someone with your best interests at heart?"

Third time's the charm, I thought. First Dennis, then Ariana, now Miriam, all telling me essentially the same thing. "Yes, there is," I told her. "As a matter of fact, I'm going to call him right now."

Chapter 29

My fingers were poised over the phone, ready to punch in Mark's number, when I realized Ariana was right. I needed to purge my mind of everything to do with the club, if only for an evening.

"I've got a proposition for you," I told Mark when he picked up. "How would you like to spend a night on the town? The Metropolitan Museum's open Saturday nights, or we could go to a jazz club, or both. I've still got the weekend section from yesterday's *Times,* so I'm sure we could figure out something."

"Sounds great. I'm glad you called, Erika. I've been worried about you – I really didn't feel right about leaving you alone last night."

"I wasn't happy about it either. As soon as you left, I realized I'd made a mistake pulling that stiff-upper-lip routine. I could really use your company."

"So what's happening? Have they figured out who killed Germaine Lavendre?"

"No, not yet. But I'm in desperate need of a break. What I'd like most is to go out, take in some good music and art, try not to think about the club and the murder, even if it's just for a few hours. I'm going to some kind of a séance tomorrow, and I'll be in much better shape for it if I can clear my mind tonight."

"What kind of séance?"

"I have no idea. I don't even want to think about it. Please, Mark, let's just go out and have fun."

And so we did. The few times he tried talking about the events at the club, I managed to steer the conversation in another direction. I could tell it bothered him, but by and large, he went along with my quest for total diversion. We spent hours at the Metropolitan Museum, exploring the far reaches of the American Wing and the galleries of Oriental art that the tourists always miss. We had a late dinner, then headed back downtown and listened to jazz till three in the morning. By the time we got back to my apartment, we were so tired that the question of sleeping arrangements barely came up. He collapsed on my couch, I crawled off to the bedroom, and we actually managed to get a few hours of sleep.

At ten he escorted Rishi and me to the club, where we met Stan, Ariana and Gloria for the purification ceremony. I let everyone in, then headed up the stairs to my office. "You go ahead," I told Ariana. "I'll wait for you here."

She shook her head vehemently as she struck a match and fired up her sage stick. "No way! This ritual is for everyone at WellSpring, not just the building. It needs all of your positive energies to make it work." Following her around the club as she waved a gigantic eagle feather, listening to her murmured incantations and inhaling the tangy scent of sage, I felt the atmosphere lighten and realized she was right.

When Ariana and I said goodbye to the others, it was already high noon. We strolled east, north, then east again, stopping every so often to let Rishi sniff landmarks en route. Then all at once we were standing before the armored black door of Stephen Wright's squat. My heart gave a precipitous lurch. "I've been here before, but I didn't know you lived here, Ariana," I said.

"Few people do know. I prefer it that way."

"Stan told me you've been working steadily for several years now. I should think you could afford a regular apartment."

"Maybe, if I scrimped and saved. But I prefer living rent-free." She turned her key in the lock, then yanked at the heavy rope handle. As the door swung open and we stepped inside, an invisible cloud of mildew, cat piss and fresh sawdust enveloped us.

Somewhere above, a chorus of dogs began to bark. Rishi pricked his ears but stayed silent, no doubt aware that he was trespassing on their turf.

Glancing back through the dark hallway toward the stairs, I remembered how they ended abruptly in midair. "Josh showed me around soon after Stephen died," I told Ariana, "but I didn't have the nerve to climb the ladders. Has there been any progress with the carpentry?"

"A little, yes. The basic stairwell is finished as far as the third floor, at my insistence. My clothes kept catching on those damn ladders, and I couldn't invite anyone over, because they were too afraid to come up. Gloria and Germaine were my first guests to try the new improved stairwell." She gave an apologetic giggle. "You'll still have to watch your step, though. Follow me."

"What about those dogs I hear? Will they attack Rishi? Or me, for that matter?"

"No, they live on the fourth and fifth floors, and their owners generally keep the ladders pulled up so the dogs can't get down. My place is on the third floor, so you don't have to worry."

As we began to climb, I groped for the nonexistent banister and peered uneasily through the gaping holes where the risers should be. I edged ever closer to the ancient brick and plaster of the wall, until my clothes brushed the surface and my hand felt its reassuringly solid roughness. Rishi climbed close beside me, his flank grazing my thigh.

As we ascended, the barking grew louder. Once on the comparative solidity of the third floor landing, I looked up to see three dogs peering down. One ghostly gray creature stood out in the darkness; I recognized him as Josh's pit bull. The other two were so dark, I could make out only the flash of white teeth.

Ariana gestured at a door draped in black and purple satin. "That's Stephen's apartment. I added the memorial swags. Mine's just down the hall. I'll go ahead and unlock the door. You'd better wait here while I let Rupert out on the fire escape."

"Rupert's your cat?"

"Yes, he's a big orange tabby – my best friend and soulmate."

I could have sworn her cat would be black. So much for stereotypes. Another stereotype shattered when she ushered me into her apartment, an austerely ordinary place with a long, skinny railroad layout and bare white walls. I would have expected something more exotic.

She flipped a light switch. "Come into my parlor," she said as she led me toward the front of the apartment. "But please take your shoes off first."

Pulling aside a curtain fashioned from an elaborately patterned Indian bedspread in reds and purples, she beckoned me into a dimly lit room that resembled something out of the Arabian Nights. The afternoon sun sifted through deep crimson curtains, giving the room a ruddy glow. The furnishings appeared pillaged from every fabric outlet, thrift store and head shop on the Lower East Side. Yards of fabric festooned every available surface. Cushions were strewn everywhere, and the walls were covered with reproductions of Oriental art and original works of unknown origin.

An enormous, rambling construction cobbled together from dozens of components dominated one corner of the room. Paintings and sculptures of goddesses, vases of silk flowers, brocade, feathers, potted plants all coexisted in a remarkably harmonious assemblage that crept onto the ceiling and spread out a good five feet on either side.

Padding barefoot around the room and lighting candles, Ariana spoke in hushed tones. "How do you like my Goddess shrine?"

"It's beautiful. I recognize some of the figures, like the Indian elephant god Ganesh and the prehistoric Venus figure, but a lot are unfamiliar. Can you tell me about them?"

"Not now. I sense an intense energy in the room, and I don't want to diffuse it. Let's get to work. First we need to sanctify the space." She placed four candles on the floor, chanted a prayer at each in turn, calling on the spirits of the four directions. Then she set two cushions in the center, settled down cross-legged on one of them, and gestured for me to do the same.

"Now we meditate in silence for a few minutes, until Bobbie's spirit pays us a visit. Once she begins speaking through me, you may pose your questions."

"You mean you're going to channel Bobbie Gruenig?"

"What I do isn't channeling, exactly. Anyway, that word has been contaminated by the mass media. I bring myself into alignment with the spirit world in hopes of hearing the voices more clearly."

Hearing voices? That was a classic symptom of psychosis. Saying nothing, I told myself to keep an open mind.

"Now you're wondering if I might be crazy, because I mentioned hearing voices."

It was a statement of fact, not a question, and I knew dissembling would be futile. "The thought crossed my mind for a second, but how did you pick up on it so fast?"

"Nothing miraculous. I sensed it from your facial expression. Now Erika, let's begin. Please close your eyes."

The ensuing silence felt endless. When at last Ariana spoke, it was in a different voice, lighter and more hesitant. "I'm here now. What do you wish to know?"

I took a deep breath to calm my butterflies. "Are you Barbara Gruenig?"

"I was incarnate in that person's body for a time, yes."

"Do you prefer being called Barbara or Bobbie?"

"I answer to both, but I prefer Bobbie. My brother preferred Barbara; he said it was more dignified."

"What is your brother's name?"

"Henry Gruenig. But he changed it to Kevin Winthrop when he went away to school. He thought Gruenig sounded too Germanic, and he hated the name Henry."

"I understand you were involved with Stephen Wright at the WellSpring Club?"

"Yes, Stephen and I loved each other very much. We were together for almost two years, but finally Kevin wore us down and we broke up."

"How do you mean he wore you down?"

"He was against our having anything to do with each other because we were both diagnosed with mental illness. He thought the WellSpring club was beneath me. He was ashamed at the idea of my going there and people finding out about it, because he didn't want me to be stigmatized as mentally ill."

"Did he acknowledge the fact that you were mentally ill?"

"Not really. He knew there was something different about me, but he hated the idea of my being labeled with a diagnosis. And he despised the mental health system. He felt I'd get better care living with him in his fancy apartment. When I was hospitalized for the third time, he fixed up a spare bedroom for me, and he made me come live there when I got discharged. Gradually he got more and more controlling, until finally he even made me stop coming to the club. He convinced me I was too sick and weak to go. And he kept me so drugged up all the time. Looking back now, I believe he may have been feeding me some kind of dope or poison. There were times I would wake up disoriented, with big chunks of my life missing. He would tell me I'd been exhausted and stressed out, and that he'd given me something to help me sleep, but I think there was more to it than that. Sometimes I'd be sore down there, as if I'd been, you know . . ."

"Raped? You believe he raped you?"

"It's possible. But when I said anything, he would say it was a delusion, and that it simply proved how sick I was." She paused, her breath coming in ragged gasps. "I can't go any further." Her eyes took on a glazed, distant look as if the life was fading out of them even as she spoke.

"Wait! I wanted to ask about the time after you left the club, and what made you take your life."

Her voice was so soft, I could barely hear her now. "I was like a fairy-tale princess, imprisoned in a tower. No one but Kevin knew I existed. There was no point in going on."

"Surely you had friends who remembered you? What about Stephen? Or Jeffrey Archer? You knew him too, didn't you?"

"Yes, he was a wonderful friend, like a brother. A real brother, not a monster like Kevin. But Kevin intercepted all my calls, my mail. Then he told them he had sent me to a hospital somewhere out west. He never told them where. In time, they forgot."

Her eyelids fluttered closed, and her body went utterly limp. I knew the interview was over.

——— ——— ———

Out on the sidewalk once more, I rummaged in my handbag, extricated my cell phone, and punched in Dennis Malone's number. True, it was Sunday afternoon, but knowing Dennis, I'd be more likely to find him at his office than home watching football and drinking beer.

I was in luck. "Dennis, I've got some exciting information," I said once I got him on the line. "Can you meet me at Tag? I could use a drink."

Half an hour later we were ensconced next to the window at the black lacquered table where we'd had our first meeting. I'd been drinking gin and tonic that day. Much too cold for that now. Craving something comforting with the hint of cinnamon and freshly harvested apples, I settled for hot buttered rum. I ordered a side of onion rings for Rishi, who was hunkered down at our feet.

Dennis sipped his bourbon in silence as I regaled him with my discoveries of the past 24 hours. Eyeing me speculatively, his green eyes narrowed, he looked for all the world like an assistant professor trying to identify some exotic species of insect.

"You don't believe a word I've said, do you?" I said at last. "You think I'm losing it."

"It's not that, Erika. I believe you uncovered an interesting connection to Stephen Wright. I believe you went to visit Ariana Birdsong, and that she told you some things about Barbara Gruenig that could very well be accurate, although she probably got her information through knowing the people involved rather than through any exotic hocus pocus. But you haven't given me anything concrete to go on. It would be hard to prove sexual abuse when there are no witnesses and the victim has been dead for three years. And I fail to see what this has to do with Germaine Lavendre's murder."

"It could have everything to do with it. If Kevin Winthrop was capable of sexually abusing his sister, he could be capable of murder. Stephen Wright was involved with Bobbie Gruenig, that much we know for sure. Maybe he and Kevin had a confrontation over Bobbie, and Kevin got into a murderous rage."

"Three years after she died? Erika, you're not making any sense."

"It doesn't make sense to me either. But it will. It's like the *Sunday Times* crossword puzzle. A word here and there, and finally it starts coming together. Except I've never had the patience for crossword puzzles – they take too long."

"Then you wouldn't make much of a homicide detective. Murder investigations take time too."

"Too much time, if you ask me. I've told you my news, now tell me yours. It's been two days already – do you have any leads on Germaine's murder? Because I have a gut feeling it was Kevin Winthrop."

"Erika, we've checked and double-checked the names of everyone who was at the open house. Granted we've probably missed a few, but we've interviewed most of them, and no one saw Kevin Winthrop there. Besides, I spoke with him yesterday at the club, and he told me he was out of town. He said he had documentation to prove it. Airline tickets, hotel receipts, that kind of thing."

"Did he actually show them to you?"

"No, but he offered to."

"Maybe he was protesting too much. Didn't it strike you as odd that he would get so defensive, offer to show you evidence that would give him an alibi?"

"Not really." Dennis chuckled. "People have a way of getting defensive when they're being questioned about a murder. I've noticed that before."

I wanted to scream. That cool, sardonic streak of his was driving me crazy. "Dennis, get serious. The club was so crowded, I still believe he could have snuck in unnoticed."

Rishi looked up, uneasy. No doubt he heard the anger mounting in my voice. I knew Dennis heard it too, and it was making him edgy. All at once he shoved back his chair and signaled the waiter. "Check, please. Sorry to cut this short, Erika, but I've got to get back to the office. We've got a couple of things going on. But believe me, we're doing everything we can to wrap this up quickly before – "

"Before what, Dennis? Before someone else gets killed?"

"I admit that's a concern. These three cases at the club have very little in common. That could mean either that the timing is an unfortunate coincidence, or that we're dealing with a very clever criminal, what we call an organized serial killer." He fell silent as he gazed into my eyes. An open, candid gaze this time, full of concern and caring. "Erika, I know I gave you the okay to open the club tomorrow, but maybe you should reconsider. Shutter the place and keep a low profile for awhile."

I rose from my chair, the better to stare him down. "I admit the idea has occurred to me. But the thought of going into hiding makes me furious, and I'd go bonkers staying holed up in my apartment. Besides, I actually feel safer at the club. We keep regular hours, eight-thirty to four-thirty, and when we're open, there are plenty of people around. Stan is always there, and Ocala's friend Howard Springhorn is coming in on an interim basis to provide some extra security. Gloria's in the front office, and Arthur usually gets there by eleven and stays through the afternoon."

Dennis rose, and we stood toe to toe. He grimaced. "Arthur Drummond? I wouldn't exactly consider him an asset. In fact . . ." He fell abruptly into an all too expressive silence.

"You suspect him of Germaine's murder, don't you?"

"Let's just say we haven't ruled him out. Erika, I didn't realize he spent that much time at the club. Didn't you tell me he shows up primarily for the free lunch?"

"Yes, but his attendance has increased ever since Franco Vanelli tried to force me into that car on St. Marks Place. I have a suspicion Arthur has unofficially appointed himself my protector."

Dennis leaned in closer, and his eyes bored into mine. "Would that job description include murder? We still haven't ruled out Arthur as a suspect in Franco Vanelli's killing."

"I know. But I can't very well just order him to stay away for no reason."

"All I'm asking is that you be extremely vigilant. Don't take anyone or anything for granted."

I shook my head in frustration. "You're asking me to live in constant fear and suspicion. That's a hell of a way to live."

Dennis placed a hand on my shoulder and squeezed. "Let's hope it's strictly temporary. But for the time being, until we catch Germaine's killer, it's the best way to make sure you'll still have a life *to* live."

Chapter 30

*N*ight was falling as I stood outside the bar with Dennis, and I could feel November waiting in the wings. I shivered. "Guess I'll have to stop procrastinating and get my winter clothes out of box storage."

He rubbed Rishi's ears. "Want me to walk you home? I trust you took my advice, and that you have someone staying with you tonight."

I'd agreed to meet Mark at his apartment, but I didn't feel like sharing that information, despite the quizzical look in the detective's green eyes. "Yes, I do. Thanks, Dennis, I'll be fine. Rishi and I can take a cab."

"Okay, if you're sure. I'll be at the office for a couple more hours." He extracted a business card from his pocket, scribbled on the back. "And here's my home phone. Call me any time, day or night."

He flagged down a taxi for me, and I gave the driver Mark's address in the East 20's. Climbing out of the cab with Rishi, I found myself standing in front of a high-rise apartment building with Art Deco detailing that had seen better days. The expansive lobby cried out for a doorman, but by the look of things, there hadn't been one for years.

I needed a few minutes of down time to collect my thoughts before confronting Mark. The morning's purification ceremony, the channeling session with Ariana a.k.a. Bobbie, then the two hours with Dennis had left me with all the vitality of a wrung-out dishrag. And the detective's warnings had left a bitter aftertaste. My natural inclination had always been to trust people unless they sent out clear signals that I shouldn't. The idea of viewing the world and its inhabitants through a dark veil of suspicion was unutterably depressing, and I needed a snatch of solitude to adjust my attitude before settling in for an evening with Mark.

To say that the talk with Dennis had been disappointing was putting it mildly. Obviously the police had no new information about Germaine's murder, and he had totally blown off my theories about Kevin Winthrop. I could understand why, because there wasn't anything concrete to link Kevin to the crime. Even so, I was annoyed at the offhand way Dennis had dismissed my suspicions.

If there was any evidence incriminating Kevin, it was up to me to find it. And since Dennis had advised me to wrap myself in a cloak of paranoia for the foreseeable future, I might as well put my suspiciousness to good use. Stephen's squat was a good place to start. The session with Ariana had been illuminating, but there was a great deal more to learn. Not tonight, though. Nine Squat was dark enough in broad daylight, and the thought of going back there now chilled me to the bone.

"Hey, lady! You look lost. Can I help you?"

I whirled to see Mark, wrapped in a loden-green trench coat and dragging a metal shopping cart loaded with bags from Gristede's. "Jeez, Mark, don't scare me like that! I was about to go for my pepper spray."

"So the afternoon's been that stressful, huh?"

"You could say that. Strange, at any rate."

Julie Lomoe

"Let's go upstairs and you can tell me about it while I cook dinner. I got a couple of T-bone steaks. I figured Rishi would like the bones."

"That sounds fabulous." I glanced down at Rishi, who was avidly sniffing the groceries. "Rishi thinks so too."

Mark's twelfth-floor apartment had a northern exposure with a spectacular view of the city. I recognized the elegant pinnacle of the Chrysler building in the distance. But the living room was cluttered with what looked like the end products of several good-sized trees. The Sunday *Times* littered the brown leather sofa and glass-topped coffee table near the windows. Ceiling-high bookshelves lined the walls, and every available surface was piled high with books, magazines and papers.

Mark grinned sheepishly. "I know, don't say it. I'm a pack rat."

"You should call the Home & Garden Channel. Maybe they could send in a crew and feature your place on one of those organizing makeover shows."

"No way. Believe it or not, there's a method to this madness. I know where everything is."

I didn't let on, but I was secretly pleased as he gave me the grand tour. There were no signs of a woman's touch anywhere in the apartment.

Over dinner and late into the night, I rambled on about Bobbie Gruenig, Kevin Winthrop and the happenings at the club. Mark was an excellent listener, but at ten o'clock I caught him sneaking longing glances at the remote control switch on the coffee table. "What do you say we catch *Law and Order?*" he said.

"Why not? It fits right in with your viewpoint. Let the cops and lawyers handle everything."

"Damn straight. Don't play amateur sleuth. Leave it to the professionals."

288

"How dare you say that!" Sliding closer on the sofa, I reached out and tickled his ribs.

He tickled me back. "So you want to play rough?"

I squealed. Rishi jumped up and came running to join the melee. "Down, boy. It's okay," I said as my hands snaked around Mark's back.

——— ———

Over the next few hours, our relationship took a giant leap forward. But by mutual consent, for all sorts of probably nonsensical reasons, we avoided taking the ultimate leap into bed. I awoke Monday morning feeling elated, and I was glad of the long walk downtown to the club with Rishi. By the time we'd covered all twenty-five blocks, I'd managed to regain some of my professional composure.

At WellSpring, the yellow crime-scene tape was gone, and Howard Springhorn was standing at the top of the stoop, conferring with Stan. Whether by design or coincidence, both men wore black denim jeans and black leather jackets, and both men looked seriously bad. Stan's height and his muscular build had always intimidated me a little, but compared to Howard, he looked like a relative pixie.

Climbing the steps with Rishi, I felt like Cleopatra addressing my generals. "I'm delighted to see you both. The club will be in good hands today."

"Yeah, we're ready to roll," said Howard with a grin.

"We were just discussing strategy," said Stan. "Howard's going to stick around the entrance, and I'll cover the inside. I'll give him a roster so he can check people off as they arrive."

"Okay. Just don't scare them too badly, Howard."

He laughed, displaying a prominent gold tooth. "Who, me? I'm a pussycat. Just ask Ocala. Seriously, though, it wouldn't hurt to have someone look over your members with a fresh eye. I'm good at sizing people up. I'll give you a heads-up if anyone seems too dodgy."

Just then Gloria arrived. Her eyes widened as she looked up at Howard. "Oooh, what have we here?" she cooed. For a moment I thought she was going to resurrect some of her Madonna moves from the cabaret.

"You remember Howard Springhorn," I said with a warning glare. "Ocala's friend."

She caught the hint and was suddenly all business. Other members began arriving, and before long the club was in session. Caught up in the familiar routine, there were stretches when I managed to forget about Germaine for minutes at a time.

Around eleven o'clock, Gloria buzzed me in my office. "Ariana's here to see you." As I headed down the stairs to greet her, the front door flew open, and Arthur Drummond stormed in. "What's that brother doing out on the stoop? He checked me off on a list and gave me the evil eye."

"He's a friend of Ocala St. Claire's," I said. "He's providing security for the time being, to insure that people feel safe attending the club."

Arthur nodded. "I saw him from the other night. He was standing in the back, watching the show for awhile. Good idea having him here. He's such an enormous mother fucker, even I would think twice before messing with him."

Ariana tittered, and Arthur glared at her. "What's so funny? You don't think I could take him?"

Sobering instantly, she threw him a sidelong glance. "I wouldn't know. I'm a pacifist, and I try not to give violent thoughts any space in my mind."

"Lots of luck," he said, as he looked her up and down. "But this is a violent world we live in, and we have to be prepared. Sometimes we have to let evil into our minds, so we'll be ready to fight back when it tries to sneak up and clobber us from behind."

Over lunch, Ariana confirmed my impression: the atmosphere at the club was reasonably benign. "See, I told you the purification ritual would help," she said.

"Either that, or everyone's simply in denial," I said.

She frowned. "Erika, have you always been so cynical?"

"I'm sorry, it's just an old defense mechanism. Actually, you've been an enormous help. I'm still feeling blown away by that session yesterday. Since things seem under control here, I'd like to go back to the squat after lunch. I want to take a look at Stephen's apartment and see if I can find anything relating to Bobbie."

"I'd help you, Erika, but I'm tied up the rest of the afternoon. We could do it tonight."

"I'd rather do it now, while it's light. Do you suppose Josh would be there to let me in?"

"Probably. Let's see, it's almost one. He should be awake by now. Why don't I give him a call and tell him you're coming? That way he can be downstairs to let you in. He'll need to walk Mugsy anyway."

———— — ————

Josh and Mugsy were sitting on the steps of the squat, soaking up the crisp autumn sunshine, when Rishi and I arrived at two. The man and his pit bull both jumped up to greet us, but while Josh was relaxed and cordial, his dog was tense and edgy.

"Mugsy's not in a good mood today," Josh said. "The other dogs have been picking on him, and he might take it out on your guy. I'd better lock him in my apartment. Then I'll come back down to let you and your dog into Stephen's place."

Ten minutes later, standing in the unrelieved blackness of Stephen's living room, I felt weighted down by a darkness oppressive enough to turn even the sunniest Pollyanna suicidal. The walls, the ceiling, the woodwork were painted a uniform matte black that sucked up the feeble light from two battered floor lamps that had probably been scavenged from the street. The lamp shades were draped in sheer black fabric, and the windows at the rear of the apartment were masked by curtains of black vinyl that conjured up memories of the body bag they'd used to take Stephen away.

I shuddered. "Ugh! How could anyone stand to live in a place like this? It's like being deep underground in a cave that's never seen the light of day."

Josh shrugged. "He liked it this way, claimed it had a peaceful, calming effect. He painted the whole apartment black after he broke up with Bobbie, and then he decided to keep it like this. I think he liked the attention. People had such strong reactions to the place that it made them worry about Stephen's state of mind. Especially women – they were always inviting him over for dinner to cheer him up."

"And did he go?"

"Sometimes. But he kept brooding about Bobbie. In fact he got kind of hyper and paranoid. He kept ranting about how Bobbie's brother was out to get him, and how he wanted get back at the guy."

Josh's tone was so laid back that he might have been describing the latest episode in a TV series. I tried to read his expression, but the murky darkness swallowed his features. "Do you know whether he actually had any contact with Kevin after Bobbie died?" I asked.

"I have no idea." He waved vaguely toward a corner where a stack of plain black books leaned against a wall. "You might try checking his journals. Maybe he wrote something about it."

I approached the journals gingerly. I'd kept journals in similar volumes of hardbound sketch paper, and the idea of opening and reading some one else's personal musings seemed like a violation of the most intimate kind. "I'm surprised these are still here," I said. "Do you know if the police looked at them?"

"I don't know. I let the cops in here after Stephen's death, but they didn't want me hanging around. They weren't here long, maybe an hour at the most."

I felt a rush of rage as I pictured them doing their obligatory walk-through. No doubt they were looking for evidence to confirm Stephen's death as a suicide, and found ample confirmation in his oppressively gloomy decorating scheme. With his history of hospitalizations for depression and in the absence of involved relatives, they wouldn't have bothered to probe further.

Picking up the top volume, I blew the thin layer of dust from the cover and opened it at random. The writing was helter-skelter and hard to decipher. I turned the page and saw a poem surrounded by abstract squiggles, while another page looked like a snatch from a short story in progress.

The black walls seemed to close in, and I felt suddenly dizzy, afraid I might faint. "I can't read these without my glasses," I mumbled.

Josh reached out an arm to steady me. "Are you okay? You look pale."

"I'll be all right. I just need some air."

"It's probably the vibes in here. Ariana's been meaning to come in and do a cleansing ceremony to help Stephen's spirit on its way. But I don't know what we're going to do with all his stuff. His apartment is already promised to some people with a couple of kids, and they're dying to get in and repaint the place."

"Would it help if I took his journals? They'd be in a safe place and I could study them at my leisure. And perhaps there's something in them worth reading or even publishing."

Josh smiled. "That's a great idea. I even have the perfect thing for you to carry them in – a plastic milk crate from some dairy in Queens. It's my end table right now, but I'll sacrifice it for a good cause."

An hour later Rishi and I were back in my apartment, with the journals spread out on my old oak dining table. Before digging in, I called the club, where Gloria reported everything was going smoothly.

I heard a female voice chattering excitedly in the background. "Ariana's still here," said Gloria. "She wants to talk to you."

"Okay, put her on." I waited for Ariana to pick up. "I didn't feel comfortable about bringing Stephen's journals to the club," I said then. "I'm concerned about confidentiality, and they're hard to decipher. At home, I can focus better and give them the attention they deserve."

"I totally understand. I'm curious – what did you think of his place?"

"It's certainly different. After awhile all that blackness felt claustrophobic, as if the room was closing in and about to squash me. I think I would have fainted if I hadn't gotten out of there."

"Erika, I feel exactly the same way!" Ariana's voice vibrated with excitement. "That confirms my hunch. You're unusually sensitive to psychic phenomena. If you want, I'd love to work with you to help hone your paranormal skills."

The very idea brought on a rush of anxiety. "Thanks, Ariana, but I've got too much on my plate right now. Can I take a rain check?"

"Of course. You need to be totally open for this kind of training to work, but with all the upset about the three deaths at the club, you have to keep a strong shield around yourself to armor your psyche. So the timing right now isn't auspicious anyway. But those weird emanations in Stephen's apartment are the main reason I haven't gotten around to doing a ritual cleansing there. Despite all the blackness, it didn't feel negative when he was alive, only after he was gone. I believe it's his spirit telling us there's unfinished business surrounding his death."

"Amen to that. And speaking of unfinished business, I'd better get started on these journals, or I'll be up all night."

Of necessity, I spent the first two hours learning to decipher Stephen's extravagant, twisted script. Then I skimmed for content, looking for major themes and trying to differentiate fact from fiction, reality from poetic license. I was bleary-eyed by sunset, but still I kept on, beguiled by Stephen's witty, lyrical style.

After the initial overview, I decided I deserved a dinner break. Scavenging the kitchen, I found half a box of wheat thins, a wedge of Brie and a bottle of Merlot. I brought my finds back to the table and resumed reading, beginning with the most recent volume.

By now I could distinguish Stephen's journaling from his poetry and fiction. The handwriting was subtly different: the works of imagination had a more flowing, calligraphic look, while the penmanship of the diary entries had a backward slant and a more angular, aggressive quality. Even before reading the words, I could sense Stephen's emotional temperature by the pressure of the pen on the page. On some pages, the large, sprawling letters and the energy of the cross-outs and corrections had an angry energy, while on others, the faint, tentative script suggested depression.

The final volume began after Bobbie's death. Stephen wrote of his despair, his guilt over giving in to Kevin's insistence that the two of them break up. Page after page he flagellated himself for his failure to insist on seeing her, his failure to confront Kevin about his abusive treatment of Bobbie. The scrawled notes identified the sister and brother only as B and K.

Stephen documented the transformational blackening of his apartment, which began as an expression of his deep depression but took on a cathartic life of its own, helping him in his healing process. As time passed, the entries about Bobbie dwindled, then ceased. For over a year he wrote nothing about her or Kevin.

Then suddenly, this past July, the preoccupation returned. He described taking some kind of hallucinogen as part of a ritual with "A," probably Ariana, and his feelings about Bobbie and Kevin resurfaced as unfinished business. "I can no longer live with myself unless I confront K," he wrote. "Her spirit will never rest unless I seek retribution for the crimes he committed against her. I must – "

Just then the phone rang. I snatched it up impatiently. "Hello?"

"Erika, it's Mark. Did we get our signals crossed? I thought you were coming back here after work."

"Oh, Mark, I'm sorry. I completely forgot. I went back to the squat and got hold of Stephen Wright's journals. I've been studying them for hours, and I think I'm really onto something here."

"You want to stop for a dinner break? It's almost nine o'clock."

"Better not. I'm afraid I'd lose my train of thought. Besides, I wouldn't be very good company. It's like I'm inside Stephen's head, caught up in a vortex. The thoughts are circling round and round, and I don't know – "

"Erika, stop it!" There was a long pause. "All this obsessing over old relationships isn't good for you. I think you should give it a rest."

"I can't, not when I've come this far."

"You want me to come over there?"

The warm catch in his voice sent all sorts of sensations rocketing through my body, and I almost said yes. But once here, I knew he would tell me to ease up on my search, to let the investigation run its course. I didn't want more lectures on the virtues of leisurely law and order.

"Not tonight," I said. "I'll be all right, I swear it. But time is running out."

Chapter 31

I wasn't sure what I meant when I told Mark time was running out, but something told me the end game was at hand. I was up all night pacing, poring over Stephen's journals. I needed an action plan, but what form would it take? I didn't have a clue.

At long last dawn rolled around. I showered and shampooed. Then, standing barefoot in my slip, I blow dried my hair. I rarely bothered, usually left my hair to its own unruly devices, but this morning I felt a need to impose some semblance of order. Maybe taming the outside of my head would help tame the tempestuous thoughts within.

I yanked a black wool suit from the back of my closet. The only black outfit I owned, something from a long forgotten funeral, but somehow it suited my mood. Mulling over the morning's agenda, I decided to call Dennis Malone as soon as I got to the club. It was already Tuesday, the day before Halloween. Four days since Germaine's murder – surely by now he'd have something to report.

Unfortunately he didn't - not about Germaine, at any rate. "We've been busy on another front," he said.

I felt the rage welling up. "Excuses don't cut it, Dennis. You've had more than enough time - "

My office door flew open and Arthur barged in, brandishing a newspaper. Rishi jumped up barking, and Arthur skidded to a stop a few feet shy of my desk.

I grabbed Rishi's collar. "What is it, Arthur? You could have knocked."

Cautiously, he held out the paper. "Look at this."

"Just a minute." I swiveled my chair away from Arthur, the better to concentrate on Dennis. "Can I put you on hold a minute? Arthur Drummond is here, waving a paper in my face."

"He's probably got the same news I was about to tell you. I don't have time to hold; I'll let you hear it from him. Catch you later." There was a click.

I swiveled back to Arthur. "He hung up on me. Can you believe it?"

He grinned. "He's probably in demand right now."

I decided to have mercy on Arthur. "Rishi, go to your closet." I pointed and my dog obeyed. Then I wheeled closer to Arthur and grabbed the paper. It was the *Post*, folded open to an inside page:

COPS NAB MOBSTER IN VANELLI MURDER

"See, I'm off the hook," crowed Arthur.

I tried scanning the article, but I was so acutely aware of his gray eyes studying me that I couldn't focus properly. Words and phrases jumped out at me: investigation . . . Detective Dennis Malone . . . gang-related . . . vendetta.

Arthur inched closer. "You thought I killed him, didn't you?"

I rolled my chair away from him, but it crashed into the wall at my back. "I'll admit it entered my mind. Arthur, why don't you pull up a chair and sit down? I don't like being loomed over."

"Okay. Sorry, Erika, I don't mean to make you nervous."

"Well you do, or did. You were so intensely interested in Vanelli's murder, I thought you had a personal stake in it."

"Damn right I did. The creep attacked you, and I still believe he had it coming. You know how I feel about you. I'd defend you if it came down to that. But I wouldn't have hunted him down and killed him. I've never killed anyone in my life."

"Glad to hear it."

Just then my inside line rang. I picked up. "Erika, it's Kevin Winthrop. Sorry I didn't get to spend more time with you when I was at the club the other day, but it was kind of awkward, what with Nancy and that detective around."

My heart began pounding faster. "Yes, I know. How are you, Kevin?"

"I'm all right. But I'm worried about you, and surprised you're open for business as usual. How's that murder investigation coming along? Have the cops made any progress?"

"They're working on it, but they don't really keep me in the loop."

"They should. You have a right to know what's going on. Plus you have some theories of your own, or at least it seemed that way the other day. That diagram you had up on the board looked pretty impressive."

I glanced up at the white board. The initials B.G. were still there in duplicate, flaming orange with a two-way arrow. How much had he registered? "Oh, that was nothing. Just doodling."

"Anyway, Erika, I didn't call to interrogate you. I wanted to invite you to dinner. Are you free tonight? I promise to keep it light, just treat you to a good meal and help distract you from everything that's going on. I was thinking of Tavern on the Green."

My intestines began writhing in serpentine knots. I'd never been bulimic, but the mere thought of dinner with Kevin was enough to make me upchuck. "I don't know," I said, stalling. "There's a lot going on. I'll have to check my day planner."

"Go right ahead. I can wait."

Footsteps sounded in the hall, and Stan materialized in the doorway. "Morning, Erika. Just checking in. Everything okay here?"

I nodded, smiled at Stan, then Arthur, as an idea took shape in my mind. "Just fine, Stan." I turned my attention back to Kevin. "I just checked, and tonight looks fine. But I've got some work to finish up first. Can you pick me up here at the club? Say, seven o'clock?"

"Seven o'clock it is."

"I still think this is crazy, Erika. It puts you at terrible risk." Stan's jaw was clenched, and his fingers drummed restlessly on his thighs.

"I think it's brilliant," said Arthur. "I say we go for it."

It was ten o'clock, and the three of us were locked in my office. We'd been over my plan a dozen times, brainstormed it from every conceivable angle, and there was little left to say. Unless I copped out – that was still a distinct possibility.

"I'm at risk anyway," I said, not for the first time. "So is everyone else at the club. I'm convinced Kevin killed Stephen, Jeff and Germaine. And he'll go on killing until he destroys the club." I stood, crossed the room to the white board, grabbed the eraser. "He had plenty of time to see this chart when he was here Saturday morning. He knows I'm onto him, I'm almost positive."

"You can't be sure of that," said Stan.

"I can't afford to take the chance." I swiped the eraser across the board, beginning with the initials B.G. It was amazing how effortlessly the board came clean.

Stan sighed. "I suppose you're right. So I'll take the closet, and Arthur will take the fire escape. You'll keep Rishi with you."

"Yes, because he'll never keep quiet otherwise."

"Are you sure you don't want to involve that security guy Howard?"

"Stan, we've been over this *ad nauseam*. He'd be duty-bound to tell Ocala, and she'd never go for this. The fewer people involved, the better. I'll take Gloria over to Gertrude Reynolds's place, so she can keep an eye on the club from the window, as a fallback plan. But it has to look as if I'm here by myself, alone and defenseless, just awaiting my dinner date with Prince Charming."

———

The day dragged unbearably. I longed to call Mark, but I knew he'd try to talk me out of my scheme. So would Dennis, and he didn't believe Kevin was a viable suspect in any event. Even so, I kept hoping against hope that he'd call to tell me he'd finally seen the light, that Kevin was a prime suspect and the police were about to bring him to justice.

It didn't happen. At four o'clock, I brought Gloria over to Miriam Goldfarb's apartment, where I gave them a bare-bones explanation. "It's probably nothing," I said, "but I'm getting weird vibes from Kevin lately. Just keep an eye on the club from Gertrude's window, beginning around six-thirty. Call 911 if you hear or see anything suspicious."

Gloria shot me a quizzical look. "But why go out with this guy if you think he's such a creep?"

"I guess I just can't pass up dinner at Tavern on the Green. Seriously, I've got my reasons, but I'll explain later. Just do it, okay?"

"Okay." She exchanged glances with Miriam. I knew they weren't satisfied, but at least they'd have plenty of fodder for gossip in the next couple of hours.

———

At seven o'clock, I was in my office playing FreeCell. Rishi dozed on the rug nearby, and the crystalline magic of Bach's Goldberg

Variations on public radio conveyed the illusion of serenity. Then the downstairs doorbell rang. My mutt came suddenly alert, and my heart lurched into my throat. Reaching beneath a stack of papers in my in-box, I clicked on my tape recorder. Then I headed for the stairs, ready to tackle my starring role in this crazy, custom-tailored melodrama.

Kevin greeted me cordially, his eyes alight with admiration. "That suit is very becoming. I've never seen you in black, and you don't usually dress so elegantly for work. Did you go home and change?"

I glanced around the deserted lobby, where cutouts of black cats and witches graced the walls. "No, I guess I was just psyching myself up for Halloween. You want to come upstairs with me? I have to shut down my computer and lock up."

As he followed me up the stairs, I could almost believe this was an ordinary date. Maybe I was all wrong about his intentions. Well, we'd see soon enough.

It didn't take long. No sooner did I sit down at my desk and reach for the mouse to log off my computer, than a knife materialized in his hand. "Sit still, Erika, and don't make a sound. We've got some talking to do." His voice was soothingly soft, his movements understated.

Hackles bristling, Rishi rose to check him out. Kevin extended a hand as if to let him sniff, made a lightning grab for his collar. With the other hand, he brandished the knife near Rishi's throat. Its long blade gleamed silver against the dog's black coat. "One wrong move, and I'll kill him."

"You wouldn't hurt Rishi. You love dogs too much."

He was silent just long enough to tell me I'd touched a nerve. "Don't count on it," he said at last in a tone of icy bravado. "Anyway, Erika, I'm sorry it's come to this. But I'll let you enjoy the company of your pooch while you can, because you don't have much time left."

My heart skipped a beat, then began a slow, heavy thudding in my chest. I'd engineered this scene, orchestrated it to the best of my ability, but who was I kidding? I wasn't ready for the reality, not at all. In a matter of minutes, no, seconds, I could be dead.

I forced myself to breathe slowly and deeply, and all at once I was in witness mode, watching myself watching Kevin as he took a seat opposite me. His threats sounded like something out of a run-of-the-mill movie, and I wondered if he'd rehearsed them ahead of time. If I were rating his performance, I'd give him two thumbs down, I decided, and the thought made me smile.

He raised his knife and ran a finger speculatively along the blade. "I fail to find anything humorous in this situation."

I wondered if this was the knife he'd used to kill Germaine. "I'm sorry." Why was I apologizing when he was the one holding me hostage at knifepoint? "Stress makes me act peculiar sometimes."

"I understand. Barbara was like that too. I imagine it's related to your bipolar diagnosis."

His tone was so calmly clinical that I could barely suppress a giggle. This whole scene was so ludicrous, I couldn't believe it was happening. "Kevin, this joke has gone far enough," I said. Experimentally and with extreme caution, I began to rise from my chair.

He let go of Rishi's collar. As the dog rushed to my side, Kevin's hand shot inside his jacket, and suddenly he was brandishing a snub-nosed pistol in his right hand, the knife still clutched in his left. "Sit the fuck down, or I'll finish you off right now! Same goes for your dog. Make him sit, or I'll blow his head off."

Was he bluffing? Finding out could be fatal, for Rishi and me both. "Sit, Rishi," I said, grabbing his collar and pulling him close as I sank back down.

Should I call out? No, something told me Kevin wasn't ready to kill me, at least not yet. He needed to talk, and I needed to listen. With a silent prayer that all my counseling skills would kick in full force, I launched into the interview that could well be a literal matter of life or death. Leaning forward, trying not to look at the weapons in his hands, I fixed my eyes ingenuously on his. "Kevin, I don't understand why you're doing this. We're friends. I thought everything was fine between us."

"It was, but on Saturday when I saw my sister's initials on that board, I realized you knew too much. I can't risk letting you live any longer."

"So I was right. You killed those people, didn't you?"

Leaning back, he stretched out his legs, resting the gun and knife casually on his thighs. "I guess it's true confessions time. I'm rather proud of my work, and I've been looking forward to sharing it with you. Quite a striking tableau the other night, wasn't it?"

"You mean Germaine on the pool table? I guess you could say that."

"You're so artistic, Erika, I knew you'd appreciate it. Very Christmasy, with the contrast of the red bustier and blood against the green baize of the pool table. And the silver duct tape added a little pizzazz, don't you think?"

He was warming to the subject, sounding like some maniacal decorator on the Home & Garden channel, but at least he was talking. "I don't understand," I said. "What did you have against Germaine?"

"Nothing, except that she was a member of the club. And the way she was tarted up so grotesquely, like the most despicable kind of slut, she happened to be perfect for my purposes."

"What purposes were those?"

"To close down the club, of course. To get retribution for the damage the place did to Barbara. If she hadn't hung out here and gotten involved with Stephen Wright, she might never have killed herself."

"You killed Stephen too, didn't you?"

His eyes darted down and away, and he was silent a moment. "Yes, he was the first. He contacted me in July, saying he wanted to talk with me about some things Barbara had told him a long time ago. Outrageous accusations, complete garbage."

"About incest, right? She claimed you abused her for years, and said she couldn't take it any more."

"Where did you hear that?"

"It was in Stephen's journals."

"Pure bullshit, I assure you. The creep was crazy, delusional. Even so, I couldn't have him spreading rumors about me. I was forced into action."

"So you lured him up to the roof and dropped him over the edge."

"No, we met by mutual consent. He was the one who suggested the roof of the club. He knew the code to turn off the alarm system and how to access the roof. Since it was a hot night, it seemed like a good idea. I had no particular plans before we met, but once we got talking and I heard the filth he was spewing about Barbara and me, I knew what I had to do. The opportunity was too perfect to pass up."

"But how did you do it? The police looked up there, and they didn't report any signs of struggle."

Kevin flashed a self-satisfied smile. "There wasn't any. I grabbed him by the belt and swept him off his feet so fast, he didn't know what hit him. Then I carried him to the edge and swung him over. I checked to make sure the angle was right, because we were only four flights up, and it was crucial that he hit headfirst. I wished him bon voyage and let him drop. He was such a wimp, he didn't even get off a good scream, just a few pathetic whimpers. But to be on the safe side, I came back downstairs and left through your office window to avoid attracting any attention on the street."

He paused, studying me expectantly as if awaiting praise for his performance in a particularly challenging athletic event. Struggling to suppress the all too graphic images that were flooding my mind, I gave him what he wanted. "You must be awfully strong. It couldn't have been easy to pick him up and handle him like that."

He grinned. "It's good to know my gym membership has finally paid off. All those years on the weight machines have helped me pack on a lot of muscle, especially in the upper body. But of course it didn't hurt that he was such a runty little guy."

"Is that why you picked Jeffrey Archer for your next victim? He had a similar build to Stephen's, slender and slight. You knew you could take him physically."

Kevin waved his hand in dismissal, shooing off the suggestion like a bothersome bug. "That was a minor consideration. I could easily dominate anyone at the club. I chose him mostly because he was a friend of Stephen Wright's and he knew Barbara. But he sealed his fate with that mural he was painting on the façade. It was getting too much attention. Odds were it would generate positive publicity for the club, and that was totally unacceptable. By arranging the artist's tragic overdose, I made sure the media would put a different spin on the story."

My loathing for Kevin intensified as he talked. I was thankful my training had taught me to keep up the open, nonjudgmental façade that encouraged frank disclosures, no matter how heinous. Clearly he was getting off on his revelations. "Have you spoken to anyone else about these events?" I asked.

He laughed. "Of course not. Do you think I'm crazy? I'm only telling you because you won't be leaving this room alive."

I leaned forward, gazing raptly into his eyes as if he'd never uttered those chilling words. "I don't think you're crazy," I said softly. "In fact in a strange way, I have to admire your cleverness. Even though the police investigations are still open, they've pretty much concluded that Stephen committed suicide and Jeff died of a heroin overdose – "

"He did. It just wasn't self-administered."

"So you've told me. Anyway, the police didn't suspect murder in either case. It must have been frustrating for you to have carried out these killings so successfully, and yet to have the quality and subtlety of your work go totally unrecognized."

"You've got that right! With your average serial killer, certain features show up repetitively, like a personal signature. They use a particular weapon, or disfigure the victim in a particular way, so the police come to recognize their work. And with all the sensationalism in the media, they eventually get downright famous. That doesn't happen if you're more imaginative and able to think outside the box. Then no one knows you exist."

Bingo! I felt a rush of exhilaration at the rightness of my last move, then remembered the high stakes of the game we were playing. "You must have felt very much alone," I said. "All that skill and imagination, going completely unrecognized. Is that why you staged Germaine's death so dramatically, to make sure people would pay attention?"

"I guess so. I haven't really thought about it in those terms before, but on some unconscious level, maybe that's true." He chuckled. "You're playing head games with me, aren't you? I've got to admit you're a better shrink than some I've met. Although of course I've never gone to one, except for some family therapy sessions with Barbara."

"The two of you must have had a very special relationship."

He shook his head, but his eyes misted over. "Oh no, I'm not getting into that. You already have your own filthy preconceptions about it."

"No, Kevin, all I have is some second-hand speculations, plus what I've sensed from the way you talk about her and the beautiful room you created for her. There was obviously a lot of love there."

Laying the weapons loosely on his thighs, he buried his head in his hands. His shoulders began to shake. "You're right," he muttered through his fingers. "I loved Barbara more than anyone, and you're like her in so many ways. I thought maybe we could build a life together. I never meant for it to end like this."

That was it. I'd heard enough, and he'd never be more vulnerable than he was at this moment. I glanced over his shoulder at the door to the closet. It stood slightly ajar.

"Sorry, Kevin, but our time is up," I said in the empathic tones of a counselor ending a fifty-minute session. Then I pumped up the volume, gave a shout. "Ooga Booga!"

Julie Lomoe

Startled, Rishi jumped up barking. Kevin lurched, and the weapons clattered to the floor. He dropped his hands, gave me an incredulous stare. "What the hell – "

He stopped short as something over my shoulder caught his eye. His back to the closet, he didn't see Stan opening the door.

The squeak and clatter of the window sash behind me told me Arthur was on the job, but I didn't dare turn to look, because Kevin was lunging for the floor, going for his gun. Clinging to both arms of my chair, I launched a lucky kick and the little gun skittered out of reach. He grappled for his knife. I kicked again, harder, connected with his hand.

Kevin howled in pain. "You bitch!" He spat out the words, his eyes bulging with rage.

Arthur's scream assaulted my ears as he streaked past me. "You creep! I'm going to kill you!" He threw himself at Kevin, pinned him in his chair.

With a roar, Stan charged across the room, grabbed Kevin from behind, chair and all. "No, you don't, Arthur! He's mine!" He wrestled Kevin, chair and all, away from Arthur, picked it up shoulder-height. He smashed it to the floor, straddled it, lowered his massive body down onto Kevin's chest. Kevin gasped, began whimpering softly.

"Cool it, guys," I said. "Nice going, but nobody's killing anybody around here. The killing is over for good."

308

Chapter 32

*D*ennis Malone stared at the weird tableau on the floor of my office. "What the hell is going on here?"

By now Stan and Arthur had rolled Kevin onto his stomach. With Stan sitting astride his back and Arthur straddling his thighs, he was pinioned in place like a beetle on a specimen board. A triumphant climax to the drama I'd staged – too bad there wasn't a camera handy.

"What's going on is that I just brilliantly elicited a confession," I said. "Kevin Winthrop murdered Stephen, Jeff and Germaine, just as I've been trying to tell you, but you wouldn't believe me. I've got it all on tape."

Kevin let out a yelp. "Tape? What do you mean, tape?" His fingers clawed the carpet, and he hazarded a few feeble kicks. "Help, officer! Get these thugs off me. They're both crazy!"

"Watch your mouth," said Arthur. "I'm not a thug. As a matter of fact, I just saved Erika's life."

"You and me both," said Stan. "Give credit where credit is due." He bounced lightly atop Kevin's back, as if posting to the trot on an

English saddle. "I agree with my colleague. There's no need for name calling."

Kevin whimpered. "I'm sorry. But officer, these men assaulted me."

"Not until you threatened my life," I said. "Dennis, look over there, near my desk. See the gun and the knife? Kevin was going to kill me. Stan was in the closet, he heard everything."

"So what?" Kevin sputtered. "He's a psychiatric patient; he's not a reliable witness. Neither is Erika, because of her bipolar diagnosis."

"Kevin, you're full of crap!" I exploded. "Unless someone has been declared legally incompetent in a court of law, he or she is considered qualified to testify."

"I'm certainly qualified," said Arthur. "I have antisocial personality disorder. I may be a sociopath, but no way am I psychotic, and I saw a whole bunch of shit."

"Quiet, all of you!" snapped Dennis. "I want you staying right where you are until back-up arrives."

Diane Olstead appeared in the doorway. "They're here now. I just saw them pull up."

"Good." Dennis stepped closer to Kevin. "Mr. Winthrop, we'll need to bring you in for further questioning. Before you say anything more, I'm going to read you your rights." He took a pair of cuffs from his belt, crouched down next to Kevin as he recited the Miranda warning. Detective Olstead stationed herself on Kevin's other side and placed her hands on his back. They looked small and delicate next to Arthur's large hands, but there was nothing delicate about the pressure they applied.

Dennis shackled Kevin's wrists together with practiced skill, double-checked to make sure the cuffs were locked securely, then glanced up at Arthur and Stan. "Thank you, gentlemen. We can take it from here."

Kevin confessed before the day was out. As Dennis told me later, he held out till his lawyer arrived but became increasingly unhinged while they huddled in consultation, insisting on claiming responsibility for the three murders, saying he owed it to Barbara to tell the truth. The videotaped confession was a painfully vivid portrait of a man falling to pieces, and a psychiatrist was called in to assess his mental status.

The forensic evidence was still being processed, but likely to be overwhelming: Kevin's prints on the knife and gun, DNA samples on the three victims' clothing. Pending a final determination, they sent him to Riker's Island. Kevin was always so fastidious, so perfectly dressed, that the thought of him in those grungy surroundings, dressed in standard-issue prison garb, almost made me laugh.

In the aftermath of his arrest, I found myself laughing a lot. An enormous weight had been lifted, and I felt positively euphoric. The club was a three-ring media circus, with reporters and video crews besieging me and the members for interviews and sound bites. Media interest had intensified with Germaine's murder, and Nancy Welcome wasn't the only journalist who had talked up the specious links between violence and mental illness. Now, with the culprit an outwardly normal man with no documented history of mental illness, they did an about-face and reported on the injustice of unfairly stereotyping the mentally ill.

Nancy Welcome called repeatedly, but I had Gloria tell her I wasn't available. She had been so intrusive, so unremittingly negative, that her brand of publicity was the last thing I needed. But relenting at last, I finally took her call and agreed to meet her for a drink at Tag. I was sipping a Margarita when she arrived. With minimal makeup and stringy hair, dressed in khaki pants and a heathery sweater, she looked haggard, as though she hadn't slept in days.

"I'm so relieved this is over," she said without preamble. "Thank God Kevin Winthrop is finally behind bars."

"But I thought you and he were good friends, that you had a relationship."

She shook her head vehemently. "We didn't, but he liked to believe we did. We went out a couple of times, but I decided not to pursue it, because there was something about him that gave me the willies. He didn't deal at all well with the rejection, and he began harassing me, sending me threatening letters and E-mails."

"Did he talk about his sister Barbara, or take you to her room?"

Her eyes widened. "Oh God, yes. He talked about her suicide, and how I reminded him of her . . ."

"He did that with me too."

"Erika, this is too much! But basically, what I wanted to tell you is that Kevin called me about the events at the club. He insisted that I cover those stories, and paint them in the most unflattering light possible. He threatened to kill me if I refused or went to the police, and I was too chicken to stand up to him or report him. If I hadn't been such a coward, maybe Germaine Lavendre's murder never would have happened."

I sat silent, momentarily stunned. She was right: she should have blown the whistle. Did her inaction make her an accessory to murder? In a way, maybe, but I could hardly blame her. She'd been justifiably terrified, a victim in her own right.

"Don't blame yourself," I said at last. "He's an extremely devious, dangerous man, and you were right to be cautious."

"Thanks for saying that. I need to make amends so that I can get on with my life."

I reached across the table and took her hands. "Consider yourself absolved. And by the way, I like you better this way than when you're in your on-air persona."

"That wasn't me. All the time I was doing those stories, I was out of my mind with fear. Of course I can't go on camera looking like this, but aside from that, I trust from now on I can be reasonably authentic. If you'll let me do another story on the club, I promise I'll put a positive spin on it this time."

"Okay. I may have just the thing for you. How would you like to cover our Thanksgiving party?"

"It's true," I told Mark that night. "We're having a Thanksgiving party. I know it's three weeks early, and we'll have a regular dinner on the actual holiday, but we want to celebrate the club's return to run of the mill, everyday normalcy."

He grinned. "Are you sure you won't be bored out of your mind?"

"Oh, I probably will, if it goes on too long, but I could do with a couple of weeks of routine. Maybe I'll spend some time in the art room, make some ceramic pots in Germaine's memory. Or a plaque for Jeff's mural."

"You do that. A little basket weaving wouldn't hurt, either." He stroked my hair, gazed at me intently. "Erika, you're a remarkable woman. You've come through a couple of months of sheer hell, and unless you're hiding it remarkably well, you've done it relatively unscathed."

I laughed. "Oh, I've been thoroughly scathed, believe me. But I'm feeling pretty good, all things considered."

"I apologize for underestimating you. Here I thought you were so fragile, and you turn out to be . . ." He paused, at a loss for words.

I snuggled closer. "A tough broad?"

"Something like that. Anyway, now that the pressure is off, maybe we don't have to be quite so cautious about, uh, I mean, getting . . ."

"You, Mark Levitan, at a loss for words? This is a first. Getting involved? Is that what you want to say?"

He nodded.

"Then by all means let's get on with it," I murmured. Then I kissed him.

———————

The Thanksgiving party had the joyful abandon of a Bacchanal. It was a small affair, strictly word of mouth – just the club members and a few guests. I'd been dubious about the idea at first, but Ariana Birdsong had insisted, knowing the healing power it could have. And she'd been right. With the death of Stephen Wright, a shroud of gloom had descended over the club, and the dark mood had deepened as the killings continued. Try as we might to maintain the illusion of normalcy, a sense of fear and foreboding had shadowed everyone at WellSpring. Now, with the confessed murderer safely behind bars, we were free to celebrate. I was surprised at the warm feeling of solidarity, and I delighted in all the congratulations from well-wishers who had doubted that the club could or should survive.

Vito Pisanello and Miriam Goldfarb stood side by side, an odd couple if there ever was one. "This club isn't so bad after all," Vito told me with a half smile. "If you ever want to expand, I might know of an additional property up the block, and I could get you a good deal."

Miriam gave him a nudge. "Now, Vito, this isn't the time to talk business. Erika, be careful he doesn't take advantage of you. This man could sell you the Brooklyn Bridge." She tossed him a flirtatious smile.

Ocala St. Claire strolled over, her beau Howard Springhorn in tow. "Erika, you know I've always believed in you. Even when things looked horribly grim for the club, I knew you had the strength to hang in there and prevail."

I smiled, wondering silently why she didn't tell me that when things were at their worst and I most needed to hear it. Just then Nancy Welcome approached, trailed by her cameraman and looking stylishly spiffy in a cranberry-red suit. We traded smiles of complicity as I turned her over to Ocala. After all, my boss was overdue for some positive media attention.

Mark made his way through the crowd, a statuesque woman at his side. "I'd like you to meet Rachel Alexander. She has some business to discuss with you."

The woman extended her hand. "Pleased to met you at last. I head up a foundation that's interested in developing a new advocacy program for the mentally ill, and I hope to persuade you to come work with us. I've heard a lot of wonderful things about you."

Arthur Drummond insinuated himself between us. Dressed in the black top hat and cape he'd worn the disastrous night of the cabaret, he looked dashingly Machiavellian. "Sorry, lady," he said, "but there's no way we're letting Erika go. We need her to keep this place afloat."

"Don't worry, I'm not going anywhere," I told Arthur. I smiled at Rachel. "I'm happy here at the club, and I'm not contemplating any career changes."

The delicate chime of Tibetan cymbals sounded close by. "Let's go to the group room for a small ritual," trilled Ariana. "I've lit some candles, and there are magic markers and squares of colored paper. Please take a few squares. Then write on them all the negative thoughts and memories about the club that you want to banish forever. One by one, we'll come up and cast them into the fire. After that, we'll make some origami birds to help our hopes and dreams for the club take flight. Any questions?"

Gloria raised her hand. "Will we get to keep the birds, or will we have to burn them too?"

"Oh, keep them by all means," said Ariana. "Or we could make a mobile out of them and hang them in the front hall for good luck."

"Speaking of birds, the turkey's almost ready," Stan announced. "It should be cool enough to carve by the time Ariana's done her thing. It's not much, just one twenty-pound bird, but consider it a preview of our Thanksgiving feast. We hope to see you all then. The luncheon will be served right after we watch the Macy's parade on TV."

Julie Lomoe

Such safe, ordinary little pleasures, I thought. Who could have imagined they would fill me with such joy?

Afterword

*W*ellSpring is loosely based on a psychiatric social club in upstate New York where I worked a few years ago, but all the characters in *Mood Swing* are entirely fictional, with one exception: the German shepherd mutt Rishi. The real Rishi, my beloved companion for over twelve years, died in 2004. I've taken the liberty of making the fictionalized Rishi considerably better behaved than the real-life version. His successor, my golden retriever Lucky, would make a far less formidable crime fighter.

The Lower East Side in *Mood Swing* reflects my own memories and experience. I lived in SoHo, not Alphabet City, but I showed my paintings on St. Marks Place and heard Hendrix and the Dead at the Fillmore East. Loisaida is more gentrified and upscale these days, and Erika and the denizens of WellSpring probably couldn't afford to live there anymore.

Stephen Wright's squat is inspired by a building on East Fifth Street where my daughter Stacey lived in the 1990's. She claims my description of the blackened windows and the forbiddingly dark stairwell is exaggerated, and that the squat was actually much more pleasant than my portrayal; perhaps my recollections were distorted by my motherly concern at the time. Yesteryear's squats have become today's condominiums, thoroughly legal and up to code, with some of the original squatters as legitimate owners.

Unlike Manhattan's Lower East Side, society's intolerance and fear of people suffering from mental illness has scarcely evolved at all. Erika's uneasiness about disclosing her bipolar disorder is all too realistic. If anything, people's acceptance of her illness after she "comes out" is perhaps too idealized. There is still a powerful stigma surrounding mental illness. And although mentally ill people are much more likely to be victims than perpetrators of crime, all too often the media – in both fiction and non-fiction – portray them as crazed, violent criminals. It's tempting to launch into a rant on this topic, but I refer you instead to my website, www.julielomoe.com.

My website also contains information about my poetry and my newest mystery novel, *Eldercide,* which draws on my experience as founder and president of a home health care agency, ElderSource, Inc., to explore the impact of end-of-life issues on elders and their families.

Acknowledgements

I 'd like to thank the members of the mystery writers' groups who believed in my work, gave me valuable feedback and helped sustain my motivation over the past several years, especially Marilyn Rothstein (a.k.a. M.E. Kemp) and Anne White of The Unusual Suspects in Saratoga, New York, and Myra Nagel, Jean Steffens and Mary P. Walker of the EmJays, an online critique group of the Sisters in Crime. Thanks as well to the poets and writers in New York's Capital Region who help provide a hospitable environment for my creative efforts. They include Therese Broderick, Marilyn Day, Lesley Tabor and Dan Wilcox.

Harriet Comfort, Director of The Mental Health Players at Capital District Psychiatric Center, has been an inspiration. But most of all I'd like to thank the many people I worked with as a therapist for over two decades, people who lived with mental illness on an intimate daily basis. This book wouldn't have been possible without their courageous examples.

319

Printed in the United States
57359LVS00004B/130-144